PRAISE FOR

NOT EVEN BONES

"*Not Even Bones* will grab you by the throat and drag you along as it gleefully tramples all of your expectations." —Sara Holland, *New York Times* best-selling author of *Everless*

"Gritty, compelling, a tale to feed the monster in all of us. I couldn't put it down." —Elly Blake, *New York Times* best-selling author of *Frostblood*

★ "A morally complex, edgy debut." —*Booklist,* starred review

"Deliciously dark and devious, with morally gray characters that make you question what is good and what is truly evil. Warning: don't read in the dark." —Rebecca Sky, author of *Arrowheart*

"The thrilling plot proves thought-provoking." —*Publishers Weekly*

"A slasher flick spliced with *Crime and Punishment,* this engrossing debut novel asks complex philosophical questions in a pleasingly hard-to-stomach way." —*Kirkus Reviews*

"Readers who are tired of the same recycled story lines will find something original here. . . . The story is so compelling that readers have to keep going to find out how, or if, Nita gets out of this mess." *School Library Journal*

MARKET OF MONSTERS SERIES

Not Even Bones

Only Ashes Remain

When Villains Rise

WHEN VILLAINS RISE

RISE

REBECCA SCHAEFFER

Clarion Books
An Imprint of HarperCollins*Publishers*
Boston   New York

Clarion Books
An Imprint of HarperCollins Publishers, registered in the United States of America and/or other jurisdictions.

www.clarionbooks.com

The text was set in ITC Legacy Serif Std.
Cover design by Sharismar Rodriguez
Interior design by Sharismar Rodriguez

The Library of Congress has cataloged the hardcover edition as follows:
Names: Schaeffer, Rebecca, author.
Title: When villains rise / Rebecca Schaeffer.
Description: Boston : HarperCollins Publishers, [2020] | Series: [Market of monsters ; 3] | Audience: Ages 14 and up. | Audience: Grades 10–12. | Summary: With her best friend, Kovit's, life in danger, Nita is determined to take down the black market once and for all.
Identifiers: LCCN 2019054998 (print) | LCCN 2019054999 (ebook)
Subjects: CYAC: Monsters—Fiction. | Supernatural—Fiction. | Mothers and daughters—Fiction. | Black market—Fiction. | Horror stories.
Classification: LCC PZ7.1.S33557 Whe 2020 (print) | LCC PZ7.1.S33557 (ebook) | DDC [Fic]—dc23
LC record available at https://lccn.loc.gov/2019054998
LC ebook record available at https://lccn.loc.gov/2019054999

ISBN: 978-1-328-86356-0 hardcover
ISBN: 978-0-358-56980-0 paperback

Manufactured in the United States of America
22 23 24 25 26 LBC 6 5 4 3 2

To all those who seize their own future,
whatever it takes

ONE

NITA STARED at the cell phone screen, her eyes wide and her mind still trying to process what she was reading.

It was eerily silent all around her. Normally, she never noticed the sounds of Toronto, the roar of cars, the hum of air-conditioning units, the honks and shouts and creaks of life. But she certainly noticed their absence when the soundproofing blocked them out. It made her uneasy.

Her breathing was short and fast as she reread the email. But the words didn't change, and the truth they told her didn't either.

Henry, Kovit's surrogate father and former employer, had sold Kovit's information to the International Non-Human Police.

Henry had sent them videos of Kovit as a child torturing people to eat their pain, which would be plenty of evidence to convince INHUP that Kovit was a zannie. As a species on the Dangerous Unnaturals List, he could be killed, and it would be considered preemptive self-defense. He would get no trial.

No jury would convict him. No judge would sentence him to prison or community service.

He would just be murdered.

Once the paperwork went through, in one week's time, his face, his name, his life would go up on an international wanted poster that would be spread across media outlets worldwide. He'd be hunted down, and when he was caught, he would be brutally slaughtered.

In one week's time, Kovit, Nita's best friend and only ally, was going to die.

Nita clenched the phone in her sweaty palm, and then angrily shoved it in her pocket, as if pushing the phone and its incriminating emails out of sight would somehow make the terrible truth go away.

Across from her, lying on a cot on the floor, was Kovit's internet friend and former colleague in the Family, Gold. Her bleached-blond hair was short and pressed flat against her scalp like a helmet, and half a dozen earrings danced up one ear. Her face had a bandage on one side from where Nita had burned her with acid, one arm was in a sling, and a crutch lay beside her cot, from when Kovit had dislocated her knee and shoulder.

"Did you know?" Nita asked, her voice tight and angry.

"Know what?" Gold rasped, still hoarse from screaming earlier.

"Did you know Henry was going to give INHUP evidence that Kovit was a zannie?" Nita snapped.

Gold was quiet a long moment, and then shook her head and looked away. "No."

Nita's shoulders slumped, and her fingers curled into her palms. She wanted to hurt Henry for what he'd done. But Henry was dead now, and there was nothing Nita could do to punish him, nothing she could do to vent her rage at this final betrayal.

No, now they had to deal with the fallout.

She turned around slowly, knowing the next step was to tell Kovit. He needed to know what had happened.

She thought of his face, the moment after he'd killed Henry. The absolute devastation in his eyes as he realized he'd broken his own rules, he'd killed someone who was like a parent to him. The rage as he made Gold scream, as something inside him broke, and he began to spiral downward into a dangerous place.

But she'd stopped him. Or he'd stopped himself. Or they'd stopped him together. For now, he was okay. Picking up the pieces of his shattered soul and forgetting his pain by causing pain to someone else.

Nita looked down the white hall at the pastel blue door at the end. Beyond that baby blue barrier, Kovit was doing what zannies did best. Hurting people and enjoying it.

Because Nita had asked him to.

She couldn't hear the screams—the soundproofing was excellent. So she couldn't hear what horrors he was committing to make himself feel better. Comfort food, he'd called it once, but she tried not to think too hard about the fact that he gained the same comfort from skinning people alive that others got from eating ice cream.

Her steps were silent as she approached the innocuous blue

door. She hesitated in front of it. Maybe she should just wait for Kovit to be finished. He'd had a hard day. He deserved some downtime. Surely this news could wait until he'd had a good meal.

She closed her eyes. Did she really want to wait for Kovit's sake, or because she didn't want to see the grisly results of her decision? She hadn't done well seeing Kovit torture an INHUP agent — the memory of his gurgling, tongueless screams was far too fresh.

Taking a deep breath, Nita knocked on the door. Then, remembering it was soundproofed and Kovit definitely couldn't hear her, she pushed it open.

The screams hit her first.

Fabricio generally had a soft, unassuming voice. It was the kind of voice that you trusted. It was the kind of voice that belonged on a gentle soul, not on a traitorous jerk who sold the person who saved him to the black market.

His screaming was high-pitched and sharp, serrated and coated in something angry. It was a scream of pain and rage, not a scream of pain and fear. Nita wasn't sure how she could tell the difference, but she could.

Fabricio slumped in his chair, wrists and ankles bound by silver duct tape. His tousled brown hair fell over his face, and the skin around his eyes was bright red from crying, the tear streaks mixing with the blood from his broken nose and painting pink lines down his cheeks.

Kovit stood in front of Fabricio, a twisted smile curling his mouth into something obscene, even as his body shivered in ecstasy from Fabricio's pain. His hands were sticky with dark red blood, though from her angle, she couldn't actually see the source of it. His black hair was glossy as a shampoo commercial, his skin almost glowing with health, his black eyes bright and hungry. The more pain he ate, the more beautiful he became, and as his body trembled with pleasure as Fabricio's pain slid through him, Nita could see the subtle changes the pain made on his appearance.

He lowered the scalpel when he saw Nita, and his smile fell a little, concern replacing the manic glee that had been there moments before. In front of him, Fabricio choke-sobbed, his shoulders heaving for breath.

Nita spoke without looking directly at either of them, her words a rush, because she wanted to get them out. "Kovit, can we talk outside for a moment? It's important. Something's happened."

Kovit's frown deepened, but he nodded slowly. "All right."

He wiped his bloody hands on Fabricio's tattered T-shirt, but not all the blood came off. The brownish dried streaks looked almost like melted chocolate.

Kovit turned to look at Fabricio and leaned forward, a hungry, delighted smile on his face. "Don't worry, we're not done here. I'll be back later."

Fabricio choked, trying to lean away, and gasped great heaving breaths that turned quickly into sobs.

Nita turned around quickly, unable to look at Fabricio any longer. It wasn't guilt she felt when she looked at him, because she didn't feel guilty. He deserved everything that Kovit was doing to him.

But she did feel *something*, and she didn't like what it was. It was different than her discomfort when Kovit had made other people scream—though there was still plenty of that too—but looking at Fabricio meant facing her own part in his screams.

It meant facing that she didn't actually feel bad about what she'd done.

She left the room, and Kovit followed her out, still shivering with Fabricio's pain, closing the door behind him and sealing Fabricio's sobs away. Nita gestured toward the reception room of the recording studio so that they could have some privacy away from Gold.

She dodged past the ultramodern reception desk and then hesitated in front of the black leather couches. Finally, she turned to him. "You better sit down for this."

Worry etched lines in Kovit's face. "Nita . . ."

"Just sit."

He sat down, and she stared at him for a moment, struck by the incongruity of the monster she'd seen a moment before, hungry and viciously cruel as he caused pain, and the young man sitting in front of her, patient and concerned. Sometimes it was hard to reconcile that all the different facets of Kovit were the same person.

She sat down beside him, their legs just brushing against each other. She could feel the warmth of his body faintly against her.

She looked down at her hands, and then forced herself to meet his eyes. "It's about Henry."

He looked away, hair falling over his eyes. "What about him?"

Nita could still hear the snap of Henry's neck as Kovit broke it. It was echoed by a snap in Kovit's soul as he broke something in himself doing it.

"After you came back to him, before he died . . ." She took a deep breath for courage. "He sold your information to INHUP."

Kovit froze, his whole body so still she wasn't even sure he was breathing.

"What?" His voice cracked slightly.

"He sent them all the videos. All the pictures. It's in processing right now, but the INHUP contact said your face would be made public in about a week."

Kovit was silent for a long moment. His voice, when it came out, was small and shattered. "Why?"

She bowed her head. "The email said he did it to make sure you couldn't leave again. So you'd be trapped with him. So you'd need his protection to survive."

Kovit laughed, a tinny, broken sound, and tipped his head back to look at the fluorescents above him. "So this is it, then. This is the end."

"This is *not* the end," Nita snarled, putting her hands on either side of his face and forcing him to look at her. "We won't let it be."

She thought of her list of corrupt INHUP agents. She thought of all the things Kovit knew about the Family he'd worked for and wondered if he could sell them for protection. Though they probably wouldn't do witness protection for a zannie.

He trembled softly and shook his head. "No one's ever

survived being up on one of the list's wanted posters. The longest anyone lasted was two weeks." He closed his eyes, and she could see him beginning to spiral into despair again. "It's over."

Nita clenched her teeth and pulled his face closer to hers. She wouldn't let him give up, not when they'd come so far. "No one had ever escaped from Mercado de la Muerte, and we burned it to the ground. No one's ever been the subject of as high profile a black market hunt as me, and I'm still here." *For now, anyway.* "We'll find a way, Kovit. Trust me."

Kovit met her eyes, and she could see he wanted to believe her, he hungered for her to be right, but he couldn't quite accept it. "It's too late. It's not like we can take the information back from INHUP."

"No," Nita agreed. "We can't. But we can prevent INHUP from publicizing it."

"How?"

Nita looked at him, from his long, dark eyelashes to his trembling lips. Beneath her hands, his skin was soft, and she rubbed her thumbs gently over his cheeks, wiping away the spots of blood that patterned his face like tears.

Finally she whispered, "I have an idea."

TWO

Nita explained her idea, and Kovit's eyes widened further and further the more she said. When she finally fell silent, he looked down at his hands, folded in his lap and streaked with blood.

"I . . ." He hesitated. "I need a moment to think."

Nita nodded slowly. "Okay."

He bowed his head, twisting his hands in his lap. He shivered occasionally, Fabricio's pain flowing through him from the other room.

Nita wondered how distracting it was for him, if the constant influx of pleasure made it hard to focus. Kovit would have to leave the building to gain enough distance to not feel Fabricio's agony. But leaving the building wouldn't make him immune to feeling every other pain of the people around him. Every hangnail, every scrape, every sprain. She shuddered at the thought, wondering how he blocked out all that feeling, kept himself from constantly twitching and shivering and being distracted.

Especially given that most pain wasn't strong enough for him to actually eat, it must get annoying. Zannies fed on extreme pain, the kind only found in torture, war zones, and hospitals. The rest of it, all those little micro pains, those were just background noise. She wondered what it would be like to always know how everyone around you hurt and to have it feel good. How it would change the way your brain perceived the world.

Had anyone ever done an MRI on a zannie? Their neural connections must be fascinating. She'd search online later to see if there were any research papers that covered this.

If there weren't, and if they survived this and she got into university one day, maybe Kovit would let her do an MRI on him and scan his brain herself. It would make a great thesis topic.

She pulled her mind away from the future before she went too far down that road. There was no *if*. She *would* be an unnatural researcher one day. Just as soon as she got the black market to stop hunting her.

She let out a breath. It had been a hard few weeks. She'd made mistakes. But she'd learned from them, she had a plan now. A multipronged one to get the black market off her back, to make herself so powerful that people thought twice before coming after her. A plan that would make her far more valuable alive and free than dead.

If it went right.

If Kovit wasn't captured and killed by INHUP first.

If Fabricio cooperated.

If if if. So many variables.

She closed her eyes. Right now, she couldn't focus on that. One step at a time. She needed to focus on Kovit, on getting him out of this mess Henry had put him in.

Finally, she fidgeted and asked, "Well? What do you think of my idea?"

"I don't know," he admitted.

"It'll work," she insisted.

Kovit gave her a look, one eyebrow arched in mild judgment.

Nita looked away, wincing slightly. "Sorry."

It had only been a few hours since they'd had their conversation about Nita pushing her ideas on him, and she was already sliding back into bad habits. If Kovit was hesitant about one of her plans, they were supposed to talk it out. It was, after all, his life on the line. He had the right to reject it.

"Okay." Nita tried to find the words. "Can you tell me why you don't like it?"

He weighed his words carefully. "You want to contact my sister."

"Yes."

Kovit hadn't seen his sister in a decade. The last time he'd seen her, he'd been ten, and she'd hid him from the INHUP agents who came and murdered their mother. His sister was human—the zannie genes had skipped her—so she hadn't been in danger the way Kovit had been. After that, Kovit had been recruited by a mafia group.

His sister became an INHUP agent.

He ran a hand through his hair. "I still can't believe she's joined INHUP. It's something the girl I knew would never do."

"It's been a decade."

"I know." He paused a moment, and when he spoke, his words were slow and cautious. "That's why I don't know if contacting her is a good idea."

Nita hesitated. "As an INHUP agent, she'll have access to things we don't. She might have ways to fix this."

Of course, none of those ways would be at all legal.

"She might." He raised his eyes, and for a moment, she thought she could see the cracks beneath the surface, the fracture murdering Henry had made inside him, but his voice betrayed none of his pain, just practicality. "But what if she doesn't want to?"

"She's your sister." Nita's voice was gentle.

"She *was* my sister. But the sister I knew would never have joined INHUP." His voice was soft. "She's clearly changed since then. What if she's in favor of the Dangerous Unnaturals List? You're basing this plan off the assumption that she'll help me, but what if instead she just wants to hunt me down? We could be giving INHUP more information that will help them kill me."

Nita understood his reluctance—almost every person he'd cared about had ended up betraying him. Gold had betrayed him. Henry had wanted to use him. Even Nita, who had never betrayed him, still struggled with some parts of him.

She didn't know if Kovit could take another betrayal on the heels of so many. Better to keep the memory of their happier years as children alive than risk destroying it.

Kovit's hands shook on his lap, and for once, Nita didn't think it was because he was eating pain from the other room.

12

She reached over and put her hand on his. "You won't have to speak with her. I'll do it. You don't even have to meet her if it doesn't work out."

He laced his fingers with hers. "But I don't want to know if it doesn't work out. I don't want to know if she says, 'Good, let him die.'"

Nita was silent a long moment, and then squeezed his hand softly. "Okay."

He stared at her, as though he wasn't sure what he was hearing. "Okay?"

"We'll think of another plan. We'll find another way to prevent INHUP from making your information public."

There were other INHUP agents Nita could contact, but unlike Kovit's sister, they wouldn't have altruistic motives for helping him. No, for them she'd need proper leverage.

Her mind began spinning plots, a spider in her web of lies and blackmail, trying to figure out a route that would tangle up INHUP and protect Kovit from harm. There were options — especially if she tied it into her plans for Fabricio. But they would be difficult. The timeline would be tight.

Even if Kovit had agreed to meet his sister, they probably would have needed to make backup plans like this anyway. Just in case.

Kovit rose, pulling away from her. He took a few steps back toward Fabricio's room, toward comfort and pain, familiarity and control. He stopped in the doorway and closed his eyes, leaning his head on the frame.

"I'm being really stupid, aren't I?" he asked.

Nita tilted her head. "No."

"She could save me. She could go in and delete everything."

"Maybe." Nita shrugged. "Or maybe she'd turn us both in. There's no way to know."

He turned to face her, and then pressed his back against the wall. He looked down at his hands. "Do you know what Songkran is?"

Nita shook her head.

"It's Thai new year. It's in April." A smile flickered across his face. "We used to have big water fights as kids during Songkran. It was a thing. One year, Patchaya—my sister—and I got water guns from our parents. Mine was neon green and white, and hers was baby blue." He laughed softly. "I can't believe I still remember what color they were. Of all the random details. I must have been . . . eight? Which means Pat was thirteen.

"We filled our water guns with water and din sor pong— a white powder." His eyes were sly. "We used to try and find businessmen, really put-together-looking people, and get them absolutely soaked until they looked like ghosts. When we had the water guns, we were practically unstoppable."

His gaze was far away. "I remember, it was near the end of the day. We were tired and heading home. Our plastic guns were empty, and we were as covered in water and white powder as our victims. We were walking along the river, and I felt it. Some man had fallen down a stairwell in the building next to us, and the pain . . . I still remember it. His, ah, scrotum, caught on a nail as he was going down and got . . . stretched. He'd cracked something in his spine, and he couldn't move, couldn't talk, but he could feel *everything*." Kovit shivered softly at the memory. "The pain was *exquisite*."

Nita shifted uncomfortably, and Kovit cleared his throat. "Anyway. I had to stop and just savor it. It was so good. I wanted to bring him home, to keep him forever because someone who can't scream, can't move, can't escape . . ."

It would be a zannie's dream, Nita thought, trying not to show that the idea made her ill.

"So Pat, she looked at me. And she asked, 'Are you hungry?' I said I was, and she tucked me against the side of the building while she went for help. She wasn't supposed to leave me alone or let me eat while I was in public, but she made sure I was safe and just let me absorb it all."

He sighed gently. "Of course, she called for an ambulance, and it ended eventually when they took him away. But I didn't begrudge her, I knew she was like that. I think that was a good day for both of us. My sister, she's always liked helping people. I think it made her feel good to save that man and to give me something I wanted at the same time."

Nita was silent for a long moment. She didn't have any idea where to start in parsing what this story said about either sibling. So she finally settled on "It sounds like a good memory."

"It is." He met her eyes. "She was always good to me. Even though I scared her. Even though I think she was too good a person for the family she was in. She was my world as a child. I'd have done anything for her." Kovit took a long, deep breath. "And she did do everything she could to save me when INHUP finally arrived."

He straightened and squared his shoulders. "Let's do it."

Nita blinked. "Do what?"

"Contact her." His mouth was firm, and his voice was calm.

"I'm not ready to die yet. I may be evil, I may deserve what INHUP plans to do to me, but I don't care. I want to live. It's stupid to reject this path. We need to try every option."

Nita hesitated, and then rose and went to him. "Are you sure?"

His gaze was steady. "I'm sure. Contact her."

THREE

O F COURSE, it wasn't that easy to call immediately. Nita didn't want to use her phone in case everything went wrong and they managed to trace her number. Which meant she needed a burner phone.

"I'll go get the burner phone." Kovit rose. "I could use the fresh air."

Nita looked at his bloody hands and raised her eyebrows. "You're going to go out like that?"

He blinked, as if just noticing the gore. "Good point."

She followed him down the hall to the small white bathroom. The water turned pink when it touched his hands, wiping away all evidence of what he'd done.

"Are you sure you don't want to, uh . . ." Nita hesitated and then carefully said, "Relax with Fabricio for a bit? I can go out and get the phone."

"You mean torture him until I'm so high on pain I can pretend the rest of the world doesn't exist?" Kovit's smile was bitter. "As appealing as that sounds, I would rather be doing something to fix the problem than pretending it'll go away on its own. Or that you'll fix it for me." He shook his head. "I've let other people control my life long enough. It's past time I started fixing my own problems."

For the first time she realized that while Kovit had broken something inside him when he killed Henry, he'd also made a choice to take control of his life back. Like pulling a blade from a stab wound, it hurt like hell, but in the end, you needed to do it to heal and survive.

Kovit needed to break the part of him chained to Henry's control, the part that could let himself be tied down that way. And now that it was gone, he could start healing the damage it had caused and building his life on his own terms.

"You're staring at me strangely." He raised an eyebrow as he turned off the faucet.

She shook her head and smiled slightly. "Nothing. I was just worried for you since . . . Well, you know. But now I see that was for nothing."

He looked away. "No. You were right to worry. I reacted . . . poorly." He sighed heavily, body shaking a little. "I can't talk about this now. Later. It's only been a few hours. I need some time."

"Of course." Nita wished she hadn't brought it up. "Whenever you need."

He nodded, but didn't look at her as he dried his hands. "I'll be back soon."

A part of her wanted to go with him, but he didn't look like he wanted company right now. And it wasn't a wise idea, even if he did.

Kovit wasn't the only one with a price on his head.

As the door closed behind him, Nita pulled out her phone and scrolled through the Toronto news. Six more missing teenagers, all of whom looked just like her. When she'd checked yesterday, there'd only been three.

Nita scrolled through the faces and clicked on the news link for an article titled GANG WAR ENSUES OVER DEAD BODY? THE BLACK MARKET HITS TORONTO.

According to the article, two rival groups had started a gunfight in Markham, just north of Toronto, over the murdered body of a teenage girl who looked like Nita, both wanting to claim it as their own. Half a dozen bystanders had been wounded before one of the groups managed to steal the body.

Nita skimmed the news and was horrified to find even the general news was now talking about how the black market was on the hunt for a teenage girl with supposed healing powers. Thank God for laws, because the news couldn't legally show the video causing all this—a video of a kidnapped minor being cut and healing wasn't public-viewing-approved in most places. But that didn't mean it wasn't going to make its way from the dark web to the regular web eventually.

Nita swore to herself. This was getting out of control. When her captor, Reyes, had first uploaded the video onto the dark web as proof of what Nita could do, Nita had known she'd be screwed. She was a new unnatural, unknown, and people would pay for that. Especially if they thought they could gain some of her power by eating her.

The emptiness where her toe used to be tingled. She'd

already had one person eat her flesh, though she hadn't seen any effects, especially not the immortality he wanted, given that he was dead now.

She rubbed her temples. She'd never imagined she'd be so in demand that gangs of black market dealers would literally have gunfights over a body that might or might not be hers.

She forced her fingers to unclench on her phone. She needed to leave Toronto. Corrupt INHUP agents had sold out her location, and it was time Nita got out, before more black market hunters found her. But running away wasn't going to fix the problem.

Luckily, Nita had several other ideas that might.

She went onto the dark net websites, scrolling through black market forums, searching up what people were saying about her. Her mother had told her she'd started to plant seeds that the video was doctored and fake, and Nita saw a few comments about that, but not enough, not nearly enough.

Her mother's idea was solid — make the video seem like a fake. Some people would always believe it, and it was already so talked about that it might not do much now, but it couldn't hurt to try. She couldn't rely on her mother for that sort of thing, though, and she made a mental note to think of ways to discredit the video.

She scrolled through other forums, picking up information nuggets like a gamer on a quest, except the consequences for this were very, very real.

Sighing, she moved her attention to the general forums and paused, eyes catching on something unusual. It was a request for information on the location of a black market dealer who went by the name Monica. Nita clicked it.

Someone was trying to buy information on her mother.

Nita frowned as she read down the list of semivague descriptions that would only make sense to someone who knew her mother. It was a list Nita recognized, because it was almost word for word what she'd been asked by a customer when she was imprisoned in Mercado de la Muerte.

Her fingers tightened on her phone, the only physical manifestation of the anger burning tight and hot within. Zebra-stripes the vampire was still hunting her mother. He'd murdered her father, and he was after her mother. She didn't know who he was, or why he was after her family. Despite the fact that INHUP had identified him to her, he wasn't listed online on INHUP's wanted list for dangerous unnaturals. Probably more evidence of corruption in INHUP. As if she'd needed more.

No matter what, Nita promised herself she would get vengeance on Zebra-stripes.

Grief trickled in when she thought about her father, soft and delicate, opening the door and tiptoeing into her heart. It felt like a wound that had bled copious amounts and just recently scabbed over. Thinking about him was like picking at the scab, little bits of blood bubbling up and trickling through her soul.

She wiped her eyes quickly, as though by removing the tears she could make the pain go away. Of course, it didn't work, and the pain lingered, a constant throbbing in her heart. It was better than before. After she'd first found out, when the pain had been almost all-encompassing and the tears had come fast and free.

She took a long, shuddering breath, banishing his image from her mind. She couldn't afford to let herself crack right now. Once she'd exacted her vengeance, once the black market was ashes at her feet, she'd allow herself the time and space to grieve.

She looked down at the ad again, and her face hardened. It was time she dealt with Zebra-stripes, once and for all.

She sent a message responding to the ad.

FOUR

KOVIT RETURNED FAIRLY QUICKLY, carrying a bag
with burner phones and two boxes of ready-to-go-pizza
from the Little Caesars down the street. Nita hadn't realized
just how hungry she was until she smelled the gooey cheese,
and she snatched one box from him and ripped it open.

"Hungry, are we?" Kovit laughed.

Nita's only answer was to shove a slice in her mouth.

Within a few minutes, both of them had devoured a whole
box, and all that remained was the oil on their hands and a few
crumbs. Nita wiped her greasy fingers on her jeans, put half
the second pizza in the empty box, and handed it to Kovit.

"Do you want to go give that to Gold while I handle Fabricio?" she asked.

Kovit made a face. "Must I?"

Nita made sure her voice was gentle, not judging, even
though she was judging just a little. "You can't avoid Gold forever. And you need to talk to her. We need to figure out to do
about her. We can't keep her here, but until we know what she's
going to do, we can't just let her go either."

"I know." He rubbed his temples and sighed heavily. "I know."

Nita put a hand on his shoulder. "Go talk to her. You were friends, once upon a time."

Until Gold realized that the anonymous boy she'd befriended in the chatroom was Kovit and betrayed him. Nita could understand if Gold hadn't known the person she'd been interacting with online was a bad person and then discovered he tortured people for fun. That was justified rage. But Gold had *known* the person she'd been sent to spy on was part of her mafia family. She'd known he was very much not a good person. She just hadn't known he was a zannie.

Even when Kovit made friends with people as horrible as he was, prejudice got in the way.

Kovit looked away. "Yeah. Once upon a time."

But he took the pizza and went down the hall toward Gold. Nita watched him until he went through the door, and then took a deep breath and picked up her box.

She stood in front of the pastel blue door to Fabricio's room. There was a strange feeling of déjà vu prickling her skin and stilling her steps. She remembered the last time she had brought Fabricio food. He'd been chained in a dog kennel in her mother's apartment, and blood had soaked the side of his face where her mother had hacked his ear off.

He'd looked at her, and he'd begged her to help him. And Nita, foolish, naive Nita, had.

And everything had gone wrong.

She swallowed. She wasn't the same girl she was then.

She was smarter now, more ruthless. And this time, Fabricio wouldn't manipulate her into ruin.

Squaring her shoulders, she opened the door.

Fabricio was slumped in his chair, still bound. He lifted his head when Nita came in. His face was striped a crusty pink from where his tears had mixed with blood and then dried. His blue-gray eyes were broken and scared, and they stared at her with a vacantness that made her shiver.

"Hello, Fabricio." Nita stepped into the room and held out the box of pizza. "I brought you some food."

He whimpered softly as he straightened his body. "I suppose you think of that as a good deed."

"Not really. But I can't have you dying yet."

His voice was bitter. "That's right. You need me to break into my father's office so you can steal his company's information."

Fabricio's father, Alberto Tácunan, ran one of the largest corrupt legal services in the world. Every monster who was anyone used his services. Legal assistants covered up crimes and got monsters off on technicalities, and shell corporations and calculated tax evasions hid money. And money, well, money told stories. Money proved crimes. Money hid secrets. And secrets were power.

Nita wanted that power.

"I told you. I don't *know* the password to get into my father's databases." Fabricio sounded desperate, his body straining forward against the bonds. "I would give it to you if I did, I don't *care* if you rob him blind. But I don't *have* it."

"I'm sure you'll remember it eventually." Nita gave him a hard smile. "After all, it's the only reason you're still alive right now."

"Forgive me if I don't jump for joy." His voice was dead. "I seem to be tied up and in the middle of being tortured. It's really getting in the way of celebrating."

Nita pressed her mouth into a thin line. "You really only have yourself to blame for that."

"Really? I somehow tortured myself?"

"Don't play the fool. It doesn't suit you," Nita snapped. "This is vengeance, and you damn well deserve it."

His head jerked up. "Are we doing tit for tat, Nita? An eye for an eye? Because I'm pretty sure we're more than equal by now."

"We'll never be equal." Nita's words were tight with rage. "You *sold me on the black market*. You ruined my life. Because of you, there's a video of me healing online that I will never escape. I can never lead a normal life. I'm constantly on my guard. I've been attacked dozens of times in the week since I escaped the market that, I remind you, *you* put me in."

"So you *poisoned* me."

"And you sent a mafia group to kill me in vengeance."

"Not in vengeance," Fabricio said softly. "I sent them because I was scared. I was scared you'd never stop trying to kill me, I was scared you knew too much about me and you'd ruin my life." He said bitterly, "And I was right, wasn't I? You're threatening me with the same thing that happened to you. To release my information online and set the whole black market on me, hoping to use me against my father."

Nita shrugged. "It would be poetic justice."

Fabricio laughed, harsh and angry. "Oh, that would be poetic justice, would it? I thought having Kovit torture me was your 'poetic justice'?"

"No. That's just vengeance."

Fabricio was silent a long moment, his whole body trembling. With rage or pain or something else entirely, Nita didn't know.

"Vengeance." His voice was cold and angry. "Is that what you're calling this?" He met her eyes. "I never pegged you for a sadist when I first met you. I guess I was wrong."

"No. You weren't wrong." Nita shrugged. "But people change. *I* changed." She leaned forward, eyes cold. "I had to change to survive because of what *you* did to me. So, this, all of this?" She waved a hand around. "That's on you."

He glared. "I'm not responsible for your choices, Nita. You are. You chose to be what you are, and you chose to do this to me. I admit, I fucked up. I shouldn't have sold you out. And I'm sorry. I really am. I've apologized a dozen times, and I mean it. But I can't change it. And it's not my fault what you've decided to do since then."

Fabricio looked away. "I have enough things to hate myself for without adding your crimes in there too."

Nita's smile was tight. "I'm sure you do."

"You can look as smug as you want, but at least I know what my crimes are." His voice was bitter and raspy from screaming. "But, Nita, do you know?"

"Know what?"

"The price of your 'vengeance'?" Fabricio raised his eyes

and met hers, rage burning dark and cold in their depths. "I think it's only fair you know, don't you?"

Nita's eyes narrowed.

"Shall I tell you what Kovit did to me?" Fabricio said softly, barely more than a whisper. "Shall I tell you what you let him do to me?"

An uneasy feeling coiled in the base of Nita's stomach. She didn't like hearing the details.

"I know what Kovit did."

"Do you?" Fabricio whispered. "Then you know that he started skinning my fingers? Slow, small strips of skin, one after the other. He peeled them off like potato skins."

Nita didn't say anything, her expression hard, trying to cover the ugly, vicious revulsion coiling inside.

"Have you ever scraped your knees, Nita? That's just a little bit of skin off. Just a small scrape. This was bigger. He scraped and scraped, and it was so painful that I couldn't even tell you my own name. I couldn't think over the pain." He swallowed. "I suppose at some point my body decided it was too much pain to bear and stopped sending so many signals. But if I twist wrong, it hurts all over again."

"Enough, Fabricio." Nita sounded hoarser than she intended. "I get it."

"Do you, though? Because I'm not done." Fabricio's blue eyes were steady. "Because he reached my nail at one point, and he slid that knife under my nail. And he ripped. It. Off."

Nita clenched her fists at her side and said nothing.

Fabricio's gaze bored into her. "Do you know what it's like

to have a fingernail ripped off? Do you have any idea how many nerve endings are in there?"

"Actually, I do." Nita could count them if she wanted to. Her own fingers tingled, as if waiting for her to do so. "It's not an insignificant number."

He blinked, his mouth slightly open. Clearly Nita hadn't responded the way he'd expected, but he recovered quickly.

"Nita, please. You're not a sadist. I know this. I remember how much it bothered you when your mother took my ear." He began to cry. "Please stop hurting me."

Nita stared at him, at his blood and tears and soft whimpers as he begged for her to have the conscience she used to, the same one she'd had when he met her.

But she didn't.

Nita wasn't that girl anymore.

The gory details still bothered her—they'd probably always bother her, she didn't think she'd ever escape that, no matter what she'd told Kovit—but she didn't feel sympathy for Fabricio anymore. She could see the points on his manipulation plan, each reaction, each word a calculated effort to pull on her strings and make her do what he wanted.

"Sorry, Fabricio. That ship sailed." Nita knelt so she was eye level with him. "You're going to have to learn how to manipulate the new me."

He met her eyes, his face damp with tears. "No, Nita. You're the one who needs to learn how to manipulate me. Because you *suck*."

"Pardon?"

"You've given me nothing to convince me to work with you. You've sicced your pet monster on me—"

"Kovit's not a monster."

Fabricio laughed then, short and sharp. "That's what you want to argue over? That? To me? Right now?"

She clenched her jaw shut.

"As I was saying." His voice was cold. "You've sicced your pet monster on me, you've threatened me if I fail. But what fucking motive do I have to succeed? Why should I help you?"

"To not die."

He laughed, sharp and bitter. "I'm going to die the minute I get back to Buenos Aires."

"Why?" Nita asked.

He looked away. "That's not important. What's important is that I'm dead either way. So why the fuck should I help you when you're just going to torture me?"

His hands twitched as he said it, breaking the scabs and causing blood to drip from his fingertips onto the floor in a steady thud-thud-thud. Nita forced her eyes away, but she couldn't stop hearing the sound, the plop as the droplets hit the carpet.

"A good businessman knows that you can't just use the stick, you need the carrot too." He met her eyes. "Hurting people if they fail works better if you reward them if they succeed too." He smiled slightly. "You need me. But I sure as hell don't need you."

"I have fail-safes if you try anything—"

"I know, I know." He closed his eyes and leaned back in his chair. "But I'm between a rock and a hard place. Dead either way. If I see an opportunity to run, you really think I won't take it, cost be damned?"

Her eyes narrowed. "What are you saying?"

"You know what I'm saying. For all your posturing, I don't think you enjoy seeing me hurt nearly as much as you pretend. I think you want to hurt me, you want your vengeance, but actually seeing it makes you ill. So don't. Stop this. The only one having a good time here is Kovit, and any time a zannie is the only one enjoying a situation, you know something's gone terribly wrong." He leaned forward. "Stop this, Nita. Before you break both of us."

"The only one breaking here is you," she snapped, and tossed the box of pizza on the floor in front of him, where he couldn't possibly reach it.

She spun away from him, hating that he was right, that he'd played her again, that this wasn't the first time she'd tossed food at him and run because she couldn't face his truths.

FIVE

N ITA CLOSED THE DOOR behind her and leaned against it, taking deep breaths. She tried not to see the parallels to the last time Fabricio had been her prisoner. It wasn't the same. It wasn't.

But she still felt uncomfortably like it was. Except this time, she was playing her mother's role.

She tried not to remember how Fabricio had screamed as her mother ordered Nita to cut off his ear. She'd thought he was innocent then, she hadn't known what he'd do to her. It was natural for her to have been hesitant. It was different now. Now it was vengeance.

And Fabricio was wrong. It wasn't breaking her to watch him suffer. She liked knowing she was getting vengeance.

But you don't like seeing it, do you? You just like knowing it happened, not facing the reality, her mind whispered.

Shut up, Nita told it.

She shook her head, forcing Fabricio's words away. He was trying to manipulate her again. That's what he did. He crawled into her head with his silver-tongued words and twisted her up until she did what he wanted, not what was best for herself.

He deserved everything that she'd done to him.

She let out a breath and walked down the hall to the other recording studio. The door opened silently, to reveal Kovit awkwardly sitting on one cot, avoiding looking at Gold, who stared at him with judgmental eyes while she slowly ate a piece of pizza.

Nita looked between them. "Did something happen here?"

Kovit shrugged and avoided eye contact.

Gold snorted. "Nothing but a zannie doing what it does best."

Kovit bristled and his jaw clenched, but he didn't say anything.

"Is that really how you should be talking right now, Gold?" Nita closed the door behind her. "Given your situation?"

"And what is my situation?" she asked, her eyes boring into Nita's. "Am I your prisoner?"

"No," Kovit said, at the same time Nita said, "Yes."

Gold raised her eyebrows. "So which is it?"

Nita pursed her lips. "What do you plan to do now, Gold?"

"Do?"

"When you leave this room, what will you do?"

Gold shrugged. "Go back to the Family, of course."

"Everyone else in your team is dead. You could easily pretend to be dead too."

"But why?" She frowned, her lip piercing catching the light. "Why would I want them to think I'm dead?"

Kovit responded, voice soft. "To start a new life."

"I don't want a new life." Gold's eyes narrowed as her gaze shifted between the two of them. "My life may not be perfect, but I like it."

"You enjoy being the flunky in a mafia group?" Nita asked.

"I enjoy being the presumptive heir to one of the most powerful and extensive crime families in North America." Gold grinned, sharp and fierce. "Someday I'm going to rule the fucking world."

Nita blinked. She had to concede, that did sound like a great life. And given her own ambitions, she couldn't really condemn Gold for it.

So instead she said, softly, "And what about Kovit?"

"What about him?" Gold asked, voice cold.

"It might be useful, if you want to rule the world, to have a zannie on your side."

Gold's mouth tightened. "I want nothing to do with monsters. When I'm in charge, I'm going to get rid of every monster in the organization and burn them all."

Nita raised an eyebrow. "The human ones too?"

Gold gave her a withering look. "Don't patronize me."

"It's an honest question. Henry was human, but I would argue he was a far worse monster than Kovit," Nita commented mildly. "He loved torture as much as any zannie, not even to eat the pain, just for the sheer pleasure of it. And he was far more ruthless and less loyal than Kovit. So, what do you consider him?"

Gold's lip curled in displeasure. "Henry was my father's right-hand man."

"I didn't ask what your father thought of him."

"What does it matter what I thought of him?" Her eyes turned to Kovit. "He's dead now, isn't he?"

Kovit flinched.

Nita crossed her arms. "And will you tell the Family how he died?"

Gold shrugged. "It doesn't really matter if I tell them, does it? Kovit's going to be up on INHUP's wanted list in a week, and there's no way he'll survive it. There's no point in wasting Family resources going after him."

Kovit's shoulders tightened, and he swallowed noticeably.

Nita frowned. "And if he wasn't on the list?"

Gold tugged at the bandage on her face. "I don't see how you could get him off it."

"This is a hypothetical question."

Gold waved it away. "I've never seen the point in hypothetical questions. Especially ones like that."

Kovit was quiet for a long moment, and then he leaned forward. "Would you tell them to kill me, May?"

Nita's heart hurt a little every time Kovit called Gold May. It was the internet name she'd used for years, commenting in a group chat and pretending to be his friend when in reality she'd been spying for the Family. It was the name of a nonexistent girl, the name Kovit clung to because he didn't want their years-long friendship to truly be gone, to have to admit that maybe it had never existed at all.

Gold turned to him, and the light glanced off her various earrings, making them sparkle in the too-bright room. Her lips thinned, and Kovit met her stare head-on.

Finally Gold looked away. "I don't see the point of answering anything. You won't believe me if I say no because you'll think it's just a ploy to escape. And I'd have to be pretty stupid to say yes under the circumstances."

Well, she had them there.

"The real question is what you're going to do with me. You're going to keep me here until you're forced to make a decision." This time her eyes found Nita's. "And I know your type. You don't like risks."

Nita's mouth pressed in a line. "No. I don't."

"Watch out, Kevin." Gold turned back to Kovit, using his fake internet name, pulling the same emotional strings Kovit had reached for. "She's going to kill me while you're sleeping so you don't have to."

Kovit stood quickly. "Nita wouldn't do that."

But there was fear in his eyes, and Gold saw it and smiled. "Sure. If you say so. A convenient carbon monoxide leak will be at fault. Or perhaps I'll choke on my pizza."

Kovit whispered softly, "You're wrong." He turned to Nita. "She's wrong, right?"

"Of course she is." Nita crossed her arms and held Kovit's gaze. "She's just trying to sow doubt between us."

Kovit nodded once, sharply. "Exactly."

And Gold probably *was* trying to sow doubt. But the best seeds of doubt were based on truth. And the truth was that Gold was a complication they didn't need, with the potential for great harm. She would need to be neutralized. Whether that meant being brought over to their way of thinking or dying, well, that was up in the air.

Kovit had already been forced into killing one of his friends. Nita couldn't let him be responsible for another. So Gold was right. Nita might need to make her have an accident. And Kovit knew it. And he knew Nita was capable of it.

Nita cleared her throat. "It's late. Kovit, why don't you and I go in the reception room and leave Gold to rest?"

He wasn't quite able to meet her gaze. "Sure."

They turned away, a hum of tension between them that hadn't been there moments before.

Gold just smiled at them both and ate another slice of pizza.

SIX

THEY MADE THEIR WAY back into the lobby, and Kovit flopped back onto the couch. Nita paced the room.

"Gold could be a problem," she murmured.

Kovit looked at her with steady eyes. "But she's one that won't be solved with murder."

It wasn't a question. It was a statement.

Nita's hands moved at her side, sharp motions of cutting with an invisible scalpel. "There are other ways to deal with her than murder."

He looked at her for a long time and then closed his eyes and leaned back into the sofa. "Good."

Nita sighed, mind whirling, clicking through all the things she still had to do. Her body was exhausted, but she couldn't rest yet. She pumped herself full of adrenaline. She still had one very important task.

She went to the bag Kovit had brought back and fished out one of the burner phones. It was crappy, so she used her own phone to bring up INHUP's website.

She stole a glance at Kovit as she scrolled through pages. "I'm going to call her now. Your sister."

He stiffened and sat up on the couch. "Do we have to do it right now?"

"We're on a bit of a time crunch. Only a week before INHUP releases your face. Do you really want to stall?"

"No, no." He ran a hand through his hair. "You're right. We should call now."

Nita met Kovit's eyes. "You don't have to be here for this conversation."

He held her gaze. "I do."

Nita went back to her phone, scrolling through pages for the anonymous tip line. When they'd seen Kovit's sister on the television earlier today, she'd been being interviewed about a murder case in Montreal involving a unicorn who had eaten the soul of a teenage girl and left her lying on the pavement, iris-less eyes staring at nothing.

She eventually found a tip number on one of the news articles about the murder, titled MONTREAL OR *MONSTREAL*? UNICORN MURDER ROCKS THE CITY. Nita rolled her eyes at the pun, but called the tip line. She flicked the phone onto speaker so Kovit could hear what she was doing.

It rang a moment, and then there was a click and a prerecorded message told her everything was confidential and that she was encouraged to give as much information as possible. She was given an option to record a message and leave it for the police or to speak to a live person. She clicked the number for the person.

The phone ticked, and then she was on with an operator.

"Hello, this is the INHUP tip line."

"Hi. I have information for Agent Vidthuvitsai about the unicorn murder in Montreal."

"What kind of information?"

"I'll only speak to her."

"I'm sorry, I'm not authorized to pass you to Agent Vidthuvitsai without more information."

Nita hesitated, then covered the receiver and asked Kovit. "What was your mother's name?"

He blinked. "Thida."

"Tell her that it's connected to the death of Thida ten years ago."

"Pardon?"

"You heard me. Pass it on, please. I'll hold."

"It may be a while, ma'am. There are a lot of tips."

"She'll want this one. Trust me."

There was a tinny click and then the elevator music started. Kovit fidgeted on the seat, and Nita paced across the room.

"What if she doesn't respond?" Kovit's leg bounced, and his fingers tapped against the seat.

"She will."

"They may not pass it on."

"They will."

He sighed, running a hand through his hair, face pinched with worry.

Nita had opened her mouth to say something when the line clicked back on.

"This is Agent Vidthuvitsai."

Across from her, Kovit stiffened at the sound of his sister's voice. His whole body stilled, and the expression that crossed his face was strange, part fear, part longing.

Nita blinked. "That was fast."

"It was an interesting message you left."

"I'm glad it got your attention."

There was a short pause and then a soft whisper, small and faint and barely audible. "Is he okay?"

Nita's throat tightened, and across the room, Kovit's face broke a little, confused joy whispering across his features, as though he couldn't quite believe his sister still cared about him.

"Yes. But not for long. Can we meet?"

"Where are you?"

"Toronto."

"Tomorrow, then." There was a short hesitation as they both realized this was being recorded by INHUP and they probably shouldn't be revealing anything incriminating on it. "I'll give you my personal cell phone number. Text me, and we'll make arrangements."

Nita wrote down the number Agent Vidthuvitsai rattled off and then hung up. She texted on the burner phone. *Tomorrow morning, 10am. The mall at Eglington and Yonge, in front of the Pickle Barrel.*

The response was swift. *I'll be there.*

Nita tucked her phone in her pocket and took a long breath.

Kovit stared at his hands, clenching and unclenching his fists, his expression a strange mix of hope and fear, pain and anticipation.

"Are you okay?" Nita asked.

"It could be a trick." His voice scraped slightly. "To lure me in."

She shrugged. "But they're not luring you in. They're luring me in. And I'm not going to give you up."

"You could be charged for hiding a zannie."

"I could lie my way out of any charges by saying you were threatening me, and they'd have no way to prove otherwise."

He laughed softly, but the sound vanished swiftly. His voice was tight. "What if she can't do anything?"

Nita leaned forward and put her hands on his shoulders. "Then she can't do anything, and we'll find another way."

He held her gaze for a moment, then his mouth quirked in a little smile. "You have an answer for everything, don't you?"

She grinned. "I'm prepared for all eventualities."

"Really?" He raised his eyebrows and crossed his arms. "Nita. Please don't tell me your backup plan is to blow up the INHUP building here."

Nita blinked. "Uhhh."

"Because that wouldn't help. It wouldn't get rid of the data, and there'd be a lot more innocent casualties than even I'm comfortable with."

She rubbed an arm and lied, "I never thought about blowing it up."

He stared at her, a mildly disbelieving look on his face.

"Okay, once," she admitted. "Maybe twice. But not seriously."

"So, these plans you have don't involve blowing anything up?"

She tossed out one of her plans. "Nope."

"Uh-huh." His look was skeptical. "Sure."

She flushed. "Look, I'm trying to think of backup plans. In case this meeting with your sister doesn't go well. Or even if it does go well, and she fails."

"I know." He hesitated for a moment, and then said, "What if you used those INHUP names you sold to Adair and started leaking them to the press?" He grinned. "No reason you can't sell them a second time."

She blinked. "The press?"

He nodded. "If you make links with reporters, if you give them reliable information and get them stories, you can maybe start tarnishing INHUP's name. And the more people start digging, the more they'll find out." He met her eyes. "There's more than one way to destroy something. Sometimes public perception can be as dangerous as dynamite."

Nita smiled slowly, liking the idea the more she thought it through. "That's very clever. Why didn't I think of that?"

"Because there's no violence," he teased.

She cracked a smile. "Maybe."

She pulled out her phone. "I should get started now—"

"There's time enough for that tomorrow." His voice was gentle as he extracted the phone from her hand.

She frowned at him. "Why? We've nothing else to do now."

His expression turned playful. "Oh?"

And then before she could blink, he'd grabbed her hand and flipped her down onto the couch. She yelped in surprise as she spiraled and then thudded into the cushion.

She blinked, looking up at Kovit. He had a smile playing

on his face, and for a moment, she thought he was going to kiss her. Her heart pounded, and her mind whirled. They'd kissed earlier today, a broken moment of pain and fear, emotions running high. She didn't know what it meant, or how things went from here, or even where she wanted them to go.

But instead he whispered, "Go to sleep, Nita. Enough planning for today. You can't scheme if you drop dead from exhaustion."

She opened her mouth to protest, but thought better of it. He was right. She *was* tired. Today had been so very long—she could barely believe it was the same day she'd woken up to. She'd murdered an INHUP agent, been arrested, freed by her mother, captured by Henry, and had a showdown with Adair. Even thinking about it all made her whole body heavy with the desire to sleep for the next decade.

But there was still so much to do.

"Nita," Kovit whispered, curling up beside her. "You need to sleep. Everything else can wait until tomorrow morning."

Finally, she sighed softly and rested her head on his shoulder. "Fine. You're right, I should sleep."

They lay down on the couch like that, curled together in a gentle embrace. Nita's eyelids were heavy, and her body sank into the warmth of Kovit's arms as sleep began to pull at her.

Before she drifted away, she murmured, "Kovit?"

"Yeah?" His voice was sleepy and relaxed.

She hesitated. "For now, let's not hurt Fabricio anymore."

There was a long silence before he whispered, "Getting cold feet?"

"No," she lied. "I'm just . . . planning."

44

He laughed softly. "All right. I won't touch him."

A small knot in her stomach released, and she whispered a sleepy thanks before she closed her eyes and drifted off.

Nita woke in the middle of the night to the snick of the front door closing.

Her mind was instantly alert, adrenaline rushing through her blood. Quietly, so quietly, she removed Kovit's arm, draped over her hips, and crawled off the couch.

There was no one in the room.

She enhanced the rods and cones in her eyes to give herself better night vision, but still, no one.

Her eyes moved from the front door to the path that led outside. She tiptoed over, turned the handle carefully, and opened the door.

Outside the recording studio, the apartment hall had bright, burning fluorescents, illuminating rows of other doorways, each painted fire engine red to contrast the beige walls. They also illuminated Gold, stumbling down the hall on her crutches, her arm in a sling, trying to make an escape.

Nita sighed and closed the door behind her so as not to disturb Kovit, and then patiently walked after Gold.

"Going somewhere?" Nita asked.

Gold froze, and then turned back around. The bandage on her face had come loose in one corner, and it flopped back, exposing the edge of a nasty acid burn Nita had given her.

Gold smiled, a bitter, cruel expression. "Oops. Caught me."

"Where were you off to?"

"Oh, you know. Out to get a midnight snack."

Nita gave her a flat look.

Gold rolled her eyes. "What does it matter where I was escaping to? The point is that I was escaping."

Nita sighed. "Did you even bother to try and save Fabricio in the other room?"

"No. Why the hell would I risk my escape for him?"

Nita wished her younger self had been as wise.

Nita leaned against the wall. She could get rid of Gold now. Kill her, shove her body somewhere, end all this. Kovit would wake, and she'd just be gone. Nita could tell him she must have escaped in the night. It wouldn't even be a complete lie.

But Kovit would never forgive her if he found out.

Nita considered just . . . letting Gold go. She didn't want to deal with the black market heiress anymore. But Kovit might still be afraid Nita had disposed of her in the night, and that was the whole point of not murdering Gold in the first place.

And Gold was bound to be a problem. Even if Nita had blackmail to keep Gold in line, like she did with Fabricio, she didn't think it would work. Gold didn't really seem to care about the practicalities of what she stood to lose by hurting Kovit. Her hatred ran too deep.

"Thinking about murdering me?" Gold asked, still smiling slightly.

"Considering it."

"Kovit would know. He'd be very angry."

"It's so fascinating that you're convinced he's both a soul-less monster and that his regret and grief over your death will protect you." Nita shook her head. "Your hypocrisy is amazing. Truly astounding. You're literally relying on the humanity you don't believe he has to save you."

Gold's smile fell into a scowl. "Fuck you."

"And you result to swears because you have no comeback." Nita *tsk*ed. "Childish."

Gold swung around on her crutches, hissing softly in pain as she did so. She glared at Nita, her eyes cold and angry. "You're one to talk. You talk about his humanity and then condone . . ." Her face pinched in disgust. "The things that happened in the other room with Fabricio."

Nita's stomach dropped, and she tried not to think of Fabricio's graphic descriptions of what Kovit had done to him.

"Kovit is evil. I've never denied it," Nita admitted easily. "But he's still human, and he has good sides. I won't disagree with calling him evil, but I will always disagree with painting him as a one-dimensional monster from a slasher film."

Gold's expression became infinitely sad. "You'll understand one day. Once you've seen more of him. Once you've seen him hurt and hurt and hurt. He punished everyone in the Family. He did it because they asked him to and because he liked it. He just turned off the part of his brain that had a soul, the part that went online and chatted about movies and consoled friends. He flicked it off like a switch, and he made people scream."

Gold swallowed. "You don't really know him. You don't know what he's like."

The words hit closer to home than Nita anticipated, and

she closed her eyes for a moment, trying to drown out an INHUP agent's screams. She replaced it with an image of Kovit holding her while she wept with grief over her murdered father.

Nita let out a long breath. "You're the one who doesn't know what she's talking about."

Gold just shook her head. "You'll see eventually." Gold tipped her head back, the fluorescents painting her face a chalky yellow. "Even if it's not me who takes Kovit down. Even if you manage to get him off the list before INHUP hurts him. Someday, somewhere, one of his victims will survive. And they will make it their life's mission to hunt down and stop the monster who hurt them."

Nita's voice was tight. "That's ridiculous. Vengeance stories like that only happen in the movies."

"Perhaps," Gold said softly. "But Kovit goes around doing terrible things, and eventually, those things will come back for him. It might not be today, it might not be tomorrow, but there will always be someone out there with more hate than logic who will try to kill him."

"Like you?"

Gold's smile was bitter. "Like me."

Nita was quiet for a beat. "Was it someone you cared about? That he hurt, I mean."

After a long moment, she said, "No."

Nita thought she'd guessed wrong, but then Gold said softly, "My father used to make me watch the recordings, you know, as I was growing up. I'd look into those people's eyes as Kovit made them scream. And my father told me, *That's how you run an empire. That's how you make people fear you. That's how you gain respect."*

Gold leaned heavily on her crutch. "The first time I saw someone try to kill my father, I was twelve. It was a woman in her early twenties. Her husband was a bruiser for my father, but he'd . . . made a mistake and been sent to Kovit. When he came home, he was missing some critical pieces."

Gold closed her eyes, and the light danced on her cheeks. "I still remember the sounds of her bones crunching as Kovit twisted them round in the socket until they popped out. My father told Kovit that she didn't need to survive, that she was going to send a message to anyone who dared go against him."

She met Nita's eyes. "People are afraid of my father. Most people, they don't dare try anything. But there's always a few who have more hate and anger than fear, who try to kill him. They've never succeeded, because my father has guards. He knows how to play the game.

"But Kovit? Kovit has you. And how long he has you, I don't know. One day, someone will have more anger than fear, and they will come, and they will kill him."

Gold's gaze was steady. "And on that day, I will light a candle for the loss of the friend who could have been, and then I will celebrate the death of the monster that was."

SEVEN

T HE *BLEE-BLEE-BLEE BLEE-BLEE-BLEE* of the alarm jolted Nita awake the next morning. It hurt to open her eyes, like there were broken grains of glass behind her eyelids, so she didn't. She pawed around for her cell phone and swiped at it blearily, hoping that she'd turned it off instead of just snoozed it.

Beside her Kovit moaned softly and pressed his face into her shoulder, as though hiding from the sound. "It's too early to get up."

"We have places to be." Nita rubbed her eyes and sat up. Her hands were sticky with duct tape glue from tying Gold up last night. "We have to meet your sister."

His eyes snapped open, and Nita regretted reminding him so quickly. His whole body was tight with nerves.

"It'll be fine," Nita whispered, gently putting a hand on his shoulder.

He gave her a shaky smile. "I don't even know what I'm more afraid of. That she hates me, or that she doesn't. That she'll still love me, and I'll only have a week to see her before . . ."

Before INHUP put his face up. Before the world turned on him and butchered him.

Nita swallowed. "Don't think of that."

His smile was bitter. "Kind of hard not to."

Nita sighed. She couldn't blame him. Wasn't she just as consumed with her fear over the black market, the release of that damn video of her online?

She rose and went to the washroom to splash some water on her face. She was tired, and she hadn't gotten nearly enough sleep because of Gold's midnight escapades. She rubbed her temples and considered healing her body of its sleep deprivation, actually going in and replicating all the things sleep did. But that would probably just make her more tired and seemed like a waste of effort.

Instead, she closed her eyes, focused on her adrenal gland, and made it start releasing more adrenaline into her body in an effort to wake herself up. She opened her eyes and immediately felt more alert, but underneath the alertness was a bone-deep exhaustion that had been building for the last week. Something was going to have to give. But not yet.

She made her way back to the lobby and found Kovit eating cold greasy pizza leftovers.

Nita sat down beside him and took a slice. "Gold tried to escape last night."

Kovit hesitated. "Is she hurt?"

"No more than she was yesterday. I tied her back up with some duct tape."

"That's good." His shoulders relaxed.

Nita sighed. Despite Gold's hatred, she didn't think Kovit

would ever stop caring for the other girl. They'd been friends once, and Kovit was far too loyal to discard someone he'd once cared so much about that easily. He'd had to be right at the breaking point with Henry, and Gold hadn't done anything nearly as terrible.

Nita rubbed her temples. "I've got her taped to the bed, but something has to change. She's going to find a way to escape again."

Kovit shrugged. "We'll just check her bindings regularly."

"Kovit . . ."

He rose. "Let's check them before we leave."

Nita followed him into the studio Gold was staying in. She was awake and lying in bed, awkwardly pinned by Nita's sloppy duct tape job.

"Good morning," she said, her voice still rough.

"Morning." Kovit smiled softly. "That looks uncomfortable."

"That's because it is." Gold's eyes were cold. "Which you already know, because you can feel my pain."

Kovit's smile fell a little. He fumbled for a moment and pulled his switchblade out.

Gold tensed and turned to Nita. "Convince him to kill me after all?"

Kovit tensed. "I'm not going to hurt you, May."

She raised her eyebrow at the switchblade.

"For the duct tape," he explained. "I'm going to redo it so it's more comfortable."

He knelt down beside her and carefully cut her bindings,

then pocketed the blade. Nita went to Gold's other side, and they each took an arm and helped her to her feet.

"This way." Nita pushed Gold toward a chair on the other side of the room.

Gold stumbled forward. She grinned, sharp and cruel. "I feel like I'm on my death walk. You know, right before they lead the prisoners to the electric chair."

Nita sighed. "Do you ever shut up?"

"I try to annoy my captors as much as possible." Gold's eyes narrowed as she smiled at Nita "Though I suppose you wouldn't understand what it's like to be a prisoner, would you?"

Nita stiffened, but didn't rise to the bait.

They retied Gold together, and Nita tugged Kovit away before Gold could say anything else incendiary. Gold was far too good at hurting Kovit, and he had enough to deal with today.

They went and checked on Fabricio before they left.

Nita pushed open the pastel blue door to Fabricio's room, and Fabricio raised his head. They'd left him tied to his chair all night, and there were circles under his eyes that told her that he hadn't slept much. Small cracked flakes of scabs had fallen off and covered Fabricio's pants like tiny bugs. Nita kept her eyes from straying to his hands. She didn't want to see what they looked like.

"Good morning." Nita's voice was forced cheery. The pizza lay on the floor where she'd left it the night before, and she picked a piece up and shoved it in his mouth. "Breakfast time."

Fabricio's huge blue-gray eyes looked at Nita steadily. Judgingly. They stared right into her soul, and they found her wanting.

It made her want to poke them out.

Nita blinked at the sudden, violent urge. Hadn't she once had nightmares about being forced to rip Fabricio's eyes out? And now she fantasized about it. How times had changed.

She turned away before Fabricio could say anything, assured that he was still trapped and wouldn't be making any escape attempts. She locked the door, just in case.

She nodded to Kovit when she returned to the lobby. "Ready?"

He gave her a tentative smile. "As I'll ever be."

They left the apartment and walked to the mall at Yonge and Eglinton—Nita had picked one of the few landmarks she knew, and part of her was a bit uneasy at the thought of meeting so close to home. Kovit stopped partway, so that if his sister was planning to turn him over, only Nita would get in trouble.

When Nita was small, her mother used to teach her tips and tricks for spotting INHUP agents, spies—people who didn't belong. How to tell if you were walking into a setup. First, go early, or have someone else go early. See who's there. Are they still there, doing the same things, half an hour later when the meetup is? How long does it really take to read the newspaper on a park bench, after all?

So Nita went early. She entered the mall beside the Pickle Barrel where they were supposed to meet up, and casually people-watched. A hostess texted at the counter of the restaurant, and an old man drank coffee by the front window. Past them, in the bookstore across the way, a man with large round glasses browsed the front tables. Nita skimmed the titles, but nothing interested her. She continued past into the mall proper. It was early enough in the morning on a weekday that there weren't too many browsers, mostly overcaffeinated retail staff.

Nita bought a bagel at a small stand and had them put it in a larger bag, so it looked like she'd been shopping. She was about to loop back around and return the way she'd come when she noticed that someone was following her around. She paused at a toy store and glanced at his reflection in the window. It was the man from the bookstore.

But why? She hadn't done anything to indicate she was the one meeting Kovit's sister, so if INHUP agents had been set up here, they shouldn't have marked her as worth watching yet.

Unless he wasn't an INHUP agent.

Nita's fingers tightened on her bag, and she turned sharply away. She needed to deal with this, find out who this person was, and handle him. In private.

Her sneakers squeaked softly on the polished floors, and she made a left, following the sign for the bathrooms down a long concrete corridor between a shoe store and a makeup store.

The man followed, slow and sure.

INHUP agent or black market hunter. But if he was a black market hunter, how had he found her? A sick feeling twisted in Nita's stomach. INHUP had sold her location out before. They could have done it again.

Except INHUP didn't know who was meeting Patchaya Vidthuvitsai. So they couldn't have sold her out this time.

Nita kept her pace even as she turned a corner and waited there. The bathrooms were just ahead, wide doors displaying clean white porcelain and pastel blue stalls. She could hear a fan going, but there didn't seem to be anyone here. It was too early on a weekday. Practically empty.

That was fine by her.

The man turned the corner and jerked back, clearly not expecting Nita to be waiting.

She smiled at him, all sugar. "Why are you following me?"

"I'm not?" He adjusted his glasses and smiled.

"But you are."

He stared at her, then looked down the hall, noticing the deserted bathroom. Since they'd turned, they weren't visible from the main part of the mall. Then he smiled.

"Stupid girl." He took out a knife. "You shouldn't confront men in dark alleys. I'm going to make so much money off of you."

Ah. He was another black market dealer, not an undercover INHUP agent. That was a relief. Her meeting with Patchaya wasn't ruined yet.

Nita smiled at him, hard and sharp. "Stupid boy. Don't follow people into dark alleys."

She brought her scalpel up from where she was hiding it and jabbed it into his inner thigh, severing his artery and slicing off part of a very tender area in one single motion.

The man jerked, gasping and opening his mouth to scream, but Nita was faster, jamming her bag with its bagel into his mouth and muffling the sound.

He fell backwards into the wall, blood soaking quickly

through his pants, and Nita muttered to herself in irritation as he bled out. She grabbed his body under the arms and dragged him toward the washroom. He jerked and struggled, but it was pointless. Nita had gotten rid of her myostatin, so her muscles had no limit on how strong they could get, and she had been training them. She had superhuman strength, and he was dying of blood loss.

She shoved him in a stall, and he lolled against the wall, eyes glassy and vacant, mouth still stuffed with bagel. Frowning, she took the bagel bag, flushed the receipt and bag down the toilet, then soaked the bagel until it was a soggy disgusting mess, ripped it into pieces, and flushed it too. She didn't want anything to be able to tie her to his death.

She locked the stall from the inside and wiggled across the floor into the neighboring stall to avoid crawling through the trail of blood. After exiting the stall, she grabbed water and paper towels and mopped up the bloody trail on the concrete.

As she scrubbed, anger bubbled in her chest. She hadn't needed this complication today. She didn't want to have to deal with this. It hadn't taken her long to handle—she should probably be disturbed by that, it was probably a bad sign how efficient she'd become at taking out black market dealers, but she didn't mind the efficiency she'd gained. She didn't even feel guilty about it anymore, it was just another task that simply had to be completed.

No, what pissed her off about all this was the fact that she was so notorious now that she couldn't walk outside for fifteen minutes without attracting a hunter.

She threw the bloody paper towels in the trash and then

covered them with clean ones. She needed to leave Toronto. This city was a death trap for her.

Part of her wanted to stay, to take every single one of these dealers out, to wreak havoc on all of them for trying to kill her and sell her. But she'd tried that, and it had only made things worse. She needed to be smart about this, and being smart meant that she had to think big, plan ahead, and not just murder everyone in her way. She needed to make them all too afraid to try to kill her.

And for that, she needed Fabricio's information. And she needed Kovit's help—she couldn't afford for him to have the whole planet trying to murder him.

Kovit. She checked the time and swore, leaving the bathroom at a brisk pace. She'd been delayed too much already.

She had an INHUP agent to meet.

EIGHT

A S SHE NEARED the Pickle Barrel, she noticed that the old man was still sitting with his breakfast in the window to the restaurant, the hostess was still texting. The man looking at books was gone of course, dead in the bathroom. Nita eyed the hostess and the man eating breakfast, but didn't let her gaze linger. There was no way to know if they were INHUP.

In front of the Pickle Barrel stood a woman. She was short, barely five feet, with long black hair pulled into a professional bun at the nape of her neck. Her brown skin was the same warm shade as Kovit's, and she shared his striking eyebrows and black eyes.

Nita let out a breath. Patchaya Vidthuvitsai had come.

But the question was, had she been followed? And if she had, was she the one instigating it, or was INHUP doing it independently of her?

You're being paranoid again, one part of her mind whispered.

Better to be safe than sorry . . . And you were *just followed and had to murder someone and hide a body in a bathroom. Is it really paranoia when it happens?*

Touché, brain, touché.

So she casually walked by and didn't even look up as she passed Kovit's sister. Once outside the mall, she tipped her head back and looked around. There was construction on the opposite side of the street, but the subway entrance was clear.

Nita crossed the street and stood under the shelter of a mesh fence, pulled out her phone, and texted the same number she'd used last night: *The subway entrance across the street.*

A few moments later, Patchaya left the mall and made her way to the streetlights. As she waited for the lights to change, the man who'd been eating breakfast at the Pickle Barrel came out the front door of the shopping mall.

Nita's eyes narrowed. It didn't *necessarily* mean anything. But Nita didn't stay alive by assuming the best. And she'd already had one brush with hunters today.

Patchaya crossed the street and approached the entrance to the subway. Nita stood just inside, out of view of the man following.

When Patchaya approached, Nita reached up and plucked her cell phone from her hand.

Patchaya spun to Nita, and Nita tossed the phone over her shoulder into the construction site. "You can come back for it later."

Then she grabbed the INHUP agent's hand and tugged her into the subway station.

"That wasn't necessary," Patchaya protested as Nita led the way down the dirty concrete stairs and into the depths of underground. The smell of industrial cleaner and urine mixed together with the occasional whiff of overperfumed commuter.

Nita shrugged. "Better safe than sorry."

On the platform, Nita pulled them onto a train as the doors opened. A few people got off, but it was mostly empty. She turned back to the stairs as the doors rattled closed, and nudged Kovit's sister.

"Do you know that man?" she asked.

The man from the Pickle Barrel descended the stairs, and Nita watched Patchaya for her response. Kovit's sister shook her head. "No. Should I?"

As the train pulled away, the man sat on one of the metal benches and opened a book and began to read, seeming totally unconcerned with the world.

Nita sighed. She really was getting paranoid.

Patchaya smiled slightly, an ironic twist to her lips. "Did you think we were being followed?"

"Can't be too careful." Nita gestured to an empty pair of seats, faded red fabric worn to nothing in several places. "Especially given the conversation topic."

"I can understand that," Patchaya said as they sat down. "I'm sure a lot of people in my office would be very angry if they found out about this meeting."

Her English had a faint accent, one very different from Kovit's. Kovit had learned English in the States from a young age, so he sounded like he was from somewhere on the East Coast. But his sister's accent wasn't like anything Nita had heard before, like each syllable was being emphasized a little more than it should.

"But INHUP doesn't have the manpower to follow me right now, even if they suspected something," Patchaya continued. "All available agents are working on another case right now. No one's going to be monitoring me."

Nita tilted her head, curious. "What are they working on?"

"Two agents were kidnapped yesterday, but only one escaped. We're trying to find the missing one."

Nita looked away, part of her mind reeling that it was really only yesterday she'd orchestrated that kidnapping. The arrest, confrontation with Henry, then with Adair, catching Fabricio — so much had happened in between that it felt like a lifetime ago.

She stared at her hands on her lap. The agent Patchaya was looking for was dead. He'd been tortured, mutilated, and murdered by Kovit in one of Nita's plans for capturing Fabricio that had gone terribly wrong. Not that she could ever admit it.

"Did — Do you know the agent?" Nita asked.

"Yeah. I know him." Patchaya gave Nita a strained smile. "I'm supposed to be working on this unicorn murder case in Montreal, but I was secretly glad you gave me an excuse to come back to Toronto and see how the search for Bran was coming."

"Oh." Nita looked at her fingers on her lap, trying not to imagine how terrible Kovit would feel if he discovered he'd tortured and murdered his sister's friend.

Nita decided it was best to change the topic before it got dangerous. She cleared her throat. "So, Agent Vidthuvitsai —"

"Patchaya. Or Pat."

"Patchaya." Nita corrected herself.

"And you are?"

Nita considered how much to say, and then settled on "I'm a friend of Kovit's."

Patchaya let out a shaky half laugh. She brushed a hair from her face with a trembling hand.

Nita blinked slowly. "Are you okay?"

Patchaya nodded sharply. "I'm fine. It's just been a long time since I heard his name. Not since . . ."

Not since their mother was killed and Kovit was left alone, ten years old and frightened, on the streets of Bangkok to fend for himself.

"How is he?" Patchaya asked, finally looking up.

Nita smiled softly. "He's all right."

"Is he . . ." She choked, as if she couldn't get the words out.

"Is he what?"

"He was always such a thoughtful child, you know. He'd do anything for his friends. He always tried to comfort me when I was scared, even though he didn't understand what was happening." Patchaya swallowed heavily. "I hoped the world wouldn't change him, that what he was wouldn't warp him. That he wouldn't turn out like other zannies. That he wouldn't become like our mother."

A weird mixture of guilt and nausea bubbled in her stomach. "Oh."

Patchaya took a deep breath and met Nita's eyes. "Did he turn out okay? Is he good?"

Nita's stomach tightened, and the lies felt sticky on her tongue, like she could taste Mirella and Fabricio and that dead

INHUP agent's screams. "He's good. He's a good person. He's not like other zannies."

Patchaya's shoulders slumped in relief, and she smiled up at Nita, eyes a little watery. "Good. That's good. I'm glad."

She wiped her eyes softly, and Nita looked down, uneasy at her own lies. But she couldn't ever tell the truth. That the "missing" INHUP agent Patchaya had been friends with had been gleefully tortured and murdered by Kovit. That he was still himself, but he was also exactly the monster Patchaya feared.

Patchaya let out a short breath. "Is he here? In Toronto?"

Nita nodded.

"Can I see him?"

Nita hesitated before agreeing. She hoped Patchaya wouldn't ask him any hard questions.

"Of course. But first"—Nita met Patchaya's eyes—"I have a favor to ask."

Patchaya's eyes narrowed in suspicion. "A favor?"

"After his—your—mother died, Kovit was picked up by a criminal organization." Nita was careful with what she said. She needed to tell the truth. Just not all of the truth. "He ran away after refusing to obey them. But they don't want him spilling their secrets, so they found evidence he's a zannie, and they sent it to INHUP."

Patchaya's expression flickered, first swelling with pride, her eyes watery, and then slowly sinking into fear and panic as the rest of the information set in. Nita had been careful to paint Kovit as sympathetically as possible while still keeping enough to the truth so that if Patchaya investigated, the information Nita gave would match up. Based on Patchaya's expressions, she'd played it properly.

"He's been outed to INHUP?" Patchaya whispered.

"Yes. We have one week before there's an international manhunt for him."

Her breath caught. "One week? That's so fast. That's the mandatory minimum time INHUP has to take to verify the information is accurate, but it almost always takes much longer. The evidence must be overwhelming."

That was *not* what Nita wanted to hear.

"One week," Nita confirmed softly.

Patchaya's head bowed. "So little time."

"We were hoping, since you're an INHUP agent and working in the dangerous unnaturals section . . ."

She shook her head. "If you're asking me to delete documents or something, I can't."

"Can't or won't?"

"Can't." Her voice was heavy. "Those kind of reports are handled by the central INHUP headquarters in France. To get rid of that information, I'd have to fly to France, wipe their servers, and then somehow stop the three to five people working on his case from talking."

Nita frowned. "Why so many people?"

"When an individual is reported to the Dangerous Unnaturals List, it's a multistep thing. First, someone has to verify the claims. That could mean DNA evidence is tested, or video files are reviewed by experts, or any number of other things.

"Part of the verification also involves sending that information to people working on cases involving zannies. For example, if there's a report on a zannie in San Diego, and a murder by horrific torture was committed there recently, the information is sent to the people working on that case to see if the culprit is the zannie."

The train doors whooshed open as they hit the next station, and Patchaya sighed. "There's also an investigation crew that usually tries to independently verify the information."

"That's . . . a lot."

"Yeah. There were mistakes in the early years. We're careful now." Patchaya looked away, mouth pressed into a thin line. "If his information has gone to INHUP . . . there's nothing I can do."

Nita's throat was tight. She hadn't truly understood the scale of INHUP operations, of how many different people in how many different places would be involved before Kovit's name went up.

The cat wasn't just out of the bag. It was long gone and had kittens.

In her mind's eye, she pictured the day the wanted ad went up. Kovit would be sitting in a hotel room, terrified to go outside, terrified to be recognized, terrified to exist. But it wouldn't matter, because the takeout place across the street would see him when they went to deliver pizza. And they'd post it on the internet, and the mob would force Kovit to pay for the crimes he'd committed.

Or maybe Kovit would be walking down the street. New haircut, fake glasses, full disguise. And then someone would see him, see through the look, and call the police. They'd surround him, dozens of cars, dozens of men in blue, guns raised high. And Kovit would look up at the sky, hopelessness writ large in those beautiful black eyes.

And he'd die.

Kovit's information was going up online in one week, and there was absolutely nothing Nita could do about it.

NINE

NITA AND PATCHAYA got off at Spadina station. As they rode the escalator up, Nita checked her cell phone for texts, but there was no reception. She wiped her sweaty palms on her pants.

Patchaya chewed her lip, a small furrow between her brows.

"Deep in thought?" Nita asked.

"Trying to think of anything I can do to stop this." She shook her head. "Short of somehow getting rid of the whole Dangerous Unnaturals List, I don't know how we'd stop it."

Nita blinked.

Get rid of the whole list.

Adair, the information broker she'd stayed with until yesterday, had told her that the list had been built corrupt, that the only creatures on it were the ones with body parts valuable on the black market. That the list wasn't there to protect people as INHUP claimed, but to make people money. That the creation of the list was, in and of itself, leading the monsters on it to commit crimes. After all, if it was a crime to be born, there was no legal way to live your life, so you had to turn to illegal ones. A vicious cycle of making monsters.

But if the list weren't there . . . well, a lot of problems would be solved.

But how could she get rid of the list?

"Are you okay?" Patchaya asked.

Nita gave her a tight smile. "Fine. Just thinking. Trying to find other ways out of this."

"I'll look into it. I don't think I can do anything, but I'd never forgive myself if I didn't at least *try*."

Nita nodded, but her mind was already past her plan to use Patchaya and working on something much better.

At the top of the escalator, people bustled through the station, shoes clicking on the tiled floors as they passed through a series of metal turnstiles. A bored attendant sat in a booth, and the faint hum of guitar music from the busker in one corner echoed just under the hubbub.

On the other side of the turnstiles, Kovit waited for them.

He was staring at his phone nervously, and he kept running a hand through his hair, mussing it. They'd agreed that if Nita deemed contact safe, she'd bring his sister here, and if she didn't, then Nita would come alone.

Patchaya paused at the turnstile. "I really should get back."

Nita raised her eyebrows. "Don't you want to see Kovit?"

Patchaya froze, mouth open, and in that instant, Kovit saw them. He swallowed, and then came over, his footsteps slow and heavy.

Patchaya turned and met his eyes. Her gaze flicked over his

face, examining all the changes, placing the face of the young man in front of her over that of the boy from her past.

He gave her a frightened, tentative smile, voice hoarse. "Pat?"

Her face crumpled, and she threw herself through the turnstile and embraced him. "Kovit."

Kovit froze for a second before wrapping his arms around her and burying his face in her shoulder. Both of their chests heaved softly, and Nita couldn't tell if they were laughing or sobbing.

Nita stepped back, suddenly feeling like an intruder. She wondered what it would be like to have a sibling who loved her that much. Who was willing to risk everything just to see her, who wept when they were reunited. She tried to imagine anyone in her life caring about her that much, and she couldn't. Her mother wasn't the emotional type. Her father . . . her father was gone. Murdered by a vampire while Nita was trapped in Death Market. A vampire Nita still needed to find and take her vengeance on.

No, there was no one who would care about Nita that way. She'd never really wanted a sibling before, but seeing the grief and love in Kovit's and Patchaya's faces, her heart ached like she'd missed out on something precious.

Patchaya pulled away and brushed a strand of Kovit's hair from his face. "Look at you, all grown up."

"Speak for yourself." Kovit's smile was a bit crooked. "Look at you, all old. You even have a gray hair."

She swatted his shoulder. "I'm only twenty-five, you brat."

Kovit laughed, light and free.

Patchaya said something in Thai, her smile still wide.

For a moment, Kovit's face was blank, and then he slowly began speaking in Thai. The words didn't sound as smooth as hers, but they came, creaking and groaning with rust and disuse. It looked like he hadn't forgotten it after all, despite his fears. Or at least, not all of it.

After a few sentences, though, Patchaya switched back into English. "Where have you been the last decade?"

Kovit looked away. "Here and there."

She raised a skeptical eyebrow. "Here and there."

He sighed, and then laughed. "How do you still always manage to make me feel guilty with that eyebrow?"

"It's a superpower all older sisters have."

He snorted. "Superpower. The only superpower you have is being an INHUP agent. How in the world did *that* happen?"

She winced slightly, mood darkening. "It's not what you think."

He gave her a sad smile, just a little broken. "Oh?"

She couldn't meet his eyes. "I just wanted to make a difference."

Nita felt bad for the two siblings. They clearly loved each other, but one was a monster and the other a monster hunter, and the disconnect of those ten years where they'd ended up on such wildly different paths was painted in the unspoken tension and the broken spaces between their sentences.

"Well," Kovit replied, his voice light and teasing. "What a terrible motive. Imagine wanting to make a positive impact on the world. The horror."

Patchaya blinked and then burst into laughter and hugged him.

Nita's heart tightened. She cleared her throat, feeling more of an intruder than ever. "I have an errand I need to run. I'll see you back at . . . I'll see you later, Kovit." She turned to his sister. "And it was nice to meet you."

Kovit frowned. "Errand?"

They'd agreed Nita would stay close by, just in case Kovit's meeting ended in some unforeseen disaster. But that was before Patchaya had said she couldn't help, before Nita's whirring mind had come up with a new plan.

"I need to check on something." Nita smiled tightly. "I need to talk to someone who might . . . know something."

Kovit's eyes widened in understanding, and his voice was careful. "Are you sure that's a good idea?"

Nita smiled. "You never know if you don't try. But if I'm not back when you're done, you know where to look."

Before Kovit could protest more, she turned away.

Her steps were heavy as she went to the one person who could tell her if her plan was possible, who had the connections to make it happen. The question was would he help her?

Or would he kill her out of spite?

Because Nita and Adair hadn't parted on the best terms.

TEN

NITA WALKED the familiar road from the station to Adair's pawnshop. The sidewalk pavement was a bit cracked, and all the buildings looked like they'd seen better days. It wasn't truly a sketchy area—she'd been in far more uncomfortable places, but the pawnshop certainly wasn't located in the nicest part of town.

It suited Adair perfectly, not just the aesthetic of it— slightly sketchy and a little uncomfortable—but because it was close to the water. Kelpies like Adair were semiaquatic, and needed places underwater to hide the rotting human corpses they ate. Though she supposed he could also hide the bodies in his murder basement.

Nita approached the front door. The sign was turned to CLOSED, but the light was on inside, and she could see shadows moving around.

She took a deep breath. She hadn't left this shop last time on the best circumstances. Adair had betrayed her, she'd tried to murder him, and in the end, Diana, his ghoul assistant, had interfered and they'd called a truce.

Adair said he didn't do vengeance. It was bad for business. And Nita believed him. Mostly. If she was wrong, he'd drag her into the underground pool in his basement and drown her and then eat her rotting corpse.

But she had to try. She didn't know anyone else as knowledgeable and well connected in the black market who actively wanted the Dangerous Unnaturals List gone. And she thought he might be willing to overlook their feud and help her with it.

She knocked on the front door and waited. Silence. She knocked again.

Diana's voice rang out from the other side. "We're closed!"

"It's me," Nita called back.

"Then we're definitely closed."

"I need to talk to Adair."

The door opened, and Diana stood there, her long dark brown hair pulled into a ponytail, her eyes tired. Her light brown skin looked gray with exhaustion and poor lighting. She reminded Nita a little of Mirella, Nita's fellow captive in Death Market and the first person Nita had heard Kovit torture.

Nita shoved her mind away from that thought.

"Go away, Nita. Adair doesn't want to talk to you."

"Have you asked him?" Nita countered.

She sighed. "I don't need to. He's furious, injured, and not in a great mood. If you go in there, he's going to kill you."

Nita crossed her arms and smiled with a confidence she didn't feel. "Well, he can try. But we know who won the last fight, don't we?"

Diana's eyes narrowed. "Because you ambushed him. He won't be tricked like that again."

Nita blew out a breath. "Look, I just want to talk. Let me in, I'll say my piece and leave."

Diana gave her a long, assessing look, and then finally opened the door a little wider.

Nita took a step in, and Diana grabbed her arm. "Nita, if you ever hurt Adair again . . ."

"You'll what? Get vengeance? You, who tried to talk me out of violence? Who couldn't kill her own family's murderer?"

Diana flinched, and Nita ripped her arm away.

Diana was quiet. "No, I was going to say I wouldn't save you from Adair's wrath again."

Nita blinked. Diana had saved her and Kovit from being thrown out of the shop and onto the streets when the hunt for Nita had been heating up. She'd stood as a wall between two angry monsters and calmed Adair down. And later, she'd stood as a wall between Nita and Adair and calmed Nita.

"That's fine." Nita's lips curled into a warped smile. "I don't need anyone to save me. I'm perfectly capable of that myself."

She took a few steps into the cluttered pawnshop. Old cabinets and tables were jammed together so tightly there was barely any room to make a path to the back counter. Glass chicken butter dishes stared at her with painted-on eyes, and a bronze statue of a general on a horse tried to stab her with its sword as she passed.

She made for the back stairwell. Two sets of stairs awaited, one leading up, one leading down. Nita and Kovit had stayed up at the top of the stairwell in a small guest room. That was where she'd left Adair last night, cooling in the bath, trying to recover from the effects of Nita's boiling water attack, which had sloughed his glamour off and revealed the monster beneath.

Nita took a step up, and Diana called out, "Not that way."

She turned around. "Where is he, then?"

Diana hesitated, then nodded to the stairs down.

Nita stared at the dark stairwell to the basement and laughed. "I didn't think you'd start in on Adair's stupid murder jokes."

"It's not a joke." Diana came over. "He had me help carry him down there last night. There's more water. He needs full submersion to recover properly."

Nita hesitated. Everything at her screamed that this was a trap, that she was being led down the stairs into an underground murder chamber. Of all the people in the world to lead her into a murder chamber, Diana was on the bottom of her list.

But Nita had been wrong before.

Diana rolled her eyes and leaned against the counter wall. "He's in the basement. You want to talk to him, that's where you go."

"Can't he come up?"

"No." Diana's eyes were hard. "He needs the water to recover from what *you* did to him."

Nita remained silent a moment. "Isn't he the one who told me never to go down there, or he'd murder me and eat my rotting corpse?"

Diana's mouth quirked a little at that. "Sounds like something he'd say."

Nita held her ground. "You can go down and get him. I'll wait here."

She shrugged. "He won't come up."

"He will." Nita took a deep breath. "Tell him I might have a plan for getting rid of the Dangerous Unnaturals List."

Diana's eyes widened. "What?"

"You heard me."

Diana was quiet for a time before finally nodding. "I'll go tell him."

She descended the stairs, and Nita leaned against the stairwell, waiting. Part of her was intensely curious what was down there in the depths of the pawnshop.

And part of her was very certain she wouldn't live very long if she found out.

She looked away, her eyes running over a curio cabinet full of ceramic salt and pepper shakers in the shapes of various animals, then moving on to a cribbage board made from an elk antler perched precariously on top of a moldy record player from the sixties. Where the hell did Adair even find some of this crap?

After a few minutes, there was a heavy thunk on the stairs, and Diana reemerged. "Take a seat. He's coming."

Nita obliged, heading over to an antique dining table. She moved a porcelain ballerina from the chair and seated herself. Diana vanished again, and when she returned a second later, she was supporting Adair.

He looked awful.

Usually, his glamour was up and strong, making him look

human. His favorite look was of a young man, white, with wavy black hair, swampy greenish yellow eyes, and a sly smile.

Now, black and scaly, Adair looked less like a human and more like a crocodile-dragon hybrid. His long, slitted yellow eyes watched her with menace, and his head was more than half mouth, long thin teeth overlapping each other, creating a toothy cage.

Seeing him like this was a stark reminder that he wasn't human, had never been human, no matter how much he pretended.

Diana helped him sit down, lowering that toothy face away from hers and easing him into the chair. Adair looked at Nita, but she couldn't read the face of something that looked like it had walked straight out of an Alien movie.

Adair tilted his head, and as Nita watched, small pockets of mucus beaded on the scales of his face.

Diana's eyes widened. "Don't strain yourself."

"I'm fine, Diana." Adair's voice was as smooth and slick and human as always, and it was disconcerting hearing it from the toothy face. "But we have a guest. I can't just come in undressed."

As Nita watched, the small beads of mucus spread over his face, and it rippled softly, like the surface of water.

And then a human face was staring back at her. Adair's face.

His hands were still taloned claws, and his body was still black and scaly, but his face was very human and very angry.

"Nita. I didn't expect to see you so soon." His smile was tight, and she couldn't forget the teeth that lurked just beneath its facade. "You'll forgive my appearance. Someone burned my skin off last night, and I'm in a bit of a foul mood. I haven't even been able to go home yet because I can't look human enough."

Nita crossed her arms. She felt a little bad, because it was her fault, but not really because he'd betrayed her to Henry. And no one betrayed Nita and got away unscathed.

"How long will it take before you look convincingly human?" she asked.

He sighed. "Of course that's what you're curious about."

She shrugged.

"I'll probably be able to get by later today, wearing a coat. But it will take a while for my skin to really grow back."

Fascinating. She'd love to dissect a kelpie one day. She couldn't even begin to imagine how unique and interesting it would be. A chemical analysis of the mucus-y substance that gave them their illusions would be illuminating—she wondered if it could be artificially replicated and used by regular people for disguises. She could make a killing on the black market with it. And it would certainly be a good way to change her face and regain the anonymity that video online had taken from her.

She hid her hands under the table, so no one would see them subconsciously reaching for a scalpel as her mind went through all the various dissections she wanted to perform on him.

Adair considered her for a moment. "Before we talk about why you're here, I need to know something."

Nita's eyes narrowed, suspicious. "What do you need to know?"

His gaze was steady. "Do you regret any of your actions over the past few days?"

Nita opened her mouth to tell him no, to bluff her way through with brash confidence, the way she always did.

But the words died in her mouth. Because the truth was, she'd made mistakes. She'd miscalculated, and she'd fucked up. And while she acknowledged that to herself, while she took her mistakes and accepted them as experiences to learn from, she couldn't quite bring herself to say the words aloud. Admitting her mistakes felt like showing weakness. She'd been okay admitting fault to Kovit, because she trusted him. Adair, she didn't trust.

But she could see it in Adair's eyes. Lying wouldn't work here. He didn't want her to bluff, to use brash confidence to fake competence. He wanted to know her thoughts, and if she didn't admit the truth, she had a feeling she'd be shown the doorway before they could have their chat.

"I made some mistakes. If I had a chance to do it over, knowing what I know now, I'd change some of my plans," Nita admitted, the words sticking a little in her throat. "But I don't know that I regret the choices I made. They seemed right at the time, and I learned a lot from them."

He raised his eyebrows. "I see. Anything else?"

She snorted. "You want me to apologize for the hot water."

"That would be nice."

Her smile was bitter. "Why don't we just agree we both made mistakes. I shouldn't have burned your skin off, you shouldn't have sold me out to Henry."

He considered, his swampy eyes strange and unreadable, before inclining his head. "Very well. We both made mistakes."

Nita could hear his unspoken *but you made more*. Which she couldn't argue with.

"You told Diana you were here because of something to do with the Dangerous Unnaturals List?" Adair asked, changing the subject.

Nita nodded. Of all people besides Kovit, Adair probably had the most invested in getting rid of the list. It was only a matter of time before kelpies were added and Adair was murdered. He'd kept his species off it with information and blackmail and who knew what else, but it was a stopgap, not a solution.

"I might have an idea to get rid of the list." Nita let out a breath. "But I would need your help."

"Of course you need my help. You always need my help." His tone was mocking, but his eyes were calculating. "Tell me more about this opportunity."

Here was the sticky part. This involved telling Adair her plans for herself too. And she didn't know who he might sell that information to.

Was it worth risking her own safety and her own plans to help Kovit?

She felt a bit bad even thinking it. She knew Kovit would gladly help her at whatever risk to himself—he had already. But she couldn't help hesitating, because nothing in the world was worth more to her than her own safety.

But she deemed the risk worth the reward, so she took a

breath and spoke. "I've captured Fabricio Tácunan. I'm going to use him to break into his father's company and steal all the files."

Adair tilted his head to the side. "And?"

"And I want to make a trade with INHUP. Dissolve the list for the contents of those files." Nita met his eyes. "You and I both know that every black market player, every corrupt politician, everyone who has something to hide and the money to do it hires Tácunan Law. With all that information to trade . . ."

"You want to take the list down?" Adair gave her a skeptical look, and then his face cleared. "Ah, no, you're not that altruistic. You want to use it to blackmail black market players so that they stop hunting you. The list is just a side note to help Kovit out."

She winced at how easily she'd been seen through. "There's no reason I can't want to do both."

"Won't work. Trading information for taking down the list, I mean." Adair sighed softly. "You think I haven't thought of something like that before? I can tell you secrets that would crush dynasties."

"But all of Tácunan Law?"

Adair leaned back. "They're even less likely to take that deal."

"Why?"

"Because to make a deal so big it would take down the Dangerous Unnaturals List . . . Do you know how high up in INHUP you'd need to be to make that deal?"

"And?"

"And the people that high in INHUP all *use* Tácunan Law."

Adair leaned forward. "Rather than dealing with you, they'd be more likely to murder you so word of their crimes doesn't get out."

Nita stared, her mind blanking for a moment.

Of course. *Of course* they wouldn't want to make that deal.

Nita had known that forces in INHUP were corrupt. She'd been paying for Adair's protection with the names of corrupt INHUP agents. Someone in INHUP had tagged her phone and sold her GPS location on the black market.

When Fabricio had fled Nita's mother, he'd gone to INHUP, but he'd known how corrupt they were and had tried to ensure that he'd be able to escape by having new documents made before he got there. He, of all people, would have had intimate knowledge of how many INHUP agents used his father's company, and he was more mistrustful than Nita had ever been of INHUP.

Adair was right. There was no bargain she could make that would convince INHUP to take that list down.

"I'm sorry about Kovit, Nita," Adair said, interrupting her thoughts.

Nita blinked. "How did you know?"

"Why else would you suddenly be looking to take the list down?" His smile was ironic. "It's not for you, and I'm pretty sure Kovit's the only thing besides yourself you care about."

"Oh." She looked away. "Yeah." She took a deep breath. "Can you get rid of his information? Prevent him from going on the list? I know you have a lot of contacts in INHUP, especially in the Dangerous Unnaturals List section."

He was already shaking his head. "It's not possible."

"I can pay." Nita's voice was tight. "I'll have all of Tácunan Law's information at my disposal soon."

"It's not about paying. It's just something I can't do." Adair gave her a bitter smile. "If I had that kind of power, my life would be a lot easier. But even I have my limits."

"Ah." It had been worth a try.

He sighed and rose. Diana, who'd been standing off to the side, rushed to help him up. "I am willing to make you another offer, if you actually manage to steal Tácunan Law's information."

She blinked. "What offer?"

"You're still looking for your father's killer, right?" Adair stumbled over to the counter with some effort. Diana reached out to help him, but he brushed her hand aside. He came back to the table with a printout of a picture.

The picture had Zebra-stripes in it.

Nita's eyes widened. "This is . . ."

"Is that him? The vampire you're looking for?"

"Yes." The picture had been blurred—it was a group shot, but all the other faces in it were blacked out. All the people were wearing semiprofessional clothes, but the style made her think older. She didn't know her fashion styles well, but shoulder pads were the . . . seventies? Eighties?

Zebra-stripes was smiling in the photo, a normal, almost human smile, his white-and-brown-striped hair parted to one side as he draped his arm over the shoulder of one of the blacked-out people.

Adair smiled slightly. "So that is him? Interesting."

"Who are the other people?" Nita asked.

Adair just continued smiling.

She sighed. "What's the price?"

"This one has . . . a lot of interesting information. The price will be high. You won't be able to pay it without getting something from Tácunan Law."

"I see." Nita considered the picture a moment before she met Adair's eyes. "Well, I know how much everyone will want that information. And if—when—I succeed, I'll have a lot of it. So since we're talking business, I'd like to hire you for something else too."

Adair raised his eyebrows. "Confident in your success, aren't you?"

Nita shrugged. "People who don't believe in their own plans never succeed."

"Indeed." He tapped a claw on the table. "What do you want, then?"

"I want you to find someone reliable to alter the video of me healing online to make it look like it's a fake. Or even someone respected in the black market circles to point out things in the video that make it look like a fake."

"You want to discredit the video?" he mused, and nodded slowly. "I know someone. The video is already up, altering it now would look suspicious. But he's considered an expert in the field. If he said it was fake and pointed out why, his word would carry weight."

"And you can make him say it's fake."

"For a price."

"I figured." Nita smiled softly and rose. "Well, think about what you want from Alberto Tácunan's databases. I'll be in contact."

Nita turned to go, and Adair called, "Oh, Nita."

She turned back. "Yes?"

"Our other deal still stands."

Nita blinked. "Other deal?"

"Our information exchange. If you find out why Fabricio, the doted-upon heir to Alberto Tácunan and his fortune, is so desperate to go into hiding, desperate enough to sell the person who saved him on the black market"—Adair cocked his head—"if you find me those answers, I'll tell you how the Dangerous Unnaturals List was created. How a list that is so blatantly about killing and selling certain valuable unnaturals for profit got legalized."

Nita tilted her head. "Will that information help me now?"

He considered. "It might. I don't know. But even if it doesn't, you want to know, don't you?"

She did. The idea of secrets fascinated her, and the information was one more piece of a giant puzzle that she was trying to piece together. She felt like she was starting to dissect a body, and Adair was offering her a bone saw. If only she let him use her scalpel in return.

"Fabricio's been reticent," Nita admitted. "But if I find anything out, I'll make that trade."

He smiled, thin and clever. "Good luck, Nita. Say goodbye to Kovit for me."

Then Diana helped him to the back, and they vanished into the depths of the pawnshop.

ELEVEN

NITA LEFT THE PAWNSHOP, miraculously managing not to trip on anything or break anything. Outside, the sun shone blue and bright, the crisp spring air making her tug her sweater tighter. The scent of just-bloomed flowers and freshly cut grass mingled together with the garbage from a craft brewery just up the block and the pervasive odor of car exhaust.

Nita couldn't trade with INHUP to eliminate the Dangerous Unnaturals List.

She let out her breath. Was she just supposed to let Kovit die? Give up?

What else was there to do? It wasn't like she could stay here thinking of new plans forever. They had one week. And the whole black market was still after Nita, hunting for her to rip her apart and sell her body. It wasn't like she could move freely.

She needed to go to Buenos Aires and steal Fabricio's father's information.

Once she did that, she'd have more options. Once she knew everything about everyone, once she had all the power that information could afford, once she could trade information like currency to eliminate the threat against herself, she'd find a way to buy Kovit off the list too.

Adair had said that Tácunan Law was full of information on higher-ups in INHUP. Surely she could use it to blackmail them to take Kovit's name off the list?

Her hand made Y incisions with an invisible scalpel as she slowly walked back toward the subway stop, mind whirling. The fresh spring air blew her frizzy curls in the wind a little, and the bright sunlight made the brown of them seem almost orange.

Blackmail was always risky. Especially with INHUP, which could, for example, add her to the Dangerous Unnaturals List. Or put out an arrest warrant.

The black market could assassinate her in a dark alley at night. But in the light of day, there wasn't as much they could do without the authorities getting too involved. She supposed they could pay off the authorities. So could Nita, in theory.

Once she had that information.

But INHUP was a problem. Would continue to be a problem. Not just the Dangerous Unnaturals List, which was questionable at best.

She used to be a fan of the list. She'd thought it was a good thing to make it legal to kill monsters without repercussions. No vampires getting off on legal technicalities or unicorns escaping murder charges for lack of sufficient evidence.

Of course, in practice, the list hadn't worked that way. Her father's killer should by all rights have been on the list, but he wasn't. INHUP knew who and what Zebra-stripes was, and whether by blackmail or something else—something Nita intended to find out when she caught him—he still hadn't gone up on the list. She couldn't keep Kovit off the list, but her father's murderer was going to get away.

She thought of Kovit, living with a sword of Damocles above his head his whole life, one wrong move away from being found and murdered by INHUP, whether he'd committed a crime or not. Adair's words from yesterday haunted her. What if there hadn't been a list? Would there be zannie doctors who could diagnose your pain instantly? Just because zannies could get their food from torture didn't mean they *had* to. An emergency room would suffice. But they chose to. Kovit chose to hurt people.

Would he still if the list was gone?

She didn't ask herself what could have been, because Kovit was right. Asking what-ifs about people stole their agency for the choices they made in this life. But what *could* be. That was another question. If the list went away and Kovit was absolved of any crimes he'd committed under it, what would he do? Would he continue to hurt people or would he walk within the lines of the law? If there were stakes, real stakes, real consequences for his actions, would he change?

She didn't know. Maybe. Maybe not.

But as long as INHUP and its list were there, neither of them would ever find out. INHUP had destroyed Kovit's life as surely as the mafia family he'd worked for had.

Her eyes hardened, and she thought about all the ways INHUP had ruined her own life. How they'd buried evidence about her father's murderer. How someone in INHUP had sold her cell phone GPS location online and sent hundreds of black market hunters after her. This entire mess in Toronto was squarely INHUP's fault. If INHUP hadn't betrayed her, she wouldn't be murdering people in mall bathrooms or making deals with murderous kelpies.

INHUP was as much Nita's enemy as the black market.

She made a new plan.

She'd been planning to use the information she got from Tácunan Law to destroy the black market hunting her. But there was no reason she couldn't use it against INHUP too. Adair had said their higher-ups would have blackmailable information in there.

Nita stood under the bright sunlight and looked up, a wild, angry smile crossing her face.

She was going to destroy everyone who'd done her wrong. The black market would grovel at her feet.

And she would annihilate INHUP.

TWELVE

NITA WAS ALMOST BACK to the subway station when she pulled out her phone and texted Kovit: *you done?*

The response came a minute later. *Yes. Waiting for you in the cafe across the street from the station.*

Nita pocketed her phone and headed back, trying not to become swamped by the hugeness of her plans. Destroy INHUP. It would be a feat that the world would never forget.

If she could pull it off. That was one hell of an *if*.

She let out a breath. Nita was the girl who had destroyed el Mercado de la Muerte, burned it right to the ground. She was the person who had evaded the black market's capture, who'd killed everyone that had tried to take her down.

INHUP was just one more thing she was going to destroy in her quest for the life she wanted.

She turned back onto the street with the subway station and immediately noticed the café Kovit had mentioned. It had a little teapot-shaped sign, and the facade was painted the pale blue of a baby shower. It looked like the kind of place little old ladies went to coo over small children and gossip over scones.

The inside proved Nita's intuition right. It looked like the living room of an old woman's house, all doilies and teapots on shelves. Cute tables with flower-patterned tablecloths and framed pictures on the wall of cats.

The whole place was packed with people. Wall to wall, they stood around, lined up for the counter. A petit East Asian girl with a high ponytail offered samples, and in the corner, a news team was packing up their cameras while a Sikh reporter chatted with an older white woman who was probably the owner.

Ads blared that this was the fourth-anniversary bake sale, and people who took selfies with the promotional banner and the cookies they bought would get a ten percent discount.

Kovit was at a table with a pink tablecloth with red hearts patterned on it, and Nita tried not to laugh at the incongruous sight of him sitting there, casually picking blood from underneath his fingernails.

He raised his head when he saw her and vacated the table, gesturing for her to follow him to the back. Nita squeezed through the crowd, trying to avoid touching people, and headed upstairs, where it was much more sparsely populated. No news crews, no crowds. Nita's shoulders relaxed.

He sat down at a table, and she sat down across from him.

"So, how'd it go?" she asked.

He smiled at her, free and happy and gentle, and for a moment he did look like he belonged in the happy, cozy teashop full of cute things. He looked, not younger, but more naive. The cruelty and hunger were washed from his face as the memory of the happy child he must have been pushed through his older features.

"It went well." He swallowed and looked down at the table-cloth. "It was really good to see her."

Nita felt a weird pang of jealousy. She'd occasionally imagined having a sibling, someone else in her life so that she wasn't always isolated in her dissection room or alone with her terrifying mother. Someone to talk to.

But as soon as the emotion came, it passed. Because the reality of having a sibling felt far too complex. Nita didn't want any of Kovit's anxieties about his sister not loving him or accepting him, his fear of judgment, or his pining for what could have been.

No, Nita was just fine on her own.

"I'm glad," she whispered, and she was. Because Kovit seemed animated again, alive in a way that she'd been scared he wouldn't be after what happened with Henry.

He ran a hand through his hair and gave her a self-deprecating smile. "I mean, it was awkward too. Ten years apart has changed us both. And it's not like I could talk about . . . you know."

"Yeah." She didn't imagine his sister would take Kovit's previous profession well.

"So I dodged a lot of questions. It was a bit stilted. But I could see her, the girl I grew up with." His voice was earnest. "Thank you."

Nita blinked. "For what?"

"For talking me into this."

Nita looked away. "This was all your choice. No need to thank me."

"No, I do." He sighed, and a bitter grimace painted his face.

"I haven't really been in the best frame of mind since I killed Henry yesterday."

Nita nodded sagely. "You've been brooding a little."

He mock gasped and put his hand to his heart. "Brooding? Me? Like a stereotypical bad boy?"

Nita tried to keep the grin off her face as she said solemnly, "Indeed. It's been very dramatic. Posed shots of you in dim lighting declaring your tragic death in one week. Mournful closeups of you trying to hide your grief in a veneer of brooding pain. Very cinematic."

His lips twitched into a smile, and his voice was soft. "I have been a little broody, haven't I?"

Nita shrugged. "I think you have a right to be. Things are fucked up. You just killed the man who was like a father to you, and even in death, he still managed to betray you one last time. You're allowed to feel shitty." Nita's voice went hard. "It's been over a week since I found out about my father's death, and I broke down and cried on you how many times? You're allowed to grieve, Kovit."

For a moment, she thought he was going to cry then, that her words would be the key that set loose everything he'd been trapping inside him since last night, and that his emotions would spill like blood on the table between them.

But then he took a deep breath and gave her a shaky grin. "I know. I did what I had to do to stay alive, to keep my friends alive, and even though it hurts, I don't regret killing him." He lowered his eyes as he whispered, "But that doesn't make it any easier."

He swallowed heavily, and just under the surface, that

broken, shattered look lurked, trying to press through his thin veneer of composure. But now she could see it wasn't a fatal break, it was the kind of break that was in her own soul too. The kind of break that stemmed from too much loss and betrayal, and you could either let the world break you or you could storm through the world and fill the cracks with the blood of those who'd hurt you until you were a semblance of whole again. Maybe not the same person, but still you, still alive, still moving forward on your own.

She'd been scared Kovit would crumble, and while his cracks were large, she trusted he would pick himself up and sharpen the broken edges into weapons.

Nita reached her hand across the table and covered his, a silent sign of support.

He meshed his fingers with hers and cleared his throat, his voice a little hoarse as he changed the topic. "What's the plan?"

She took a deep breath. "Okay. I have an idea for getting you off the list."

"And?"

She kept her gaze steady on his. "I want to use the information at Tácunan Law to take down INHUP."

He stared at her, mouth slightly open. "What?"

"You heard me."

He looked at her in concern. "But, Nita . . . it's the police. I have my issues with INHUP, but I don't want to destroy the police."

"Countries have their own individual police forces and laws. They don't need INHUP. They were fine before INHUP, and they'll be fine after it."

"I suppose." He shook his head, disbelief marking his features. "You really want to take on the black market *and* the police?"

"I do."

He burst into laughter. He tipped his head back, and when he smiled at her, it was vicious and cruel and delighted.

"What the hell? Why not. Go big or go home." He considered. "Well, for me it's probably go big or get dead."

The waitress had been approaching, sort of shyly eyeing Kovit while he was being adorable about his sister, but when she saw that laugh and grin, full of darkness, her eyes widened, and she quickly returned the way she'd come.

"You're not going to die." Nita's voice was fierce.

"No," he whispered, and she could almost see him shoving the fatalism aside and smashing the determination on top of it to keep it down. "I'm not."

For a moment, they were silent, letting their energy hang in the air between them, a promise of survival. They'd made it this far. They would make it to the end.

"When are we leaving for Buenos Aires?" he asked.

"As soon as possible." She checked her phone. "There's a direct overnight flight leaving at midnight tonight."

He nodded. "Can we be ready for that?"

"Yes. It's just . . ." Nita took a deep breath. "We need to discuss what we're going to do about Gold when we leave. We can't take her with us."

Kovit's eyes narrowed. "You want to kill her."

"No," Nita lied. "But she is a complication. We need a solution."

Kovit watched her carefully. "It would make things worse if she died."

"How?"

"Her father is the head of the Family. He knows that Henry and Gold are hunting me. If Gold dies, he will move heaven and earth to find me and kill me."

Nita snorted. "You've already got INHUP after you, how much worse can it get?"

He gave her a bitter smile. "Trust me, you don't want to find out."

"And if Gold lives and tells him Henry is dead?"

Kovit shrugged. "I suppose it depends on the way Gold tells the story. He might still move heaven and earth to kill me. Or he might not."

Nita was silent for a long moment. "You want to let her go."

He met her eyes. "I do."

She hesitated. "She could ruin us."

"She could." He didn't sound bothered by this. "But if we don't tell her where we're going, and we let her go right before we leave for the airport, by the time she calls people and gets assistance, we'll be long gone."

Nita didn't like this plan. She didn't like it one bit. It was broken and flawed and messy, and there were far too many points to possibly account for. It was unpredictable beyond belief.

It relied on assuming Gold would pay back Kovit's kindness with kindness. And in Nita's experience, the exact opposite was more likely to happen.

It was a monumentally stupid decision.

But it wasn't her decision to make.

She let out a breath. "And this is what you want?"

"Yes." Kovit's gaze was steady. "This is what I want."

"All right." Nita sighed. "We'll release her right before the flight, then."

Nita didn't like it, but it was Kovit's life, and she'd already pressured him enough about killing people he cared about. Even if Nita was right and it was a mistake, it was Kovit's mistake to make.

No matter how the outcome might hurt Nita in the long run.

"I'll book three tickets for tonight, then." Nita pulled out her phone and looked up. "Does Fabricio have his passport with him?"

"It was in his pocket when I searched him last night."

"Good." Nita looked down at the phone and let out a breath. "Then there's only one thing I need to do before we leave."

Kovit raised his eyebrows. "Oh?"

Nita met his eyes. "I need to go see my mother."

THIRTEEN

THE AFTERNOON SUN was high in the sky, and it was a cloudless day. Sweat trickled down Nita's back, and not just from the heat.

She'd arranged to meet her mother at the park near the police station where they'd last met. The gravel pathway crunched beneath her feet, the shade from the trees providing a brief respite from the sun. The air smelled of freshly cut grass and some flower, little bits of pollen floating along on the breeze and catching in her curly hair.

A few people wandered about, families with small children, couples holding hands. Nita couldn't imagine wandering a park with her mother as a child. She could barely believe she was meeting her of her own volition, without the threat of her mother's punishment motivating her.

Her last meeting with her mother had gone well. Better than Nita had ever imagined. Nita wasn't even that scared of seeing her again.

No. That was a lie. She was still scared. She would probably always be scared. One good meeting didn't change years of ingrained terror.

Nita turned a corner, coming to a small clearing with a picnic table. Her mother sat on one side, legs crossed, red-and-black-striped hair falling in straight, sharp lines along her jaw. Her lips were too red, and her eyes were too dark, making her ghostly skin look even whiter.

She rose when she saw Nita and smiled. Her smiles always unnerved Nita, because there was something sharkish about them, sharp and hungry and predatory.

"Nita, I'm so glad to see you again."

Nita stood awkwardly a few steps away. "Yeah." She couldn't think of anything else to say, so she just dove right into the main point. "Did you bring my passport?"

Her mother pulled it out of her pocket and waved it, but stepped back when Nita reached for it.

"Now, now. Don't be so hasty." Her mother gestured at the picnic table. "Why don't you sit down? We can have a chat. I'd love to know where you're planning to go."

So this was how it was going to be. "I have things to do."

Her mother sat and placed the passport in front of her. "I'm sure you do. But you can spare a moment to ease a mother's worries, can't you?"

Nita gave in and sat. "I'm just leaving the country."

"Because of the bounty hunters?"

It would have been easy for Nita to say yes. Toronto was still swarming with black market hunters trying to find her and kill her and sell her. She'd already killed half a dozen people, including a man just this morning, had an altercation at the police station, and murdered an INHUP agent to hide evidence.

But she didn't want her mom to think she was running. She didn't want to seem weak.

So instead of just agreeing to the assumption like she knew she should have, she said, "No. I have a plan to get them off my back for good. I need to leave the country, though."

"Oh?" Her mother leaned forward. "I do love a good plan."

For a brief moment, Nita considered telling her mother everything, explaining her entire plot to raid Tácunan Law and then use the information contained therein to systematically destroy the black market dealers targeting her, to bring fear into the heart of the market when they heard her name, to become untouchable as her enemies burned.

But Nita's mother might be one of the people who hid secrets in Tácunan Law. And Nita was very sure she wouldn't want those secrets to be exposed.

Nita just smiled and shook her head. She reached over and snagged the passport from in front of her mother before she could react.

Her mother's eyes narrowed as Nita pocketed it. "Not planning to tell me?"

"I'll tell you when we're done."

Nita realized her mistake the moment the words were out of her mouth.

Her mother's eyebrows shot up. "We?"

Nita remained silent.

"Who is this 'we'?" Her mother slowly leaned forward, like a shark scenting blood in the water. "Nita, darling, did you make a friend?"

Nita swallowed. She didn't like the way her mother said that. Didn't like the fear that fluttered in her stomach when she thought about her mother meeting Kovit. Because all her mother would see was an opportunity for money. Kovit would be dead and dissected before Nita could blink.

Nita rose. "I need to go."

"Sit down."

Nita froze at her mother's tone, flint and iron. That was not a voice you disobeyed. That was a dangerous voice.

Nita looked around, but they were alone in this part of the park. No one to help. No one that her mother had to perform for. Nothing to stop her mother from being her mother.

Nita sat down.

Her mother smiled, hard and flat. "Good girl."

Nita flinched at the endearment. Like a pet dog.

"Now, tell me about this friend."

Nita shrugged and remained silent, avoiding her mother's gaze.

Her mother *hmm*ed softly. "Well, that's interesting. I know you didn't have a friend before you were kidnapped, so you've met her—"

Nita tried to keep her face blank, but something must have been telling because her mother course-corrected.

"Him. So you've met him since then. So that leaves meeting him here or before, at the market."

Her mother tilted her head and considered. "Given that

102

you've been so hunted here, and you've had such success at repelling attackers, I'm inclined to believe you've had help. Which means you met him at the market."

Nita's heart thundered in her chest, and she didn't move, trying not to give anything away.

"But you came back claiming no one had survived the market. If your friend had been another captive, then you would have led him to INHUP with you. You came to INHUP alone, I checked in on that. Which means whoever this was couldn't go to INHUP. So not another harmless unnatural victim."

Her mother's smile was long and thin. "And there was no one else at the market except dealers and monsters."

Nita clenched her fists in her lap, under the table and hidden from view.

"Given the black market kerfuffle over you now, I can't imagine you'd have befriended a dealer. Or that you'd trust one. And I don't see how you'd have had the opportunity to meet one during your captivity, except your own. And I doubt you befriended them. So that means it's a monster who's not a dealer. Someone who's willing to help you hide from hunters, someone you must have had frequent contact with at the market."

Her mother was squinting at Nita, trying to read her face. Nita tried to force her legs to move, to get up from the table and run, run as far and as fast as she could. But she couldn't seem to make her body move.

"There was a zannie in the video of you healing, wasn't there?"

Nita's poker face broke.

Her mother shook her head. "Oh, Nita. A zannie?"

Nita squeezed her eyes shut. "Leave him alone."

"It's a zannie, Nita. It tortures people. It's evil."

You're evil too, and you don't even have being a zannie to use as an excuse, Nita wanted to say.

Instead she said, "I don't care."

Her mother rolled her eyes dramatically. "Is this one of those dreadful misguided Romeo and Juliet teen romances I hear about? Have you been watching too many mafia-sponsored vampire dramas? Do you think your purity and goodness will cure him of his evil appetites?"

"No." Nita snorted at the absurdity of it. Nita was many things, but good and pure weren't any of them. And no one could change Kovit except Kovit. "Nothing like that."

Nita didn't say anything more, because her relationship with Kovit was complicated, and anything she said would only feed into her mother's theory.

"Nita, darling." Her mother sighed, long and slow. "My poor child. You're so naive about the world sometimes."

Nita bristled. "Stop patronizing me."

"Fine." Her mother's mouth tightened. "But let me tell you a story. And then you tell me who's the fool."

Nita's gaze was flat. "Fine. Tell your story."

Her mother cleared her throat. "A long time ago, well before I had you, before I'd even met your father, I had a good friend who was a monster hunter."

Nita snorted.

Her mother glared. "What was that for?"

"You. Having a friend. I don't believe it."

Her mother laughed then, throwing back her head, and then she leaned forward and smiled gently at Nita. "Yes, I know, it's hard to believe I was that young and foolish. Never fear, I grew out of it, and you will too."

That wasn't a comforting thought, but Nita kept silent.

"Now," her mother continued, "this friend of mine was very good at killing monsters. Even better than me, if you can believe it. Her great love was the challenge of the hunt, and so she'd take dangerous, wild jobs no one else would touch. She was fearless, and people paid her well to kill their monsters.

"But one day this friend fell in love. With a monster. One she was supposed to be hunting."

"And what?" Nita asked. "It killed her?"

"No." Her mother's eyes went sad, and her voice soft. "It did something much, much worse."

Nita blinked, because the emotion in her mother's eyes was old and worn but real. Nita had been thinking of this as a fairy tale. But the grief etched in the lines of her mother's face was genuine. This person had existed. Her mother had cared about this person.

And it hadn't ended well.

"The monster was smart. It knew just killing my friend would solve nothing. That would just make all her monster-hunting friends come after him. So he was clever. He ingratiated himself. For years, he was protected from the monster hunters of the world because of his relationship with my friend. He pretended he was different, that he wasn't a killer. And because of my friend, they . . . Well, even if they didn't believe him, they didn't dare hurt him.

"So by day he schmoozed with monster hunters and conned my friend, and by night he murdered and did everything terrible that monsters of his ilk do."

Nita was silent, leaning forward slightly, caught up in the story despite herself. "And what happened?"

"Monster hunters started disappearing. They'd go out to hunt, and they wouldn't come back. Their traps stopped working. Their plans were foiled at every turn. One by one, they were being picked off. And as they were picked off, the monster whispered in my friend's ear, telling her that the problem had to be coming from close by, that there was no way the monsters could have known when and where and how these hunts were happening. No way it could have been monsters doing the killing. It had to be other monster hunters. Or someone close to them. Someone in the know."

Her mother's expression was bitter. "And so my friend turned on the monster hunters, and they turned on each other, and the monster watched and laughed as all his enemies killed each other.

"And at the end, when he had killed all his enemies, he turned on my friend, and he killed her too."

Nita rocked back, the pain in her mother's voice shaking her as much as the story.

Her mother took a long, deep breath. "He'd always intended to kill her. Years of relationship were all a sham. He was thinking of himself, of changing the world hunting him to suit his needs. He never cared about her, only what she could do for him."

Her mother met Nita's eyes, hard and cold and angry. "So

tell me, Nita, are you doing anything for your monster? Has he talked you into any harebrained schemes that benefit him more than you?"

Nita stared at her mother and thought about all the running around she'd done, the desperate risks of meeting INHUP agents, the modifications to her plans, all trying to find a way to save Kovit.

"You're wrong," she whispered. "He's not like that."

Her mother smiled, sharp and hard. "The answer is yes, then. He's roped you into trying to save him from something."

"I volunteered. It was my idea."

"Was it? Or were you made to think it was your idea?"

Nita thought about all the conversations about the list, Adair's revelations about its origins, all the tumbling thoughts that had gone through her head, and the truth was, she couldn't be sure if she'd been led into anything or if it was a natural consequence of the lives she and Kovit had been leading.

But she didn't think Kovit was manipulating her.

Her mother, on the other hand, was notorious for manipulating Nita.

Nita rose. "Thank you for the story. It was very interesting. I'm leaving now. Don't follow me."

"You're making a mistake."

"So what? It's my mistake to make."

"And it's my job to protect you." Her mother rose. "You're my daughter, and I won't let you fall into the same trap my friend did." Her voice went low and sharp. "I will kill this monster before it has a chance to betray you."

Goose bumps prickled along Nita's skin. "I'll never forgive you if you hurt him."

"I don't need your forgiveness, Nita. I need your survival."

Nita didn't know how to respond to that. Finally, she just whispered, "Please. Please leave him be. He's not the monster that hurt your friend."

"No, but monsters like that are all the same." Her mother's eyes were hard. "I know their type. And these things, they never change."

"Please," Nita whispered.

Her mother just smiled gently, as though Nita was a small child again. "Don't worry, Nita. I'll kill this monster before anything happens to you."

FOURTEEN

NITA STUMBLED AWAY from the park as fast as her shaking legs could take her, glancing back every few steps to see if her mother was following—even though her mother had smiled when Nita fled, not moving, just watching with this mildly amused and utterly unconcerned expression, as though Nita running away wouldn't change a single thing.

Nita's lungs felt tight, like she couldn't get enough air, and her head felt like it was full of helium, ready to float away and leave her bloody corpse behind.

She got on the first bus she saw, sitting down and fisting her hands in her lap to try and stop the shaking. Nita looked outside, almost expecting her mother to be standing on the sidewalk watching the bus leave, but no one was there. It didn't calm Nita's nerves at all. She wasn't sure where this bus headed, but she knew she couldn't go straight back to the recording studio. She had to make sure her mother couldn't tail her.

She couldn't let her mother find Kovit.

She leaned back in the bus seat and closed her eyes. How had she fucked this up so badly? She'd been so careful up until now, and one careless slip and everything was exposed. Her mother knew about Kovit. She would find him and kill him and think she was doing Nita a favor.

The bus rumbled beneath her, and she looked up at the escape hatch on the ceiling. She needed to escape. She needed to grab Kovit and run, far and fast. That Buenos Aires flight tonight couldn't come soon enough.

Her chest hurt when she thought of how she'd added another person to the list of threats against Kovit. She was the worst friend. Every time she tried to help him, all she did was make everything ten times worse.

Swallowing, she looked out the window as the bus turned onto the highway and carried her far away. As her heart rate slowly calmed, she considered the story her mother had told about a woman conned by a monster. To Nita, the hardest part to believe was that her mother actually had a friend. She couldn't picture the calculating, manipulative woman who'd raised her befriending someone. But there were a lot of things she didn't know about her mother.

There was one thing she did know. Whether the story was true or something her mother made up to try and keep Nita away from Kovit, she wasn't going to let her mother win. If it came down to a choice of her mother or Kovit, well, Nita knew who she would pick.

By the time Nita got back to the apartment, it was almost time to leave for the airport. Kovit was waiting in the reception room, pacing. His hair was mussed from running his hands through it too much, and his eyes had shadows under them. He sagged in relief when she came in.

"I was worried. Did you get my messages?" he asked.

Nita shook her head. She hadn't checked her phone on the last bit of her journey. "No, I'm sorry."

"We need to get going."

She nodded, all business. "Do we have everything we need?"

She looked around and realized they didn't really have anything. No clothes—everything they weren't wearing was bloody. Just passports, some money, and their phones.

He smiled as though he was thinking the same thing. "We're good."

Nita sighed. "I suppose we should untie Fabricio."

"Oh, I did already."

Nita raised an eyebrow. "Oh?"

"We can't have him going on a plane looking like he just got kidnapped and tortured. I got him some new clothes and some bandages and antiseptic. He took a shower and is just changing now."

Nita tilted her head to one side. "That was . . . nice of you."

Kovit shrugged. "I didn't see the harm in letting him have a shower."

For a moment, Nita was catapulted into the past, when she was a prisoner in the market, when she had tried to slowly build a relationship with Kovit by asking for small things. A towel. A shower. All a ploy to learn more and get him to let his guard down so she could betray him and escape.

"Did Fabricio ask for a shower?" Nita asked.

"Yeah, why?"

"No reason."

He didn't see the similarities. Well, Nita wasn't going to

point it out. Yet. But sneaky little Fabricio had already started spinning his web to escape. He'd already identified the same weak spots in Kovit that Nita had, and was starting to build on them.

It disturbed Nita a little to find that she and Fabricio thought so similarly. She didn't want to be anything like him. If someone had saved her life, she never would have betrayed them.

But even as she thought it, she wondered. Because if it meant survival, there was very little she wouldn't do. She just couldn't see how Fabricio selling her out was a survival tactic.

Kovit interrupted her musings. "I need to say goodbye to Gold before we go."

Nita resisted the urge to rub her temples. She still wasn't happy that he was choosing to let a wildcard like Gold go. But she couldn't think of anything to sway him away from his foolishness.

So all she said was, "All right."

She followed Kovit as he went into Gold's room. Gold lay on her cot, gently rubbing pain-numbing cream on her previously dislocated shoulder. She wasn't bound anymore, so Kovit must have been in here earlier. Nita sighed, thinking of both their prisoners unbound and running around asking Kovit for things and taking advantage of him. Kovit really was a terrible jailor. Nita, of all people, should have known better than to leave him in charge of prisoners.

Kovit shivered as he entered the room, and Gold tensed as she watched him eat her pain.

"Here," he whispered, taking out his switchblade. "Let me."

Gold stiffened, but Kovit made a small cut on his finger as he approached her, before reaching over and spreading his blood on her wound. The tension went out of both of their bodies, even though Gold remained wary. Zannie blood was a powerful anesthetic.

Eventually, Kovit lowered his hand and cleared his throat. "I came to say goodbye."

Gold gave him a bitter smile. "Finally going to kill me?"

"No. Of course not." He looked away. "I know you hate me, but I still think of you as a friend, May. I'm not just going to throw that aside."

Gold was quiet for a long moment before she said, "Where do we go from here, then?"

"Nita and I are leaving. You're free to do whatever you want. I've left your phone in the front hall. It's dead, I'm not sure where your charger is. If you can't find it, just knock on one of the apartment doors in the building. I'm sure someone will let you borrow theirs."

Gold blinked at him, long and slow. "You're really just letting me go?"

"Yes."

She opened and closed her mouth, her face a picture of confusion. "I don't understand."

Kovit sighed. "You don't have to understand, May. It's okay. I hope you have a good life."

He gave her one last smile, took a deep breath, and turned back to Nita. "Okay, let's go."

Gold watched them leave with huge eyes as the door closed behind them.

Kovit's steps were heavy as they crossed the hall to Fabricio's room. Nita wanted to say something, anything to make him feel better, but she didn't know what. She didn't think she could understand the emotions that led him to release a threat, that led him to care about a person who so clearly hated him.

She tried to imagine that their roles were reversed and she'd been betrayed by a friend. But Nita didn't have any friends except Kovit. She imagined it was her mother who betrayed her instead.

Well, that wasn't too far from the truth. Her mother was always disrespecting Nita and doing evil shit. And if it was a choice of Nita's life or her mother's, Nita would pick her own without question every single time.

In many ways, that was the big difference between Nita and Kovit. Nita would always pick her life over anyone else. And Kovit . . . Kovit would always pick his friends' lives over his own. More than anything, that convinced her that her mother's threats about Kovit betraying her were utter bullshit.

She couldn't find the words to make Kovit feel better, so she put her hand on his shoulder, and he looked at her, eyes soft and sad. Then he smiled gently at her. It was enough.

Nita took a deep breath and opened the door to Fabricio's room.

Fabricio lay on the floor, unbound and free. His brown hair was still wet from the shower, and it clung to his forehead as he lay on his back and stared up at the fluorescents above him. His hand had been carefully bandaged, so that there was no sign of the horror beneath. He'd taped his broken nose, though he couldn't hide the swelling or the black circles under his eyes from pooled blood. He turned his head when they came in.

His eyes were tired. "Nita. Kovit."

Kovit blinked. People didn't usually acknowledge his presence with a name. Just a fearful expression or a desperate plea for Nita not to let him hurt them, like Kovit was a vicious dog and Nita held the leash.

"Fabricio." Nita stepped forward. "It's time to go. We have a flight to Buenos Aires waiting."

He turned away. "Is there anything I can say to talk you out of this? Anything to make you reconsider trying to rob my father?"

"No."

He sighed heavily, and began the laborious process of getting to his feet. He winced when he moved too quickly, and Kovit twitched with his pain.

"I thought about what you said, Fabricio, about the carrot and the stick." Nita gave him a smile.

"And?" he asked.

"And I'm taking it under consideration. But for now, I want to make sure we get to Buenos Aires without problems."

Fabricio eyed her nervously. "Wait, what—"

Nita darted forward and stuck the needle in his arm. The last vial she'd gotten from Adair yesterday, the drug she'd used on Quispe and the other INHUP agent. She couldn't take it with her, so she might as well get one last use out of it.

Fabricio stared at her a long moment before his eyes moved down to the needle in his arm. Finally, he whispered softly, "We're all going to die in Buenos Aires."

Then he crumpled to the floor.

Nita rolled her eyes. "So dramatic."

She hoisted him over her shoulder, his head flopping against her back, and the three of them left the apartment behind.

FIFTEEN

THE AIRPORT was much easier with Fabricio unconscious. They put him in a wheelchair when they arrived. Online check-in meant that they didn't have to go to the counter, and they went straight through the priority security lane.

When they hit customs, Fabricio was groggily beginning to wake, but he was completely looped. Kovit went through separately, and Nita pretended to be Fabricio's cousin. They didn't look much alike, but they both had Spanish names, and Nita kept all her conversation with Fabricio in Spanish. The customs agent didn't speak it, couldn't hear that their accents were completely different. Nita's father was Chilean, and she'd been raised in Madrid until she was six, so her Spanish was an unusual blend of the two accents that most people struggled to parse initially. Fabricio spoke standard Argentinian Spanish, his *y* sounds whispering into *sh*.

The customs agent side-eyed Fabricio drooling in a wheelchair, only half conscious and talking nonsense in Spanish, but she approved them. After all, Fabricio did have an Argentinian passport, and it looked like he was going home.

By the time Fabricio was fully awake and less drug-addled, they were already in the air.

They'd given him the window seat, and Nita realized the drug had worn off when he sighed and said, "I really should have expected the drugs after our conversation. Like mother, like daughter."

Nita flinched at that, remembering that was how her mother had kidnapped him and taken him on a plane too.

He didn't say anything else after that. Part of her expected him to start screaming, "Kidnapping!" in the middle of the plane to get it to turn around, but he was eerily silent. Plotting, probably. If she were him, she'd be plotting—more than just trying to manipulate Kovit when Nita wasn't there.

"He's being too well behaved," Nita whispered to Kovit after Fabricio plugged in his earphones and groggily watched an in-flight movie.

"Maybe we scared him enough?"

But Fabricio didn't seem scared of them. He didn't flinch when Kovit leaned over Nita to plug his charger in beside Fabricio. He just occasionally stared at both of them with these flat, angry eyes, his gaze boring into them with more judgment than Nita had thought a look could have.

"I don't think so." Nita looked over at Fabricio's form and scowled. "He's definitely biding his time and plotting something."

Kovit shrugged, unconcerned. "Then we'll deal with it when he makes his move."

Nita sighed and settled back, accepting the truth of Kovit's words. There was nothing she could do with just suspicions. Yet.

The plane ride was long, more than ten hours, and Nita slept for most of it. She woke up occasionally to check that Fabricio was still curled up in his seat, and then fell back asleep.

They cleared customs easily, no visa required. The airport, a glass-and-white-tile clone of every other airport in the world, was bustling with people. Nita flinched when people came too close, sticking as tightly to Kovit as she could. She was surprised to see Fabricio cringe every time people looked their way, shrinking in on himself, trying to make himself small and unnoticeable. The black circles under his eyes from his broken nose were stark in the harsh light, and his eyes flicked back and forth, trying to look at all the faces of the people around him at once, as though he might spot someone he knew.

He didn't look like he thought that person would rescue him.

She wondered if it was his father he was so afraid of. If this was like her and her mother. Nita tried to imagine robbing her mother, and her whole body chilled at the very thought. She imagined how her mother would smile when she caught Nita, so wide, too wide, and she would whisper, "Someone's been a bad girl."

Nita didn't want to think about what would come after.

She jerked her mind away from that path and looked back to Fabricio. He'd mussed his hair across his face so it covered as much as possible, but his bangs were too short to hide much more than his eyebrows and the top of his eyes.

For the first time in a long time, she pitied him. She knew what it was like to be that afraid of family, she knew how parents could warp you as a child. But it still didn't excuse what he'd done to Nita.

Nita stepped closer to Fabricio. "Relax."

He turned to her with large red eyes. "Excuse me?"

"You're with Kovit and me." Nita gave him a cold smile. "If anyone you know tries to take you from us, we'll make sure it's the last thing they try to do."

Fabricio blinked, and then a small, sly smile came over his face. "Are you trying to comfort me, Nita?"

She stiffened. "Of course not. Just stating fact."

His smile fell from his mouth, but his eyes were steady and solemn. "Thank you."

She jerked away. "I wasn't comforting you."

People like him didn't deserve comfort.

Her words clearly had relaxed him a bit, because he was less jumpy as they boarded the bus into the city. The drive was long, and the houses and soccer fields and trees all blurred together in her jet-lagged mind. Kovit napped, head resting against the window.

Nita stared out the window, mind whirling, thinking of how she was going to break into Tácunan Law and steal the information. She'd need to scope out the building—she'd have to do something about the security cameras, certainly. She didn't want any record of their escapades existing. And there would likely be guards, so she'd need to think of a way to handle them. She'd need a hard drive too. With that much information, she might need several, all of the best quality she could find.

Beside her, Kovit gasped, and Nita blinked herself out of her thoughts and looked out the window. A massive stone fountain loomed beside them, rearing horses elaborately carved to be leaping out of the water, their legs turning into sea foam.

"It's amazing," Kovit whispered, face pressed against the glass.

Fabricio smiled, his eyes soft and dreamy. "Isn't it? There's nowhere quite like Buenos Aires."

Nita wasn't sure what she'd thought Buenos Aires would look like. Maybe something like Lima, smaller office buildings in the business core, wide streets, lots of Spanish colonial architecture that had evolved over the years into something else, something a little unique and different. Colectivos running up and down the roads calling out destinations. A long beautiful path along the cliffs overlooking the ocean, floripondio trees and overpriced shopping malls lining the water.

Buenos Aires looked nothing like Lima.

On one side of the bus was the water of the Río de la Plata glinting in the sunlight. Boats crowded the small docking area, and massive skyscrapers of steel and glass, an ode to the modern world, speared into the sky, seventy or eighty stories high. On the other side of the bus, monolithic Greek columns held up a building that looked like the Parthenon, marble statues reared up in the roundabouts, carved horses leaping up and leading their stone riders to victory.

One side of the bus was the past, beautiful European

architecture lining the road and springing up in the distance, breathtaking in its size and majesty. On the other side, towering steel monuments to capitalism.

"It's stunning." Kovit's breath fogged up the glass and he wiped it away, eyes wide. "I've never seen anything like it." He turned to Nita, a bright, happy grin on his face. "I've seen pictures and movies set in Europe, but never actually, you know, been anywhere like this."

Fabricio looked over at him curiously. "Where did you live before . . ."

"Before I joined Nita?" Kovit's eyes were glued to the passing city outside. "Bangkok until I was ten. And then I was part of the Family, and they had a compound just outside Boston. But I didn't really get to go outside, they didn't like that. Occasionally they'd drive me into the city for work, though. It was nice." He made a face. "And then they sent me to the jungle. But I was only there for a month before I met Nita and we escaped."

A look flitted across Fabricio's face Nita couldn't quite understand. It wasn't quite pity, it wasn't quite sympathy. It was just a flicker, a moment of some sort of sadness, and then it was gone.

"You've only been free a week?" Fabricio asked.

Kovit nodded, silent.

"Is it everything you wanted?" Fabricio's question was soft.

Kovit hesitated. "I . . . I don't know. I never realized how hard it would be when I had to make my own choices. I have the opportunity to be whoever I want to be, but all I can seem to do is the same things I always did." He gave a short, sharp laugh. "But I got to see my sister, which I never thought I would again. And I'm getting to see Buenos Aires. So, yeah. It's not perfect, but I'm glad I got out."

Fabricio nodded slowly. "They say that people are creatures of routine, and even if you put them in different settings, they always end up repeating the same habits."

"I hope not." Kovit's voice was soft. "I don't want to go back to the life I had."

"Me neither," Fabricio whispered. He stared out at the city with sad eyes, his face part fear, part longing.

They were all silent for a time, while Nita tried and failed to figure out what was going on in Fabricio's head.

Kovit glanced over at Fabricio, his voice containing a little bit of wonder. "Why does the city look so . . ."

"European?" Fabricio didn't turn, eyes still fixed out the window. "Lots of waves of immigrants from Europe who wanted to re-create the Old World. There was a time when Argentina was very rich, we had a lot of resources that were in demand. We spent a lot of that wealth trying to build a city to rival the famous ones in Europe. To put Buenos Aires on the map." He smiled slightly. "People call it 'the Paris of Latin America.'"

Nita considered, looking out as they passed ever more strange and innovative buildings—down some streets, she could see tall brickwork buildings with metal gratings that looked like they belonged in 1930s New York, elaborate fountains that reminded her of pictures of Italy—all of them stunning, none of them matching.

"It doesn't really look like Paris. It's too eclectic," she commented.

Nita had visited Paris a couple of times with her mother when they were living in Germany a few years ago, just before they moved to Vietnam. Her memories of the city were fuzzy, she spent a lot of time dissecting in a small apartment in the south of the city, but she'd got out for a day and wandered around all the famous tourist areas with her mother, trying to burn the images into her memory.

It was one of her few good memories of traveling with her mother.

"They are eclectic, aren't they?" Fabricio's expression was fond, and his eyes seemed more vibrant, happier, than she'd seen them before. "It's because buildings were built in whatever style was most popular at the time. Or most beautiful. There are buildings here built a few years apart, and one looks like a concrete block, and the other a German palace."

Fabricio's voice was wistful, and not for the first time, Nita realized that he loved this city, this strange, eclectic place he'd grown up. He was just very afraid of it. Or of someone in it.

The bus let them off at the side of a major street, across from a massive raised park. Green trees blocked the sun, and a clocktower arched up to the north of them, standing in front of another mass of modern glass and steel buildings. To their other side, the water of the port glinted in the light, reflecting the skyscrapers just beyond.

It was warm outside, a pleasant temperature that was just shy of hot. It was strange to go from a chilly spring in Toronto to a warm fall in Buenos Aires. The sky here was clear and brilliantly blue. Nita felt like her body had whiplash from all the different countries and temperatures she'd been through in the past week.

"Where are we going?" Fabricio asked.

Nita took out her phone and checked her Airbnb reservation. "Here. It's just south of Plaza de Mayo on the map."

"Monserrat? San Telmo?" Fabricio looked over her shoulder and pointed south. "Ah. I see. That way."

Nita wasn't thrilled about letting him lead, but he knew where he was going, and she followed their progress on an offline map to ensure they were heading the right direction.

As she walked, she turned her attention from the buildings to the people. They were *tall*. Much taller than she'd expected, taller than anywhere else she'd been in Latin America. Fabricio and his gangly height fit right in.

The people were also, for the most part, whiter than she was used to seeing. Toronto had been a diverse city, lots of people from all over—at least, the central parts she'd been in. Lima had been primarily full of people whose skin was varying shades of brown, interspersed with dollops of white, black, and Asian people.

Buenos Aires was much whiter than both of those cities. Many people were white or had the slightly browned skin that people called "olive" or "tan" in the Mediterranean, and "ethnic" if they were from outside of Europe. There were certainly plenty of people who weren't white on the streets, but it was less than Nita would have expected, given their location.

Fabricio blended in easily with the other people in Buenos Aires, as did Nita, her mixed heritage making her fit in for once. Kovit stood out a *lot*.

Kovit noticed it too. "Great. I can be one of three Asians in the city."

"I'm sure there's more than three," Nita said, though she didn't see anyone else in their immediate area.

Fabricio agreed. "There's a whole Chinatown."

Kovit looked around at the people walking on the street. "Yeah, not in this area." He shifted uncomfortably. "I feel . . . conspicuous."

No one seemed to be staring at Kovit, which was what usually happened to Nita when she went somewhere that wasn't used to people who looked like her. Which probably didn't make Kovit any more comfortable about standing out, but at least no one was being openly rude.

They continued walking, crossing a massive square. On one end, a large pink building surrounded by gates, and on the other, a wide road encircling a monument. In front of the building, dozens of protesters with large banners had camped out, yelling inaudible things into megaphones and banging something metal around, even as a song wafted from speakers. More came down the road, like this spot was the end of a march of some kind.

She looked at the banners, but she couldn't quite read them through the mass of people, and the wind was blowing them at the wrong angle. She turned to Fabricio. "Are there a lot of protests here?"

He nodded. "Many people remember what it was like to not have a voice, so they use it whenever they can. We're very politically active. We protest, we vote, we talk politics a lot."

Someone walked by selling ice cream and water, and then

they were across the plaza and into one of the smaller streets. From this angle, she had a clear view of one of the protest signs, but it was all catch phrases and talking points she didn't have the cultural reference points to understand.

Nita found herself asking, "What are they protesting?"

Fabricio jerked away and continued walking. "What am I, your prisoner or your tour guide?"

Nita tilted her head. "Can't you be both?"

He glared at her.

Kovit sighed. "It's not important. Let's just get to the apartment."

They continued walking, and after a few moments Fabricio said, "They're protesting the rules around claiming veteran's benefits for soldiers of la Guerra de las Malvinas."

Nita knew of the war. In the 1980s, Argentina invaded the British-occupied islands after negotiations to return them to Argentina broke down. Argentina was thoroughly routed.

"Guerra de las Malvinas?" Kovit repeated, mangling the Spanish.

"The Falklands War," Nita translated.

Fabricio's eyelid twitched, and his jaw clenched when he heard the F-word, and Nita immediately wished she hadn't said anything. Her father once told her that the surest way to get in a fight with an Argentine was to claim the Islas Malvinas weren't theirs. Nita had a rule about the Falklands—keep her mouth shut. She didn't want to get in a fight over something she only had the barest understanding of, especially when most of what she knew was from her Chilean father who had little love for Argentina.

She needed to change the subject, and quickly.

"Nice weather today, right?"

Wow. She was really great at this.

Fabricio gave her a mildly exasperated but also a little amused look like he knew exactly what she was trying do. Kovit looked at her like she was speaking gibberish, since he had no idea what a minefield topic this was.

"You should try alfajores while you're here," Fabricio said, pointing at a display of white cookies in a bakery window. "They're delicious."

Nita's shoulders loosened, relieved he was playing along.

"I will," she promised. "I hear the gelato here is good too?"

They continued prattling on about innocuous dessert items as they strolled along the cobblestoned roads. The narrow streets were one way, closed off and small, a perfect little bubble that made her feel like she'd gone back in time. Small café tables cluttered the sidewalks, full of people reading books and drinking coffee. Nita saw a big sign for something called a submarino, which, if the sign was to be believed, involved putting a whole chocolate bar into hot milk and letting it dissolve to make hot chocolate. She made a mental note to try it while she was here.

Kovit was so busy staring at a building nearby with old-fashioned balconies that he nearly stepped in dog poop. Nita and Fabricio both kept one eye on the ground and neatly avoided it. Even this small similarity between them annoyed Nita.

It didn't take long to find their Airbnb. Kovit had booked it with Fabricio's money, money he'd gotten selling Nita on

128

the black market. It was only fitting Nita used that money to advance her own goals now.

The Airbnb apartment was small but serviceable. It had a double bed in one room and a pullout sofa beside the kitchen. The walls were white with small pink flowers, and the floors were well-worn hardwood. The windows looked down on the street, with metal shutters that could be lowered over them. The room was light and airy, and the flat-screen TV on the wall was so shiny it could be used as a mirror.

Fabricio looked nervously between the couch bed and the main bedroom. "There's two beds."

"And?" Nita threw her bag in a corner and pulled out her phone to connect to the Wi-Fi.

"And there's three of us."

"So we'll share."

Fabricio tried to play it cool, but Nita could see how tense and tight his body was. "Am I sharing with Kovit?"

Kovit raised an eyebrow. "You don't like me?"

Fabricio held his bandaged hand tight to his side. "No offense, Kovit, but you're not my type."

Kovit blinked at him, clearly not expecting the conversation to go there, and then burst into laughter. He ran his hand through his hair, and his eyes lowered to Fabricio's injured hand. His smile fell a little.

Nita interrupted, not liking the pensive, slightly unhappy look on Kovit's face. "It's fine. I'll share with Kovit."

Fabricio looked between them, slight smile forming on his face. "I didn't realize you two were . . ."

"Were what?" Nita's voice was soft and dangerous.

He gave her an innocent look. "So close."

Kovit laughed softly. "Good save."

Nita rolled her eyes.

"Enough play time." Nita turned to Fabricio. "It's time to make yourself useful. We're going to break into Tácunan Law. What do we need?"

Fabricio sighed. "You need someone with security clearance and door codes."

"Which you have."

"Yes." Fabricio plopped himself on the sofa.

"Let's talk security cameras." Nita crossed her arms. "What do you know?"

"They have them? I don't know much more."

"Guards?"

"There's always some." He shrugged. "If we go in the side entrance, you shouldn't encounter any, but they'll come if they hear noise."

Nita nodded to herself, already making a mental list of things she'd need to do. "How far can your codes get us?"

"I can get you into the building, I can get you right to the computers that can access all the information you need. But that's as far as I can go. I don't have the passwords to get into the mainframe."

Nita crossed her arms and stared at him. "Really?"

"Really." He ran his uninjured hand through his hair. "Look, if I could get into my father's information, don't you think I would have done so before now? I would have left Buenos Aires years ago. I'd have sold some random information, taken the money, and run."

"Why?" Nita met his eyes. "Why would you have run?"

His mouth snapped closed. "I have my reasons."

"If you really wanted to run, you'd have tried, money or not."

"I did try. Once."

Nita blinked. "Pardon?"

"I tried. When I was . . . thirteen? Fourteen? I can't recall. I didn't make it far before I was recaptured." He shuddered softly. "Let's just say your mother wasn't the first person to remove some body parts."

Nita stared, remembering the first time she'd seen Fabricio, with his bare feet, missing toes. Her mother had told her they'd been sold online by the collector who owned him. But there had never been any collector, just his father.

Nita didn't want to think too hard about what that said about Fabricio's father, or how she felt about that, so she barreled ahead. "Fine. So you don't have the passwords to get us in. Who does?"

He looked away. "My father."

Nita shook her head. She didn't want to go directly against Alberto Tácunan unless she absolutely had to. "Who else?"

"That's it."

"That can't be it. He can't run the entire company by himself. Other people need to have access."

"People have access to individual things they're working on." Fabricio shrugged. "But you want everything? Only one man has the password to get all the information."

Nita pressed her lips together. It wasn't ideal, but she was prepared for this.

She smiled at Fabricio. "Then I guess we're going to have to get the password from your father."

"You'll die."

"Perhaps." Nita tilted her head and met Fabricio's eyes. "Or maybe he will."

Fabricio just stared at her before a bitter smile crossed his face. "If only."

Nita knelt so she was face-to-face with Fabricio and grabbed his chin in her hands. "You wanted a carrot? Something to motivate you to work with me?"

"Yessss." He dragged the sound out, but his voice was nervous.

She forced his eyes to meet hers. "Here it is, Fabricio. If you do everything in your power to make sure Kovit and I get this information, I'll do everything in mine to make sure your father is never a problem for you again. And when the dust has settled and all the blood's been spilt, we'll call it even once and for all. No more blackmail. No more pain. No more threats. We just walk away. Deal?"

Fabricio looked down at his bandaged, bloodied hand before he nodded. "Deal."

SIXTEEN

FABRICIO ASKED IF he could have a shower, and Nita didn't see any reason for him not to, so he retreated into the bathroom. She suspected it was less that he wanted a shower and more that he wanted an excuse to be alone for a while. She didn't blame him.

She also didn't trust him. He'd seemed genuine in taking her deal, but she knew firsthand how superb an actor he was. But there was nothing she could do about it for now—she needed him, and he knew it.

Kovit leaned against the counter. "What now? How are we going to get the password out of Alberto Tácunan, of all people?"

Nita rested her chin on her hand. "If this were a movie, I'd leave you in a room with him for an hour and we'd have all the answers we wanted."

"You know torture doesn't actually work like that."

"I know. He'd probably give us gibberish, make up things to get it to stop." She sighed. "But it's a nice fantasy. That things are so easily solved, answers so easily obtained."

Kovit smiled dreamily. "It would be fun. Answers or no."

Nita shivered at his expression, full of innocent delight at what she knew would be something truly terrible. "I'm sure. But we need a better plan."

His eyes came back to this world, and he raised his eyebrows. "Do you have one?"

"Sort of." She chewed her lip. "We lure him somewhere, we make him talk."

"We make him talk how?"

"That's the part I haven't figured out yet," she admitted.

He nodded slowly. "I see."

She rubbed her temples. "I mean, there's a lot of pieces I haven't figured out yet."

"Like?"

"Where to start?" She counted them off on her fingers. "How I'm going to get that password. How I'm going to use this information to get rid of INHUP. Backup plans. You know. Stuff."

He considered. "Speaking of getting rid of INHUP, what's happening with that vampire?"

Nita looked up at him. "Zebra-stripes? What about him?"

"INHUP didn't put a wanted poster up for him."

"No, they didn't." Nita frowned, seeing where Kovit was going with this. "Zebra-stripes must have something on INHUP. Something so powerful that it's kept him off the list."

Their eyes met, and a slight smile curled on Kovit's face. "Blackmail powerful enough to keep him off the list would be good to have."

"It would," Nita agreed, reaching for her phone. "It would be an excellent thing to have, in fact."

It might even be enough to keep Kovit off the list.

And Nita really did want answers. And vengeance.

She went online, onto the big black market websites, and checked her inbox. Kovit leaned forward and peered over her shoulder.

There, sure enough, was a response to the message she'd sent the ad asking for information on her mother. The account that was likely from Zebra-stripes.

She'd pinged it with an offer when she'd last been online, just to see if it responded — she knew her mother's location, but wanted half upfront to guarantee she'd get paid. It was a common practice, and Zebra-stripes had accepted. Nita downloaded the money.

She exchanged a glance with Kovit and took a deep breath, her fingers hesitating over her screen. Then she told Zebra-stripes that her mother was in Buenos Aires.

"Done."

Kovit nodded. "Good. Now we just need to make sure he goes where we want him. We don't want him running all over Buenos Aires not knowing where he'll go."

Nita grinned, an idea sparking in her mind, tangling up with her other plans. "Then we'll give him a direction."

Kovit raised his eyebrows, but Nita just smiled at him.

Nita scrolled through the internet, searching for anything interesting happening in Buenos Aires she could use. Her fingers paused a few hits down from the top. Apparently, there was a multigovernment meeting about laws regarding unnaturals starting tomorrow and going on all weekend. It seemed like the sort of thing people in the black market might take an interest in.

The kind of place she might be able to set a trap for those people.

As she clicked through, she learned more. The conference involved trade ministers and representatives from Peru, Colombia, and Brazil. Since Peru wasn't a part of INHUP, they were often a haven for black market dealers who took advantage of the different laws to run their trade. The article on the conference said it was a meeting to discuss how to enforce stricter laws against unnatural trafficking and get rid of the pervasive black market influence.

Nita let out a long breath. She wondered if this conference had been sparked by her burning down the big black market on the Amazon, el Mercado de la Muerte. She hadn't thought anyone would care. The idea that she'd done something that could cause so many ripples, change so many things, was a bit overwhelming. She kind of liked it. It made her feel powerful.

But as she scrolled down, she realized that no, this wasn't her doing.

It was Mirella's.

Mirella, the girl who'd been a prisoner at the same time as Nita, who Kovit had tortured, who'd lost an eye to the market, had been using pods of dolphins to disrupt all the trade along the Amazon. According to the article, the protests had gotten so bad and businesses were losing so much money on trade that the governments had decided to do something.

They'd chosen Buenos Aires as neutral ground, since actors from a variety of factions would also be there and didn't feel safe meeting in a country under the control of the people they were protesting.

An uneasy feeling bubbled to the surface, a thought popping up like a virus, and she immediately checked the attendees roster for the pink-haired girl. But Mirella was still in the Amazon, fighting. She'd made a statement last week that she wouldn't be attending because the conference refused to guarantee her safety. Apparently assassination attempts had been made.

Nita let out a heavy breath of relief. That was one complication she really didn't need.

She went to the conference hotel and booked a room for tomorrow night under one of her mother's more well-known aliases. One that Zebra-stripes was surely familiar with.

Tomorrow morning, she'd check into that room and build a trap.

She smiled to herself. This time, she wouldn't be rash, she would think ten steps ahead, she would plot and maneuver and make sure she'd examined everything from all angles before she went forward. She wouldn't let this end up like Toronto. She'd learned, and she would see her enemies destroyed before the end of this.

"What are you up to, Nita?" Kovit rose from the couch where he'd been texting and sat down on a stool by the counter near her. "You've got quite the expression right now."

She gave him a grin, fierce and free. "I'm engineering some destruction."

He smiled at that, but it fell away quickly, and he sighed and tipped his head back and looked up at the lights. "Do you really think this will work, Nita? That we'll be able to rob Tácunan Law, take down both INHUP *and* the black market? It just seems so . . . big."

"It will." She set her jaw. "We'll make it."

"I wish I had your confidence."

"It's not confidence." Nita's voice was soft as she leaned against the counter beside him. "It's determination. I *will* make it work, one way or another. If this plan fails, I'll try another one. And another, and another and another." She put her hand on his face and turned it so he was looking her in the eye. "I won't let INHUP kill you, and I won't let the black market kill me. We will be feared, and we will be untouchable."

Then, before she could hesitate or think too hard about what she was doing, she closed the gap, leaning forward and kissing him. It wasn't a soft kiss, it wasn't gentle or romantic or sweet. It was hard and firm, full of power and a need to express it.

Nita didn't know why she'd kissed him before, when Henry died, couldn't untangle the snarl of emotions inside her. It had felt right at the time, like she was full of emotions and she needed a way to express them, to show him just how much he meant to her, and the only way she'd ever seen those kind of big, complicated feelings expressed was through romance.

But this? This was something different. This was about power. Showing it, sharing it.

Kovit made a small sound in the back of his throat but rolled with it, matching her vicious kiss with equal force, as though taking the power she was pressing into him and drinking it in until he was as vicious as she. His fingers curled around her body for a moment, digging into her shoulders almost painfully before he pulled away.

Nita blinked, her mouth tingling, and her body somehow both hot and cold at the same time.

He ran his hand through his hair. "Nita, I . . ."

She frowned, concerned. "What is it?"

He stared at the ground, searching for words that didn't come.

Nita tried to defuse some of the tension, even though she was still nervous. "Kovit, just tell me. Whatever it is, I'm not going to be mad, or abandon you, or throw plates, or whatever it is they do on those overdramatic sitcoms."

He laughed at that, a grin spreading across his face. "But, Nita, what if I confess that I'm actually a long-lost identical twin who has woken from a decadelong coma to replace the original Kovit and that I'm madly in love with another?"

"Yeah, you're actually in love with Gold." She rolled her eyes, then paused. "You're not, are you?"

He burst into laughter, clutching his stomach. "No, God, no."

"Oh, good. That would have been awkward."

He sighed softly. "No, you definitely don't have to worry about *that*." His face went solemn. "It's nothing that simple."

Nita shifted slightly, giving him space while still remaining close. "Okay. Do you want to try and explain it to me?"

He mussed his hair. "I . . . I'm not really sure what I'm feeling about all this. All the relationships I saw in the Family were —

well, let's just say they're not the sort I ever want to emulate." His smile was bitter. "And my other point of reference is movies, and whatever we have, it's certainly not something you'd find on Disney."

Nita snort-laughed at that, imagining Kovit as Prince Charming. In her head, he looked like Aladdin but with more gore.

He swallowed. "When I was a child, I used to be terrified of turning into an adult, because all everyone could talk about was how they lost control to their hormones, and the idea that I would just one day wake up and suddenly not be able to control myself was . . . Well, it was terrifying."

"That's just an excuse people use to justify bad decisions. No one's a slave to lust," Nita pointed out.

"I know that *now*." He shrugged. "But it really got to me. It terrified me. All I have is control. If I lose control, what am I but the mindless monster the world paints me as? The thought of willingly participating in something where I would give up control was abhorrent to me."

Nita understood. For someone like Kovit, who always maintained such tightly wound control, such care in every action he took, in every shiver he suppressed, in every choice he made — for him, control was everything. There was so little in his life he'd ever had control over that he clung tightly to anything and everything within his power. He couldn't bear the thought of losing it.

"Anyway." He laughed a little. "Turned out I need not have worried. I've never really been, you know. Interested. Maybe all the puberty hormones skipped me."

"Well, if they did, then they skipped me too." Nita shrugged. "I've never been particularly interested in sex either." She considered. "I suppose I might try it someday to see what all the fuss is about."

A little of the tension left his shoulders, but some remained. "I guess it's more common than I thought. The noninterest."

"Probably." Nita watched him carefully. "Is that what was worrying you?"

"Part of it," he admitted. "But it's more than that. It's just—this, us, it's so new and so different from any kind of relationship I've had before. I don't want to hurt you if all of this life-and-death stuff ends and it turns out I don't think about you that way. You know?"

"You won't hurt me." Nita's voice was gentle. She hadn't truly thought about the impact of her actions. She couldn't really get a handle on her emotions, she'd just been following instinct. It had seemed right to kiss him, so she had. But what did she actually *feel*?

After a moment, she was forced to confess, "I'm not . . . I'm not sure about what I feel either."

He tilted his head, a question.

Nita flicked her eyes to his and then away. "I just . . . I have feelings, and sometimes I feel like they need an outlet, a physical form of telling you how big they are. I don't even know if they're actually romantic. I don't even know what romantic feels like. All I know about relationships is what I've seen on television. And on TV, everything ends in a kiss." She considered. "Or a cut to a softcore porn scene."

He laughed at that. "Ouch. Too true."

She looked down, suddenly feeling empty and a little dark. "I'm not really sure what people mean when they talk about love sometimes. I loved my father, but obviously not, you know, *that* way. And I guess I've just never understood how romance was different from a friendship? I mean, aside from the kissing?" She looked away. "I don't . . . I don't know what any of these things are supposed to be like. I don't understand what I'm feeling," she admitted, and then she bit her lip and whispered, "But I don't think I'm experiencing it right."

He frowned. "What makes you say that?"

"I don't know. I just don't think my feelings match what people say they're supposed to be." Nita couldn't explain it more than that. There was a disconnect between what she thought her feelings were supposed to be—big, all-consuming, rose-tinted glasses, giddy with love—and what she actually felt. Something strong and warm and fierce, but not really . . . that. She didn't feel lust, she didn't want to rip his clothes off. She didn't feel like he was perfect, his flaws were all still striking and real. But she did feel warm when she was with him, content and relaxed.

He hesitated, then leaned forward and put his hand on hers. "We're quite the pair, aren't we?"

She choke-laughed. "Yeah, we are."

They stayed like that, hands just touching, a unanimous decision to link themselves together, even though neither of them understood what kind of link it was.

SEVENTEEN

AFTER A TIME, the shower stopped, and Fabricio came out. He had changed back into his clothes, but his hair was sopping wet and dripped all over the floor where he stepped. He froze in his tracks when he saw them sitting silently at the table. "Uh, am I interrupting something?"

Kovit lifted his head, irritation crossing his features. "Your jokes are getting old."

Fabricio held his hands out, palms up, for peace. "Sorry, I didn't mean it."

Nita went to the window, and tilted her head as she looked at the street below. Cars cruised down the street, an odd mix of old boxy models and new luxury brands. People laughed and chatted as they puttered down the sidewalk. A little girl ran ahead of her parents, carrying a blue balloon.

Nita turned back. "Fabricio."

He gave her an uneasy look. "Yes?"

"There's an international conference starting tomorrow dealing with unnatural trafficking along the Amazon." She crossed her arms. "Would your father come?"

He considered. "Probably not. He'd send someone to see how it went, though."

Nita tapped a finger on her leg. "Would he come to meet a high-profile client there?"

"Maybe. Depends on the client."

"With only a day's notice?"

"Notice isn't an issue if the person is important enough."

Nita nodded to herself. "I figured as much." Nita turned to Kovit. "We're going out."

He blinked at her. "Now?"

"Yes."

Fabricio ran his hand through his hair. "Where?"

Nita raised her eyebrows. "You're not going anywhere. You're staying right here. Kovit, get the duct tape."

Fabricio raised his hands again, palms out. "I thought we were working together?"

"We are. But I don't want to leave you here unbound. Who knows what plans you could set up behind my back?"

Fabricio's shoulders slumped as Kovit led him to a chair and began duct-taping him to it. Fabricio gave Kovit a mournful look. "Can you tape me to the couch instead? It's more comfortable."

Kovit shrugged. "All right."

Nita rolled her eyes. "Kovit, you need to stop doing everything your prisoners ask."

"There's no harm in letting him be comfortable," Kovit protested.

Nita sighed dramatically.

Fabricio plopped on the couch and held out his hands for

Kovit to tape. "You're not a great team player, Nita, you know that?"

"I don't particularly care."

He muttered something inaudible over the squeak of the duct tape being peeled off its roll.

When Fabricio was bound, Nita and Kovit headed for the door. "Don't worry, Fabricio, we'll be back in a few hours."

"And if you die?" His voice was caustic. "I'll be stuck here in a duct tape cocoon until I die too."

"Nonsense, the Airbnb is only booked for three days. They'll discover you when they come in to clean it. You can survive without water for at least that long."

"That's not exactly comforting."

Nita waved it away. "Not my problem."

She closed the door behind her before Fabricio could voice any more complaints.

Nita and Kovit made their way toward the conference hotel, following the map on Nita's phone. They walked north, up a wide cobblestoned pedestrian street full of clean, pricy shops interspersed with bookstores and fast-food chains. There must have been three McDonald's in just as many blocks. Glass windows and modern blocky buildings mixed with massive stone archways and turn-of-the-century European construction styles. All along the streets, manteros had laid mats on the ground and spread jewelry, wire animals, sandals, belts, and an assortment of other things up for sale.

The echo of currency exchange people calling, "Cambio, cambio, cambio," mixed with the roar of the nearby roads and the chatter of hundreds of people on the crowded street, many of them exchanging their unstable pesos for dollars and euros, currencies with less fluctuation.

Nita stuck close to Kovit, trying to distance herself as much as possible from the crowds of strangers. She curled her body away each time someone brushed past and clenched her fists at her sides.

She kept her head low, trying to avoid notice. It was only a matter of time before the black market realized she was in Argentina. INHUP had leaked her location before, but she hadn't traveled with INHUP this time. Did whoever had leaked her information last time have access to flight manifests? Passport control records? She didn't know.

Her hair fell over her eyes and watched the people around her carefully. She couldn't let her guard down just because they were in a new city.

Nita and Kovit eventually turned toward the water, crossing a series of massive highways to get to a bridge. The bridge was designed all in white with tall ridges on one side that made it look like a sail floating across the waves. The wooden boards creaked as they walked across, and the sound reminded Nita too much of the groan of the wooden docks in Death Market.

Ultramodern and ultra-expensive, the conference hotel resembled nothing more than a cubed fishbowl. Nita hated buildings like that, they made her feel like she was back in a glass cage again.

The lobby was as plush and modern as the building promised, all circular white couches and pristine white desks. A stairwell on the far side of the lobby led up to the second floor, and pleasant-looking signs were posted in gold at various points, directing people to different rooms.

Nita pulled up her list of major dignitaries attending the conference and showed it to Kovit. She'd weeded through it earlier and picked out the people who seemed important enough that Alberto Tácunan would take notice. "We want one of these men."

Kovit scrolled through the list, examining the pictures and smiling slightly. "Does it have to be one of these guys, or will any rich middle-aged man do?"

Nita rolled her eyes. "You know they won't."

The two of them took lobby chairs facing reception so they could watch who was checking in. With the conference starting tomorrow, there were a lot of people arriving today, and it was only a matter of time before one of her targets showed up.

They settled in for the long wait, and Kovit idly twirled one of the free pens on the table. A stocky young white man walked by talking on the phone in English.

Kovit watched him, his mouth turning down.

Nita frowned. "Do you know him?"

He shook his head. "No. He just looks a little like Matt."

"Oh." Nita looked at the young man again. He had a loud, brash voice, and he was exclaiming at someone on the phone. His muscles were too large, toned past the point of being attractive and into the point of being a bit creepy. He had that square jaw and football-player look that was popular in movie stars, but Nita had always found unattractive.

"Did I ever tell you?" Kovit asked softly. "What Matt did that made Henry so angry?"

Nita turned to him. "No."

Kovit's eyes were on the stranger. "Matt was supposed to kidnap a man and bring him back to the compound. The target was checking into a swanky hotel just like this one." His smile was bitter as the Matt-looking young man hung up and walked to the elevator. "Matt was supposed to follow him up to his room and snatch him. He had a large suitcase ready to stuff the body into—a beige and purple flowered one that looked like an old lady's curtains."

"What happened?" Nita asked.

"The person he was supposed to kidnap resisted." Kovit shrugged. "Matt had a violent streak. He pulverized the man's head, murdered him. Brought the body back. Oh, man, Henry was mad. They were only planning to scare the man, give him a good rattling. They didn't want him dead."

Kovit sighed heavily. "It wasn't the first time something like that happened, and well . . . Henry decided Matt was a liability."

"And asked you to get rid of him," Nita finished.

"Yeah." Kovit looked around the room, his eyes dark, lost in the past. "It's still so hard to wrap my head around. That Henry killed him, after everything. It doesn't feel real?" He ran his hand through his hair and gave a sharp laugh. "I never saw the body. I don't know how or when it happened. And I'm in a strange place, so there's no memories of him here, nothing to remind me that he should be here too but isn't." He closed his eyes. "Sometimes, I feel like he was just a dream, a phantom I made up to be not so alone in the Family."

Nita was quiet a long moment before she asked, "Is it easier? To pretend he was a dream?"

"Easier? Maybe. But it makes me feel like a shitty friend."

Nita didn't have much to say to that. She'd felt similar when grieving for her father. She still felt it now. Anytime she let the world distract her, let her mind slip away from the pain, she'd suddenly see something and be struck by the realization that her father was, indeed, still dead. And she'd feel like she betrayed him every time she forgot, even for those brief moments.

"What about Henry?" Nita asked.

Kovit's expression darkened. "What about him?"

Nita hesitated. "You've been avoiding talking about him."

"I don't want to grieve for him. He betrayed me in every possible way. He ruined my life, he treated me like an object, and he murdered my best friend. I shouldn't grieve for him."

"But you can't help it," Nita said gently.

Kovit swallowed heavily. "Why does he get so much space in my mind? Matt was a friend, a real friend, but Henry's the one whose death haunts me, who plays over and over in my head." His voice was bitter. "I wish I could just turn it off, shut out all these feelings. I don't want them. He doesn't deserve them."

Nita bowed her head. "It would be a lot easier if we could stop caring about the people who hurt us."

She thought of her mother, and her dark promise to get rid of Kovit, and shuddered softly. Why did Nita always go back to her? Why couldn't she have remembered her passport the first time?

"It would," Kovit agreed. He ran a hand through his hair. "I just keep coming back to that moment we realized he'd sold me out to INHUP. If he couldn't have me, no one could. Like those pet owners who'd rather put down their pets when they move than let another person adopt them. Like he thought he owned me."

"I think," Nita said carefully, "in his mind, he did."

Kovit sighed. His eyes were dry, and his expression was calm, but she could see that he was hurting underneath it all. She didn't blame him. He'd be some sort of superhuman if he could get over murdering his surrogate father in only two days.

She'd opened her mouth to say something when he elbowed her gently, a wicked grin coming over his face, breaking the spell of grief.

"Look," he whispered, eyes hungry and violent and full of delight.

Nita followed his gaze and found a man checking in at the registration desk. A slow smile crept across her features.

Kovit pulled out his switchblade and smiled, cracked and dark and promising agony for all those in his path, and he whispered, "Time to have some fun."

EIGHTEEN

NITA KNOCKED on the door to room 403. Kovit stood just to her side, invisible through the peephole. There was no answer the first time she knocked, so she did it again, and called in Spanish, trying to mimic Fabricio's strong Porteño accent, "Mr. Almeida, you left your credit card at reception. We've been trying to call your room phone, but it doesn't seem to be functioning."

There was a muffled thud, and then the door opened to reveal a sweaty middle-aged white man glaring at them.

"What?" His Spanish was heavily Portuguese-accented. "Are you sure?"

Nita just smiled and smashed two knuckles into his throat.

He choked, stumbling backwards, and Nita stepped into the room, closely followed by Kovit. She closed the door behind them, and Kovit smiled as he watched the man gasp and sputter. "You're getting better at this."

"Thank you." Nita returned his smile, flicked her phone onto its loudest setting, and played some death metal from

YouTube, loud off-key screams reverberating around the room just under the heavy base.

Almeida stumbled to his feet, but Kovit casually grabbed him, twisted his arm behind his back with one hand, and seized his throat with the other. Almeida couldn't get air to scream as Kovit twisted the arm, forcing Almeida down.

Nita took out the duct tape, and they set to work taping him firmly to the chair.

When they were done, Nita sat down on the bed across from Almeida.

"Do you know who I am?" she asked.

Kovit had covered his mouth with tape so he couldn't scream, and Almeida just shook his head, eyes wide with fear.

"That's fine, then. You don't need to." Nita fished through his briefcase, searching for his laptop. She pulled it out and opened it to a password screen. "But if you want to get out of this alive, I'll need your laptop password."

He started to shake his head, and Kovit pressed his switchblade into Almeida's throat. "Think carefully."

Almeida swallowed, and the switchblade pressed a little harder, drawing a thin trickle of blood. Almeida's eyes flicked between them, and he tried to say something through the duct tape.

Nita smiled softly. "Let me get that for you. And remember, if you try and scream, my friend will cut your vocal cords right out, and I'll make you write the answers to my questions."

Almeida flinched, either at Nita's calm words of horror or the duct tape ripping off his skin, Nita wasn't sure.

"It's my girlfriend's birthday." Almeida's voice was hoarse as he gave them the date.

Nita typed it in and then went straight to the email icon. "Do you work with Alberto Tácunan?"

His eyes widened. "Uh."

"Never mind, I found the emails." She smiled slightly, scrolling through his inbox. She'd organized it by sender, and she skimmed boring emails about tax forms and offshore accounts and funneling money. "Any plans to meet him while you're here?"

"No."

Nita ordered the emails by most recent and decided he was telling the truth. So she composed an email to Alberto Tácunan, marked as urgent.

Something has come up. I need to see you in person. I'm at the summit tomorrow. Can we meet?

She considered adding more details, but decided the vaguer the better, and hit the Send button.

She glanced through the emails, and Kovit retaped Almeida's mouth and asked in a hungry, hopeful voice, "Can I play with him?"

Nita kept her face calm even as her stomach turned. "Not yet. We still might need him."

Kovit sighed and flopped on the bed beside her to read over her shoulder. On the chair, Almeida began to struggle, but it was pointless, and both Nita and Kovit ignored him.

Kovit watched as Nita flipped through emails with Tácunan Law, scrolling through Almeida's files. Offshore accounts, check. Funneling campaign money into personal accounts, check. Running a brothel in São Paulo, check.

"What a sleazeball." Kovit's voice was layered with disgust.

"Agreed." Nita casually copied the relevant emails and sent their details to one of the Brazilian nonprofits trying to end corruption.

Kovit pointed at one of the email headers. "Look, did he ask his superiors to be the representative to attend this summit?"

Nita blinked and clicked on the email. He had indeed requested it. She skimmed the email, then the next. It looked like Mr. Almeida had significant holdings in the black market. He'd lost a lot of money when el Mercado de la Muerte was destroyed — a lot of bribe money, specifically. He'd wanted to come here to ensure that whatever happened, this summit failed.

"Wow." Kovit's eyes were wide. "I'd realized the black market had a lot of reach — they must have to keep Death Market running so easily — but this . . ."

"I know," Nita whispered. "It's a lot."

"Look there." Kovit reached over her shoulder and clicked an email. "Is that a hit? He put a hit on an activist?"

Not just any activist. He'd put a hit on Mirella.

Her companion in captivity in el Mercado de la Muerte. The girl who'd had her eye gouged out and sold, who'd escaped with Nita, who'd been shot on the dock. Who Nita had thought dead until she came and wreaked bloody vengeance on the people attempting to flee the market after Nita burned it to the ground.

It was hard to imagine Mirella as such a powerful activist that she could cause a summit like this. That she could inspire assassination attempts. Mirella was always trapped in Nita's mind as the victim, powerless and angry. A victim of Reyes, who sold her for parts on the black market, a victim of Boulder, who'd stolen her eye and eaten it.

A victim of Kovit, who'd tortured her.

Nita shivered at that thought and tried not to think too hard about Kovit leaning over her shoulder, reading up on assassination plans for Mirella.

"Wow, this activist person is impressive." Kovit scrolled through the email. "She really pissed these people off."

Nita blinked. "You still can't say her name?"

"Whose name?"

"Mirella."

He looked at her blankly.

And Nita realized: he didn't remember Mirella's name. She was nothing to him but another faceless victim in his past. He had no idea who Nita was talking about. Mirella was so unimportant to him that the memories had already faded into nothing.

Nausea rose in Nita's stomach. Mirella's screams had haunted Nita's nightmares, and Kovit, the instigator of those screams, didn't even remember her. Nita had always known he dissociated from his victims, refused to name them, refused to make them people in his mind. But seeing him looking between Nita and the email in confusion after everything he'd done made her ill.

Kovit occasionally frightened her. She hated watching him

eat, seeing the perverse pleasure he got from others' pain. But seeing this, right here, this lack of recognition, was somehow so much worse than when he'd ripped that INHUP agent's tongue out in front of her. Worse than Fabricio describing what Kovit had done to him.

"Dolphin girl," Nita tried. "You remember, in the market?"

He continued to stare at her blankly, and a chill ran down Nita's spine.

She turned away quickly. "Never mind. It's not important."

Even though it really was.

She clicked through the emails and found that this latest assassination attempt was going to be the third by Almeida alone, never mind other organizations. Mirella was apparently *very* effective as an activist.

Nita sighed. All that power, and all Mirella had managed to do was paint an even bigger target on her back. Nita couldn't help but sympathize — they were stuck in similar situations, targets of people more powerful than they. In some ways, it felt like they'd never escaped the black market at all. They'd just gotten out of one cage and into another. And this one didn't have clear walls or ways to see your enemies. You couldn't shoot them or burn them, because you didn't always know who they were. And even if you did, Nita imagined if Mirella murdered high-ranking government officials, it would have consequences.

But the key difference was, Nita hadn't chosen this life.

Mirella, on the other hand, was fighting for people she didn't even know. For other people still trapped in markets, for girls she'd never met. Why did Mirella care what happened to

156

other girls? Mirella had escaped — she should have lain low and survived. By sticking her neck out for all these other faceless, voiceless girls, she only put herself in danger. It boggled Nita's mind.

Nita might need to fight the black market, might need to take on INHUP or the police or even the world, but the only person she fought for was herself. And occasionally Kovit.

Certainly not people she didn't even know. What a waste of effort.

This was why she'd never liked Mirella. How was she supposed to understand someone like that?

"We should see if we can warn this girl," Kovit said, skimming through more emails. "She could use a heads-up."

Nita stared at Kovit as if he'd grown a second head. "You want to help her?"

"Yeah." He seemed confused by her reaction. "Why not? It costs us nothing."

"I . . ." Nita shook her head. "No, you're absolutely right, we should try and send this to her. I just . . ."

"Nita, you're acting weird, what *is* it?"

"Kovit, you *tortured* her." Nita's voice broke a little. "You made her scream until she could barely talk. She *hates* you, and with good reason."

"I . . . What?" He leaned back. "I did?"

"How can you not remember? She had grayish skin? She and I were in the cages together."

His eyes widened, and something dark and incomprehensible crossed his face. "Oh, her."

For a moment, he looked haunted, as though he could

157

actually see Mirella as a person and realize the atrocities he'd committed on someone he'd expressed admiration for not a minute earlier. And then it was gone, something hard coming into his eyes. Nita could almost see as he built a wall, forcing himself to dissociate from Mirella, forcing himself to forget she was a person.

"I don't see how that's relevant." He shrugged. "Are you done yet? I'm hungry."

Nita opened her mouth, part of her not wanting to let him change the subject like this, wanting to bring Mirella up again. But she didn't. She'd known who he was when she teamed up with him, and she'd known what he'd done to Mirella. Nothing had changed.

So she went back to the computer, screen-shot all the evidence, and then went online to find out how she could get in touch with Mirella. Her activist cause had a website with a contact form, and Nita pasted all the information and sent it, hoping Mirella would look. There was an email required at the bottom, and Nita hesitated before creating a new account just for this. She picked a username that couldn't be traced back to her and then sent the information off.

Nita checked back on Almeida's email and found that there was a response from Alberto Tácunan.

Saturday, 4pm. Hotel restaurant.

Tomorrow. Nita could deal with that. She fired back a response.

Sensitive subject. Meet in my room. 403.

After a moment, there was another response.

Fine. See you then.

Nita grinned, wild and fierce. Victory.

Step one of this plan was a go. If all went well, she'd have a password tomorrow and have the data by the end of tomorrow night. She closed her eyes and imagined all that information, all that power at her fingertips, and she licked her lips. She liked the way that idea made her feel. Liked the idea of being right at the top, of pulling all the strings that made the black market move, of making all the people who'd tried to hunt her whimper and grovel at her feet in fear.

She shivered slightly and tried to push the feeling away. She wasn't there yet. She needed to stay focused, not get caught up in fantasies.

She checked Almeida's schedule and found nothing for this evening, so she closed his computer and looked up at Kovit. "We're done here."

He was staring out the window, lost in thought. He blinked and refocused on her. "Okay."

She turned to Almeida, still bound and gagged in the chair. "We don't need him anymore. You can do what you want to him."

Kovit's attention turned to Almeida, hunger in his eyes, fingers white-knuckled on his switchblade. He slid off the bed, movements lithe and precise and predatory.

Nita took the laptop and went to the door. "I'll wait down in the lobby. Come down when you're finished." She looked around the room, the beige carpet and white bedspread. "Try not to make a mess. I didn't think to bring plastic tarps. Blood-less is better."

"No evidence left behind. Not a problem." He smiled, wide

and creepy and playful, his gaze never leaving the terrified man bound to the chair.

She quietly closed the door behind her, cutting off the man's grunting, struggling attempts to scream through his duct tape and Kovit's delighted laugh as he got to work.

NINETEEN

NITA TOOK THE LAPTOP to the lobby and spent the next hour or so looking through Almeida's emails and messages, trying to get a firmer grasp of the scope of the black market. She also went onto his banking account, easily accessing it using passwords from a conveniently labeled folder on the desktop, and sent herself as much of his money as she could without triggering the antifraud software.

Afterward, she closed the laptop and went into her phone's contacts list and messaged Diana. She might be Adair's right-hand woman, but she was a good hacker, and Nita was sure there'd be something at Tácunan Law that she could pay Diana with, if she didn't want any of the money she'd just stolen from Almeida. To deal with security cameras at Tácunan Law, Nita would need a hacker. She'd also need to contact Diana on her own, without Adair knowing. Just in case.

A couple of minutes after she sent the text, her phone rang. She checked the caller ID, found it was from Toronto. She hesitated for a moment — she really hated phone calls, why couldn't people just text? — before she finally picked up.

"Nita?" The voice on the other end was soft. "It's Diana."

"Oh. Hi."

"You messaged me about the security camera system at Tácunan Law?" Diana sounded unsure, her voice a little high.

"Yeah." Nita took a deep breath and leaned back. "I want to know if it's hackable."

Diana was quiet a moment before she asked, "Why should I help you?"

Nita sighed softly. "I'm trying to take down the DUL with the information I get there — why *wouldn't* you want to help me? You've spent years haunted by the fear that ghouls will go up one day, that you'll suddenly be on a kill list when you've never hurt anyone. It's in your best interest to get rid of that list, the same way it is mine."

"I know." Diana's voice was hard. "I know that very well."

Nita's voice was firm. "If it's money you want, I just got a nice payment from a corrupt Brazilian diplomat. Easily enough to pay college tuition for you."

With plenty left over to pay for my own tuition. Nita wouldn't have made the offer if her own future wasn't secure. She would go to college, but with Almeida's funds. She could afford to be magnanimous and send Diana as well.

Diana hesitated, then whispered, "I don't want money. I mean, I do. But more than anything, I want a promise that no matter what happens, you won't ever try and hurt Adair again."

Ah. So that's what this was about.

"I've no interest in hurting him. Unless he does something that puts me in direct danger, you've no reason to worry for him."

Diana let out a little sigh of relief. "Okay. All right. Good."

"So, will you help?"

Diana hesitated, then asked softly, "You really think you can take down the Dangerous Unnaturals List?"

"I'm damn well going to try."

Diana hesitated another moment, before whispering, "All right. What do you need me to do?"

"CCTV. I don't want the cameras picking me up. Can you hack them?"

"Well, every system is hackable. CCTV is especially vulnerable, actually — did you know most of them have software and security that's over a decade outdated? And lots just feed directly into the internet. Sometimes Adair has me search for CCTV from gas stations that feeds into the internet and then I hack it and I can read credit cards, and he steals the numbers."

"That explains a lot." Nita had been wondering how he paid for things when he clearly took most of his payment in information. Toronto wasn't cheap. "Does that mean Tácunan Law's CCTV is feeding onto the internet?"

"In all likelihood. But if they've got half a brain, it'll be locked up tight." The click of computer keys echoed in the background. "I'll poke around and see what I can do. Normally, for a company like Tácunan Law, I'd say hacking anything is impossible. But CCTV is a weird special case. It might be possible."

"What do I need to do?" Nita asked.

Diana considered. "Nothing right now. I'll contact you if I need anything from you."

Nita agreed and hung up, uncomfortable at leaving

something completely up to another person, passing off that little piece of control. But she needed to accept that she couldn't do everything herself.

She adjusted her mental list of things to do. If she could get all this working, then she would just need to find a way to deal with the guards, if there were any. Or other potential witnesses in the building.

Kovit came down shortly after. He glowed with health, his hair as shiny as a shampoo commercial, and his skin looked so soft and smooth she wanted to reach out and touch it.

"All done?" she asked.

"Mmm." He nodded, his eyes sleepy and contented. "All done."

"Good." Nita rose and tucked the laptop under her arm. "We've got a couple of errands to run on our way back."

Nita used Google Maps to find Tácunan Law. It was only a fifteen-minute walk from the hotel, so they set off along Puerto Madero, the sun high and hot above them. The sunlight made the water glint too brightly to look at, and the boats bobbed up and down in the port, mostly sailboats and yacht-looking things in this part. People Rollerbladed by, and a pair of street performers did an impromptu tango show beside the water.

When they came to Tácunan Law, Nita found it was exactly like all the other buildings around it, tall and glass, a monstrosity of steel and chrome.

Kovit looked at it skeptically. "The whole thing is a law firm? Or just one floor?"

Nita frowned. "Good question. It does seem a little overkill to own an entire building."

She stared up at it, pretending to be another awestruck tourist bumbling around. What she really wanted was a look at the area around it. Escape routes. Visibility. A sense of place.

Dozens of security cameras peppered the side of the building, and she really hoped Diana could hack them — otherwise, their break-in was going to be very short and very unsuccessful.

Kovit went inside and checked the public floor plan. He came back out and shrugged. "It looks like they're only in three floors of the building. But it's called the Tácunan Building, so I'm guessing Alberto Tácunan owns it and leases out the other floors."

Nita nodded. That would make sense. It would both provide more money, as well as a good cover and front of respectability.

But it also meant that when she stole the information, the chance of other people being in the building was high. And she didn't want witnesses.

"Any other companies in there we should be aware of?" she asked.

"I took a photo."

He showed it to her, and she peered at the names with suspicion, but she didn't recognize any of them. They could be anything from harmless accounting firms to fronts for more of Tácunan Law's illegal operations. She made a frustrated sound at how useless all this was.

As they headed away, Nita was so lost in thought, she almost didn't hear the beep of her phone. She pulled it out, thinking it was Diana with more information on the security cameras, but it wasn't.

A small notification alert informed her that a new name and face had been uploaded by INHUP's Dangerous Unnaturals List division.

It was Kovit.

TWENTY

NITA STARED at the screen, unwilling to believe it. Kovit's face and name were up on INHUP.

She clicked on the link, just to confirm, because maybe it was a mistake, it was too soon, there was supposed to be a week waiting period, this wasn't supposed to happen. But she knew even before the INHUP page loaded that it wasn't a mistake.

The entire world was going to be hunting for him now. Millions of people subscribed to the same alerts she did. And those who didn't would watch the news tonight and see Kovit's face — it was rare for someone to be added to the list — so it always ended up being a big story. Most of the time, the police killed monsters before this kind of thing needed to go public.

She imagined all the people sitting in their homes as the news told them the atrocities Kovit had committed, their eyes glued to the screen as they watched the videos that Henry sent to INHUP. In her mind's eye, the citizens swarmed over Kovit like a horde of zombies, hands grabbing, hungry for state-sanctioned blood. Kovit would flick out his switchblade, but it wouldn't be enough to fight them all off. Eventually he'd be crushed by the press of bodies, and then he'd be the one screaming in videos posted online.

Nita forced her mind away from that image. She wasn't going to let that happen.

"Nita? What is it? Is something wrong?" Kovit asked, leaning over and trying to see what she was staring at.

She winced. A part of her wanted to hide it, to shove her phone in her pocket, lie, and say it was nothing. Pretend that everything was all right. But she wouldn't let herself be that person. She wouldn't hide this from Kovit, she wouldn't become the manipulating information hoarder her mother was.

So she raised her head, and tried to tell him. But the words wouldn't come, they caught in her throat like she'd swallowed an egg whole.

She held out her phone, wordless, and he looked down at the notification. She'd only looked at the top, where the picture was, too scared to scroll down and see what details they'd put in about him. He looked a bit younger in the photo, maybe fifteen or sixteen, but it was very distinctly him. In the picture, his eyes were narrowed at something offscreen, his head tilted at a three-quarter angle, and the slightest hint of a sneer pulled at his features. It was not a flattering photo.

He stared at the picture a long moment, his face terrifyingly still. Then he leaned against the concrete barrier protecting people from falling into the water and slowly slid down so he was crouched against it, a small, soft keening sound emanating from his throat.

Nita knelt beside him, hovering, wishing she could do something but not knowing what to do.

"I'm sorry," she finally managed, her voice cracked and broken. "I'm so, so sorry."

His face broke, that perfect stillness shattering into a million glittering shards of grief. "Why is it out early?"

"I don't know," Nita whispered. "It was supposed to be a week. Your sister even said that was how long verification took." Her mind scrambled. "New evidence? Confirming evidence somehow?"

Or maybe her mother had figured out who Kovit was and pulled strings with her contacts to make it go up early.

The idea made her nauseous. But if anyone could find a way around the rules and get Kovit onto the list early, it would be her mother. A sick feeling settled in her stomach.

She shoved this aside. If it was her mother, so be it. She would handle it later. Right now, it wasn't important why or how Kovit had been added to the list. What was important was dealing with it.

Kovit trembled on the ground, his chest heaving as though he couldn't quite get enough air. "I'm going to die."

"No—"

"*Yes*, Nita. My face is up. No matter what you do, even if you destroy INHUP, it's too late. My face is *already up*."

He ran his hands through his hair, fingers curling into his scalp, and Nita knelt beside him and grabbed his hands before he could scratch his skin off with his fingernails.

"It's not over until it's over." Nita's voice was hard and sharp and desperate.

He laughed brokenly, his voice high and a little hysterical.

"Nita, no one has escaped the list once their name and face are on it. *No one.*"

"No one escaped Death Market either."

"Nita, this is not something you can *fix*." His voice broke, and he took a moment to collect himself, his chest heaving, his throat gulping for air. "My name is out there. It's over. It doesn't *matter* anymore."

"It does. It always matters." She pressed her hands to his cheeks. "Kovit, you can't give up. You *can't*."

"Why?" His smile was bitter. "All my misdeeds are coming back to get me."

Nita snorted. "You, of all people, should know there is no karmic justice in the world. There's no meaning. You can spend your whole life being a saint and still get murdered in a random shootout," Nita snapped, thinking of the real estate agent who'd taken a bullet meant for Nita in Toronto, her eyes widening as she cried out and fell. An innocent casualty in a war she didn't even realize was happening. "And you can be the most terrible person in the world, and as long as you have money and power, no one will touch you.

"The world isn't *fair*, Kovit." Nita pressed her forehead to his. "Maybe you do deserve to die. Maybe you're irredeemably evil. But I don't *care*, and neither does the world. And God damn it, I'm not going to let INHUP take you from me."

His breathing was shaky. "How? How can you stop this?"

Nita pulled away and tugged her cell phone out, giving him a gentle, careful smile. "You think I didn't plan for this eventuality?"

He blinked. "What?"

"You gave me the idea. Back in Toronto. When you said I should start cultivating relationships with newspapers by selling off those corrupt INHUP names. So we could more easily release any information we got from Tácunan Law."

"Yeah . . ." He frowned. "What about it?"

"Well, I thought about it a bit. I've been building a good relationship with an editor from the *Washington Post*." She hesitated. "And then I realized I could do something like this."

She showed him the email she'd been preparing, just in case.

He looked at the email, and his eyes widened. "I wondered why you wanted Pat and me to go to that café. There were so many people and reporters. You'd been trying to keep a low profile . . ."

Nita smiled slightly. "There's a reason for everything."

Kovit was silent a long moment. "Why didn't you tell me what you planned?"

"I didn't want to mess up your big day with Pat." She looked away. "And I kind of hoped I'd never have to use this backup plan. For obvious reasons."

His mouth pressed into a thin line, and his eyes were not quite looking at her. "What happened to discussing plans beforehand?"

She bowed her head, guilt twisting in her chest. How quickly she slipped back into old patterns when she wasn't thinking. "I'm sorry. You're right. I should have told you. I'll do better."

"Do you have other plans I don't know about?" he asked softly.

She shook her head. "No. Just this one."

"Did you think I would veto it?"

"You still can." Nita put her phone away. "I haven't done anything yet. I won't press Send until you tell me it's okay. This is your life we're talking about."

He closed his eyes for a heartbeat, shaking. Finally, he pulled away from her and looked down at the email.

"If you send this . . ." His voice caught. "Pat will be in as much danger as me. If the mobs find out we're related, even just that she knows me . . . it paints just as much of a target on her back as on mine."

"Not just as much," Nita said, though she'd thought something similar when she'd first crafted this plan. Perhaps that was the real reason she hadn't talked to him about it—because at its core, it endangered his sister, and Kovit wouldn't want to do that, even to save his own life. "It's still a crime to hurt her. Many people won't want to deal with murder charges."

"And many won't care about the consequences."

"Perhaps." Nita met his eyes. "But Pat can take care of herself. And besides, she's your sister. Do you really think she wouldn't do anything she could to help you?"

He bit his lip. "We can't make that decision for her."

"She's already said as much. She said she'd do anything to help you when I spoke to her." Nita inclined her head slightly. "But you know her better than me. Do you think she'd take this risk?"

Kovit hesitated, then looked away. "She would. I know she would. But that doesn't make it right. I can't . . . I can't let my sister share my fate."

Nita let out a long breath, then grabbed Kovit's chin and turned him to face her. "Kovit. You're going to die if we don't discredit the list. We can hide, and we can fight, but we won't make it. We can't go small. We have to go big. You've already admitted Pat would do this to save you. I'd do anything to save you. Why won't you let us help you?"

He blinked watery eyes and gave her a soft smile. "Because I'm not willing to trade my life for yours or hers."

Nita made a frustrated sound. "Please, Kovit. It's not a trade. It's just a risk. She hunts unicorns, for fuck's sake. You really think associating with you is more dangerous than unicorn hunting?" Nita arched an eyebrow. "High opinion of yourself, huh?"

He snort-laughed, then was quiet for a moment. "Do you really think this plan will work?"

"I don't know." She tilted his chin up with one finger. "But I'm not going to sit here and let you die. And I think it has a chance, so I damn well want to at least *try*."

He pulled away, and stared down at his fisted hands, his whole body still shaking from fear or adrenaline or someone's pain on the street, Nita didn't know.

Finally, he whispered, "Okay."

"Okay what?"

His voice was heavy but firm. "Send it. Let's try."

Nita's body slumped in relief, and she put her hand on his shoulder and gently squeezed. "You're making the right choice."

"No, I'm making the selfish choice." His smile was small and bitter. "But I don't want to die."

Her chest tightened.

"You won't," she promised, but she was scared she was lying.

Kovit held out his hand, scrolling through the email, taking one last look at the pictures included in it. All of them taken by Nita as insurance when they were in Toronto. Kovit and his sister hugging in the train station, the two of them smiling and laughing as they chatted. A link to the CBC news segment of the café's anniversary, with Kovit and Pat figuring obviously in the background chatting. And also the pictures of Kovit's sister talking on the news, the banner underneath advertising her status as an INHUP agent. And lastly, just now, Nita copy-pasted the link to Kovit's entry on the Dangerous Unnaturals List.

She didn't say what their relationship was, didn't draw any conclusions. Just commented, INTERESTING THAT AN INHUP AGENT IS SO FRIENDLY WITH A ZANNIE.

Finally, his finger rose, hovering above the Send button. He held Nita's gaze for a moment, and she saw the fear and guilt battling there together for a moment before the resolve won out and he pressed the button.

She let out a breath as he put the first nail in INHUP's coffin.

TWENTY-ONE

T HEY SAT TOGETHER for a little while, backs against the concrete barrier as Kovit tried to gather himself, wiping his eyes ferociously, as if he could wipe away all the evidence of his humanity. But the more he swiped at them, the redder they looked, and the more broken and human his face became.

Nita just sat next to him, quietly leaning against him for support while he put himself back together. There wasn't much else she could do.

When he finally took a deep breath and stumbled to his feet, Nita rose with him.

"Ready to go back to the Airbnb?" she asked.

"Yeah."

"I think both of us could use some sleep. We've had a long day, and the flight wasn't ideal for rest. Things will look better once you've had a nap."

He didn't seem convinced. She linked her arm with his, just to feel his warmth and signal silently to him that she was there, she wasn't going anywhere. He leaned in, almost as though he was using her as a crutch, even though he didn't put any of his weight on her, and they headed back.

The return walk was tense. Kovit kept glancing nervously at people, as though expecting them to jump out at him at any moment. His eyes darted around with an almost manic fear in them, and he kept clenching and unclenching his hands.

"Relax," Nita whispered to him as they crossed the bridge. "The post only just went up, most people won't have seen it yet. And even if they did, no one would think to look for you here."

He nodded sharply, but his body remained tense and concerned.

Just in case, though, she bought a pair of sunglasses for him at a stall. With them on, he blended in better, his ethnicity more ambiguous.

When they returned to the Airbnb, Nita double-bolted the door behind them, and Kovit finally let the tension drain from his body.

Fabricio was still tied up on the couch, and he looked up when they arrived, his hair mussed from the nap he presumably had while waiting for them. He tilted his head. "Can someone untie me so I can go to the bathroom?"

Kovit snapped his switchblade out and approached. To Fabricio's credit, he didn't flinch at the sight, despite everything that had happened to him. He held very still while Kovit cut the duct tape, his whole body tight with tension. Once he was free, he thanked Kovit, went over to the kitchen, put on the kettle, and then went to the bathroom.

Kovit flopped onto the couch where Fabricio had been and put his head in his hands. "What now?"

"We rest." Nita's voice was gentle. "Nothing important is happening until tomorrow."

"But we should . . . I don't know. Do something?" He sighed. "Do you have any more ideas for what to do next?"

"Maybe," Nita admitted. "I've been thinking on the way back. But nothing will work until the article about you goes online. We need to wait for people to start talking about why an INHUP agent was meeting with you on such friendly terms."

"When will that happen?"

"Everything I sent is easy to verify, so . . . soon?"

"How soon?"

"Let me check." Nita pulled out her phone, and sure enough, there was a response from the reporter.

I've confirmed the identity of the INHUP agent and zannie through multiple sources. That cafe event sure was popular! Do you have any information on why the two of them were together, and why they seemed so close?

All I can tell you is that INHUP knew about the two of them and looked the other way, Nita replied. *I'm sending these pictures out to other sources tonight, so if you want the scoop, you have the rest of today to publish.*

She looked up at Kovit. "Not sure. Hopefully this afternoon."

He nodded and stared down at his hands.

Fabricio exited the bathroom. "What's this afternoon?"

"Nothing." Nita's response was automatic, hiding information a second nature to her.

His tone was skeptical as he went into the kitchen. "Nothing, huh. Doesn't sound like nothing."

Kovit swallowed and looked away, and Fabricio looked between him and Nita. "Something happened."

Nita admitted, "Kovit went up on the Dangerous Unnaturals List."

"Ah." The kettle boiled and automatically turned off with a pop. "I see. I'm sorry, Kovit."

Kovit jerked slightly. "No, you're not. You're happy I'm going up on the list. One more monster who the public will righteously kill."

"Hardly." Fabricio looked through the cupboards absently. "The list is a scam. The worst monsters have always been able to find a way to buy their way off the list. Just like everything else."

"But it'll get rid of me," Kovit responded.

"So?" Fabricio raised his eyebrows at Kovit as he pulled out packets of tea, and a large bag of maté.

"So that will make you happy."

"You don't know me very well if you think that," Fabricio said placidly.

Kovit blinked, a confused frown forming on his face. "What does that mean?"

Fabricio sighed, clearly not wanting to talk about this. "There are very few things in this world that would make me happy. Your death really isn't one of them. Would I be relieved if I never had to worry about you hurting me again? Sure. But would I be happy? Not particularly." His lips pressed into a thin line, and it looked like he was debating saying more before he decided against it. He turned to Nita and asked, "Would you like some tea?"

"So you can poison me with chemicals you found in the bathroom cupboard?" Nita snorted. "No thanks."

He rolled his eyes. "I'm not the one who uses poison here."

"Nonetheless."

He shrugged. "Would you like something, Kovit?"

Kovit quirked a smile. "Is it actually poisoned?"

Fabricio rolled his eyes. "No. I'll drink out of it too to make you feel better, if you want."

Kovit was silent for a long moment as he watched Fabricio before he said, "All right."

Fabricio turned back and pulled two cups from the pantry. One was a regular mug, which he plopped a tea bag into, and the other was brown and looked more like a little gourd than a mug. He put a metal straw in the gourd with a filter on the bottom.

"What is that?" Kovit asked.

"Maté. I love it, but it's an acquired taste," he said, filling both cups with water. The maté cup looked to be ninety percent leaves, ten percent water. No wonder he needed a straw with a filter to drink it. "I figured you'd probably prefer the mint tea packet." He tilted his head at Kovit. "You're free to try the maté, though."

"Is it bitter?" Kovit asked.

"Very. But I'm sure there's sugar here somewhere."

"That's fine. I'll stick with the mint."

Fabricio held up the mug to show Kovit and then took a sip. "Good enough?"

Kovit smiled slightly. "I'm satisfied it's not poisoned."

Fabricio brought it over to Kovit, holding it carefully in

his bandaged hands. Kovit took it and just held it. He looked down into the depths of the tea and finally cleared his throat. "Thank you."

"You're not supposed to say that until you're done." Fabricio's voice was light. He seated himself across from them, bringing a thermos full of water with him to refill his maté cup.

Kovit finally looked up. "Why are you being nice to me?"

"I made you tea, that's all."

"But why?" Kovit put the cup down. "I've hurt you."

"Yes." Fabricio sipped his maté. "I recall, thanks."

"So, why are you being nice to me?"

"Would you prefer I be mean to you, Kovit? Scream and run around the room flailing my arms?"

Kovit snorted softly. "No."

Fabricio sighed and put down his cup. "Fine. You want to know why I'm being nice to you? I'll be blunt. I don't want you to hurt me anymore. I figure if I treat you like a human, maybe you'll treat me like one."

A bitter smile crossed Kovit's face. "So it's all fake. You're just pretending I'm human to manipulate me."

Fabricio gave Kovit an disgusted look. "You *are* human. I can't pretend something that's already true."

Kovit blinked. "Pardon?"

"I'm just pretending you don't scare the shit out of me, and I'm trying to pretend what happened in Toronto was a bad dream so I can function normally around you." Fabricio picked his maté back up and held it close. "But I'm hardly pretending you're human. That's just a fact."

"I'm a zannie." Kovit's voice was soft. "Not many people consider that human."

Fabricio shrugged. "You said you grew up in captivity in the black market, right? No offense, but I don't think you exactly met the most exemplary side of humanity over there."

"I met plenty of people who weren't part of the black market too." Kovit's eyes went dead. "They didn't consider me human either."

Fabricio's lips quirked. "Ah. Well, if you treat people as less than human, then you shouldn't be surprised when they treat you the same. You dehumanize them as much as they dehumanize you."

"So what? You think if I'm nice, they'll be nice back?" Kovit's smile was deeply amused. "You're living in a fantasy world. I eat pain, and that scares people."

"Sure it does. But lots of people are scary—terrorists, fascists, racists. That doesn't mean they're not human, much as some people might wish." Fabricio's eyes met Kovit's. "You're a sentient, thinking being. You choose who you hurt, and if you hurt someone." Fabricio made a frustrated noise. "You're not a fucking avalanche mowing down everything in its path."

Kovit looked down at his cooling tea. "I think you're vastly underestimating people's fear of what I am. I suspect the average person would much rather die in an avalanche than meet me." Kovit gave him a small smile. "But I appreciate the thought. And the tea. Thank you." Kovit rose. "I think it's time I slept some of that jet lag off now."

Fabricio raised his eyebrows and sipped his tea as he watched Kovit vanish into the bedroom.

Nita stared between Fabricio and Kovit, uneasiness growing. She could see, clear as day, Fabricio's plan. Humanize himself to Kovit, make himself a real person so Kovit wouldn't be able to bring himself to hurt Fabricio again.

But Fabricio didn't understand Kovit's rules, didn't know how carefully Kovit had crafted them to keep himself sane, didn't understand that by twisting and breaking them, Fabricio might inadvertently destroy the glue that had held Kovit together for the last decade. Glue that had started melting when Kovit killed Henry and hadn't had a chance to properly re-form.

And if that glue melted apart, Nita had no idea what would happen to Kovit. But she didn't think it would be good.

TWENTY-TWO

NITA STARED AFTER KOVIT, but didn't rise.

"That was very well done," she admitted, looking at Fabricio. "You've learned how to pull his strings quickly."

Fabricio smiled slightly. "I'm good with people."

"Good at manipulating them, you mean?"

He shrugged. "Isn't that what all human interactions are? We want people to think certain things, behave certain ways. Believe us to be certain types of people. For example, I imagine you could have hid the fact that Kovit went up on the list from him. Well, for a day or two. But you didn't want him to think you were lying or hiding things from him. You wanted him to think you were honest and forthright, so you told him when you found out." He sipped his maté. "Isn't that a form of manipulation too, then? You wanted him to see you a certain way, so you behaved accordingly."

Her eyes narrowed, but her palms sweated at the truth of his words. Were her actions truly so transparent? "Not all human interactions are as calculated as you seem to think."

"No? Perhaps not consciously. But every interaction you

have, every decision you make, all of that is subconsciously determined by who you want people to see you as. Or what you want to hide. Or how you want people to perceive others."

"Maybe in some interactions, but certainly not in all." Nita's voice was steady, even as his words burrowed into her mind like weevils. "Some interactions aren't that complicated."

"Aren't they?" His eyes were open and honest, but his smile was clever. "When I was younger, my father used to order these elaborate Starbucks drinks. Half sugar, shots of syrup, almond milk, low-fat whipped cream, all that stuff. He'd get angry when they got it wrong, and his request was always so complicated they often did. I always ordered something really simple, even though I wanted whipped cream too. But I didn't want the barista to think I was like my father, demanding and inconsiderate." He looked down into his maté, as if it were a window into a past that made him sad. "It was, as you say, an uncomplicated interaction. Just an order at Starbucks. But even in that, there are layers."

Nita was silent. She'd never thought too much about the casual considerations that went into everyday encounters. Now that she was, she found she didn't like the picture Fabricio was painting.

"So you see, Nita, to some extent, all our interactions are manipulations of some sort or another. We're all playing a part, and how we deal with people is a trick to show them what part we want them to think we're playing."

Nita's eyes narrowed at that. "Is that so? Well, I see what part you're playing with Kovit."

"Do you? Because if you really did, I don't think you'd be so angry." Fabricio smiled slightly and set down his maté. "Speaking of, I imagine you want to follow him now. It's about the right time for you to play the good friend. That's your role, isn't it?" He rose and went to the couch Kovit had vacated, pulling one of the blankets draped over the top onto his shoulders. "And it's about time for me to go to bed. I still have some drugs to get out of my system."

"Please." Nita rose. "Those wore off hours ago."

He curled up on the couch. "So you say, but I doubt you've ever experienced being drugged. Not fully. The moment you can think clearly, you can heal it. I, unfortunately, can't." He closed his eyes and rolled away from her. "Good night, Nita. Kovit is waiting."

She hesitated, wanting to say more. But she didn't know what to say or how to counter his arguments. She didn't even know that she disagreed with him, she just felt like she should say something.

But why do you want to say something? Do you just want Fabricio to be wrong because he's Fabricio? asked a small voice in her head.

No, Nita responded, then hesitated. *Maybe.*

She looked at Fabricio's back, his body curled away from her. He'd pulled himself into the fetal position even though it clearly wasn't the most comfortable position on the couch, and she wondered, not for the first time, what his life had been like before she met him. Because the more she spoke to Fabricio, the more she saw the cracks in him, saw that he was just as broken as she and Kovit, maybe even more so. He just knew how to hide it better.

She turned away. She could ponder Fabricio and his warped

manipulative mind later. For now, he was right — it was time to go see Kovit.

Nita walked to the door and tapped softly on it. "Kovit? Can I come in?"

"Sure."

She opened the door, slipped inside, and closed it behind her. This was a private conversation. She didn't need Fabricio eavesdropping and figuring out how to manipulate them even better.

Kovit sprawled on the bed, the tea by his side. His shirt had ridden up, exposing a thin line of skin, and his whole body glowed with health and beauty from the pain he'd just eaten. Draped across the bed, he looked achingly beautiful and not quite real, like a model on the cover of a magazine. Glossy and a little bit alien.

Nita slowly sat beside him. "You know Fabricio's manipulating you. He just doesn't want you to hurt him again."

"I know." He shrugged. "It doesn't stop it from being effective."

Nita raised an eyebrow.

He gave her a self-deprecating smile. "Nita, relax. I know you're worried Fabricio has some diabolical motive for the things he said, but even I can see his plan. He laid it out pretty bluntly."

"Is it working?"

He hesitated, then looked away. "You don't want me to hurt him anymore, right?"

"No."

"Good. Then it doesn't matter if it's working or not."

She snort-laughed. "If you know what he's doing and why, then why are you letting it affect you at all?"

Kovit sighed, closing his eyes. "Because for all his manipulation, he *saw* me. He looked at me, even after I hurt him, and he didn't see a monster. He saw a human to be understood. He might be manipulating me, but he thinks I'm a real person." His voice was small. "You've seen how rare that is."

She had. Henry used him like a tool, Gold saw him as nothing more than a monster. People they'd attacked had referred to him as "it" and assumed Nita could command him, like a trained dog.

Nita snorted. "Are you telling me that his attempt to manipulate you worked because he acknowledged that he's manipulating you?"

Kovit laughed. "Pretty much."

"You do realize that just because Fabricio sees you as a person doesn't mean he won't betray you." Nita's voice was full of barely contained anger.

Kovit's smile was warped and twisted. "Oh, I know."

They were silent a long moment, both looking up at the ceiling, lost in bitter thoughts.

Nita hesitated. "Are you thinking about what Fabricio said? About how people will treat you like a human if you treat them like a human?"

He considered. "A little. But I'm not naive enough to believe it would really happen that easily. Even if I turned into a saint tomorrow, never hurt another person, got everything I needed from emergency rooms and physiotherapy clinics or whatever, it wouldn't really change things. There's still decades of INHUP propaganda about dangerous unnaturals, multitudes of crimes committed by other zannies, and people's assumptions, never mind my own past, if it ever got out."

Nita nodded. As much as she'd have liked to tell him it really was that easy, do good unto others and it shall be done unto you, or whatever the hell the Bible thumpers said, the truth was it wouldn't. The most selfless act Nita had ever done was to free Fabricio — and all it got her was sold on the black market.

The world wasn't fair. And it didn't operate on a karmic cycle, much as people wished.

She flopped down beside him and gently poked the crease between his eyes. "Then what is it that has you thinking so hard?"

He smiled slightly and playfully batted her hand away, like a small kitten.

She raised her eyebrows, and he sighed heavily before admitting, "I just feel like I'm slipping back into old patterns."

"Old patterns?"

He stared up at the ceiling, brow furrowing. "I've escaped from Reyes, from Henry, from the Family, but a part of me feels like I haven't *really* escaped. This is all I did in the Family. Hide away until I was needed, and then I'd terrify the Family's enemies. I'd hurt them, punish people for their transgressions. Nothing's changed." He met her eyes. "Even though I've escaped, all I've done is the exact same things I did when I was in a cage."

Nita bit her lip, because he wasn't wrong. "You don't have to stay with me. You've always been free to leave."

"Nita, I'm not going anywhere." His voice was gentle. "It's not about you. We're partners, and you've been doing better about not asking for things I can't give. I appreciate it."

"Then what can I do?"

"Nothing." He sighed heavily. "We're in a bad situation right now. We have to get through it to survive, and it will be ugly. I know that." He rubbed his temples. "But it doesn't make me feel less trapped. I feel like a hamster on a wheel, running the same route over and over. And even though the wheel is gone, all I've ever done is run, but now I don't know where I'm running to or what I'm running on. I'm just running."

He ran his hands over his forehead and fisted them in his hair. "I want to get off this wheel. I want to try and figure out who I am outside of that life."

"How?"

"I don't know yet." He closed his eyes. "I just want to try something different, force myself outside of everything I've ever lived." He shrugged. "Maybe I'll hate it, but at least it would jolt me off the wheel, so I can figure out who I am for myself."

Nita lay back and considered. "What kind of different?"

He gave her a small self-deprecating grin. "I have no idea. I guess it's something I'll have to figure out."

Nita linked her fingers with his. "Whatever you decide, I'll be there for you."

His smile was soft and genuine, and he shifted slightly to press their foreheads together for a moment and whisper, "Thank you."

Nita wrapped her arms around him in a tight embrace. "Always."

They curled up like that, arms wrapped around each other, as they slowly drifted to sleep.

TWENTY-THREE

NITA WOKE UP in the late afternoon when her alarm went off. Kovit moaned beside her, and she sighed softly, unwilling to move from her position curled against his warm body.

He gave her a sleepy look. "Is it time to get up now?"

"You can rest a little longer. I'm going shower and get ready before we go back to the hotel."

He nodded drowsily and nestled back into the pillow.

She rolled off the bed and stretched, her muscles stiff. She scooped up her phone and checked for messages.

There was one, from her mother.

Nita swallowed, then clicked it open.

You should come home now. Your little monster will be dead soon, it read, followed by a link to Kovit's DUL listing.

Nita deleted the email, her hands shaking. She'd wondered before if her mother was responsible for Kovit's name going up faster, if she'd pulled strings and manipulated connections. The more she thought about it, the more sure she was. But whether it was her mother or not, her mother now knew *exactly* what Kovit looked like.

And she had the whole world on her side, wanting to kill him.

Nita logged out of email and forced herself to move on to more productive lines of thought. There was nothing she could do about her mother right now.

The *Washington Post* reporter Nita had contacted had posted the article, clearly not wanting to miss the scoop on INHUP's misconduct. It included the photos of Kovit and his sister that Nita had sent, but it also included multiple short video clips. Some were from local Toronto news channels, some from Instagram feeds, which had obviously been found by scrolling the promotion hashtag. Kovit and Patchaya were caught on camera chatting happily in the background of dozens of videos.

Nita smiled slightly, pleased it had worked out so well.

She scrolled through the comments, some of them wondering if the clips were fake, others wondering if INHUP was trying to trap the zannie, others wondering if he even *was* a zannie.

Other articles had sprung up, all asking how an INHUP agent could be going on what looked like a date with a zannie. Some speculated that this was a romance gone wrong, and an INHUP agent had abused her power to put her ex-boyfriend on the list.

Nita hadn't planned for this to look like a lover's quarrel, and she imagined some intrepid reporter would figure out the truth soon enough, but for now, she liked the romance angle.

Romance gone wrong always got a lot of attention in the tab-loids.

For once, the stereotypes against zannies worked in Kovit's favor. The video clips, while short, showed him laughing and smiling and acting perfectly adorable. It was a bit of a shock — usually in public Kovit was mildly terrifying, people steering clear of him without fully understanding why. But in the video he seemed so happy and joyful, and if he had his danger aura, it didn't come through.

No one believed someone who looked so genuine could be a monster.

Nita skimmed through comments and tweets, a little creeped out by how many people commented on Kovit's looks and attractiveness, like that was some kind of metric for inno-cence.

But a lot of people were angry. Petitions had been made, investigations had been called for. Someone had dug up the fact that Kovit had been added to the list before the manda-tory weeklong verification period was completed, and this had incensed the public even more. People were demanding Kovit be taken off the list until a thorough inquiry had been done.

Nita smiled as she read through the articles. It was going well, better than she'd expected. Soon people would start to ask how many other innocent people had been put on the list. Investigations would be called, people would demand account-ability. The list would grind to a halt during the investigation, everything on pause as the world watched.

Who knew how long an investigation might take. Months? Years? Indefinitely?

Her glee was tempered by wariness. She couldn't get cocky. INHUP wouldn't go down that easily. That was fine, though. She'd be ready for whatever they threw at her next.

Beside her, Kovit made a strangled sound. His eyes were glued to his phone screen, and Nita could almost see the life draining out of him.

"What is it?" she asked.

He hesitated, then looked away, his voice a whisper. "My internet friends. They saw the news. They recognized me. They're asking if it's true."

"Ah." Nita's voice was heavy with understanding. The only real friends he'd had, shielded from him by a virtual screen. People who'd supported him without knowing at all who he was. The group Gold had infiltrated to spy on Kovit for Henry.

"What do I say?" Kovit looked down at his hands. "I never wanted them to know."

"You could lie. Say it was a look-alike."

He shook his head. "And then what? The lie wouldn't hold forever."

"Then tell the truth. Your version of the truth. Before Gold gets in there and poisons them all with hers."

After a long moment, he whispered, "I'm scared."

Nita's heart broke a little at the sound, at the fragile cracks in his voice.

"They'll probably hate me forever. This will be . . . It will be the end." He looked at her, lashes casting dark shadows on his cheeks. "And I don't want it to end."

Nita didn't know what to say to that, because there wasn't much she could say. She could tell him that he had other support now, that he wasn't alone anymore, a scared child trapped in a cage with only the friends on the other side of the screen to keep him sane. But that wouldn't change how much these people meant to him or lessen the blow of their loss.

So instead, she just squeezed his hand gently, letting him know she was there.

He looked back down at his phone and finally started typing, his fingers slow and heavy as they slid across the screen

She turned to her own phone. She hadn't actually read through Kovit's listing, and she wondered what it said. What horrors his friends were imagining. She found her fingers flicking across her screen before she could stop herself.

It didn't say much. Just that he was there, he'd committed multiple crimes against humanity.

And that he was currently in Buenos Aires.

Nita swore. Viciously.

Kovit raised his head from the screen, hair flopping across his face. "What is it?"

She sighed and leaned back. "Nothing. Just an annoying complication."

He groaned softly. "How bad?"

"The listing puts you in Buenos Aires."

He frowned. "But . . . how?"

Nita's lips pressed into a thin line. "I don't know. I only told one person where we were going." She met his eyes. "Adair."

Kovit shook his head. "He wouldn't sell our location to INHUP. He hates the list."

195

"I know." She pulled out her phone and put it to her ear, voice grim. "But I have to ask. Especially since he's still furious at me for melting his skin off."

Kovit stared at her with a mixture of horror and fascination. "You melted his skin off?"

She nodded.

"Did it hurt?"

Of course that was what he was concerned with. She shrugged. "I imagine so."

Kovit looked like he wanted to ask more, but the phone clicked and the ringing stopped.

"Hello?"

Adair's voice was tinny over the phone, losing much of its smoothness. It was strange to hear him without seeing his teeth, knowing that beneath his mask, a monster lurked. Just hearing him over the phone, she could pretend he was as human as anyone else.

"So I saw that somehow Kovit's location got on the dangerous unnaturals listing," Nita began with no preamble.

"Nita?"

"Who else?"

"Indeed." Adair sighed. "I didn't expect to be hearing from you so soon."

"Really? You didn't think I'd call when I saw the listing?" Nita leaned against the wall and tried to keep her voice measured, even though she was angry. Angry that everything kept going wrong, angry that she hadn't prepared for this, angry that Kovit was in danger and she wasn't powerful enough to do anything about it. "You're the only other one who knew I was going to Argentina. You're the only one who could have given my location to the black market."

There was a short pause, and Nita could hear the click of his computer keys. "Oh, yes, I saw that post this morning. But I'm not the one who told them you two were in Argentina."

"And why should I believe you?"

Adair snorted. "Believe me or not, I don't care. But I'm not so wasteful as to post valuable information for free. If I'd leaked it, you better bet I'd be getting paid."

Of course. Whoever had done this had just posted the information for free for all the world to see. There was no gain here, unless it was some personal vendetta. And even if Adair was pursuing vengeance, he would still want to get paid.

"I see that silenced you." Adair's voice crackled over the phone. "Look, Nita. I don't know who else you've told or not, but I wouldn't have compromised your suicide plan, because on the small chance you actually succeed, I very much want that information, and I'm more than willing to trade for it. I'm not stupid enough to toss away this chance out of petty vengeance."

Nita bowed her head. She'd figured as much, but she'd needed to hear him say it. "Then who did it?"

"I don't know." There was a loud bang and a muffled voice. "Ah, I have to go. Lovely hearing your baseless accusations as always."

He hung up before Nita could respond. Nita stared down at the phone for a long moment. If it wasn't Adair, who could it be?

Kovit cleared his throat beside her, his expression pained. "It wasn't him, was it?"

She shook her head. "No."

He rubbed his temples. "I was thinking about it, and there is one other person who could conceivably have figured out our plans."

"Who?"

He winced. "Gold."

Nita stared at him. He was right. Gold had stayed with them for a day, she'd had plenty of opportunity to sneak around and eavesdrop. Even if she hadn't, she'd known they were keeping Fabricio prisoner, and she could put two and two together.

As soon as Kovit said her name, the rightness of the answer settled on Nita. Kovit had done a good deed, talked Nita into doing a good deed, and she was being punished for it. That was how the world worked. Good deeds got you nothing but pain.

Kovit closed his eyes. "I'm sorry."

Nita flopped on the bed. Her voice was resigned. "I told you."

"I know," he whispered.

"I warned you that she'd turn on you."

"I know." Kovit ran his hand through his hair and fisted it there. "I just thought if I let her go, maybe she'd see I wasn't all evil. She'd remember that once upon a time, we'd been friends. Before she knew who I was. I wanted to remind her that I'm not just a monster. I thought she'd . . ."

"Be your friend again?"

He shrugged, looking away. "I guess."

Part of Nita wanted to yell at him, to berate him for his

naivety and stupidity. For risking everything so that he might look better in a childhood friend's eyes. But the other part of her just felt sorry for Kovit, for his shitty life and his shitty friends and his sad, small attempts to be good going terribly wrong.

Sometimes, she felt like both of them were damned no matter what they did, good or bad. That any choice they made led to ruin.

But she couldn't let herself think that way. There's was always a way to victory. Always a path to survival. Maybe it was ugly and painted in blood and grief, but it was there. She believed it. She had to believe it.

She put her hand over his gently. "It's okay, Kovit."

He looked at her, his eyes dark. "I'm so sorry, Nita. I never meant for this to happen."

"I know," she whispered, leaning her head against his shoulder. "I know. But it's okay. It's an extra complication, but we've faced worse. And even if your location is out, so what? People are questioning the entire validity of the list right now. It won't be long until a full-scale investigation is launched."

He perked up. "Really?"

"Really." She handed him her phone with all the articles. "Take a look."

He did, scrolling through the information, body loosening the more he read. Nita took the time to wash and get dressed as she mentally prepared for the next stage of her plan. All these things were distractions, Kovit, the list, all of it. She had come to Buenos Aires for two reasons: Alberto Tácunan and Zebra-stripes.

And today she was going to destroy them both.

She dressed and went out to the main room. Fabricio was still sleeping, but he woke when she entered the room and watched her through slitted eyes.

"Off somewhere?"

"Taking care of something. Kovit and I will be gone most of the night." She pulled out the duct tape and smiled at Fabricio. "You know what that means."

Fabricio gave a long-suffering sigh. "Can I go to the bathroom first?"

She let him, and afterward, duct-taped him back to the couch.

Kovit came out a few minutes later, looking much calmer and more put together. He was wearing the sunglasses, and he'd used water to slick his hair into a smooth part that made him look older. It wasn't the best disguise Nita had ever seen, but it hit the main points. Kovit was shorter and darker, so he might be able to pass as Latin American with his eyes covered. Definitely not Argentinian, though—he moved through the world in a different way. Nita did too. It was like the city had a rhythm, and she and Kovit were w   ng to a different song, always a step off beat.

But the hairstyle aged him, as did his serious expression, making him easily able to pass for late twenties instead of the twenty and a few months he actually was. She was hopeful that even if he couldn't blend in, at least it wouldn't be obvious who he really was.

"Are we ready?" he asked.

Nita sighed, tying her hair back in a more mature style so

that she could look older than her nearly eighteen years. She didn't want to ruin Kovit's disguise by looking too young. Though, older men with younger women wasn't that uncommon, just gross.

"As we'll ever be," she said, adding a few age lines to her face for good measure. There. Now they looked like a pair of late-twentysomething tourists.

It was time to get some answers.

TWENTY-FOUR

I T WAS ALMOST eleven in the evening when Zebra-stripes finally came.

Nita nearly missed him, she'd been sitting so long on the couch in the hotel lobby staring vacantly at the entrance. She knew he'd arrive today based on his message when she sold him her mother's location, sometime after sunset, but she hadn't known what time, which meant a lot of waiting.

He entered quietly, unassuming in brown slacks and a thin beige coat. He'd tried to cover the distinctive white stripes in his brown hair with an old-fashioned-looking hat, the kind she expected on people who dramatically swept it off and bowed when introduced, kissing a lady's hand in greeting. Despite the fact that all his clothes looked a little out of date, they all looked newly made and clean, and the effect was less that he'd walked out of a period drama of 1930s Chicago and more that he was young with a bit of a retro, quirky style.

His movements were slowed down, so that they looked almost human, not the too-fast, impossible actions she remembered. It still made her shudder when she recalled how he'd moved, like she'd blinked and missed something.

But he wasn't trying to scare her now. He was trying to pass as human, and it seemed to be working.

He walked to the front desk, and Nita nudged Kovit. He nodded, and the two of them separated, shifting into position. They knew where Zebra-stripes was going.

Nita went over to the elevator banks. All of them were at the lobby, and she pressed the top floor in each one except one, sending them shooting up and away. Then Nita got in the final one, just as Zebra-stripes turned the corner.

She smiled at him, her face a mass of wrinkles from her disguise, her hair tucked up under a wig she'd bought on the way there. She'd swapped disguises, afraid that Zebra-stripes might recognize her from the market if she looked young. But now, to all intents and purposes, she looked like a seventy-year-old woman.

"Going up?" she asked, holding the door open.

"Yes." His voice was low, a little on the deep side, a little too deep for his face, which seemed young, mid-twenties. It was a lie, of course. Vampires didn't age the same as humans. Their faces froze at some point in their lives and then after that, you could only tell their age by their hair.

The more white in their hair, the older they were—though it wasn't really white, it was an ethereal, almost translucent, sparkling color that resembled white. They could live as long as seven hundred years, but they grew older and frailer as they aged. When they were young, they were preternaturally strong and practically unstoppable. The old ones were weak as kittens.

His hair was covered, but Nita remembered how much white Zebra-stripes had. She'd placed him between one and three hundred years. A dangerous age to be. Wise from their years and still strong with youth.

That wasn't going to stop Nita from taking him down. Nita was strong too. And she had a lot more riding on this.

The elevator doors clicked closed, and he pressed the sixth floor, as she'd known he would. Soft music began to play, and Nita leaned forward and pressed the button for the eighth floor, dropping her bag as she did so.

"Oh, goodness," she croaked, making her voice raspy and old to go with her wrinkly skin. "Dear, could you get that for me? My knees aren't what they used to be."

Zebra-stripes didn't say anything, just knelt to pick up the bag.

And Nita used the opportunity to drive a knife into his spine.

She'd been very careful with her planning—she didn't want to kill Zebra-stripes, not yet, but she couldn't take on a vampire. She was realistic.

But she'd dissected many a vampire. She knew their biology well.

The knife slid in just below the base of his skull between the C1 and C2 vertebrae, immediately paralyzing him. Blood slipped out, coating the knife handle and painting Nita's fingers red.

The only sign of his surprise was his widening eyes as his

body collapsed beneath him in a single moment. Paralysis was a beautiful thing—you could survive it, and it made you completely vulnerable. Vampires had superb healing, though, so Nita didn't take the knife out as he collapsed. She left it in to prevent his body from naturally healing the damage.

He grunted when he hit the ground, and Nita drove the knife in deeper.

He glared up at her, his eyes so pale they seemed almost white. "Who are you?"

Nita smiled at him, reached down, and shoved a gag in his mouth. "We'll talk soon."

The elevator dinged on the sixth floor, and Kovit was waiting with the plastic tarp. They rolled Zebra-stripes onto the tarp quickly, seconds ticking by, eyes wide, hoping no one turned onto the corner and saw them.

Blood dripped off the plastic tarp from the wound, not a lot, but some. Kovit had some cleaning supplies, and he darted into the elevator while Nita dragged the body across the hall to the room she'd rented under one of her mother's aliases.

Kovit held the elevator doors open and looked at the stains with concern. "Really, Nita?"

"I did my best."

He gave her a look. "You'll be okay while I deal with this?"

She nodded, edging the door open and tugging the body into the room.

Inside, the room looked like a serial killer's playhouse. She and Kovit had draped everything in plastic and taped it there so that all the evidence could be bundled away and destroyed afterward. She dragged Zebra-stripes across the room and hauled him onto the bed with her enhanced strength. He grunted but couldn't say anything through the gag.

She used industrial-strength chains to bind him to the bed by his hands and feet, even though he was paralyzed. Then, as an extra precaution, she shoved a needle in his jugular. The needle was connected to a long plastic tube that led into a massive cooler.

Vampires could self-heal, but it took a lot of energy. Eventually, his body might find a way to heal around the knife in his back. She didn't want that. So she drained his blood out, knowing his body would divert energy to replenishing his blood to keep him alive and delaying his healing time and reducing his physical abilities if he did escape.

He glared at her, and she let out a breath. It was done. She had caught him.

The monster who had murdered her father. Who had somehow managed to con the DUL and escape justice for it.

It was time for answers.

She stared down at the pale vampire, his deceptively youthful face twisted in anger. But she could see the fear that lurked underneath the anger, because Nita had made a vampire's worst nightmare out of this room.

Vampire blood was highly prized—a sip a day kept death away, or so the saying went. It wasn't quite true. You couldn't become immortal from drinking their blood. But you could delay aging. A small amount every day for years built up in your system, and you'd age slower and slower over time. There was anecdotal evidence of people living to two hundred years with vampire blood.

Nita didn't put much stock in nonscientifically tested rumors, but most people did, and vampire blood was a booming industry. A vampire at full health could heal its body for up to a week when blood was being constantly drained from it before it died. If you occasionally fed it? Well, it could be in your blood-draining factory forever. Plenty of blood for you to live an extra century, and plenty of blood to sell online.

Her mother hadn't drained any vampires Nita knew of. Too much of a time commitment, too much of a hassle to feed. But Nita had dissected and packaged more than a few for sale, since eating their flesh was said to have a milder but similar effect. Probably from the residual blood in it.

Nita crossed the room and checked on her container. Filling up nicely. Plenty of extra cash when this was over. If she was going to capture a vampire anyway, and needed to keep it weak, she might as well earn a bit of money off it as well. She certainly wasn't going to just throw the blood out. What a waste that would be.

Zebra-stripes grunted on the bed, trying to speak through his gag, and Nita went over to him and looked down at him as she shed her disguise. Off came the gray wig, and she tightened her skin back up until she looked like herself again.

Zebra-stripes' eyes widened in recognition, and Nita smiled down at him. "We meet again."

His eyes narrowed.

Nita sat down on a chair beside the bed. "Don't worry, I'll take the gag off soon. I just wanted to make it clear how things were going to go here first."

He glared.

"See, I really just wanted to murder you at first. I'm not really the forgive-and-forget type. But then I realized that you probably have a lot of answers that I need, and I have a lot of questions. So here's the deal: answer my questions, and I'll let you go."

He snorted and rolled his eyes.

"You don't believe me, that's fair," Nita agreed. "But what have you really got to lose? If you don't answer them, I'll just kill you. If you do answer them, I might be telling the truth and will let you go." She paused. "Obviously I won't let you go while I'm in the room. I'll be long gone. But I'll call whatever number you want to have someone come to find you."

He tried to speak through the gag, and Nita leaned over and plucked it from his mouth, arms fast, careful not to give him an opportunity to bite her.

He licked his dry lips, his chin brushing against the plastic tubes sucking his blood out. "Fine. I'll answer your questions."

"Excellent."

"But first, answer one of mine."

Nita shrugged. "All right."

"What did I do that you want vengeance for?"

Nita blinked. "Pardon?"

"You said you wanted vengeance, that you're not a forgive-and-forget kind of person." He blinked slowly. "But I don't know what I've done. I'd like to know."

She stared at him. "You . . . what?"

"Was it because I came to visit you in the market?" He sounded curious. "Are you getting vengeance on everyone who came to see you?"

"What? No." Though eventually maybe she would. She hadn't really thought about that. She wondered how many of the people who'd visited while she was in the market were hiring people to hunt her down now. A lot, probably. "You killed someone important to me."

"Oh." He considered. "Who were they? I've killed a lot of people over the years."

"You killed him two weeks ago. Just before you went to the market. In Chicago."

His cold eyes blinked at her. "I see. And who told you I killed him?" He sighed, veins standing out blue on his pale, bloodless face. "No, wait, let me guess. INHUP?"

Nita blinked. "Yes."

His smile was bitter. "How convenient that all their enemies die by my hand. You know, if I'd committed all the crimes INHUP claims I did, I'd never have time to sleep."

"Vampires don't sleep."

"That's beside the point."

Nita crossed her arms. "So you want me to believe you're innocent?"

He shrugged. "You can believe whatever you want."

Nita considered the possibility. She did only have INHUP's word for it. But if Zebra-stripes believed being innocent would keep him alive, he'd obviously lie.

She put the thought aside now and moved on. Whether he was innocent or not, it didn't change what happened next. He had answers to her mother's past, her father's death, and, most importantly, he had information on INHUP that must have kept him off the list.

Nita intended to find out what it was.

"My turn for questions." Nita crossed her arms. "Firstly your name."

"Andrej."

"Andrej what?"

He hesitated. "Smirnov."

Nita raised her eyebrows. "Like the liquor?"

He smiled, but it seemed fake. "Exactly."

He was lying. That definitely wasn't his real name.

She brushed it aside. It wasn't important.

"Why are you hunting Monica?" she asked.

"What's she to you?" he asked, considering. "You have the same ability, so my guess is you're her daughter. Though I never saw Monica as the motherly type. More as the eat-her-own-young type."

If Nita had needed proof that the two of them knew each other, that would have sealed the deal. That was one of the most accurate descriptions of her mother she'd ever heard.

"How long have you known my mother?" Nita asked.

"Oh, a long, long time." Andrej made a face. "She ages better than I do."

"You don't age."

"My point exactly."

Nita crossed her arms, something unhappy squiggling in her chest at the implications. "So why do you want her dead?"

Andrej stilled, so completely, perfectly, inhumanly still, it made the hairs crawl on Nita's skin. Then he quietly hissed, "She murdered someone very important to me."

That didn't surprise Nita. At all. "Who?"

"My . . ." He considered. "We were never married, but it feels like a disservice to call her my girlfriend. We were together almost forty years."

Nita raised her eyebrow. "Also a vampire?"

Given how many vampires had ended up on Nita's dissection table over the years, it really was a miracle none of their friends had come for vengeance before now.

"No. Human."

Nita blinked. "Why would my mother bother killing a human?"

Andrej hesitated, and then said carefully, "She was a very important human."

Nita raised her eyebrows, waiting. She could feel something here, something that tugged on her memory. She'd wondered if Andrej had been the monster in the story Nita's mother told, but she hadn't been sure. But in that story, the monster was the killer. Her grief had seemed genuine, but who could tell with Nita's mother?

Andrej seemed just as angry and grief-stricken. Which could also be an act. But they couldn't both have killed the same person. Though she supposed they could both blame each other for her death?

"How did she die?" Nita asked.

Andrej looked away. "Trickery and lies."

Nita rolled her eyes. "That is the vaguest answer I've ever heard."

Andrej glared at her.

Nita shrugged. "I mean, if you don't answer, I'll just kill you. Cooperation buys you time."

His jaw tightened like he was imagining ripping her throat out, and she suppressed a shiver. She was in control here. She was the one with the power. She wouldn't be afraid.

Andrej tilted his head up so the light bounced off his clear eyes, and he said, "It's a long story."

"I have time."

He sighed softly, his face still eerily still. "Fine. I first met my girlfriend in the 1960s. This was before INHUP, before anything even like that existed. She was a monster hunter for hire, and she was damn good at it."

Nita nodded. This was fitting perfectly with her mother's story. Nita would have to question which version was right when they started to diverge, but the things they had in common, she thought it was safe to take as truth.

"What was her name?" Nita asked.

"Nadya." He sighed softly. "But I suppose you'd know her as Nadezhda Novikova. The founder of INHUP."

TWENTY-FIVE

INHUP'S FOUNDER.

Nita tried to wrap her head around it. Not just that INHUP's founder had been having a thing with a vampire for forty years and no one knew—no, actually, it wasn't possible no one knew. How could INHUP not *know*?—but also the idea that Nita's mother could have possibly been friends with INHUP's founder. Nita's mother *hated* INHUP. She was constantly deriding them, always wary of them. She despised them. Nita could never imagine her working with them.

But a dark, frightened part of her whispered that the most violent hate is born from the tightest love. And betrayal.

She cleared her throat. "Wait. Wait a minute. Nadezhda Novikova isn't dead. She's still head of INHUP."

"Technically, she is." Andrej agreed. "But she's been a figurehead for the past, oh, twenty years or so, hasn't she?"

"Yes . . ." Nita agreed slowly, dragging out the *s*. "But that's just because she's getting old. She's got to be in her . . . eighties? By now."

"But have you seen her at all, in any event, in the past

twenty years? Surely an eighty-year-old could cut a ribbon at a ceremony, or give an interview."

"I haven't looked into it," Nita admitted. Unsurprisingly, the head of INHUP hadn't been someone she was interested in. She'd never really researched her.

Nita tried to think of any pictures of Nadezhda Novikova she'd seen, but all of them were too old. She seemed young, in her thirties, in most of the pictures Nita could recall. But most articles used pictures of people in their prime, so that was no surprise.

"If Nadezhda Novikova was dead, the world would have mourned. We'd all know. There'd have been a huge public funeral," she pointed out.

Andrej sighed. "Well, she's not . . . *dead* dead. She's brain-dead. Her body has been in a coma for the last two decades, and for legal reasons, no one can unhook her. So everyone is just keeping it all under wraps for now, and hoping she passes away naturally soon."

"Surely people would know, though."

"You don't think INHUP can hide one person in a coma? Have you seen how extensive some of their research and medical facilities are?"

This Nita did know. She'd researched INHUP's research facilities extensively, because she'd researched everywhere with good unnatural science programs. There were a lot of internships at INHUP for an unnatural researcher. Not that Nita would ever work there.

Well, maybe. If the right research project came along.

"I have. It's possible," Nita admitted. "But why would they cover it up in the first place?"

"Because they don't want people to ask questions." His voice was bitter.

"Like how she ended up in a coma?"

"That they can lie about. Even tell the truth about, or a version of it. No, the issue becomes when people want to visit her body. Then things get tricky."

"How so?"

"Nadya looked very young for being in her sixties. I imagine by now, age has caught up a bit, but she'll probably still look in her mid-forties when she hits a century."

Nita thought for a moment, then realized. "You'd been feeding her your blood. To slow down her aging."

"Every day for forty-odd years. That empty body will easily live to two hundred."

Nita's mind whirled through the implications. "It would be obvious she'd been drinking vampire blood. Very regularly. There's nothing else that has that effect on humans."

He nodded. "And how would that look to the rest of the world? The head of INHUP, addicted to vampire blood."

"Was she addicted? I didn't think it was addictive."

"It's not." His head jerked slightly, as though he'd gone to make a hand motion before realizing he was paralyzed. "But people are addicted to power and looking young, which makes it more addictive than cocaine to certain personality types. And the media *would* spin it that way."

They would. Nita could see the headlines now. INHUP

FOUNDER ADDICTED TO MONSTER BLOOD. WHAT
HAS SHE BEEN SACRIFICING TO GET HER FIX?

"So they've kept it under wraps." Nita's eyes narrowed. She
still wasn't quite sure she believed him. "But how did she end
up in a coma in the first place, then?"

Andrej was quiet a long moment. "Your mother is
how."

Nita raised her eyebrows, thinking of her mother using the
same hateful, disgusted voice when talking about how Andrej
had killed her friend. "Do tell."

"When I first met Nadya, she'd been hired to kill me, but
somehow things worked out differently."

"I'll say."

"She was riding off her fame from killing Bessanov," he
continued, undeterred. "She was getting calls from all over the
world asking for her help. But she couldn't be everywhere, so
she was giving the jobs to other hunters she knew, including
your mother, and taking the trickiest, most dangerous ones for
herself. She loved her risks."

"And you were a tricky, dangerous job?"

His eyes fixed on hers, eerie and clear. "Yes."

Nita's body stiffened in terror, and in that moment, she
absolutely believed he was exactly as dangerous as he sounded.

"But, as I said. Things went differently. When she sug-
gested forming INHUP to gather and train people, to cen-
tralize everything, I agreed to help. When we realized some of
the corruption among the hunters, she decided to start making rules—which eventually became laws—about hunting
unnaturals. There's a big difference between someone who's

trying to get rid of a serial-killing unicorn and someone who wants to try eating a ningyo because they think they'll gain immortality."

His eyes assessed Nita, cold and cruel. "But the more rules she put in, the more fame her organization got, the angrier certain elements became. Elements like your mother. They joined to kill things, and they didn't like being told there were things they couldn't kill."

Nita leaned forward, fascinated despite herself. "And?"

"And things came to a head eventually. Twenty years ago. Your mother decided I had too much influence over Nadya. She couldn't get rid of Nadya, she was the face of INHUP. But she could get rid of me."

He closed his eyes. "I want to say I escaped, or that I won the fight, but the truth was I lost, and I'm only alive because your mother was interrupted before she could behead me. The people who interrupted her were under the impression I was human, and I was buried."

He licked his lips. "It took me a while to get out. I was badly hurt, and weak, and climbing out of a coffin buried six feet underground is hard even when you aren't starving and nearly dead. By the time I got out . . ."

"What happened?"

"Your mother—she went by Monica then, I don't know if it was her real name. I don't think so." He swallowed. "Monica had confronted Nadya. I guess she thought if I was gone, she'd be able to regain her influence over Nadya. But Nadya knew what she'd done and was furious. They fought, and your mother was banished from INHUP." His smile was bitter.

"Officially banished, anyway. She had too much sympathy among the ranks for it to work, really."

His voice went soft. "So when she snuck back into the building later, no one stopped her. And she found Nadya and murdered her."

The grief on his face was so familiar, so much like her own heart-wrenching pain from her father's death that it stole her breath. She could see the pain in his eyes, and the scars in her own chest throbbed in response. She understood this pain, and she knew, without ever asking, that he'd truly loved Nadya.

Her mother had claimed Andrej killed Nadya. Andrej claimed her mother did it. Both of them looked like they'd genuinely cared about this woman. So what was the truth?

"Why?" she asked. "Why kill Nadya?"

"I'm not in her head. I don't know." He met her eyes. "But if I had to guess, it was because she's a fucked-up control freak who'd rather murder her best friend than let said friend make her own life choices."

A chill went all the way down Nita's spine, and she took a step back, heartbeat loud in her ears.

She suddenly saw just how stark the parallels between her own life and Nadya's were. Her mother had killed Nadya's boyfriend to regain control of her friend. It hadn't worked, and she'd committed the ultimate act of control—taking Nadya's life.

And now, decades later, her mother was doing it again. She was coming after Kovit. And when Kovit was dead, and Nita still refused to return to her mother, would her mother kill Nita too?

That, more than anything, made Nita believe Andrej's side of the story. Because he couldn't possibly know about what was happening with her mother and Kovit, and the parallels were too strong to be a coincidence.

Andrej continued, oblivious to Nita's slowly mounting horror. "Afterward, your mother had her pet lawyer propose a bill."

"Her pet lawyer?" Nita asked, clinging to the distraction, something else to focus her mind on while her subconscious worked through the truths she was faced with.

The "pet lawyer" had to be her father, a legal consultant and her mother's partner in the black market industry. A person Andrej had only minutes before denied knowing the existence of, never mind the murder of.

Liar.

"Yes. He made the first proposal for the Dangerous Unnaturals List. It claimed if even *I* could kill Nadya after we were together for forty years, no vampire could live without murder. The council was full of old hunters already angry at Nadya for curtailing their murder sprees, and they passed the bill. The DUL was born with vampires at the very top." His voice was bitter. "Followed closely by every other creature your mother used to enjoy killing and thought she could make money selling."

Nita stared at him, mouth open. This couldn't be true. Her mother couldn't be responsible for the Dangerous Unnaturals List. It simply wasn't possible.

Except it was definitely something her mother would do.

Nita kept her tone mild. "It sounds like you had quite a grudge against all the people involved."

"Oh, I do. I've spent the last twenty years trying to kill them all. Those wretched INHUP hunters. Her wretched pet lawyer. And especially your mother."

And there it was. Everything made clear and in the open.

In all probability, her father's killer was in front of her. The signs pointed to it, even if he hadn't confessed it outright. She should feel vicious, want to carve his heart out. She should press him on his slip-up, bully a confession out of him.

But all her mind could do was keep going back to her mother, and that terrible story about Nadya and how her mother had destroyed so many lives in order to keep control of her friend.

"Is my mother still part of INHUP?" Nita asked.

"Yes. She's one of the few original board members still alive." His lips curled. "But so many of the board members are younger now. They grew up with INHUP, they aren't hunters by nature. They're changing the organization, and she doesn't like it. She's losing control, and there's nothing that enrages her more."

Nita's brain clunked sluggishly along. Here, here was the source of INHUP's corruption, the broken wheel that had started everything. Here were her answers.

"There's warrants out for my mother's arrest," she pointed out, trying desperately to poke holes in his words, to prove them lies.

"Indeed. Warrants for a thirty-year-old woman named Helen. Or a forty-five-year-old woman named Valerie." His hair caught the light and gleamed like diamonds. "But the board doesn't know what she is. No one knows that thirty-year-old Helen and eighty-seven-year-old Monica are the same woman."

Nita wanted to protest, to ask how they couldn't know, but she didn't. Because it would be easy. If her mother really was that old, really could heal age . . . Well, Nita had seen her stack of fake passports. She knew how many identities her mother had. Why couldn't one of them be INHUP's board member?

She swallowed suddenly, a terrible thought occurring to her.

"How much would my mother have access to in INHUP?" Nita's breathing became fast and hard. "Could she have expedited a name being put on the Dangerous Unnaturals List?"

"Of course."

A sick feeling welled up in her chest, as more and more pieces clicked together.

"Could she have gotten someone to install bug software on a refugee's phone?" Nita asked, the words heavy on her tongue.

"I don't see why not."

Nita's hands were shaking, and she couldn't seem to stop them. Had Nita's mother been the one to sell her location on the black market when she was in Toronto?

Nita tried to think back to when her information had gone up. She'd rejected her mother. She'd left the restaurant. And then, right after, her phone's GPS location had been posted online.

Almost like a response to Nita running away.

She'd thought it had to do with leaving INHUP—that was the safe time for the corrupt INHUP agent who'd bugged her phone to sell her information. But she'd left her mother at the same time. And her mother had tried to use the danger of Nita's location being revealed to force Nita to come back. To weasel her way in, to make Nita flee to her for protection. To put Nita back in her control.

And her mother had guessed Kovit's existence so easily — if she'd bugged Nita's phone, she'd know Nita was meeting someone.

The thought made ugly, sludgy emotions rise up in her chest. She remembered how proud her mother had said she was when Nita fended off the black market. Was all that a lie too? A trick to get Nita to come home again?

Nita tried to talk herself out of it — she'd suspected her mother of terrible things before, and she'd been wrong. Her mother hadn't sold her on the black market, Fabricio had. But the idea had wormed its way into her mind, and no matter how she tried to talk herself away from the thought, it only burrowed deeper.

And the story about Nadya was just too close to what Nita was living.

People never really change. They repeat the same patterns over and over in their lives. And this was not a pattern Nita could risk ignoring.

Nita took a shaky breath as things became clear. She'd been fighting the black market. She'd been fighting INHUP. But the truth was, they were actually the same enemy. She'd only been fighting one person this whole time.

Her mother.

Fury burned in Nita's stomach, anger searing her soul as everything that had happened started piling up, her mother's list of crimes growing longer and longer. All of this to force Nita back, to return to her mother's control.

Fuck her. Nita was going to live her own goddam life.

Nita raised her eyes as she came to a decision, her gaze hard and cool as she looked at Zebra-stripes, supposed victim of her mother and weaver of tragic love stories. He might not be evil. He might even be a better person than her or Kovit. She might even be able to use him more if she kept him alive, his quest for justice might be useful to her plans.

He might even be innocent. She didn't think so—she was reasonably sure that, in this at least, INHUP hadn't lied to her. Zebra-stripes was probably her father's killer.

And if he wasn't, so what?

If Nita released him, he'd just kill her. Keeping him alive and a prisoner was a liability, and she didn't think she'd get any more useful information out of him.

More and more, Nita was realizing she didn't give a fuck about what was right or justified. She cared about herself and the people important to her. And him being alive put her and them in danger.

"Thank you for the information." Nita's voice was calm, perfectly calm, despite the emotions that ran rampant through her soul. "That's all I needed."

He looked at her, eyes tired. "You're not going to let me go, are you?"

"No. Like I said, I don't forgive." Nita picked up a scalpel from her pocket. "And I don't forget."

She brought the blade down.

TWENTY-SIX

KOVIT STOPPED BY BRIEFLY, and she sent him away to find them dinner while she dealt with the body. She needed time, time to think, to contemplate her next steps. To internalize what she'd learned.

She also needed time to be alone, just her and her scalpel and the body, to appreciate the peace of dissection, the calm and the clear-headedness she could only truly achieve when she was elbow-deep in a chest cavity.

Before she dissected, she knew she needed to verify some of the things Andrej had said.

She turned to Google. The Wikipedia page for Nadezhda Novikova informed Nita that she was still alive, but hadn't been seen in public for the past twenty years, which fit with the story.

The internet at large was full of conspiracy theories — she saw a number referencing how young she looked twenty years ago at age sixty, and how many people thought she was some sort of unnatural that had gone into hiding. There were also some that claimed she'd been murdered and INHUP covered it up, which Nita didn't like. The closer people's stories were to internet conspiracy theories, the less she trusted them.

She switched tactics, realizing she might actually know what Adair's photo was from now. She searched for INHUP founders' images and scrolled through blurry photos from sixty years ago, trying to find — there.

Nita pulled up the photo, the same one Adair had shown her. Except this time the other faces weren't blurred out.

Andrej stood in the middle, grinning, an arm casually wrapped over Nadezhda Novikova's shoulders. There were half a dozen people Nita didn't recognize. And one she did.

At the top corner of the photo, Nita's mother toasted the photographer with a glass of champagne. Her smile was wide and bright and perfectly happy. It transformed her face, made her look less like her mother and more like . . . more like Nita.

Nita shuddered. That was a terrible thought.

But here it was. Photographic evidence that both of them had at one time been part of INHUP. That her vicious, murderous mother might actually be at the head of the organization Nita was trying to destroy.

Nita had always known her mother had contacts in INHUP. She'd assumed they were bribed or threatened or whatever. But she'd never expected this.

She put her phone away, put her dissection gloves on, and did what she did when her mind couldn't process things, when she was stressed and needed to work through her pain.

She dissected.

She'd cut Andrej's head off to ensure his death — no easy

feat with nothing but a scalpel and brute strength. It had also made quite the messy splatter, she was glad she'd put the plastic down as a precautionary measure.

It was always best to be *extra* sure with vampires. So she made a Y incision, peeled back the skin, and cracked open the rib cage so she could pull out his heart. It was shriveled and black, like a giant raisin, and it smelled like it had been dead for a hundred years.

Death confirmed, she began carefully removing the organs, one at a time, gloved fingers slicked with blood. Her fingers slid against the interior flesh of the chest cavity as she hollowed it out, careful and slow.

Nita immersed herself in the calm methodical act of taking a person apart piece by piece, lining up the organs by her side, their smooth surfaces slick with blood. Time lost meaning as she let all her pain at her mother's betrayal slide away into the perfect serenity of dissection.

When she was done, when the body was all taken apart and packaged up in sealed plastic bags for disposal and there was nothing left to do, she rose and cracked her back, working off the stiffness in her body. Smiling slightly, feeling calmer and more grounded, she went to the bathroom, washed her hands, stepped into the shower, and washed her whole body, the blood rinsing away in a pink pool before disappearing down the drain.

She put on the new clothes she'd prepared, left her hair in a towel as she put her bloody clothes in another sealed bag—more evidence to be disposed of—and went back into the main room.

She pulled out her phone and texted Kovit. *All done. You can come up now so we can start disposal.*

Then she took one of the bottles of red wine she'd bought, poured about half into the sink, and filled the empty space with blood she'd collected from Andrej. Vampire blood went bad notoriously fast, and alcohol worked as an excellent preservative. People had been mixing blood and wine for centuries. It kept the blood fresh, it was an inconspicuous way to transport it, and it improved the taste.

Nita corked the bottle and swished it around so that it was nice and mixed before she opened the bottle and took a long drink.

A knock on the door made her pause, and she went over and peered through the eyehole, then opened it. Kovit slipped inside, shoulders tight, nervous expression on his face. But when he peered in and saw there was no sign of the body, only bags, he relaxed and smiled.

"Find out what you needed to know?"

"Yes." Nita took another swig of the blood wine.

Kovit raised an eyebrow. "Is that blood? Are you literally drinking the blood of your enemies now?"

"Yes." She passed him the bottle. "Want some?"

"Yes." He took a long swig.

"Good?" she asked.

"Terrible." He wiped his mouth and handed the bottle back. "Who knew immortality would taste so bad?"

She grinned as she sipped it. "Nothing comes for free."

He rolled his eyes and snatched it back to take another drink.

She sat down on a chair and looked up at the lights as he drank. Her head felt a little muzzy from the alcohol, but she could feel the blood working on her body, slowing her age. She focused in, internally watching what the vampire blood cells did to her body, seeing if she could replicate it. Could she simulate the effects of the blood and make herself immortal?

She studied the chemical composition and decided, yes, she probably could. Maybe not immortal, but she could slow her aging a lot.

And combined with her healing power . . .

She wondered how long she could live. She wondered how long her mother *had* lived.

"So, did you find out anything interesting?" Kovit asked.

She nodded. "My mother is one of the heads of INHUP."

He stared at her, lips still bloody from the wine. "What?"

"She's probably the one who expedited your reveal." Nita's voice was soft. "I'm sorry. This is my fault."

He shook his head. "No, it's hers. And I would have been revealed anyway, and that would have had nothing to do with you."

She let out a breath. "Nonetheless, I'm sorry."

He sat next to her, his body close, so close, and wrapped his arm around her shoulder in a half hug. She leaned into it, grief bubbling up softly.

"It's her fault my location was outed online in Toronto." Nita's voice trembled.

Kovit squeezed her shoulder tighter. "I'm sorry."

"I'm going to kill her," Nita whispered, looking up at Kovit, the alcohol giving her the ability to say the words she couldn't even bear to think when sober.

"Are you sure?" Kovit's words were gentle. "She's your mother."

"I don't care." Nita clenched her jaw. "She's trying to control me, and if she can't, she might even kill me. I wouldn't let Reyes keep me in a cage, why would I let her?"

Kovit was silent at that, probably thinking about Henry, and how hard a decision that had been for him.

"It's not like you and Henry," Nita whispered. "This isn't a hard decision."

Nita was lying. Not just because this was her mother, and she knew her mother loved her, even if that love was warped beyond all reason into something dark and terrible. But because Nita was absolutely terrified of going against her mother. A lifetime of ingrained fear rested in her soul, and she didn't have the slightest idea how she would ever overcome it.

When Nita was a child, she'd misused her power, not understanding how it worked. Too many hospital trips later, her mother decided to teach Nita how to use her ability properly. Nita read a book on human biology, learned more than any child should ever know about the chemical processes that occurred in her body, and her mother quizzed her.

Then the practical part began.

Sometimes her mother would break Nita's bones, cracking her wrist in one, two, three places. Sometimes she'd pulverize Nita's hand. Sometimes she'd cut Nita, her knife sliding along Nita's skin and the blood dripping onto the carpet, and

Nita would be expected to heal it with her ability, or suffer for months letting it heal naturally.

At the time, she thought this was perfectly normal. After all, how could she use her ability if she didn't learn and practice? Only now, with the benefit of age and hindsight, did Nita understand that it hadn't just been about teaching—it had been about making her afraid.

She pushed the thought away, and all the other ones that came after it, a lifetime of memories that built on that fear. Dead animal bodies in her bed, Nita's dreams getting crushed the way her hand had been.

She didn't want to think about it now, didn't want to face the monster her mother had always been. Because at her core, Nita truly had believed her mother loved her.

But maybe the truth was that her mother had never loved Nita. She'd loved the high she got controlling Nita.

"It can't be easy, going against your mother." Kovit's voice brought her out of the past and into the present. "It won't be easy."

He was right, he was always right.

Nita took another swig of wine. "No. It won't."

You'll never win against her, a small part of her mind whispered, and no matter how much she told it to shut up, it kept coming back.

Kovit tilted her head up to face him. "I can do it, if you want. I don't mind."

For a moment, Nita wanted to say yes. She wanted to leave her mother in a room and let Kovit deal with her. To not face the problem, to just let Kovit do what he did best and bask in her freedom afterward.

But she didn't think Kovit could contain her mother. She didn't think he had any better chance of taking her down than Nita did. And she'd never forgive herself if she let Kovit try to solve her problems and he died for it.

She sighed softly, regret coloring her voice. "Thank you. But I need to do it myself."

"I understand." His voice was gentle.

And he did, she knew that. And she loved that he accepted her choice, he didn't press. He'd be there if she needed him, and that was everything she wanted.

But as she leaned against him, her mind continued running in terrified circles, unable to contemplate a single scenario where she faced her mother and won.

TWENTY-SEVEN

IT WAS ALMOST DAWN by the time they finished getting rid of Andrej's body. Nita didn't have a proper refrigeration unit to store all the body parts, and selling them would take time and tools she didn't have. So she just threw the pieces, wrapped in plastic bags, into one of the many massive trash bins in the city. The trash compacter would come around that evening and deal with it.

The blood wine she kept. Easier to store, easier to transport, and better benefits.

Kovit checked his phone occasionally on the way back, and she thought he was checking for updates on the DUL, but when she asked, he admitted he was just reading group chat messages from his online friend group.

"They've decided to kick Gold and me out," he admitted softly.

"I'm sorry." Nita's voice was gentle. "I know how much they meant to you."

He shrugged, but she could see the pain in his eyes. "It's

okay. I never expected . . . They're good people. I knew, when the news came out, that I would lose them."

"It doesn't make it hurt any less."

"No," he whispered. A sad, slightly amused smile crossed his face. "I guess Gold didn't think it through, though. She's having an online meltdown that they're kicking her out too. I told the group what happened in Toronto. I guess Gold didn't realize that spying and trying to bring me back to a torture cage would *maaaaaybe* horrify the others."

Nita sighed, a sound part amused and part exasperated. The more she thought about Gold, the more she began to feel like she might finally understand the angry, vicious daughter of a mob boss.

"I think Gold is in severe denial," Nita finally said.

Kovit tilted his head. "About?"

"Herself." Nita's gaze shifted to her hands. "I suspect she's done and seen a lot of bad things, and she can't square the things she's done with the way she views herself. So focusing on zannies, on unnaturals, on making them evil, she can at least believe she's the *better* person, even if she's not good."

Nita licked her lips. "If she accepts that you're as human as she, then she loses that slim moral high ground, and she has to face her own monstrosity." Nita sighed, lost for a moment in her own bloody past. "Losing that moral high ground means taking responsibility for what you've done, for what you've been avoiding thinking about. And that's hard."

Kovit blinked, hesitating a little. "I've never thought of it like that." He considered. "I think . . . I think you're right. I think she clings to the idea that she's at least not as bad as me, that in this one thing she's better, to avoid facing what kind of person she's become over the years."

Nita nodded. She could understand that. She had a lot of experience avoiding the truth of her own crimes. Facing her own guilt had been hard, but she didn't regret it.

"Maybe this rejection will force her to face it," Nita mused.

"Maybe," Kovit whispered, but she could tell he was trying not to hope too hard.

They walked the rest of the way in silence, both of them lost in their own thoughts.

By the time they returned to the apartment, it was full-on morning, and Nita and Kovit were both exhausted from all the body dumping and carting crates around. Nita opened the door and was greeted with the buzz of the local news programming. Fabricio had managed to wiggle far enough to reach the television remote and was watching the news.

Nita scowled. "What are you doing?"

Fabricio gave her a steady look. "Watching INHUP defend putting Kovit on the list."

Kovit darted forward so he could see the screen. "Wait, what?"

The announcer onscreen was speaking in Spanish, and Kovit made a frustrated sound. "What's he saying?"

Nita closed the door behind her and listened closer. "They've moved past the INHUP stuff and are on to some sort of financial analysis."

Kovit pulled out his phone and started googling, and Nita peered over his shoulder.

One of INHUP's directors, a tall man in his forties, had made an official statement. Kovit clicked the video and turned up the volume.

"... While we acknowledge that the one-week mandatory verification period wasn't respected, this was because we found it unnecessary due to overwhelming evidence against the zannie in question." The man assessed the crowd as cameras flashed and the INHUP logo towered over him in the background. "We were unaware of any relationship with the agent in the photos, but have suspended her pending an investigation, the results of which we will make public after the inquiry."

"What is this overwhelming evidence?" called a voice from the crowd of reporters. "Can we see it?"

"At this time it is classified."

"Why?"

"The videos all involve graphic scenes of torture as performed by a minor. Our legal department is working on the legalities of releasing one or two to the public, and we hope that we can allay your suspicions shortly."

The man waved at the reporters and then walked offstage, and the video ended.

"Can they release the videos?" He looked at Nita nervously.

"Probably," Nita admitted. "But we can counter this."

Fabricio interrupted them. "Can you counter the testimony of one of Kovit's victims who's come forward?"

Both of them turned around to face Fabricio. Nita stared at him. "Victims?"

"The pink-haired girl. I saw her on television earlier." Fabricio shrugged. "She's making quite a fuss."

Mirella. Mirella was on television.

"Thanks, we'll look at that now." Nita smiled tightly at Fabricio and then dragged Kovit into the bedroom, closing the door behind them so that Fabricio couldn't snoop on what happened next.

Nita clicked through the news links on her phone until she found the one she wanted. It was titled WOMAN COMES FORWARD CLAIMING TO BE ZANNIE VICTIM.

Nita hesitated, eyes flicking to Kovit as her finger hovered over the Play button. His jaw was tight, and he nodded sharply. "Play it."

She did. Mirella came onscreen, her long pink hair tied back into a professional bun, her left eye covered by a black patch like a pirate. Her skin was gray and contrasted starkly with her too-pink eye. High cheekbones and a square face made her determined look seem more steely and hard as she spoke. Nita clicked the subtitle button beneath the video so that Kovit could see the translation, since he didn't speak Spanish.

"I want to clarify, for all those people doubting that this man is a zannie. He absolutely is, and he's absolutely the monster your nightmares are made of. He was one of my jailers in el Mercado de la Muerte, and he abused his power frequently to torture me whenever he was bored." Her eyes were hard. "If you see him, don't hesitate. Kill him."

The video ended there, and both Nita and Kovit were silent afterward. Nita had always assumed that Kovit had hurt Mirella more than just the one time Reyes had asked him to, but hearing Mirella actually say it, putting words to

236

the monstrosity she hadn't dared quite imagine made Nita feel nauseous and a little lightheaded.

Kovit was very still, and he blinked slowly before whispering, "Fuck."

Nita pursed her lips and closed the window. "Mirella has no proof, and anyways, this isn't a trial right now. We can still fix this."

"Even when the videos come out?" Kovit sounded skeptical.

"Even then." Nita opened the fake email account she'd created when they sent Mirella the information about the assassination and found a response.

Thank you, whoever you are, for this information. It saved my life. If there's ever anything I can do in return, let me know. —Mirella

"Translate it for me?" Kovit asked, and Nita did. His smile was bitter. "So we actually saved her, and she decided to go do this?"

"She doesn't know we're the ones who sent the information." Nita's voice was soft.

"Would she have refrained from making that video if she knew?"

Nita considered, remembering Mirella, fierce and angry and full of hatred for all the people who'd wronged her. Nita recalled the way she spoke of Kovit, the violence that dripped from her words, and she thought of the video she'd watched. Kovit hadn't just hurt Mirella once. He'd done it often, who knew how often, before Nita came. She didn't think Mirella would ever forgive Kovit. Nita didn't blame her.

"No," Nita said. "I don't think it would have changed anything." She looked down at the email. "Do you want me to tell her who her savior was?"

Kovit stared at the email for a long moment, then shook his head. "No. If it won't make her recant her statement, there's no point."

Nita lifted an eyebrow. "You don't want her to think you feel guilty?"

"Why should I care what she thinks of me?" He sounded genuinely baffled. "If you think that me pretending to feel guilty will make her switch to our side, I'll play whatever tune you need me to. But I see no point in making her believe I feel guilty when I don't and there's no benefit."

Nita let her fingers fall. Sometimes Nita thought Kovit might actually feel some sort of guilt for his actions, especially after he'd sent the warning to Mirella yesterday. But then she would be reminded starkly that he really didn't, and all her thoughts about that were just Nita projecting, wishing he felt guilty because it would make everything a little less terrible.

"All right," Nita said, and didn't press further.

Kovit sat down on the bed and then lay back, staring at the ceiling. "I should have killed her."

"We'd be dead too, then," Nita responded absently, flipping through the phone she'd taken from Henry. "She's the reason we made it to the docks at Tabatinga after the market blew up. She unwittingly saved your life."

He didn't respond, and Nita didn't expect him to.

Nita went to the cloud where she'd first seen all those videos Henry had been blackmailing Kovit with. There were hundreds of them, spanning years. She didn't know if the whole file, en masse, had been shared with INHUP, but this looked like all the recordings he'd ever taken. Which gave her an idea.

"Look, right now, Mirella isn't important." Nita turned to him. "She's a revolutionary in a fringe part of the world most people don't know or care about. People are already online calling her accusations lies to get attention for her cause. What's important is INHUP, which will release videos of you soon. What's important is that we control the narrative they're trying to build." Nita's voice was firm. "They need time to make sure everything is in order before releasing the videos. We don't."

He frowned. "What are you saying?"

"We're going to release them first."

Kovit stared at her, face blank. "What?"

"Everyone is questioning INHUP right now. It's the perfect time to show them how broken the Dangerous Unnaturals List is."

"By showing them videos of me as a child torturing people?" He laughed, high and light. "Somehow I don't think that will make them sympathetic."

Nita smiled softly. "It won't. Not if INHUP decides on the videos to release. But if you and I pick just the right video, we can change the narrative."

"How?"

"There are hundreds of videos here. You worked for the Family for years." She licked her lips and then gently asked, "Was there any time you refused to hurt someone? Any time you resisted?"

He gave her a skeptical look. "I rather enjoyed those torture sessions. They were the best part of my life."

"I'm sure," Nita said, sliding past that and trying not to think too hard about it. "But you have rules. Henry must have broken them once or twice before Matt. Didn't you tell me once about a Family member who wanted you to torture some girl who didn't want to have sex with him?"

Kovit blinked slowly, thoughtfully. "There were a few incidents."

Nita handed him the phone. "This is all Henry's videos on the cloud. Find one. Find one we can use to paint you as sympathetic. The younger you are in it, the better. I want it to look like you were beaten into this path, not like you were willing. Coercion of a minor is a crime—if they can prove force, you're not culpable."

He gave her a look. "I'm very culpable."

She rolled her eyes. "I know that." She leaned closer. "But the truth doesn't matter. We're crafting a story. They're going to try and prove you're a monster, so we want to try and make people believe you're a tragic victim instead."

He frowned down at the phone. "Do you really think people will believe that?"

"People will believe what you tell them to believe. You're young, attractive, and have a tragic past. We can spin this. People *love* a tragic past and a reformed monster." She shrugged. "I know it's not true, but it's as true as the monster mask you wore in the Family."

The more Nita thought about it, the more she wondered if life was just a series of masks you wore. Kovit was a different person with her than with Fabricio than with Henry than with his victims than with his sister. All the masks were him, just not all of him, only a piece.

Nita was the same, behaving differently in different situations. She wondered if it was impossible to be all of yourself at the same time, because yourself was too complicated. So people broke it down into bits and pieces and wore some of them some days and others different days.

"I see what you're getting at." He considered. "I can pretend to be good and tragic or whatever. I think. I've never really tried before. What do good people do?"

"They feel all angsty and guilty about all the terrible things they did." Nita grinned a little, voice wicked. "You're going to have to practice your dramatic brooding, after all."

He gave her a long-suffering face. "People always look constipated when they brood."

She laughed, and he started flipping through the files on the phone. "Can you think of a video to use?"

He nodded, eyes glued to the tiny thumbnails. "I know just the one."

TWENTY-EIGHT

NITA WATCHED THE VIDEO Kovit chose. Or at least, she watched the start of it. He helpfully paused it before it got too dark.

Kovit was young in the video, ten, maybe eleven, but small and round-cheeked enough that he could probably pass for younger if he wanted. Like the other videos, it took place in a room with white walls and white floors and a steel table in the middle with a person tied on it.

The person on the table was young, maybe twelve, a boy with short blond hair and huge blue eyes. His mouth was taped, and he was trying to scream through his bindings, but it wasn't working.

Kovit walked in, but this time, he was accompanied by Henry, who was clearly visible—Nita was pretty sure that meant this particular video hadn't been sent to INHUP. It was part of Henry's personal collection.

It was hard for Nita to watch the rest. Tiny child Kovit refused to hurt the boy, his English broken and heavily accented, a stark reminder of how out of his depth Kovit had been when the Family had taken him in.

Henry hadn't taken it well.

Nita flinched at every blow to child Kovit and every time his small, broken body jerked from a boot, or his tiny face turned toward the camera, blood covering his features and face swelling and blackening. With every rejection small Kovit gave, and every blow that followed, her heart broke a little.

In the end, Henry gave up and agreed he'd deal with the child himself, but he still forced Kovit to stay in the room while he made the boy scream, skin fluttering to the ground in thin strips as Kovit gasped and rolled on the floor, a combination of ecstasy from the child's pain and agony from his own.

Nita uploaded the video and sent the links to all her new-found media contacts.

Then she closed the phone and quietly turned to Kovit. "I never realized . . ."

He shrugged, clearly uncomfortable with having shared the video. "It didn't happen often. Henry didn't bring me more children. He realized I got difficult with them. I think he thought I'd get over it in time. He taught me a lot. He really was a great mentor." He paused a heartbeat, before clarifying, "Most of the time."

Nita didn't argue with him. Kovit had murdered Henry to save himself, and if he wanted to cling to the illusion that his childhood had happy moments instead of acknowledging that it had been ruled by an abusive, controlling monster, then she wasn't going to break his image.

She wasn't exactly one to talk.

She tried not to think about the parallels to her own upbringing. Her mother never forced her to torture people. But her mother did leave the bodies of small animals in Nita's bed when she disobeyed her parents, broke Nita's body to teach her how to heal it, crushed all her dreams, all her hopes of leaving, created an aura of terror that still made Nita flinch whenever she thought about disobedience.

Kovit closed his eyes. "I can see your face, judging me."

"I mean, he was pretty awful from what I saw."

Kovit was silent a long moment. His breathing was deep and slow, and when he finally opened his eyes, he admitted, so softly that she could barely hear him, "You're right. He was awful."

Nita was silent, watching.

"He betrayed me. He manipulated me. He murdered my friend." Kovit squeezed his eyes shut tight for a moment and ran his hands over his face. "But I can't seem to stop this rose-tinted view of him from creeping back in. I can't seem to stop feeling shitty for having killed him."

Nita sat beside him and sighed. "Brains are weird like that. It's common to gloss over the bad things, or think it wasn't all that bad after it's over. It's not like you can actually go back and look and see what the reality was anymore."

"Yeah. I guess." He looked at her, head tilted. "Is there anything you still romanticize that way?"

She went to shake her head, but paused, thinking. Her conversation with Andrej had brought a lot of ugly questions into her mind, and the one she'd avoided facing was what all of this said about her father.

Her father. Who loved her. Who cared for her.

Who'd helped her mother murder the head of INHUP. Who'd passed a law to create the DUL. Who Nita hadn't really, truly seen since she was a child. Who was wholly and completely her mother's person. And for all that in Nita's mind he stood up for her, the truth was, he never went against her mother. He was calming and could sometimes mediate. He loved Nita and would do things with her.

But he never stopped her mother from hurting her. He never gainsaid her mother.

He was powerless, and as much as she hated to admit it, she wondered how much of her love for him was real and how much she'd built up in her mind over the years, a lifeline to cling to when things got ugly.

She didn't say anything, though. If she voiced those concerns, then they'd be real. If she kept them quiet, maybe they would die in the dark. Because her father was dead and gone and never coming back, so even if he hadn't stood up for her, hadn't protected her in all the ways she wanted him to, what was the point in dredging it up? He wasn't there to confront. Wasn't there to talk to. He was gone, and the truth went with him.

So it was better to just let herself have that rose-tinted view. Whether it was real or not didn't really matter anymore.

"Nita?" Kovit asked, voice concerned.

"Sorry, lost in thought." She shook her head. "No. I don't

think I have a rose tinted view of much of anything in my past anymore."

Kovit lay back on the bed. "You know, the strange thing is, even though I still have all these ugly, awful feelings about what I did, and even though the whole world is hunting me, I feel . . . freer than I ever have before. I don't think I realized that I was slowly being strangled to death by him, and when I cut him down, I felt like I was breathing for the first time in a long time."

Nita lay down beside him, and said softly, "Sometimes freedom comes at an ugly price."

He was silent for a moment before he whispered, "I don't think this guilt will ever go away. I don't think I'll ever not feel awful about killing Henry."

"But you don't regret it?"

"No." He swallowed. "It had to be done."

"Then it's okay," Nita said gently. "If you didn't feel at all guilty, I'd be a bit worried about you. It's human to feel terrible about something like that."

He sighed softly. "I know. I just wanted . . . I made the right decision. I just wish it weren't so hard. I wish that making the right choice wasn't so painful. If it's the right decision, it shouldn't leave you feeling like shit, you know?"

She smiled bitterly. "If only the world worked like that."

"If only." He let out a soft sound, then closed his eyes. "But it's okay. I'm learning to deal with the guilt. I did something terrible, and it's okay to feel bad about it without regretting my choices. I will always love Henry, just a little, despite it all, and that's okay too."

Nita didn't know how to respond to that. Kovit had done an awful lot of other terrible things in his life, much worse than killing Henry. But she just squeezed his arm gently, understanding that some crimes might be objectively less terrible but emotionally much more impactful.

There were still plans to be made, set ups to be done for meeting Alberto Tácunan later today. But for now, there was just them and the understanding that sometimes people you loved betrayed you, and sometimes cutting them out of your lives was the only way to heal yourself, even if you lost a piece of your soul doing so.

TWENTY-NINE

THEY NAPPED FOR A BIT, then ordered delivery. Kovit released Fabricio, and the three of them ate in silence, tense for what had to come next, the whole point of their trip to Buenos Aires in the first place.

In two hours, they were meeting Alberto Tácunan.

Fabricio's whole body was tight with tension as he ate, and he kept staring blankly at the pizza and then shuddering slightly. Occasionally, he'd take slow, calming breaths, and Nita wondered what memories he was reliving that haunted his expression so. She thought of asking, but she didn't think he'd answer. And she wasn't entirely certain she wanted to know.

The walk to the hotel was quiet and charged. They had to stop at a few places for Nita to pick up supplies, and the whole time Fabricio's shoulders were tight, and he hunched over slightly, trying to make himself smaller. His eyes flicked around, his expression a strange combination of terror and determination. Nita kept close to him in case he got cold feet and decided to make a break for it.

But he didn't. His forehead gleamed with nervous sweat, but his mouth was set.

She wondered at the three of them, all terrified of the people who'd raised them, all warped and twisted and destroyed in some way or another by the black market as they grew up. She wondered if they were like trees that started growing sideways young and could never straighten out, would always be deformed in some way, or like chameleons, who could lose a tail and just grow themselves a new one given enough time.

As they walked, Nita noticed the hunters. Normal people on the way to work, their eyes nervous and sharp as they scanned the streets. Baristas in coffee shops, their eyes too focused on each person who came in, examining their features as though wondering, *Is that the zannie?*

A shorter, slightly round young man walking along got accosted a block ahead of them by two civilians, who demanded he take off his sunglasses prove he wasn't a zannie. Nita could hear the man's indignant protests, asking how they could mistake him for Thai when he was so obviously Argentinian.

Nita linked her arm with Kovit's and turned them away. Kovit's eyes didn't leave the scene until they turned a corner, and his body was stiff with fear.

Walking together offered him some protection, since eyes passed over them, as though people couldn't imagine a zannie traveling with others, or having a girlfriend, or whatever they looked like to the outside world.

But the Dangerous Unnaturals List was everywhere, printed and pasted on walls, up on everyone's phones, and Nita shivered, wondering how many innocent people who resembled Kovit had already been attacked, like the girls who looked like Nita back in Toronto.

She tried not to think about it.

The hotel lobby was pristine and clear. Kovit fiddled with his sunglasses but didn't take them off, even though they were indoors. It made him stand out, but it was still less risky than having him take them off and be recognized.

They headed to Almeida's room. Nita had disposed of the diplomat's body at the same time she'd disposed of Andrej's body last night. She didn't want the stench of rot to give away all their plans, and she didn't want any bodies found in the hotel.

Of course, after tonight, she didn't care if they found bodies. She just needed everything to look normal until she had the password from Alberto Tácunan.

Inside Almeida's room, the faint smell of corpse remained, a combination of urine and a hint of rot. Nita found the smell of it comforting. Decay and death had always been her life's work. And this death was a piece of her success.

Fabricio wrinkled his nose as he walked in, and Kovit closed the door behind them. They were early for the meeting, and Nita sat down on the single bed, the plush surface sinking beneath her. Kovit sat beside her and Fabricio made for the chair, but paused, looking closely at it.

"Is that blood?"

Nita shrugged. "Probably. We murdered a man there yesterday. I didn't see the point in cleaning that part until we were done with your father, though." She considered. "I hope the maids don't ignore the DO NOT DISTURB sign I put up."

Fabricio didn't respond, just quietly backed away from the chair and stood leaning against the wall.

"So, anything we should be aware of?" Nita asked. "Before we ambush him for the password?"

"Not really."

"You're an unnatural. Is he?"

"No." Fabricio looked down. "My mom was."

Nita tilted her head to one side. "Where is she?"

"Dead." His voice was soft. "When I was young."

"I'm sorry." Nita wasn't really, she didn't care, but it was something you said in these circumstances. "How did she die?"

He hesitated, then admitted, "Cancer."

Nita was silent, curiosity sated, but Kovit commented, "That must have been hard."

Fabricio shrugged, a sad little smile playing on his mouth. "It was a long time ago. I don't really think about it much anymore."

The seconds ticked by, Fabricio fidgeting nervously, eyes flicking to the door. Kovit twirled his switchblade in his hand, pensive, and Nita ticked through the to-do list items on her plans, trying to see if she'd missed anything, trying to plot where things could go wrong.

When the knock finally came, Fabricio nearly jumped out of his skin. He wiped his sweaty palms on his pants, his breathing harsh and frightened.

Nita felt a moment of pity for him. She recognized that terror. It was a feeling she knew well.

Before she could think through her action, she put her hand on Fabricio's shoulder. "We got this."

He stared at her, breathing slowing, and he gave her a slight smile. "Nita, you're trying to comfort me again. Careful, I might think you have a heart."

She scowled and jerked her hand away.

Then she went to the door and opened it.

A man in his early fifties stood at the entranceway checking his phone. His gray hair was smoothed back from his face with a bit of gel, and he was clean shaven with cold brown eyes and lightly tanned skin, a little darker than Fabricio. His clothes reeked of money, all of them tailored to fit, and his watch alone probably cost more than the hotel.

He blinked when Nita opened the door, then frowned.

"Ah, I must have the wrong room," he said, voice deep, his Spanish the same cadence as Fabricio's.

"No." Nita smiled, reaching forward, grabbing his hand, and yanking him inside. "You came to the right place."

Kovit descended the moment he was inside, knife at Alberto's throat, hand twisting one of the older man's arms behind his back painfully, voice whispering threats of all the things he'd do. Nita shut the door behind them as Kovit led their prisoner to the chair Almeida had died in yesterday. Alberto was rigid with fear, Adam's apple bobbing against the knife, and his movements were stiff as he followed Kovit's directions. He didn't scream or flail or fight, he just watched and obeyed, all his movements careful and calculated.

They bound him quickly with duct tape while Fabricio watched, frozen, his whole body stiff with terror. His eyes, wide and nervous flicked to his captive father and then away, as though he couldn't quite face what he was doing. Nita wondered if he was having second thoughts. Too late now.

After Alberto was tied up and gagged, Nita stepped back to examine her work. Not a single hair had shifted out of place, and his shirt was barely rumpled from Kovit's twisting his arm. His eyes were furious, flicking between Nita and Kovit before settling on Fabricio. A rage came into his gaze, a fury like Nita had rarely seen. There was pure hatred in those eyes, and Nita wholeheartedly believed that if this man got out, the things he would do to Fabricio were more horrible than even Kovit could imagine.

But he wouldn't be getting out.

Nita turned to Alberto and smiled. "I'm sorry for the subterfuge, but this was the only sure way to request a meeting with you. I have some questions, you see."

He made a sound of rage through his duct tape gag, and Nita nodded. "Yes, I know the gag is annoying. Don't worry, I'll take it off shortly. It will be hard for you to answer questions with it on, I'm sure. Be patient. I just want to establish what's going to happen today first. Some ground rules, if you will."

Sweat beaded on Alberto's reddening face, and he glared silently.

"Now." Nita gestured for Kovit to come forward. "Perhaps you've seen the news? A new zannie added to the Dangerous Unnaturals List?"

Alberto's eyes widened in recognition, and Nita could almost see his mind matching Kovit's face with the picture on the news.

"If you don't cooperate, I'll give you to Kovit here. He's had a lot of experience with uncooperative people, you see." Nita didn't actually intend to torture Alberto—torture wouldn't work, she knew that. The threat was sufficient in this case. "He's also very eager to demonstrate his skills to you."

Kovit gave Alberto his very best monster smile, all laughing glee and dark promises. Alberto didn't flinch, but his jaw tightened and he swallowed heavily.

"Now that you understand how things are going to work, we're going to start asking you some questions." Nita leaned forward and ripped the duct tape off his mouth.

"I'm going to kill you," hissed Alberto.

"Good luck with that," Nita said mildly.

"Not you." His eyes moved to Fabricio. "I'm going to kill you, Fabricio."

Fabricio's face was gray, but his voice was steady. "You've already done far worse to me."

Nita's eyes narrowed, and she spoke to Alberto in a slow voice, like one used with a child. "Now, now, no one needs to die today, as long as you answer the questions."

His eyes swiveled to her, full of hate.

"First question. What is the administrator password to access all the files at Tácunan Law?"

He ground his teeth. "I can't give you that."

Nita's gaze was flat. "Kovit?"

Alberto sneered at them both. "That won't help. I can't give it to you because I don't *have* it."

"Of course you do." Nita rolled her eyes. "You're Alberto Tácunan. It's called Tácunan Law. It's literally your company."

254

His eyes shifted to Fabricio and then back to Nita, full of controlled rage. "I'm not Alberto Tácunan."

Nita blinked, then stepped back. "What?"

That was not an excuse she'd foreseen.

Alberto was looking at Fabricio again, eyebrows drawn, gaze dark. "There's only one Tácunan in this room, and if you want the passwords, you're going to have to ask him for them."

Nita turned around slowly to look at Fabricio.

He trembled slightly when he looked at not-Alberto, but his jaw was set and his gaze was steady as he met Nita's eyes.

"Is it true?" Nita asked. "Have you had the password all along?"

He nodded, once, sharply. "I have."

"And your father?"

He laughed, a small, broken sound. "My father is dead."

Dead. Alberto Tácunan was already dead.

Nita stared at him, and then turned back to not-Alberto, his face still pulsating with rage. "Then who the hell is this?"

THIRTY

Nita stared at Fabricio, mind trying to process what was happening but coming up blank. Alberto Tácunan was dead. Had been dead for a while, in all likelihood. She couldn't quite grasp what that meant for her, but she had a feeling it was very bad.

All she knew for certain was that Fabricio had tricked them somehow. All along, Nita had thought she was the one in control, the one with the prisoner, but he'd been playing her the whole time.

She'd been a fool.

Fabricio was giving her a look that was a little sheepish, a little clever, and a little sad. He almost looked guilty, but not quite. There was a layer of fear underneath it all that was genuine. Whoever this man was, Fabricio was terrified of him. But everything else? She didn't know. He was so good at faking emotions, at playing people's strings. She couldn't trust what was real.

"Fabricio." Nita's voice went low and dangerous. She was

angry at him, angry at herself, angry at their situation. "I asked you a question. Who the hell is this?"

"His name is Ricci. Martin Ricci." Fabricio's voice was soft and vicious, something dark and hateful creeping into his words. "And he's the man who murdered my father and masqueraded as him for the last five years."

Nita's mind whirled. "How? And why?"

Fabricio's hateful eyes went to Martin Ricci. "Power. Isn't it always power with people like these?" Fabricio's laugh was brittle and broken. "He saw what my father had, and he wanted it. So he murdered him, hid the body, made the fact that the crime ever happened disappear, and then tried to take my father's place."

"But . . ." Nita trailed off. "People would know. People who'd met your father . . ."

"Were few and far between," Fabricio said bitterly. "My father liked his privacy. He was always a behind-the-scenes kind of person, and he enjoyed his anonymity. Sure, there were some people who knew him by face. But they were easily dealt with through bribes and a few 'accidents.'"

Ricci interjected. "He's lying. His father died in a car accident. I raised this ungrateful little brat after his father died. I took care of the company. I kept it from collapsing from his father's loss. I made sure that the investors and the clients didn't annihilate us when he died."

Fabricio's voice was cold, and his voice so full of derision and revulsion that it felt like it should be toxic to hear. "You had power over me, and you fed me and kept me alive, but that doesn't mean you raised me."

Nita nearly flinched, not just at the tone, but at the cold truth of those words when she thought about her own life.

Fabricio turned to Nita. "My father was very smart. He knew that if anything happened to him, I'd be in trouble. A man like him, with a lot of money and a lot of power? Everyone wanted a piece of what I'd inherit. So he set things up so that the company couldn't run without me. The mainframe needs my fingerprint to be activated. I'm the only one alive now with the admin passwords. If I die, or if I don't check in often enough, all security goes down, and everything goes online."

Nita's eyes widened. "What?"

"It was a security measure to ensure no one would get rid of me to take over the company. I'm necessary for this damn company to function. And only I can change the settings to make myself *not* necessary." Fabricio smiled bitterly. "Of course, my father wasn't a fool. He knew that pressure could be applied to make me tell people the passwords. Which is why I don't have the passwords to change any of the settings. Even if I spill passwords that I do know, the machine still needs a fingerprint from me. All the information on how to reset the fingerprint password and such was sealed away in a vault I couldn't access until I turned eighteen."

It was a brilliant insurance policy, Nita had to admit. If anyone wanted to run the company, they needed either Alberto or Fabricio. It meant that even if he died, his son would stay alive.

It was a touching gesture, even if she had the sinking idea it hadn't ended well. Fabricio's father had at least tried.

Fabricio closed his eyes and took a deep breath. "The first

few months after they killed my father, Martin and his flunkies pampered me. I stayed in my nice, swanky room in my father's penthouse. I ate everything I wanted, and anything I asked for, they gave me. But I refused to give them access to anything. And when we had to do updates or change things, I refused to enter the codes on anything unsecured, anything that they could use to steal the passwords I had."

Fabricio's voice hardened, his whole body going still. "Then they got mad."

A chill ran down Nita's spine at his tone.

"They locked me in a small, dark room. A basement somewhere. They starved me for a while. Occasionally they beat me. They hired a zannie for a few weeks — that's the real reason I lost my toes." He smiled bitterly at Kovit. "Sorry, Kovit, you're not the first one here. I know all the tricks for getting through the pain."

Kovit gave him a look of horror. "Weeks?"

Fabricio's smile was broken, and his whole expression looked a little cracked, like he was trying to make a normal expression but didn't quite know how, it had been shattered into a thousand pieces and he'd taped them back together to try and approximate normalcy. "Twenty-three days. It felt like longer, but I counted the time, the seconds and minutes and hours, one, two, three. I put them to a beat in my head, music helped me focus on things besides the pain."

Kovit swallowed, eyes wide, and Nita tried to hold back her revulsion at the thought, tried to block her brain from imagining thirteen-year-old Fabricio in the dark day after day, screaming and singing to try and take the pain away.

"On my fourteenth birthday, they finally gave up and let me out." Fabricio's gaze turned inward. "I did the bare minimum to keep the company afloat, which was mostly just be alive and make necessary authorizations. I kept the penthouse suite, and no one hurt me anymore. And we all just waited for my eighteenth birthday to roll around, because then I'd have access to all the passwords, even the reset ones — and Martin would have access through me. He could just go to the bank with me, look over my shoulder, and it would all be over. After I turned eighteen, he'd be able to finally get rid of me."

Fabricio laughed a little, his voice hoarse and sad. "My life has been a ticking clock, a countdown to my death."

Nita licked her lips. "When is your eighteenth birthday?"

"Last week," he admitted. "While I was in INHUP custody in Bogotá."

Pieces clicked together in Nita's mind. "This is why you were so desperate not to go back. Because you knew if you were sent back—"

"They'd bring me to the bank, I'd open the sealed vault, Martin would take the information." He closed his eyes, breath whooshing out as he whispered, "And I would die."

Nita was silent a long moment. Across from them, Martin snorted.

"Turning yourself into a tragic hero, Fabricio?" Martin looked up at them all with cold brown eyes. "Using that silver tongue of yours to spin the very best tale possible, make yourself the hero of this story. Always the tragic fucking victim, aren't you?"

Fabricio's smile was bitter. "You can curse me all you want, but I've only spoken the truth."

"Oh, I never said you lied. You just strategically omitted things, the way you always do." Martin turned to Nita. "What he didn't tell you here is that he learned on his daddy's knee. That he's actually been a major force in preventing people from finding out his father is dead. I'm the fake face of Alberto Tácunan, but he's the behind-the-scenes Alberto Tácunan."

Fabricio shrugged. "It's true. If the world found out my father was dead, and the situation with Tácunan Law, the monsters would descend. A million people would want to kidnap or kill me for the same reason you did, Nita. I'd never survive. And God knows Martin here didn't have the knowledge to pass as my father."

Martin ground his teeth. "Snotty as ever, I see."

"I guess you shouldn't have hired a zannie to torture me when I was thirteen, then. Maybe I'd be nicer."

"Get over yourself."

"Get over my — no. I'm not doing this again." Fabricio's face was a mask of rage, and his whole body shook. He turned to Nita, stiff and sharp. "There. You finally have the truth."

Nita stared at him, mind racing. "So. In summary, you've had the passwords. You've always had the passwords."

"Yes."

"Then why the hell did you want me to kidnap him?" she snapped, gesturing at Martin.

Fabricio blinked. "Isn't it obvious? I want him dead. He's the one running Tácunan Law now. He's the one who's going to murder me if things go wrong. He killed my father."

"So you made us kidnap him?"

Fabricio corrected her placidly. "I created a situation where you have no choice but to kill him."

Nita raised her eyebrow. "No choice, huh?"

"Well, he's seen your faces. You've tied him up and threatened him. You don't think someone like him will forgive and forget that, do you?"

Nita's jaw clenched. He wouldn't.

Kovit voiced her thoughts. "Fabricio's right, Nita. He's seen too much. He has to die."

Nita didn't really care that Martin had to die. She'd been planning to kill him from the start. What she cared about was that she'd been manipulated into committing a murder she had no stake in. She'd been used, played, and tricked into doing Fabricio's dirty work.

"Fine." Nita's voice was hard. She'd had enough of this. "Kill him."

"No, wait—" Martin cried, but the sound was cut off by a sickening crack.

Kovit released Martin's head, and it lolled at an impossible angle, eyes staring.

Nita turned to Fabricio. "He's dead now."

"Yes." Fabricio's gaze was glued to Martin's body, something cold and hard in his eyes. "Thank you."

"Now you're going to give us the information we need."

"Yes," Fabricio agreed. "I'll break you into the office, I'll put in the password, you can take whatever information you want. I don't care. Rob the company blind."

Nita narrowed her eyes, and Kovit watched them both with wary eyes, as though afraid not just of what plan Fabricio might have up his sleeve, but what Nita might do about it.

"Fine," Nita said, not trusting him at all. "Lead the way."

THIRTY-ONE

THEY LEFT THE HOTEL, leaving Martin's dead body still bound and gagged in the chair. Nita would clean it up later. Her fingers ached for a scalpel, and her hand twitched involuntarily. What she wouldn't give to just spend a few hours crawling through this man's chest cavity, ripping out his organs and putting them in jars, all clear lines and still bodies.

She'd only dissected a few hours ago, but it felt like an eternity—the calm and stillness it had brought had been shattered by the real world, with its noise and tricks. There were no clear lines and still faces in living people. Just lies and scams and deception.

Fabricio, instigator of those lies, walked slightly ahead of her out of the hotel and onto the street. The sun shone down on him, making the golden brown highlights in his hair gleam. He tipped his head back and looked up at the sky and smiled, as though a great burden had been lifted from him.

Nita scowled. A great burden had been lifted from him, and he'd conned Nita into doing it. Her eyes narrowed as she watched him, wondering what else he had in store for her and

Kovit. He'd said he'd get them in and give them the password, but she didn't trust him, not at all. Had she ever?

A little, she realized. She'd trusted that he had his own self-interest in mind, and she'd banked on that. The problem was, she hadn't known enough about him to realize what was in his self-interest. She still didn't.

The thought sent a chill down her spine.

No, he couldn't turn on them completely. She could still ruin his life with a few clicks of a button, send all his information to the internet and let the black market descend. It would be everything he feared. He wouldn't let that happen.

But the uneasiness lingered as she fell into step beside Kovit, following Fabricio into the light.

They left the hotel and walked south along the water of Puerto Madero. Joggers ran past, and Rollerbladers skated around each other, laughing. A woman leaned casually against the railing over the water, rows of ships lined up behind her, as a college-aged young man took pictures using a tripod and a teenager held up a portable hairdryer so the model's hair would blow in the nonexistent wind.

Glass and steel skyscrapers looked down on them, silent and powerful, blocking out the sun in places, as though the buildings were trying to obtain the dark, shadowed atmosphere of Toronto, but the sun in Buenos Aires was too bright, the sky too blue, and there were too few skyscrapers.

Nita fell into step beside Fabricio. There was something lighter in the way he walked now, as though with each step he shed a piece of the fear that had been weighing him down for years. Someone passed too close to him, and for a moment he froze, then relaxed again. He bent down, hands on his knees, and took big gulps of breath.

Nita leaned away from him and gave him a suspicious look. "Are you okay?"

He laughed, a short, high burst of sound, almost disbelieving. "I am. He's dead. He's finally dead." Fabricio took a gulp of air. "It's just taking a moment to sink in. I keep watching the street, looking out for anyone who might be working for him, who might come kidnap me and bring me back, but then I remember: he's dead. It doesn't matter. It's over."

Fabricio was shaking with relief, and he looked close to tears.

"It's over," he whispered again, as though by repeating it to himself, he could make himself believe it.

Nita went to say something and was surprised when Kovit intervened instead.

"That stage of your life is over. He can't hurt you again." Kovit's voice was soft, but hard. "But that doesn't mean it's all over. You have to get us into Tácunan Law."

He nodded, straightening, "I know."

"And, Fabricio." Nita raised her eyebrows. "Remember, if you betray us, I still have all your information set up to automatically post if I don't stop it."

His smile was bitter. "I know." His gaze was steady. "You held up your side of our deal—you killed the man ruining my life. I'll get you the information you want. I don't give a fuck about this company, I never have. When this is over, I'll never go back. It can go down in a ball of flames for all I care."

Nita almost flinched at the sheer hatred in his voice but kept herself still. "So long as we understand each other."

He started walking again. "We do."

They continued down the port, but Nita wasn't reassured. Fabricio had proven himself an incredible liar and manipulator, and she couldn't trust which of his emotions and reactions were real, and which were designed to maximize her sympathy, tug on her trust, manipulate what she wanted.

Kovit tilted his head so his sunglasses met her eyes, and she knew he understood. He was wondering the same thing.

Nita wanted so much to just rip the information out of Fabricio's brain, to strip it out in pieces and consume it like French fries, so that she could do this herself, so that she didn't need him. But as people said, if wishes were unicorns, most of the world would be dead.

Now that Nita thought about it, she wondered if that was actually a real saying or just something her mother had made up. She'd never heard anyone else use it. Speaking of her mother, since Fabricio was finally shedding some of his lies, she might as well ask him some questions she still needed answers to.

Maybe he'd even tell her the truth.

She picked up her pace slightly so she was walking beside him, her legs moving a little quicker to keep pace with his longer strides.

"Can I ask you something?" Nita's voice was softer than she expected.

Fabricio blinked. "All right."

"Before, back in Bogotá, you told me my mother kidnapped you because she wanted to blackmail your father, but you didn't know why. That was a lie, wasn't it?"

"Why do you say that?"

"Because you turned eighteen last week. A week after my mother kidnapped you. That's a pretty big coincidence."

His shoulders slumped slightly and he nodded. "Yes, it was a lie."

"I thought so." The water glinted in the light of the setting sun, orange tinted. "So, why did my mother kidnap you?"

He sighed, long and hard. "Because I was stupid and desperate and made a mistake."

"What mistake?"

"Martin kept me locked in an apartment. I had access to the internet, but though I could view things, I couldn't comment. I couldn't *do* anything. And while I had complete control over the Tácunan Law computer system, it's locked. There's no internet. No one can hack in if you're not connected. So one day, when he brought me into the company for something, I logged into the system and just stole some random information that had been marked as valuable. It was in a separate file. I figured I could sell it online for money."

"Information on my mother?"

He hesitated. "On your father, actually. Apparently your dad used to work for Tácunan Law. Did you know that?"

Nita hadn't, but it was certainly plausible. He'd been a legal consultant as long as she could remember, he had to get that legal expertise from somewhere.

"Anyway, so it had information on your father. His current

address, current clients, all sorts of things like that. Your mother was only tangentially mentioned." He swallowed, eyes flicking to her and then away. "I didn't have access to the internet, so I bribed one of my jailers. I said we'd split the profit fifty-fifty if he posted the information for sale online."

Fabricio's smile was bitter. "He did. But of course, I didn't get a penny of it. It all went straight to his bank account." He laughed, cruel and angry. "Though it didn't help him in the end. He died before he could use that money. It was only a day after he got paid that your mother showed up at my apartment and killed my jailers, including him."

Fabricio's mouth twisted. "The rest you know. She kidnapped me to blackmail my father into taking the information on your father down, not realizing my father was already dead and I was responsible for the information leak."

And in the meantime, Andrej had bought that information on her father online, and then killed him in his quest for vengeance.

Fabricio was just as responsible for her father's murder as the man who actually killed him.

Nita thought she'd feel anger, that her rage at Fabricio would bubble back up, so large it would devour her whole. But she didn't feel mad. She just felt tired. No, not tired. Relieved. She finally had her answers, she'd finally figured out the start of the domino chain that had ruined her life, and she could feel her shoulders relaxing a little, her body loosening.

She had her answers.

They didn't come with anger. They didn't come with pain. They came with clarity, perfect, wonderful clarity. Nita would murder Fabricio for everything he'd done, of that she was sure. But she wasn't angry at him anymore. It was just one more inevitability, one more thing to do on her checklist.

So much murder, so little time.

They turned away from the water and toward the towering steel and glass towers of Puerto Madero, each of them lost in thought. So much so that Nita almost didn't notice when Fabricio stopped.

"We're here," he whispered.

THIRTY-TWO

THE SUN WAS SETTING. It was a Saturday, and the office was closed, most of the lights off. Nita didn't take any chances, though, and called Diana.

Diana picked up on the first ring, and Nita dove in without preamble. "I'm here, is everything ready?"

Diana's voice was nervous, and a little excited. "Yes. I mean, it took a bit of work, Tácunan Law isn't easy to hack, you know, but CCTV really is a joke security-wise and—"

"Is it off?" Nita interrupted.

"Oh. Not yet. They'll notice when it vanishes. Do you want me to loop it instead?"

"Please."

The sound of keys clicking echoed tinnily on the phone, and Diana said, "Okay. Annnnnnd, you're good."

"Excellent. Call me if there's any issues."

"Will do."

Satisfied that the cameras were taken care of, Nita hung up. Her googling had revealed that Tácunan Law leased out most of the lower floors in the building, but that the upper ones, where the firm worked, were completely inaccessible from the lower floors. It had its own elevator, stairwell, and security.

Which was fine by Nita. It made things less dangerous. If there were people in her way, she knew they were employees of Tácunan Law and should be dealt with accordingly, not random employees of Habitat for Humanity who decided they should work on Saturday for some reason.

She tucked her bag close. She'd prepared for any security they found.

Nita turned to the others and nodded to Fabricio. "All right, lead the way."

Fabricio didn't go to the front door, he went around to the side of the glass and metal monstrosity. Nita and Kovit followed, both watching his every movement.

An emergency stairwell exit blended into the side of the building so well it was almost invisible, innocuously placed behind an artistic patch of flowers. It was the same gray as the rest of the building, and if Nita hadn't known it was there, her eyes would probably have skimmed right past it.

Fabricio typed some numbers into the small covered keypad beside the door. The door beeped twice, and the lock clicked off.

Fabricio hauled the heavy metal door open and gestured to the entrance. "Coming?"

Nita and Kovit exchanged a look, then entered.

They ascended the stairs slowly, sterile concrete steps that went round and round, up and up. They looked like they'd barely been used, and a fine layer of dust covered the railings.

"There's no elevator?" Kovit asked, huffing as he passed the eighth floor.

"There is." Nita answered before Fabricio could. "But if there are security guards in the building, they'll notice the elevator. I want to keep this under wraps if possible. We'll kill them if we need to, but I'd rather just avoid the risk."

Kovit grunted in acknowledgment and continued up the stairs.

She kept her blood highly oxygenated, and she thanked her past self for building muscles and getting rid of all the chemicals that inhibited muscle growth. She was the only one in the trio who wasn't panting with exertion.

As she went, she reminded herself why she was doing this. She thought of all the valuable information she'd get from this office. All the things she could use to blackmail the black market, to bring down INHUP, to control the people who were trying to kill her and sell her body online. The key to getting rid of all her enemies lay in the building, and she was so close she could almost taste it.

It made her nervous. Every time she was this close to anything, something went wrong.

She swallowed, trying not to think of all the problems she'd still have to deal with after she got the information. She'd actually have to implement it. She'd have to twist it and craft it to get rid of the DUL, to take down the black market players.

And no matter what the information here said, it still wouldn't help with her biggest problem, the one she still didn't know how to face.

Her mother.

Nita shuddered softly and pushed that thought from her mind. She'd deal with her mother later. After. When she had the information and the power that came with it. Maybe it would even the playing field a bit.

But even as she thought it, she knew it was just an excuse to avoid the fact that she was no match for her mother, and she had no idea how she'd survive if her mother wanted Kovit dead and Nita back in her power.

When Fabricio finally stopped on the twelfth floor, he leaned against the wall and gasped for breath. He wiped sweat from his brow before turning to the door. Another keypad with another code. He unlocked the door and they were in the office building.

The overhead lights were off, but all the walls were windows, and the sunlight provided more than enough light to see by. The floors were polished white reflective tiles, and the offices and meeting rooms had short, fuzzy black carpets. The walls between rooms were all made of glass, as were the doors, so all the rooms looked like fishbowls. Nita shuddered at the thought of working in a place like this. Big Brother always watching.

She looked around, but there were no guards. No people at all. The whole floor was deserted. Would they really just trust that security cameras and PIN codes would be enough to keep people out?

Nita paused, eyes narrowed. She didn't buy it.

"Where are the guards, Fabricio?" Her voice was soft.

He hesitated, then admitted, "I don't know. There's usually always a few."

On cue, the elevator dinged, and Nita's eyes widened. She gestured for the others to hide before realizing there was nowhere to go because literally every wall was glass.

Instead, she pointed to either side of the elevator door, and Kovit nodded, smoothly moving to one side, while Nita took the other. Fabricio, realizing what was about to happen, wisely ducked out of range beneath a desk.

The elevator doors slid open, and Kovit flicked his switchblade out.

When the first guard stepped out, Kovit darted forward, stabbing him in the neck, instantly severing his spine and killing him.

Nita swung around, darting into the elevator before the body had fallen, her scalpel raised. The guard reached for his gun, but never made it, her blade going into his eyes and up into his brain as she buried it as deep as possible. Kovit stepped in and slit the man's throat for good measure.

They dragged the bodies out of the elevator, and Nita swore as she tried to pry her scalpel from the dead man's eye socket. It was sticky and wet when it came out, and she wiped it absently on his clothes.

From under the table, Fabricio squeaked, "Is it over?"

"It's over." Nita's voice was hard. "Let's get going before more show up."

Fabricio crept out from under his desk, studiously avoiding looking at the dead bodies as he led them down the hall to another office, this one obviously more important because it was huge. Through the glass walls, Nita could clearly see two couches, a coffee table, a massive desk larger than their Airbnb bed, with three monitors on it, and a wall of bookshelves — the only non-glass wall in the whole floor.

Fabricio input another PIN code, and the glass door buzzed open.

The three of them stepped into the room, and Fabricio headed directly for the desk. He powered on the computer and stared at the blank screen for a moment, expression inscrutable, then shook his head, as if dislodging an unpleasant thought.

Nita went around his shoulder, a memory bank in hand. She'd found one that claimed to hold fifteen terabytes — she hoped it was enough. Even if she couldn't get everything, she would be able to get a massive amount of data.

Fabricio entered a series of passwords, pressed his thumb into the scanner, and finally the computer appeared to deem him acceptable and the home screen came up.

Nita plugged the memory bank in and gave Fabricio a look. He shrugged and set the device as a backup machine for what was on the computer.

"Most of the information is on servers, which we host here." Fabricio typed in another password. "But this is the only terminal in the building that can access it all. My father was more than a little paranoid."

"With good cause, it seems," Kovit commented.

"Indeed."

The computer chimed, and then a small window with a

loading bar came up. Time until download completed: thirty minutes.

Nita let out a breath and leaned back. Thirty minutes.

Kovit took off his sunglasses and put them on the desk, rubbing his eyes before sitting on one of the couches on the other side of the room and cleaning his switchblade. He made an unhappy noise when the blood didn't come off. "Is there a sink somewhere I can clean this?"

"The washroom is just down the hall," Fabricio said.

Kovit rose and slipped away, still trying to rub the blood out of the grooves of his switchblade.

Fabricio sat in the plush leather chair across from Nita, hands in his lap. He turned to her. "Is there any information you want to look at before it finishes downloading?"

She hesitated, then nodded. "Yes. INHUP. Anyone associated with it." She pulled out her phone and showed Fabricio the picture of her mother, Nadezhda Novikova, and Zebra-stripes from an old photo. "Especially anyone from this photo."

"Are there names to go with that?" He asked, opening a search bar.

Nita listed off several of her mother's aliases, but none of them came up. Then out of curiosity, even though it didn't matter anymore, it was over and he was gone and never coming back, she had him search her father's name.

The hit was instant, and most of the information was older than she was. She scrolled through a case where he got a serial-killing unicorn off on a technicality years before the Dangerous Unnaturals List was put up. He'd covered up evidence in multiple unnatural trafficking cases. He'd helped set up dozens of offshore accounts for various companies to avoid paying taxes.

Nita had known her father wasn't a good person. He worked with her mother, he helped run the business side of their operation, and he'd never really had an issue killing or selling unnaturals. He'd hidden their money, he'd avoided taxes and the law.

But he'd loved her, and she'd loved him. Even if she was slowly coming to understand that his love hadn't truly included protecting her from the person hurting her the most.

Nita sighed softly. She'd always thought her father was good, but it was nothing but childish illusions. Finding out the depth of his crimes didn't change how much she loved him, didn't rock or shift that core in her heart. It just made her feel lost and a little sad for the naive child she'd been who'd seen her father as the only good person in her life. Who couldn't recognize that "good" was a relative term, who couldn't understand that just because someone loved her didn't make them good.

Nita wasn't sad to see the last of that child disappear, didn't regret letting her illusions finally die. Because even though it made her admit her father was a terrible person, she felt like she could at least see him as a person now. A flawed, weak person, but a person nonetheless.

Fabricio left the desk and wandered to the bookshelves while she read more. He ran his fingers over the spines of the books and finally said, "This was my father's office."

He wore a wistful, sad expression, and Nita asked, "Do you miss him?"

"Every day." Fabricio swallowed and looked down. "I

thought it would get better, you know, the grief. And I suppose it has—it's not as sharp, not as constant as it used to be. But sometimes it comes back full force, and it's like I lost him yesterday."

Nita's chest tightened, thinking of her own father. Gone. Stolen forever.

"Were you close?" Nita asked.

"We were. I was his only kid, and since my mother was gone, we spent a lot of time together. He always took Sunday off, and we'd do something fun. Go to a movie or to see a fútbol—soccer—game, or to Montevideo to lie on the beach." His eyes were sad. "I think he wanted to make sure I didn't feel the loss of my mother. That I had a full childhood, even without her."

"He sounds . . . nice," Nita admitted.

"My father used to try and comfort me about my mother's death by telling me good people die young. They're too good for the darkness in the world." His smile went cruel. "You know what I used to think whenever he told me that?"

"What?"

"If being good means you're going to die young, why would I ever be good?"

Nita blinked, unnerved to hear her own thoughts echoed back at her. "Pardon?"

"Never mind." The computer beeped, and Fabricio nodded at it. "Download's finished."

Nita unplugged her hard drive and tucked it away.

Fabricio looked up and seemed to come to some sort of decision. "I know you don't believe me, but I'm sorry, Nita. I really am. It's my fault you were sold, it's my fault your father was found and killed. I thought I was doing what I had to do to survive, but I didn't really think through the consequences."

Nita's mouth formed a thin line. "So you've said."

His smile was sad. He knew she didn't forgive him, wasn't capable of it. "I hope the information in here is enough to make up for it, but I have a feeling you want blood. I've done so very much to survive, though, and I'm not willing to die yet, even if I deserve it." He met her eyes. "So I'm sorry for this too."

That was when the alarm began to ring.

THIRTY-THREE

NITA WHIRLED AROUND, looking for the source of the alarm, some way to shut it off, *anything*, and in that moment, Fabricio ducked into the adjacent room and locked the door.

Nita stormed over and smashed her fist into the glass surface separating them. "You little shit, what have you done?"

Fabricio shrugged. "I told you, I don't want to die. When you had what you wanted from me, I figured you'd kill me. Vengeance, tying up loose ends. Both."

Nita clenched her teeth. He was right, but that only made her angrier.

"You should run," he said gently. "These glass doors are bulletproof, and you'll waste a lot of time trying to get in here to kill me. Tácunan Law has a security force on standby for situations like this, and they're probably on their way. You should go before they get here."

"And what about when they find you here?" Nita snapped.

Fabricio blinked, then gave her a sad smile. "Me? I'm the

son of the owner. Brutally tortured for the password." He looked down at his hand bitterly, still covered in bandages from Kovit's "ministrations" three days ago. "I've even got the evidence to prove it."

Her fists clenched at her sides as the alarm rang louder and louder. She'd been played again. When would she learn?

"You're a traitorous asshole," she hissed.

"No. I gave you the information you wanted, didn't I? The computer is even wiped—I bet you didn't know that one, did you? I set it so once the backup was done, the servers would be wiped clean. Not even Tácunan Law has the information you have anymore." He gave her a clever smile. "You're the only one in the world with that information."

Nita frowned. "Why? Why would you do that?"

He laughed softly, but there was something almost hysterical in the sound, like he couldn't quite comprehend the magnitude of what he'd done. "To end this company. To destroy it, completely and utterly, so no one will ever hurt me because of it again."

Nita stared at him a long, hard moment. "I'm going to release all your information online. I don't go back on my threats."

"That's fine," he agreed amicably. "I don't see the issue with that now. Martin is dead, he can't send people to bring me back. Tácunan Law has been robbed—and the computers wiped—so I have no information the black market cares about." He considered. "I suppose now that I'm eighteen I'll inherit my father's fortune, though I imagine the collapse of

Tácunan Law will eat up most of it. There's better rich kids to kidnap and ransom."

He grinned at her. "Thanks for getting rid of everything tying me down, Nita. After this, I really can start a new life." His face cleared, and for a moment, he looked like he'd just seen paradise and he wanted to weep from the sight. "I'm finally free."

"You . . ." Nita couldn't even find the words to express her anger. Because he was right—she had nothing on him anymore. Nothing. He'd played her like a violin to deal with all his problems, and now she had nothing left to hold over him.

And even now, played and manipulated and furious, she still felt a little bad for him. There was something so utterly pathetic about his situation and his goals that made her pity him.

She tried to push that emotion away, because that was just another part of his manipulation too. But the emotion persisted, mixing with her anger into some new emotion she didn't fully understand.

Kovit ran into the room, his eyes wide. He grabbed Nita's hand and tugged her toward the door. "Nita, why are you standing here? We need to run!"

Fabricio smiled and tapped his finger on his wrist, indicating a nonexistent watch. "The more time you waste here yelling at me, the less time you have to escape."

"He's right." Kovit pulled Nita away from Fabricio. "We need to go, Nita. Now."

Nita hated that they were right, and she let Kovit pull her

away. She shot one last murderous look at Fabricio before she left. "This isn't over, Fabricio."

He sighed softly, slumping against the glass. "It never is with you."

And then Nita was running, Kovit yanking her along. They sprinted back down the office hallway, nearly crashing into a glass door they could barely see before they got to the stairwell. Nita grabbed the door handle and yanked the massive metal monstrosity open in a single sharp motion. They ducked under the FIRE EXIT sign and pelted down the stairwell, round and round, feet slamming on the concrete stairs.

It would probably have been faster to use the elevators, but Nita didn't want to get caught in them. If they froze or the power was cut, she and Kovit would be trapped, sitting ducks in a metal box.

The alarm blared, and Nita was near frantic by the time they reached the bottom of the stairs. They burst out the side door and ran for the street, hoping security hadn't reached them yet and that they still had time to vanish among the crowds enjoying the evening in Puerto Madero.

The air outside was warm and muggy, even in the darkness of evening, and the sound of tourists chattering and the excited music of a violinist busking whispered through the air.

Nita grabbed Kovit's hand and tugged him toward the water and the bridges that crossed over to reach the rest of Buenos Aires. The sound of an overpowered car engine roared closer, and a massive four-by-four shrieked toward the building, followed by several more.

Kovit swore, and the two of them sprinted for the safety

and anonymity of the tourist sector. Surely they'd be safe with witnesses. Tácunan Law wouldn't want to get the police involved.

They reached the main seawall and quickly vanished into the crowds.

She glanced back once and saw the men going into the building through the front door. She let out a long breath. They'd gotten away in time.

Beside her, Kovit's shoulders relaxed a little. He lifted his head and grinned at her, and she smiled back.

Then she realized: he'd forgotten his sunglasses. His hair was a mess from running.

He looked exactly like the photo that had gone up online.

Her eyes widened, but before she could even form the words, she heard the sound she'd dreaded since he went up on the list yesterday.

"ZANNIE!"

It was impossible to see who'd screamed in the mad crush of tourists and locals. The whole mass of them froze, like the entire world had been put on pause. A woman in a Yale sweater held her umbrella in front of her like a weapon, and cell phones went up immediately, recording whatever was about to happen next. Panicked faces searched the crowd.

And all their gazes shifted to Kovit.

It wasn't because he was the only obviously Asian person there, though maybe that was part of it. But in her panic, Nita had forgotten that Kovit's clothes had been spattered with blood from the guard he killed, and they painted him with a bright red bull's-eye.

"Fuck," Kovit whispered.

Behind them, someone in the crowd pulled out a gun. People nearby saw and dove out of the way, clearing a straight path for the bullet.

Nita shoved Kovit to the side as the first shot went off. The moment after the shot was perfectly silent, like time had stopped, and all that was left was the ringing in her ears.

Then time started again, and she and Kovit stumbled sideways as the bullet smashed into a garbage can behind them, sending it toppling to the ground and rolling across the pavement, spilling trash as it went.

Nita's and Kovit's eyes met, and she whispered, "Run."

And they did, pushing their already tired limbs to new speeds.

The pedestrians came out of their stupor as soon as Nita and Kovit started to run, and quickly divided into two camps. Those who ran screaming in the other direction.

And those who decided it was a good day to hunt a zannie.

The man with the gun was quickly joined by other people. Young men on Rollerblades, tourists in sun hats wielding selfie sticks like batons. Old and young, foreign and local, people began to mass behind them, a slowly forming mob of humans shedding their surface veneer for the once-in-a-lifetime chance to let their inner monsters free without consequences.

A hamburger flew through the air and smacked into Kovit, but he wiped it off and kept running, ketchup smearing across his face and mixing with the blood. A Rollerblading kid zoomed toward them, and Nita tripped him, sending the kid flying into the concrete barrier separating the walkway from the port. Blood spread red along the gray of the barrier, but Nita didn't turn back to see the damage.

Ahead, a massive bridge with old, nonfunctioning cranes loomed, a chance to cross and vanish into the tumbling melee of the rest of the city.

Nita licked her lips and hissed, "Go. Run. Hide. I'll hold them off and meet up with you later."

He didn't question her, just put on a burst of speed.

Nita put on her own burst of speed as Kovit elbowed through crowds of confused tourists who had no idea why he was being followed by an ever-growing mob. Her eyes were glued on a motorbike casually parked by the side of the road.

Nita was very strong. She had no myostatin limiting her muscle formation, and she'd been working on her strength for a long time now.

So when she grabbed the motorbike, she swung it round and round, her body dizzy from vertigo, and then threw it at the mob.

People screamed, ducking out of the way, but they were too tightly packed, and the bike smashed into them and plowed a path through their midst. Voices rose high in panic, and blood coated the sidewalk.

The blood seemed to snap some of them out of their mob mentality, and they backed away, then sprinted off in various directions in panic. But it made others scream louder, eyes wide and unseeing, full of violence and rage that had nothing to do with rationality and everything to do with a hunger to hurt someone that was just as strong as Kovit's.

Nita didn't stick around to see what the swarm did next.

The second after the bike hit, she raced away, feet pounding on the pavement, across the bridge and into the city proper, hoping Kovit had eluded his pursuers and terrified by the knowledge that even if he had, there'd always be more.

THIRTY-FOUR

S HE COULDN'T GO back to the Airbnb because Fabricio knew about it, ditto with the room in the conference hotel. Nita had been using Fabricio's money to buy things while he was their captive, but now that he'd escaped, she didn't want him able to track her, so she used her own stash of money—most of it stolen from that diplomat she'd murdered yesterday—to pay for a hotel room.

She texted Kovit the address, but he didn't respond. She tried not to let the fear creep in, but it was hard. She checked the news, but his name was still on the list, and none of the local channels or social media mentioned his death. Yet.

She took a deep breath and tried to be practical. He would survive or he wouldn't, and there was absolutely nothing she could do about it either way right now. She needed to focus on the things she could do.

She doubled back to stop by the conference hotel to pick up the blood wine and the diplomat's laptop she'd been using. Information from a hard drive wasn't much use if she didn't have a device to read it.

The new hotel was a cheaper one, just off Florida Street. When Nita checked in, the bored hotel clerk gave her two cards and then went back to scrolling through his phone at the reception desk.

Waiting for the elevator, two tourists, women in their late teens or early twenties, were whispering excitedly to each other.

"Did you hear there's a zannie in town? He was spotted by the port!"

"I know! Do you think they've killed him yet?"

"I dunno. I hope not. I really want a chance to see him first. Gosh, I wonder if there's a hashtag tracking him? Think of how many followers I'd get if I could get a video of him being killed!"

"It'd definitely go viral," the other woman agreed, and they all stepped into the elevator.

Nita's fingers dug into the crate of blood wine, and she tried to keep her anger off her face. None of it was real to these people. To them, Kovit wasn't a human, he was just something they could watch from a safe distance, a piece of entertainment, his life only as valuable as the followers they gained from his death.

She hated people.

She got off on her floor and tapped her keycard on her room. The door opened, and she immediately put the wine down and assessed their new space. It was small, with a queen-sized bed, a desk, and not much else. Faded red curtains matched a faded red blanket on the bed.

She closed the door and sat on the bed. It groaned ominously.

She yanked out her phone, but still nothing from Kovit. She texted him the room number, and waited for something, anything.

Finally, she shoved the phone aside. She had things to do, and sitting here worrying wouldn't get them done.

She plugged the laptop in and connected the hard drive. She had a terrible fear that the information hadn't transferred, that something had gone wrong.

But when she plugged the hard drive in, it was all there, all thirteen terabytes of it, an impossibly large amount of information she couldn't imagine where to even *start* parsing.

She stared at it a long moment. This was it. This was the power she craved. Here was the information that could crumble nations, destroy powerful men, change her life.

She had no idea how to use it.

The words blurred in front of her. She didn't know any of these names, didn't know who she needed to blackmail to stay safe, didn't know how to best deploy this information. Didn't know what was important and what was junk, didn't know who was at the top and the bottom.

She let herself be overwhelmed by it all for a moment, the sheer magnitude of what she didn't know, of what she had to learn.

Then she pulled herself together and took out her phone.

Adair picked up on the first ring. "Hello?"

"It's Nita." She forced herself to sound cool and confident. "I have the information. I successfully robbed Tácunan Law."

There was silence on the other end of the line before Adair finally whispered, "Well, damn."

A smile crept across Nita's face at his impressed tone. Just hearing those words made something ease in her chest. She had done something incredible. She could do anything she put her mind to. She would figure all of this out.

"I didn't think it was possible," he admitted. "I'm impressed."

"You shouldn't have doubted me."

"Of course I should have. I'd doubt anyone trying to rob something as big as Tácunan Law. Even if they were a professional. I'm sure people have tried before."

Nita had to admit this was true. "But they didn't have Fabricio."

"Precisely."

For a moment, she thought of just how dangerous it must have been to be Fabricio, knowing that all anyone wanted him for was a chance to steal his father's fortune in information, and she remembered his look of pure happiness and relief as he explained that with no more Tácunan Law, he was free.

"I have the only copy of the information now," Nita told Adair. "The servers there have been wiped."

"And that will be the end for it." Adair's voice was soft. "It's been around longer than I've been alive. It'll be strange to see it go. I wonder what will take its place."

Nita shrugged. "Don't know. Does it matter?"

"Not at the moment." There was a short pause and then he said, "Well, I have some information I want, and you have some misinformation you want me to spread, so shall we get started on this exchange?"

"Let's."

"Do you have anything on Arlene Qiu?"

"Spell that?"

He did, and Nita searched her hard drive. She found the file and clicked on it, horror mounting as she realized that she had more than forty thousand pages of text on file. Documents, court records, account details, correspondence, audio recordings. An impossible number. It would take her a year just to get through one person's data.

How was she even supposed to begin sorting this?

"Do you have anything?"

"I have . . . a lot."

"Define a lot?"

"If I printed it all out and stacked it up, it would probably be as tall as your pawnshop."

He paused. "I know what I'm looking for. Send it all."

"All of it?" Nita's voice was mildly incredulous.

"That's my price. Everything you asked for. I'll have your video with Reyes debunked as best I can. When people come to me to buy information on you, I'll tell them it's fake and that your time in the market was all a clever scam to get in, rob them, and burn it all down. I'll tell them whatever you want to be known for." He paused. "And all the information you asked for, on INHUP, on the list. Anything I know."

Nita was silent a long time. She didn't know how to use the information she had. These documents were probably worth far more than what Adair was giving her for them. But she needed what he had, she didn't have the influence or power to make things happen. All she had was information, and valuable as it was, she didn't have the knowledge to make a counteroffer. Things were only as valuable as they were useful to you.

So even though Nita knew she was getting the bad end of the deal, she said, "Fine. How do you want me to transfer the data?"

He sent instructions on how to upload her files to a private server of his, and she followed them carefully.

"It's going to take a while," Nita said, watching the progress bar crawl along. "There's a lot."

"That's fine." Adair was calm.

The sound of voices laughing in the hall drifted through the small hotel room, almost but not quite covering up the hum of the air-conditioning unit.

"So." Nita kept her voice steady. "I want to know everything you know about Andrej and INHUP and the Dangerous Unnaturals List."

"I see you've found some of the information on your own." A hint of amusement laced his words.

"Yes."

He sighed softly. "All right. So, here's what I know for certain. Nadezhda Novikova had a lover, who was also a founding member of INHUP. He went by the name Andrej Smirnov, but that's likely an alias. I don't know what his real name was—he probably discarded it a long time ago."

Nita turned this over, determined it wasn't important, and said, "Go on."

"They were in a long-term relationship, and they're both listed as founders. Smirnov—no, I'll call him Andrej, I feel like I'm talking about vodka when I say Smirnov—Andrej was never, and can never be, put on the Dangerous Unnaturals List because of all the public pictures of him at INHUP functions. The public doesn't know he's a vampire, but they certainly would if his face made the list. And wouldn't that cause controversy." Adair's voice was bitterly entertained. "That's why he wasn't on the list even though he killed your father and why information on that case was classified. Speaking of, INHUP apparently found video of your father's death. I'm still working to get it, but I should have it soon."

"I see." Nita pursed her lips, trying to push away all the emotions that wanted to boil back up when she thought of seeing a video of her father dying. A part of her wanted it desperately, wanted to see the truth for herself, wanted to know for sure she'd gotten his killer. And a part of her crumbled at the very idea of seeing him die. She didn't want to watch that.

She shoved those thoughts away for another time, and asked, "And Novikova? What do you know about her?"

"In a coma for the past twenty years after a failed assassination attempt. The doctors say she's brain-dead, but pulling the plug requires consent they can't get."

Nita licked her lips, and even though she knew the answer, she needed to hear it. "Who tried to kill her?"

"Ah, there's no actual proof, but I believe it was another founding member of INHUP, a woman who goes by the name Monica Veer. Not her real name, which, I suspect you already knew," Adair said softly.

Nita didn't rise to the unspoken question, and simply asked, "How did Novikova survive at all?"

When Nita's mother went to kill someone, usually they stayed dead.

"Novikova had been drinking vampire blood for nearly forty years. She healed faster and was more durable than any regular human. If she hadn't been drinking so much blood, she'd be dead," Adair explained. "There's so much aggregate vampire blood in her system that she hasn't visibly aged since she was in her mid-thirties."

An idea formed in Nita's head, and she asked, "Do you know where they're keeping her?"

"An INHUP research facility in southern France, near Nice."

Nita actually knew the one he meant. They'd been publishing groundbreaking papers on the long-term effects of vampire blood in humans. Now she knew where they were getting their data.

Nita was silent a long moment, mulling things over. Her computer beeped, and the file transfer was completed.

"Can you access the files I sent?" she asked.

"Yes, I see them." A short pause. "You really weren't kidding about the volume, were you?"

"Nope."

Adair was quiet before asking in a carefully modulated tone, "What do you plan to do with all this information?"

Nita hesitated. "Use it."

"To?"

"Intimidate the market. Take down INHUP and their list."

"Okay." His words were slow and precise, as though chosen

with deliberation. "Do you know what information will do that?"

The words echoed Nita's earlier thoughts so precisely that she wondered if kelpies could read minds.

She opened her mouth to brush him aside, to tell him she had it handled, but what came out instead was the truth. "No."

He sighed softly, a brush of static over the line. "I thought as much." A soft rustle of noise. "Nita, I'm going to make you an offer."

"I won't sell it all."

"That wasn't the offer."

"Oh." She cleared her throat awkwardly. "Go ahead."

"You don't know the value of this information. You don't know how to sell it. You don't know how to use it to its best effect. You overpaid me today—by a lot."

Nita rubbed her temples. "I figured as much."

"I know how to use it." Adair's voice was steady. "I know how to stretch it and manipulate it and leak it and whisper it in the right places to make things happen." He took a deep breath. "Work with me."

Nita thought she'd misheard. "Pardon?"

"I'll partner with you. You have the power, but I know how to use it."

Nita stared at the wall, at the cracks in the plaster that looked a little like a fibula bone. Her first instinct was to reject him, to push Adair and his offer away. She didn't share her power. She needed to be in control—only when she was completely in control would she be safe.

But she forced the instinct down, because it was wrong. She wasn't her mother, obsessed with control at all costs. She *couldn't* do this alone. She *didn't* know how to use the information. Adair was right, much as she hated to admit it. Adair was almost always right. The very thought left a bad taste in her mouth, but she knew it to be true.

"You don't even like me. I nearly killed you." Nita's voice was hard. "What's stopping you from killing me and stealing my information?"

"I told you, Nita, I don't do vengeance. What's past is past. We're both still alive, and this isn't about liking. This is a business partnership, not a marriage proposal. Like doesn't factor in."

"Betrayal does," Nita said. "What's to stop you betraying me?"

He was silent for a long time, then said, "Diana."

Nita blinked. "Pardon?"

"Diana. She wouldn't let either of us betray the other. She may not hold much sway over you, but I won't do anything to make her angry."

His admission came out grudging, and Nita frowned slightly. "You like her, don't you?"

"Of course I like her, I work with her every day. You think I'd hire her if I didn't?"

"No, I mean, you *like* like her."

Adair was silent for a long moment and then said, "I've never understood people's obsession with romance. Why can't I value her for who she is without there being something romantic?"

Nita blinked. She hadn't really thought too deeply about it, or even thought too deeply about her question. Now, though, she wondered. Why *had* she assumed that?

Adair sighed softly, a crackling burst of static on the other end. "People love to think that if you have strong emotions for someone, that if you care for them deeply, it must be romantic. But that's not true. I care about Diana a lot. But not that way."

Nita was quiet. She understood, in a deep, foundational way, what Adair meant. Growing up, she knew there were friends and romances. Life hadn't prepared her for anything else, and whenever she thought about Kovit, and the emotions around him, her mind said it must be romance, because surely a friendship couldn't be that strong. If she felt this powerfully, then it must be something else, something "more," as though friendship wasn't enough and there was a next level of importance.

But what Nita felt for Kovit wasn't necessarily romantic. That didn't mean it wasn't powerful.

Hearing Adair say those words, hearing him give voice to the confusion in her soul released something deep inside her, gave her permission she hadn't known she'd been seeking to understand something within herself.

She cleared her throat. "I understand. I need to think on your offer."

"I have time."

Nita nodded and hung up, then stared quietly at the phone and the information, lost in thought.

THIRTY-FIVE

NITA SAT THERE letting the thoughts tumble around her mind for a while before a knock on the door pulled her out of her stupor. She hesitated, heart racing as she asked, "Yes?"

"Nita?" called the voice on the other side.

Relief flooded her systems, muscles she hadn't realized were tight with tension loosening, and she opened the door and let Kovit in. He wore a giant floppy tourist hat that obscured half his face, and a pair of ugly shades that covered the rest. He'd got a jacket somewhere and had used it to cover the bloodstains on his shirt. He was breathing heavily, from heat or exertion or both.

"Are you okay?" Nita asked, closing the door behind him.

He nodded. "I'm fine. I smell like dead bodies and hamburgers, but I'm fine."

Her breath whooshed out. He took off the hat and the glasses and the coat, and he stumbled over to the bathroom and started washing the dried ketchup and blood from his face.

"What happened?" Nita asked, following him in. "How did you get away?"

"I ran. For a while. I swear every time I thought I'd lost them, they'd find me again and there'd be more of them. But I managed to lose them for a few minutes, and I found some sunglasses in the trash. I can't believe how much these things help." He ripped his shirt off and stuck it under the sink, scrubbing at the blood. "It made it easier to hide from the mob with the coat. I bought it at one of those artisan stands. God, it was hot, though."

"I imagine." Nita leaned against the wall and crossed her arms. "I don't think you can go outside for a while."

"You think?" His voice was bitter, and he wrung the water out of his shirt. It was a little pink. "I'm going to have to live in this room for the rest of my life."

"Hardly," Nita said, but she wasn't sure.

He spread out his shirt, looking at it critically. The stains were mostly gone, and he put it back on, still wet.

"What did I miss here?" he asked.

Nita hesitated, then admitted, "Adair offered to partner with me. He knows how to use the information we got, and I . . . don't."

Kovit nodded. "It's not the worst idea."

Nita raised her eyebrows. "Working with a kelpie who's betrayed me before?"

"Adair's not the worst you could do. He's ruthless when he has to be, but he doesn't hold a grudge, he's damn clever, and he's reasonably sympathetic, for a murderous black market information broker."

Nita sighed and flopped back on the bed. "I know."

"But?"

She hesitated. "But is it . . . is it weak to take him up on it?"

He sat beside her. "Weak?"

"I don't have the knowledge. If I work with him, maybe I can learn it. He can use it more effectively than I can." She closed her eyes. "But I would basically be giving over power to someone else. I worked so hard for this, and the idea of just letting it go . . ."

Kovit hesitated, then slowly said, "I suppose it depends on your goal."

"Goal?"

"You once told me you wanted to be an unnatural researcher." Kovit turned to her, his wet hair dripping on the bed as he lay beside her. "Can you really do that if you're scrambling to try and use this information right? Working with Adair will make it easier — much easier — to pursue that goal safely, and faster."

Her mouth dried. "Yes, it would."

"You'd be giving up power, but was power your ultimate goal? I thought you wanted it so that people wouldn't hurt you, so that they would be too scared to go after you. So you could live your life."

"Yes," she admitted.

He shrugged. "Do you really think you can live your life, the one you claim this is all for, *and* become an information broker more powerful than Adair at the same time?"

Nita was silent for a long moment, thinking. Because Kovit

had a point—what use was power if she couldn't use it to do what she wanted?

She still wanted to be an unnatural researcher. But she also wanted to be so powerful that no one would ever dare try and mess with her again. Giving the information to Adair felt like shifting responsibility, trusting that he would take care of protecting her instead of Nita using the power to protect herself.

She didn't like it.

She put it out of her mind for now. "Let's see how the world is taking our videos."

She pulled out her phone and went online. Kovit scooched closer so he could see the screen, their arms touching and their heads tilted together to look at the news.

The video of Kovit being beaten had created a massive online controversy. Marches protesting the Dangerous Unnaturals List were being scheduled, and several branches of INHUP had been mobbed by angry people on both sides, pro- and anti-DUL.

INHUP posted their own video from Henry's archive after they had, but instead of proving Kovit was a monster, it only authenticated Nita and Kovit's video. At least three legal cases had been brought up.

An avalanche of other stories had started coming out. Anonymous vampires who said they'd never killed anyone, they lived off their significant others' and friends' donations, but feared for their lives. A story about a pair of grieving parents whose neighbor had broken in, murdered, and mutilated their five-year-old son because he was a zannie.

A research firm had done an analysis last year of the damage resulting from the DUL kill-on-sight policy and found that there were twice as many regular people killed by it as dangerous unnaturals. Through mistaken identity, casualties of mob violence, cases of people shooting at suspects and missing, hitting innocents. The mobs formed often committed other crimes after killing their target, and property damage was also high.

"It looks promising," Nita said.

Kovit sighed. "Yeah, but will it actually do anything?"

Nita shrugged. "Time will tell."

He reached over and clicked one of the links. "What's that?"

The article popped up. It was titled VIDEO OF MAN BEATING CHILD ZANNIE LEADS TO ARREST OF MULTIPLE MEMBERS OF MAJOR EAST COAST CRIMINAL FAMILY.

"Holy shit." Kovit leaned forward, eyes wide as he skimmed the article. "They arrested a bunch of members of the Family because they ID'ed Henry from the video."

They scrolled through the article until they got to the bottom and stopped. The reporters had managed to get a sound bite from Gold when she was trying to post bail for the rest of the Family. It looked like she hadn't been arrested with them. Yet.

"Miss Pullman! Miss Pullman!" called a reporter. "What do you say to the claims that your father was grooming you to take over his criminal organizations?"

"Alleged criminal organizations." Gold's tone was frosty, and it was clear that was the end of that topic.

"What do you think of the allegations of coercion and abuse he's facing for forcing a zannie to torture people?" another reporter piped up.

Nita expected Gold to say what she always did: *a zannie is a zannie, it likes torturing people, there's no coercion involved,* or something equally dismissive.

But instead, Gold lowered her eyes, and for a brief moment, she looked infinitely sad. Her voice was steady when she finally answered, "I think that's an issue for the courts to decide."

"But surely you have an opinion on the accusations?"

Gold gave them a bitter smile. "No. I've been forced to face a lot of hard truths recently. I don't know what I think anymore. But I know I'm not the right person to pass judgment."

The reporters tried to ask more questions, but Gold turned and walked away.

Nita and Kovit both stared at the screen, eyes wide.

"Did she just . . . admit she was wrong?" Nita asked.

"Maybe." Kovit's finger hovered over the replay button. "I wonder if something finally got through to her. If having our internet friends kick her out and call her as much a monster as me finally made her face all those things she'd been ignoring."

Nita considered. She found it hard to believe a friendship breakdown could be the final thing that forced Gold to face herself and see her hatred for Kovit as what it truly was—

misdirected self-hatred. But then again, Nita had never really had many friends. Maybe they did have that much power.

"I don't know. Maybe."

Kovit nodded, and his expression was soft and a little sad. "I hope she figures things out."

"Even if she does, I doubt she'll want to be friends with you again," Nita cautioned.

"That's okay." He gave her a slight grin. "As long as she's not hell-bent on murdering me, I'll count it as a victory."

Nita snorted, but she was secretly relieved for the same reason. She hadn't wanted to have to arrange an "accident" for Gold in the future, and she'd been worried she'd need to if the girl continued to try and take down Kovit.

"I'm sorry, though. I know you wanted to fix it, to be friends again," Nita said gently.

He turned to face her, and suddenly they were nose to nose, and he smiled a little. She was so close she could see the shadows cast by his eyelashes across his cheeks.

"It's okay," he whispered, and squeezed her hand. "I lost her. But I gained you."

For a moment, the urge to lean forward and press her lips against his was impossibly strong. To show him that he meant the world to her, that she was always on his side.

Instead, she leaned forward and pressed her forehead against his. It was warm, and they were so close she could feel the heat radiating off his body.

"Nita . . ." he whispered, eyes searching hers.

"Shhhhh," she murmured. "I've been thinking about us. About what I want. About what I feel. About what we are."

His eyes were nervous, fear and longing all tangled together in an expression that made her heart tighten. "And?"

"And you mean the world to me," she whispered. "And you were right. Kissing, romance, sex, all of that. I don't really want it. But I do want *you*. I want this." She waved her hand at him, the room, everything. "I want to lie here with you, talking. I want to curl up next to you while you sleep. I want to rest my head on your chest when I feel bad, and I want to lean my shoulder against yours just to feel you there."

He stared at her a long moment, the soft lines of his mouth curling into a slight smile, his sharp eyebrows drawn, his dark eyes on her. Something shifted in his expression, but she couldn't read what it meant.

She gave him a nervous smile. "Say something."

He looked at her, those beautiful black eyes soft. "I've been thinking too. About what I want. About who I am. About who you are to me. And I still don't know that I've figured it all out yet. Maybe I never will, not completely. But I think, before, I was scared about how it would go wrong. About how everything I didn't know and didn't understand yet could end up making things between us worse. That was flawed logic—it won't go wrong as long as we talk about things, as long as we work together and communicate what we want."

Nita agreed. "I think we've been doing a good job of that lately."

"We have."

He leaned forward then, slowly, and wrapped his arms around her, pulling her body tight against his own, and all her muscles relaxed, because sometimes you didn't need words to understand, and Nita cuddled up against the warmth of his chest, pressing her face into the rumpled fabric of his T-shirt.

His hands were wrapped around her back, and he turned his face into her hair and whispered softly, "What you said, about touching, about supporting, about being near." He swallowed heavily and tightened his grip on her, fingers warm and gentle on her back. "I'd like that. I'd like that very much."

She smiled into him, her head on his heart so she could hear it beating a soothing rhythm, her uncertainty fading as she took his words and held them close. She knew exactly what they were to each other, and she didn't need a word for it. They were themselves, terrible, vicious, and united, and they understood each other and what they each wanted, and that was all that mattered.

They lay like that, a perfect tableau, both smiling as they whispered to each other until they drifted off into warm dreams.

THIRTY-SIX

T HE NEXT MORNING, Nita rose and showered so she could go out and find them breakfast. Kovit, who was essentially trapped in the hotel room, lay in bed, his hair mussed and his eyes bright, drinking vampire blood wine from the bottle while he read through comments on the videos of him. Every once in a while he'd mutter something along the lines of "that's not anatomically possible, asshole." She'd tried to get him out of the comments section, but it was no use, so she left him to it.

She made her way outside. The day was too hot, like every other day, and the streets buzzed with excitement. Whispered conversations swirled around her.

"—they still haven't caught that zannie yet—"

"—heard there's talk about suspending the DUL—"

"—all bullshit to me—"

Nita went to a pizzeria across the way and sat just outside while they made her pizza. Pizza for breakfast was the sort of quality lifestyle independence afforded her, and she enjoyed taking advantage of it.

"Hello, Anita."

Nita froze, her whole body turning to a small, frightened statue at the sound of that voice. She turned, slowly, like she was in a horror movie, until she faced the person behind her.

Her mother.

Her mother, who was trying to kill Kovit. Trying to take Nita back, control her life. Who'd sicced the black market on Nita. Who'd murdered her own best friend.

Her mother's hair hung loose, just touching her shoulders, the red so vivid against the black that it looked more like fresh blood than hair dye. Her eyeshadow was dark blue, as was her lipstick, a blue that almost looked black. She looked like a gothic mermaid, not the kind that sang in Disney movies, but the kind that stole your voice by ripping your vocal cords out with her bare hands.

"Anita, darling." Her mother grinned, thin and sharkish. "How are you?"

Nita opened and closed her mouth like a fish, before managing a choked "Why are you here?"

"Now, now, is that any way to speak to your mother?" Her mother was smiling, but Nita could see the mockery just under the surface.

Nita didn't know how to respond. So she just remained silent.

Her mother's smile widened. "I heard about the mob that ran through the city yesterday, hunting a zannie. Pity they couldn't get him."

Nita's breathing was harsh and sharp, and her heart was loud in her ears. Something bad was about to happen. She could feel it, deep inside. Worse than the dact incident, worse than when Nita had freed Fabricio, worse than anything her mother had ever done to her before.

"Please," Nita whispered, her voice soft.

"Please?" Her mother laughed. "Please what? Please fix what that incompetent mob couldn't accomplish?"

"Please leave him alone," Nita whispered.

"Oh, darling," Her mother tut-tutted. "It's too late for that."

Nita's eyes drifted across the street to the hotel. *Too late?*

She needed to get back to Kovit. Now.

Her mother's hand reached across and grabbed Nita's shoulder. "You're not thinking of running off without me, are you?"

Nita swallowed, part of her wondering if she could break her mother's iron hold, the rest of her knowing it was impossible.

Her mother slid an arm around Nita's shoulders. Nita kept her back straight and tried to lean away as she was yanked close to her mother. "Why don't we go up and visit him together?"

"Let go." Nita tried to make her voice firm, but it came out as a squeak of terror.

Her mother held on tighter. "I don't think so."

They walked back across the street, Nita's steps stumbling and awkward as they entered the hotel and boarded the elevator.

"You know, Nita," her mother said, shaking her head, "I tried to be nice. I tried to give you a little bit of freedom so you could understand why coming home was important. But you just kept running off on your own and talking about not coming back. It was terribly rude."

Nita didn't say anything, her throat too choked with fear, her mind too occupied running through escape plans, each more elaborate and doomed to failure than the last.

"You've led me on a merry chase, but it's time for it to end." Her mother's voice was hard.

The words were out of Nita's mouth before she could stop herself. "And if I don't fall in line, you'll kill me like you did Nadya?"

Her mother raised her eyebrows. "Well, someone's been talking to people."

"You didn't answer me."

"If you're smart and see the wisdom in coming home, I won't have to resort to drastic measures." Her mother's tone was steady, but Nita could hear the anger underneath. "Nadya was too corrupted by her time with that monster. But you're younger, you've been influenced less. I'm sure it won't come to that."

Nita couldn't help the small, hysterical laugh that bubbled up.

Her mother was delusional. Absolutely, completely delusional. She was so lost in her own world, so focused on controlling every piece of the people around her, that she made up these elaborate reasons why no one would come back to her. She couldn't acknowledge that no one ever wanted to be under someone else's control—especially not someone like her mother.

"What's so funny?" her mother asked.

Nita just shook her head, fear bubbling in her chest. "So, what? Are you going to shoot Kovit?"

"Nonsense." Her mother smiled as the elevator dinged on their floor. "I have something much more illuminating in mind."

Her mother dragged Nita down the hall and stopped not in front of Nita's room, but the room next door. She shoved Nita inside roughly. The moment they crossed the threshold, her mother drove a knife into the back of Nita's neck.

Nita opened her mouth to cry out, but she was completely paralyzed. The knife had gone between the C1 and C2 vertebrae, where Nita had stabbed Andrej, except her mother had pushed the knife right through her voice box, effectively muting Nita.

She collapsed bonelessly to the floor, completely powerless, and her mother stepped over her limp body. "I can't have you trying to run off now," her mother commented, pulling up a chair to face the wall. "I prepared a show especially for you, and it would be a shame for you to miss it."

Nita tried to open her mouth, to say something, but only a thin line of drool trickled out. She focused her body, trying to heal the damage, but the knife was still wedged in there, blocking her from healing it.

The irony that she'd used the exact same tactic on Andrej wasn't lost on Nita.

Her mother hauled Nita up onto the chair facing the wall. She flicked on the television, and to Nita's horror, it showed her and Kovit's room. There must be hotel security cameras in each room, and her mother had hacked the feed.

Kovit lay sprawled on the bed, scrolling through his phone, completely oblivious.

Someone knocked on the door.

Kovit looked up. "Nita? Is that you?"

A beat of silence passed before a voice whispered, "No. It's me."

Kovit blinked, clearly startled, then rose and walked to the door and opened it.

His sister stood on the other side. She wore plain clothes, a T-shirt and jeans rather than the impeccable business suit Nita had last seen her in. Which made sense, since Nita was pretty sure INHUP had fired her.

Her mother leaned forward, and whispered in Nita's ear, "You have no idea how much fun I had setting this up."

A chill whispered down Nita's damaged spine, and tears of frustration pooled at the corners of her eyes. Something terrible was about to happen, and she was powerless to stop it.

"Pat!" Kovit smiled hesitantly as his sister stepped in and he closed the door behind her. "What are you doing here? How did you find me?"

Patchaya's hands were curled into fists, and she whispered softly, "You killed him, didn't you?"

Kovit frowned, his eyes concerned. "Killed who?"

"Bran. You killed him."

Kovit didn't look any more enlightened. "Who's Bran?"

She whirled on him, her eyes watering, rage in her voice. "Don't fuck with me! I spoke to Agent Quispe. The moment you went up on the DUL, she came forward and identified you as one of the kidnappers! She said you were the one in the driver's seat, that she saw you right before someone tranquilized her. You kidnapped Fabricio, Quispe, and Bran, and Bran is the only one who hasn't reappeared."

Kovit's eyes widened, and he whispered, "Pat—"

"Don't you 'Pat' me!" she shrieked, voice rising. "He was my best friend! We went through basic training together, we'd known each other for years! He was the only one I ever told about you, he would have helped get rid of the DUL! He would have been on our side! And you—you—"

Her voice broke, and she burst into tears, as though she'd been bottling up all her pain and fear and anger and grief and it had exploded out in a wave of sobs, choking on her own emotion.

Kovit looked stricken, and he took a step back. "I didn't know. Pat, I'm so sorry."

"Sorry? You're sorry?!" Patchaya stepped forward, hands gesturing wildly. "You're sorry about *what*, Kovit? What did you do to him?"

Kovit looked away. "You really don't want to know."

Patchaya flinched like he'd slapped her. "Oh, God. You—I didn't—oh, God."

"Pat—" He took a step toward her.

"Don't come near me!" she snarled, and suddenly her gun was in the air, and Kovit froze. "Stay back!"

"I'm sorry, I didn't know." Kovit's voice was soft, and Nita knew he was remembering the way he'd made that INHUP agent scream. "I'm so, so sorry."

"No, you're not." Her voice was suddenly flat, and Nita's skin prickled. It was not a good tone. "You're not 'sorry.' You don't regret your actions. The only thing you regret is that I found out."

Kovit blanched.

Patchaya took a step forward. "You don't feel bad for what Bran went through, what *you* put Bran through. You don't feel bad for what I've gone through, the loss of a friend, the grief at knowing his final hours must have been horrific. No." Her voice turned vicious. "You feel bad that you have to face consequences for it. You feel bad because now you have to look me in the eye and admit what you've done."

"I'm sor—"

Patchaya interrupted, her voice calm, so calm. "No, Kovit. You're not."

In the silence that followed, Nita's mother curled her fingers over Nita's shoulder and leaned forward to whisper in her ear. "Here it comes."

Nita didn't want it to come. Because she could already see where this was going to go.

"You're a monster, Kovit," Patchaya said evenly. "I'd hoped, I'd really hoped, that you wouldn't end up one. That you'd be able to maintain control, that you wouldn't give in to your violent urges and become a serial killer like every other zannie."

"I'm not a serial killer," Kovit said, voice soft. "I haven't lost control. I'm still me. Just . . . just a little darker."

Patchaya's laugh was bitter and sharp. "Kovit, you're deluded if you think you're in control. Do you think control means you pick who you hurt? Because that's not control. Control is when you don't hurt anyone, when you resist the violence within. Control isn't just picking your victim."

Kovit was quiet. After a long moment, he looked down at the gun in Patchaya's hand and whispered, "Are you going to kill me?"

Patchaya laughed, wet and broken, her fingers tight on her gun. "I came here to stop you. To avenge Bran, to put an end to this."

Kovit swallowed. "Pat—"

"Shut up."

They stood there for a heartbeat, then two, completely silent, Patchaya's chest heaving as she steadied herself, gun high, and Kovit stared at her with dark eyes.

Finally, Patchaya lowered her gun and turned away, tears streaming down her cheeks. "Don't talk to me, now or ever again. As far as I'm concerned, my brother died ten years ago."

Then she spun around and left, slamming the door behind her.

Kovit stared after her, before slowly falling to his knees on the old carpeting.

Nita's muscles loosened. It was okay. Patchaya hadn't been able to go through with it. Her mother's plan had failed. Kovit was all right.

Nita's mother clicked her tongue, jerking Nita's attention away from the screen. "Well, that's annoying." She sighed heavily. "But as they say, if you want something done right, you have to do it yourself."

Then she raised her own gun and shot through the paper-thin wall into the room next door.

THIRTY-SEVEN

KOVIT HAD BEEN SHOT BEFORE. When they'd both been trapped in a cage together in Death Market, they'd tried to escape their captors, a fight had ensued, and a stray bullet had caught Kovit in the side. Nita had stitched it up, he took antibiotics, and he recovered.

But a stray bullet is not the same as a bullet shot by her mother aiming to kill.

It didn't matter that it was through the wall, or that they were watching through a TV screen. Her mother had practice and aim, and Kovit went down in a spray of blood.

Nita tried to scream, but she was paralyzed, and all that came out was a terrible, broken croak.

Her mother nodded approvingly as Kovit choked onscreen, his body sprawled across the floor, blood seeping out and pooling around him.

"I've still got it." Her mother laughed, harsh and cruel.

Tears streamed down Nita's face at her own uselessness.

On the screen, Kovit gasped, hand weakly coming to cover his wound, even as the blood pooled around him.

A sudden sharp pain rocked Nita's spine, and it took her a heartbeat to realize her mother had pulled the knife out. She immediately started healing the damage.

"Go say goodbye to your little monster. I imagine you'll need a little bit of alone time to think through things. I'll be waiting for you in my hotel." Her mother's eyes hardened. "Don't make me wait long."

Then with a cheery wave, her mother was out the door and gone.

Nita didn't focus on the future, on what she'd do about her mother, she spent all her energy healing her spine, re-fusing vertebrae and nerves. The moment she could move, she was out the door and smashing into her and Kovit's room.

Kovit turned to her when she entered, his face spattered with his own blood, eyes unfocused. "Nita?"

"I'm here," she whispered, yanking out her phone and calling 911. "I'm here, Kovit. It's going to be okay."

His eyelashes fluttered like butterfly wings, and he gave her a cracked smile. "I don't think it is."

The blood was pooling around him, and the stain on his shirt was a deep, dark red. His chest was rising and falling in jerky motions, and his breathing was wrong. There was a strange, sucking sound coming from his chest when he inhaled, and glops of blood burbled against his shirt.

"Don't talk like that," Nita hissed. "You're going to get through this."

He just smiled slightly and fumbled for her hand with his bloody one. "Thank you, Nita. For everything."

"Stop talking like that." Her voice rose in panic, because the more he spoke, the more real it made things.

His eyes fluttered closed. "It's okay. This is how it was always going to end for me."

"Bullshit!" she screamed, hating that he was so accepting, that he wouldn't fight back against the path that the world had put him on. "That's bullshit, and you know it!"

But he didn't respond, his chest gasping and gaping, and his head lolling limply.

Then she was connected to the emergency line, and she had to listen to them rather than to Kovit. She covered his wound with a piece of duct tape to keep the blood in and the air out. The person on the other end of the line was calm and collected even as they said things like "punctured lung" and "sucking wound" and "critical condition."

When the EMTs finally came, they hauled Kovit onto a stretcher and calmly wheeled him to the elevator bank. The police had arrived at some point, not that Nita cared. She just hoped no one decided to shoot him again because he was a zannie.

She choked on the thought and stuck close to Kovit, praying that they'd help him, that the people here were anti-DUL, that they'd let him live.

One officer came over to talk to her, but paused when he saw Kovit's face, doing a double-take. Kovit had been recognized. His hand went to his weapon, but another man put his hand on the policeman's arm.

"Didn't you see the notice this morning? The DUL is temporarily suspended pending investigation."

Nita had won. She'd gotten the DUL suspended. Kovit being alive wasn't a crime anymore.

A part of her wanted to laugh at the irony of it all. So much time and effort fighting to get the DUL suspended, all her manipulations and plans finally came to fruition.

But it was too late.

What did it matter now? Maybe the hospital wouldn't legally be allowed to kill him, but he could die in surgery anyway, and Nita would never know if it was murder or not. No one would.

Nita had won everything and somehow lost what she was fighting for in the first place.

She linked her bloody fingers through Kovit's limp ones, not knowing if she was trying to comfort him or herself as the policeman joined them with the EMTs in the elevator.

Part of her wanted to scream at the EMTs. They were so calm and slow and methodical and *slow* and she just wanted them to move *faster*, help him *more*. But they remained slow and steady as they all climbed into the ambulance and sped toward the hospital.

The officer tried to ask her a few basic things while they were in the ambulance. Did Nita know who shot Kovit? No, it was someone in the room next door. The officer nodded like he expected as much and remained silent. The EMTs cut Kovit's shirt off and exposed the gaping hole in his chest. They shoved tubes down his throat with sharp precision and connected him to an IV drip.

"Do you know his blood type?" one of the EMTs asked her.

Nita stared at him for a moment, and then touched her

bloody hand to her mouth, making Kovit's blood a part of her, letting it dissolve on her tongue. And when it was a part of her, she could identify it, she could manipulate it, same as any other part of her body.

"B positive." Her voice was hoarse.

He made a note, and Nita swallowed her panic, a desperate idea taking form. "I'm type O negative. Does he need blood?"

He did indeed need blood, and they set up the transfusion bag as the ambulance screamed toward the emergency room.

Nita wasn't actually O negative, but she could manipulate her body to be anything, and she changed her blood as it filtered into the bag, hoping desperately that all those fools on the black market were right, that consuming her body really did give a person immortality or faster healing or anything remotely useful. She'd never wanted any of the marketing scams around her to be right before, but at this moment, she wished she were made of magic, that everything said about her was true, that it was within her power to save Kovit.

Drops of her blood filtered into his veins, but his eyes remained closed, and his wound remained open and vicious.

At the private hospital the policeman had insisted the ambulance go to, the halls were sterile and strangely empty, making it feel creepy and haunted. Nita had expected a big crowded hospital with thousands of people and beds in the hall, overworked and underpaid staff. This place gleamed with money, and a small part of Nita wondered how she was going to pay for this. But that was a problem for later, and she shoved it aside.

Nurses wheeled Kovit away, right into surgery. Nita

grabbed the doctor as he followed beside Kovit, and she whispered, "Will he be okay?"

The doctor looked at her, and she knew, she just *knew*, in that moment, that Kovit would not be okay. That no one here believed he would survive this.

But all the doctor said was, "We'll try."

And then they wheeled the stretcher away, and he was gone.

THIRTY-EIGHT

NITA STARED AFTER KOVIT as though if she watched the white surgery doors long enough, she would develop x-ray vision and be able to see what was happening beyond. A nurse directed her to a short row of chairs and a small table with pop culture magazines on it.

"You can wait here," the nurse said, her face lined and her eyes soft. "It will be a while, but I promise, the minute I have news, I'll come tell you. Okay?"

Nita didn't respond, only sort of hearing what the nurse was saying. The nurse gave her a gentle pat on the shoulder and then quietly retreated.

Nita stood there, staring at the wall, hands covered in blood, Kovit's blood, wondering if she'd just seen him for the last time. The nurse returned at some point with wet wipes, a towel, and a pair of scrubs. Nita took it all in her bloody hands and let the nurse lead her to the bathroom.

The nurse spoke slowly and carefully, as though if she said too many words too fast, Nita would just shatter from the pressure. "You take all the time you need. Wash the blood off. You'll feel better after you're clean, I promise."

Then Nita was left in the bathroom. It was a handicapped one, large, with sparkling clean white tiles and walls. Nita dripped dark blood on the floor as she stumbled in, marring the pristine surfaces. She put the scrubs on a small shelf by the door and wandered over to the sink.

Her reflection stared back at her from the mirror. She looked dead. It wasn't just the blood on her face or the waxiness of her skin. It was the expression in her eyes. The expression of someone who has lost everything. The expression of someone broken.

Kovit wasn't going to make it.

Part of her demanded that she shouldn't think like that, that he wasn't dead yet, but she'd seen the doctor's look, the EMTs' expressions. She knew the chances were low.

And even on the slight chance he did make it, her mother wouldn't let it last. Was her mother here at the hospital even now, waiting for a chance to sabotage the surgery? How would she go about it, Nita wondered, thoughts almost clinical. She could cut the power. Or poison Kovit. Even just take his IV out. Swap the blood bags.

Or she could just tell the staff to look at the news. They'd all see he was a zannie, and even though the Dangerous Unnaturals List was suspended now, someone would take matters into their own hands, thinking they were doing the right thing. There was always going to be someone.

A choked sob made its way from Nita's throat, scraping the

skin at the back of her throat with its force, and she crumpled to the floor, blood on her hands staining the towel she'd been given, coloring the pure white with death.

She thought of Kovit, with his beautiful black eyes, the way he smiled just for her. Not his creepy smile, his weaponized grin of violence and fear. No, she thought of the soft one he gave her when she laid her head on his chest, the gentle one that was full of childish wonder. The genuinely sweet one that was all him, none of the darkness seeping in.

She swallowed heavily, a barrage of memories playing through her head of all the different Kovits she knew, all the different faces he wore. She thought of the expression he made when people were cruel to him, internalizing his hurt so that no one could see it. She thought of all the conversations they'd had, how little he felt he truly knew himself, how much he wanted to learn.

She remembered the pure joy on his face when he'd seen Buenos Aires. And she remembered the cracked and broken soul he'd worn on his sleeve after he killed Henry.

She closed her eyes. They'd managed so much together, from escaping and destroying the market where they'd met to evading black market hunters and setting Kovit free of the Family. It seemed so unfair that here, at the end, when they were so close to a fresh start, when the list was crumbling and the future was full of possibility, that it should all end. They'd always had the cards stacked against them. She supposed it was only a matter of time before they were dealt a losing hand.

She clutched the towel close, pressing it to her chest like it could stem the blood flowing from the wound in her soul, trying to imagine what she'd do without Kovit. The hard truth was, she could still do everything. Her life wasn't over. She could still go to college. She could still have power over the black market. She could still live her life.

But it felt empty. Hollow. Like the whole world had lost its color. She didn't need Kovit to achieve her dreams. She didn't need his help against the market. Kovit wasn't a tool she'd lost, or a change of plans. Kovit was Kovit. He was the person who held her when she cried. Who entwined his enemies with hers, so that she wouldn't be alone. He bought her breakfast and told corny jokes. He slaughtered the people who tried to hurt her. He made her smile.

There, on the floor of the bathroom, Nita finally broke down. She curled in a puddle of his blood, clutching the towel, as the wound in her soul bled her dry, spilling out in her tears until she was empty inside.

THIRTY-NINE

WHEN NITA FINALLY CAME OUT of the bathroom, she was a little more put together. She wore the scrubs and had washed most of the blood from her skin. Her face was still waxy, and her eyes were still dead, but she wasn't covered in the blood of her best friend anymore, and that made a lot of difference.

A policeman was waiting for her in a chair by the bathroom, and he rose when she approached.

"Can we talk?" he asked. He kept his voice slow and gentle, and it was clear he was trying to be considerate of her shock.

All she wanted to do was tell him to fuck off. To slide Kovit's switchblade across his throat. He was an obstacle in the way of her one and only goal, the last thing in this gray world that had any color in it.

Kill her mother.

That was all that was left. Kill her mother, end this once and for all. Get vengeance for Kovit, vengeance for herself, end her mother's brutal control over Nita's life.

After that . . . Well, there wasn't an after that. Nita couldn't envision it. She knew it wouldn't bring back the color, knew it wouldn't fix what was already broken. But she'd feel goddam good doing it.

"Señorita?" The policeman sounded worried.

Nita forced her hands to unclench, forced her mind away from the switchblade and her mother. If Kovit did survive, she wanted him to have a chance. On that slim possibility the world would be good to her, she needed to cover for him. She needed to protect him.

So she nodded and forced herself to reply with, "Yes. We can talk."

The policeman led her back to the waiting room chairs, giving her worried glances. She seated herself on a black plastic chair, and he brought her a cup of water. She didn't drink.

"Am I correct in assuming that's Kovit Sangwaraporn in surgery right now, the zannie all over the news the past couple of days?"

There was no point denying it. "Yes."

"And you are?"

"Nita."

"Nita . . . ?"

Nita tried to remember what name she was using with INHUP. She had so many aliases, it felt weird to actually use her real birth name. "Anita Sánchez."

He waited a moment for her to give the rest of her name, but she didn't have more. They'd used American naming customs, so she only had her father's surname.

"And what's your relation to Kovit Sangwaraporn?"

"He's . . ." Nita chose her words with care. "He's my friend."

The officer nodded slowly. "How did you meet?"

"On the black market. We'd both been kidnapped and were up for sale."

The policeman was taking notes. "And you're . . ."

"I'm harmless," Nita lied.

"How did you two end up for sale on the black market?"

"I was kidnapped. Wrong place, wrong time," Nita whispered. "Kovit had been a prisoner of a mafia group for years. They finally got tired of him resisting their demands and decided to sell him."

"Demands?"

Nita met his eyes. "You've seen the videos."

The policeman stilled. "I have."

"I don't really need to explain what his life was like, then, do I?"

"No." The man sighed softly. "No, I got it." He cleared his throat. "So what happened next?"

"We escaped, and we both made our way to INHUP."

"Both of you?"

"Yes," Nita lied, weaving her story to match as closely to the truth as possible but adding her own flavor to it. "He had a lot of information on that mafia group in the States. The one recently arrested after the videos came out. They were . . . bad. Really bad. I think he knew INHUP would probably kill him anyway, but I think he also felt like he had to stop the people who'd hurt him for so long, who'd made him hurt others."

The policeman had started recording her. That was fine. Nita didn't want to have to tell the story again. She hoped it got leaked. She should have recorded it herself.

"What happened at INHUP?" the policeman asked.

"I don't know all the details. We didn't get to see each other much after I went into protective custody. The news keeps talking about how he was dating that INHUP agent, but that's not true. She's his sister. But they'd been separated when INHUP killed their parents a decade ago." Her eyes flicked to the policeman and then away. "Kovit was in some sort of INHUP witness protection thing for a while, and they spent a lot of time together while he informed on the mafia group that had kept him prisoner. But after INHUP had all the information they needed, she turned around and betrayed him. She put him on the list and—" Nita swallowed a huge gulp of air, not needing to fake the shaking in her hands. "He got shot."

The officer was silent, before he responded slowly. "That's a pretty hefty accusation."

Nita snorted, then wiped her nose because it was snotty from crying. "I haven't got any proof either. I mean, I'm sure there's records in INHUP but . . ."

"INHUP wouldn't release them," agreed the police officer. "You said you went to INHUP too?"

"I stayed with them in the Bogotá office for a while. My case worker was Agent Ximena Quispe."

The officer made a note, and Nita twisted her web of truth and lies tighter and tighter. If he went and investigated, if anyone did, they'd be able to prove a lot of this—just not all of it. And the parts they couldn't prove would be the parts INHUP would want to hide.

It wouldn't hold up in a court. But it might hold up enough to keep Kovit safe. If he survived.

Even if he didn't. Even if her mother won, even if Kovit was gone forever, and she could never get him back, at least she'd be able to take down the Dangerous Unnaturals List. Surely that would be something? A sad conciliatory prize, but something.

He swallowed, then said carefully, "I've not seen you on any of the other coverage about the DUL."

"No. I was filmed on the black market demonstrating my ability, and now I'm worth a lot of money. I've been in hiding — or trying to be in hiding. I was in Toronto, and things got . . . violent. Black market hunters everywhere trying to kill me. INHUP was useless at protecting me. So I've tried to stay out of the limelight. I don't want them to find me again." Nita took a deep breath, then continued, "Kovit was helping protect me. People are scared of zannies, and he can fight well. After the disaster where INHUP betrayed him and couldn't adequately protect me, we met back up so we could keep each other safe."

The officer was silent for a long moment. "That's quite a story."

"I know."

"I'll need to talk to my superiors. Do you need a protective detail here?"

Nita shook her head. "I don't want anyone to know I'm here. I'm scared. Kovit's already got enough attention without the black market finding out about me being here."

"I see."

Nita hesitated. "But Kovit will need one. If . . . if he survives."

The officer sighed. "I'm aware. We've got some people here already."

It made Nita uneasy, having the police so close. But she couldn't see any alternative, so she just nodded. "Thank you."

The officer looked down, frowning. Nita couldn't tell how much of her story he believed. But he'd believe a lot more once he started researching Nita. She hoped.

She rose. "I'm going to go get some food from the cafeteria. Do you have any more questions?"

He shook his head. "No. Do you have a phone number?"

She gave it to him, and one of her burner emails, then said quietly, "But you won't need to use them. I'll be here, at the hospital until . . ."

Until the end.

He grimaced, understanding her unspoken words. "Thank you for your cooperation. We'll be in touch."

Nita stared at the floor as he walked away. Lies upon lies upon lies. She wondered how long it would take the world to untangle them all. Hopefully long enough that Nita would have vanished without a trace by the time they realized how much wool had been pulled over their eyes. Long enough to keep Kovit safe in the hospital.

But there was only one thing that could ever truly keep her safe.

Nita rose and headed for the doors.

It was time to end this.

FORTY

OUTSIDE, THE SKY was still blue, and the sun beat down. The air was warm, and the city was bustling with noise and laughter. It was a beautiful day. The kind of day people wrote poems about, did their wedding shoots on.

The kind of day people died.

Nita took the subway south. She got off at Catedral station and walked the twenty minutes the rest of the way to San Telmo. Wide roads gave way to older cobblestoned streets. It was Sunday, and a massive antique market sprawled down all the side streets, people selling leather books and maté cups, artisanal dulce de leche and candles. Inside the buildings, more shops had been set up, these ones full of antiques and curiosities, nineteenth-century microscopes sitting next to Barbie dolls still in their packaging. The antique shops reminded her a bit of Adair and his strange pawnshop, and a part of her longed to be back in Toronto with Kovit, in simpler times.

Nita paused at one shop, full of antique weaponry, ancient pistols and swords and knives, all of them polished and sharpened, ready to find a new home. She considered them for a moment, imagining herself walking into her mother's hotel room with a double-bladed axe strapped across her back. While the image was tempting, it would ultimately be pointless.

Nita couldn't beat her mother in a straight fight.

Her mother had decades of experience on Nita and had been hunting and killing unnaturals far more powerful than herself for years. In terms of skill, strength, and ruthlessness, Nita would never win in a straight fight.

Which was why she had a very different plan.

Her mother had emailed Nita the hotel address and room number. It was in the heart of the San Telmo district, surrounded by colorful historic mansions crammed together in a sea of faded glory, and a few blocks away from Plaza Dorrego, the center of the Sunday market and the home of tango. It was a huge tourist trap, and Nita hated how crowded it was as she squeezed her way between people on the narrow cobblestoned streets.

The hotel was old but well cared for, and it had an aging, retro feel to it that made it seem quirky rather than dated. The bottom looked like it had once been part of a grand house, and the top floors were a newer addition, made of brick that didn't match the lower level.

She took the elevator up to the eighth floor. Her own reflection stared back at her in the mirrored elevator walls, shadows under her eyes and something both very empty and very dark caught in the reflection of her gaze.

She walked down the long hallway to the end and stood in front of the door for a long moment. This was it. The moment she'd never thought would actually come, yet somehow had always known had to happen. She expected to feel some sort of regret or resistance. This was her mother, after all, and for so long, she'd been the only person in Nita's life. Nita had truly believed her mother loved her.

And maybe she did, in her own way. But that wasn't the kind of love Nita wanted.

But though she'd expected some reluctance in her heart when she stood here, there was nothing. Only cold, stony determination.

She adjusted her backpack and knocked on the door.

Her mother opened it quickly, a broad smile blooming on her face. She'd reapplied her lipstick, and it was a bright vivid red, like an artificial candy.

"Nita." Her mother opened the door wider. "I see you've seen sense."

"Yes," Nita agreed. "I have."

Nita stepped into the room. It had two beds, each with a baby blue comforter. Sheer white curtains covered the window, and a small electric kettle sat on top of a mini fridge. A hard-case carry-on suitcase was tucked in the corner, the same blood red as her mother's fingernails.

Her mother closed and bolted the door. Nita barely suppressed a flinch at the sound of the bolt sliding home. It felt too much like she'd walked back into a cage, and the bolt was the lock sealing her inside.

Her mother breezed past. "So, I've been thinking we should move to India next. So many unnaturals there to hunt, and I've never really had a chance to explore the country. What do you think? We could kill some nagas—you know their venom goes for a high price online."

Nita imagined the idea of being in her lab, a half snake person on her dissection table, and a part of her delighted a little at the idea of dissecting something new.

Her mother had always known how to appeal to Nita. To throw the carrot in with the stick, as Fabricio would have said.

"Whatever you think is best," Nita commented noncommittally.

Her mother laughed. "Oh, someone's in a mood. Are you angry about this morning?"

"No," Nita said. She wasn't angry. She was something, all right, but the emotion had long since transcended anger and formed into something entirely new. Determination? Resolution? "I'm not."

Her mother paused and looked Nita up and down. She frowned. "You really aren't, are you?"

Nita shrugged.

"Well, good." A smile, wide and sharkish. "That makes things so much easier."

Nita didn't respond. She put her backpack on the bed, and it bounced gently before settling. Then she quietly walked to the window to pull the curtains back and look out at the view below. It looked over the roof of another building, and the building beyond that blocked any hope of seeing the rest of the city.

Her mother eyed the backpack. "Is that everything you have?"

"Yep. Just two changes of clothes, a book, and a laptop."

Her mother's tone suddenly dropped into something dangerous. "You know you're not allowed a laptop."

Nita did know that. Her mother hated the idea of Nita having her own computer. She'd always hogged the one they did have, doling out uses of it sparingly, always keeping control over Nita's internet time and access.

Her mother didn't want Nita getting ideas, after all.

But Nita just stared at her with dead eyes. "It's mine."

Her mother's jaw tightened, and her voice was cold. "I see you've learned some sass out there in the world. We're going to have to fix that."

Nita flinched, a fear as old as she was crawling through her heart and settling in her chest, making her nauseous. That was the tone that meant dead animal bodies in her bed.

Her mother went to the bag and scooped it up, her expression cold and angry. Nita had no doubt she had some dramatic demonstration of control planned. Shattering the laptop over her knee. Throwing it in the toilet. Something to show Nita who held the power here.

Her mother always had to be in control of these things.

Nita knew that. So when she'd decided to finally end this, she'd taken what some might call the cowardly way out. Nita called it practical.

Google had told her easy ways to make a bomb using household chemicals, and she'd spent the last hours carefully building the device inside her backpack.

When her mother ripped it open, she severed the lining

keeping two different chemicals apart. Their molecules mixed, and the chemicals bonded to each other, starting a chain reaction.

Nita ducked behind the desk near the window as the bomb exploded.

The blast wave hit her before the sound did. She'd made the bomb as powerful as she could, knowing her mother's ability to heal and knowing that Nita herself would be farther away and would also be able to heal.

She might have gone a little overboard.

A ball of fire smashed outward, crashing through the window and into the world beyond. Nita braced as the force ripped the skin from her hands, her bones shattering and her muscles melting. The desk she cowered behind was crushed, and flying shards of glass rained down on her. She'd held her breath so the flames wouldn't get inside and melt her from within, but her flesh was blackened and cracked.

If she were human, she'd have died instantly.

But she wasn't, and she'd been prepared. She'd shut off all her ability to feel pain, which allowed her to focus on healing herself quickly, rebuilding melted muscles, fusing shattered bone, regrowing layers of skin that had been scorched off.

She'd closed her eyes and covered them for the blast itself to avoid having them boiled too badly, and when she opened them, the whole room was black with ash. Black walls, charred beds, ash all over the floor. It looked like a dragon had breathed fire across the room.

Nita healed her burst eardrums, and sound flooded back

into the world. The fire alarm rang tinnily, and the faint sounds of screams from outside echoed through the room like the voices of ghosts.

Her mother was gone.

Chunks of cooked flesh were spattered across the room, charred beyond all recognition. A few pieces of a spinal column lay on the floor, and one of her mother's boots was still mostly intact, though the leg it had been attached to was gone.

There was nothing else.

She let out a shuddering breath, stumbled to her feet, and took a tentative step forward, needing to see, to make sure that her mother was gone.

But not even bones, only ashes remained when Nita rose. Not even her mother could put herself back together after being blown to literal smithereens.

Nita's mother was dead. And she was never, ever going to hurt Nita again.

Nita let out a long breath. She'd expected to feel relieved, but she didn't. Just vaguely satisfied, like she'd finally completed a long overdue task.

She walked slowly across the room, kicking a fragment of skull out of her way, and left through the shattered hole where the door used to be, down the blackened hallway, its walls on fire, and to the stairwell.

Her mother would never control Nita's life again.

FORTY-ONE

NITA SPENT the next three days at the hospital by Kovit's bedside.

Kovit had a room to himself in the far corner of the hospital. Normally, hospital rooms were shared, but because of Kovit's notoriety in the news, other patients' misgivings, and the fact that he unconsciously fed on the pain of everyone around him, the hospital had agreed to give him his own room.

A policeman stood outside the door, and Nita wasn't sure if it was to make sure Kovit didn't escape or protect him from the zealots, reporters, and curious bystanders who kept trying to swing by his room. Either way, while Kovit was unconscious and helpless, it was a boon to have the police presence — it saved Nita a lot of effort.

When he'd come out of surgery, Nita had asked the doctor his prognosis.

"It's too early to tell. Honestly, I never thought he'd survive the surgery. He shouldn't have." The doctor had frowned softly. "I've never worked on a zannie before, though. Do they have healing skills like vampires?"

"Not that I'm aware of," Nita had whispered, but she'd thought about the vampire blood Kovit had drunk that morning, known to improve healing and lifespan, and her own blood running through his veins. Maybe it had been enough.

"Ah. Well. He's been lucky so far." The doctor had given her an encouraging smile. "We'll see if it continues. We're not out of the woods yet."

Nita hadn't been able to return the smile, or any of the other optimistic comments the doctor had made in the days since then. She just listened to the steady beep of the heart monitor and watched as Kovit's sleeping face grew more and more hollow.

Outside the hospital, the world changed and morphed. Countries suspended INHUP operations pending investigations, exposés were done on various INHUP founders. The Dangerous Unnaturals List was taken down in most countries — most, but not all. Never all.

Nita had leaked what information she could to the press, and a reporter had been able to get access to INHUP's research facility in France, where he'd filmed and photographed a comatose Nadezhda Novikova. She looked young, far too young for her age, and rumors and theories flew fast and furious. The pictures were analyzed, and old scarring on her neck made people scream vampire, but it wasn't until one of the scientists at the research facility spoke out that the theory was confirmed.

For days, headlines blared articles with titles like DANGEROUS TO US, OR DANGEROUS TO INHUP'S INTERNAL POLITICS? THE DUL HISTORY EXPOSED. And in the center of it all, the scandal around Kovit raged, information and misinformation flying fast and free. A transcript of Nita's first conversation with the police right after Kovit was shot was leaked to the press and made more headlines, igniting further speculation. Kovit's sister had been fired from INHUP and had vanished. Reporters and private investigators tried to hunt her down, but so far no one had found her, and she wasn't speaking out.

Police had come twice more to visit Nita and ask her questions. She kept her story as consistent as she could, making sure all the lies she wove in were things that only INHUP could prove false. INHUP, which was currently under investigation in multiple countries, with operations in some parts of the world completely suspended. The world was caught up in a frenzy of INHUP-related scandal, and the organization began to crumble internally from the pressure. The acting head resigned amid a tax fraud scandal — something Nita had exposed with her new information from Tácunan Law.

Everything went exactly according to Nita's plan. INHUP was collapsing in on itself, she'd taken out her mother. Adair had been as good as his word, and black market forums had started questioning the legitimacy of the video of Nita circulating. Her involvement in the end of el Mercado de la Muerte, and the theft of files from Tácunan Law had been leaked as well, and the conversation online had shifted.

People were still hunting her. But they were more cautious now. They were waiting to see her next move. It wasn't the power Nita needed, but it was a step in the right direction.

To all intents and purposes, she'd won.

Except it never really felt like it.

Her eighteenth birthday came and went, and she spent the day by Kovit's side. She forgot it even was her birthday until the next day, when some spam arrived in her inbox promising her a fifty-percent-off birthday discount.

Adair emailed her a video file he'd managed to get from INHUP in the midst of the scandal. It was from her neighbor's security camera, and it showed Zebra-stripes and her father fighting. Nita couldn't watch the whole thing, it hurt too much, so she skipped to the end, where Zebra-stripes stood over her dead father.

She expected to feel relief, to feel satisfied at this proof that she'd killed the right person, that her father had been avenged. But it only made her feel more empty and hollow inside.

Through it all, Kovit slept. He had a breathing machine, and his chest rose and fell as it dictated. His chest was a mess of bandages. At one point, his pulse skyrocketed, and the nurses dragged him away for another emergency surgery.

When he came back, he looked even more waxy and still, his hair losing its gloss and his eyes becoming sunken. Sometimes, in the dead of night, Nita would enlist the help of her police supervisors to help her drag Kovit's bed through the hospital to the emergency room to let his body absorb some of the pain. His color always looked better after that, though the police escort always looked unnerved.

On the third day, she had a new visitor.

Agent Quispe walked through the door wearing a crisp

business suit and a cold expression. Her brown skin looked taut and a bit waxen, and her buzzcut had grown out a little. The officers at the door had relieved her of her gun, and she crossed her arms when she entered the room.

Nita rose from her seat beside Kovit, eyes wide. "Agent Quispe."

"Nita." Nita had never heard Agent Quispe's voice so cold. Usually it was firm and commanding, occasionally gentle, but never angry, especially not this stony calm sort of anger.

Nita gave her a patently fake smile. "What brings you here?"

The INHUP agent's face remained still with rage. "I'm here to confirm the identity of the man who participated in the kidnapping of two INHUP agents and a minor under our protection." Quispe's eyes met Nita's. "And why are you here?"

Nita's smile fell under Quispe's expression. She could see the agent had put the disparate pieces together, had puzzled it all out well before she came to Buenos Aires. She'd realized Nita and Kovit had been working together from the start, and she wasn't surprised to find Nita hovering over his bedside. She'd come to prove her suspicions, and there was nothing Nita could do or say to allay them.

It made Nita a little sad, she realized, to burn her bridge with Agent Quispe. She actually liked the INHUP agent. Quispe had seemed to honestly care about Nita. Her promise to expose the corruption in INHUP had seemed genuine.

Nita just shrugged softly. "Why ask questions you already know the answer to?"

Quispe's expression darkened.

They stood there staring at each other for long moments, before Quispe finally said, "You've made a fool of me."

"Not intentionally." Nita's voice was soft.

"You had me searching for corruption in INHUP when it was you all along."

Nita snorted. "When it was me all along? Give me a break. Did I sell my own location on the black market? Not a chance. No, INHUP is exactly as corrupt as the news says, and you know it. You knew it before you met me."

Quispe didn't flinch, but her mouth turned down, and that was as close as Nita was going to get to an acknowledgment. "You led me to believe that an INHUP leak exposed Fabricio's travel information."

"Ah, you mean Fabricio Tácunan?"

Quispe's eyes widened slightly, and Nita smiled at her small victory.

"You hadn't figured that part out yet, had you?" Nita crossed her arms. "In fact, despite what you seem to think, there's a lot you haven't figured out."

"Then why don't you tell me?"

For a moment, Nita was tempted, but then she shook her head. "Whatever confession you're hoping to tape here and use as evidence, it won't work."

"This isn't being taped."

But Nita knew she'd guessed right by the way Quispe's hand shifted ever so slightly to her left pocket, where no doubt something was recording this conversation.

"Sure." Nita sat down again and turned her face to Kovit. "But I've nothing more to say."

Quispe was silent a long time, long enough that Nita wondered if she'd left and Nita hadn't noticed, when the click of her shoes approached. She looked down on Kovit, eyes traveling over all the tubes he was hooked up to and settling on his face.

"Why?" Quispe finally asked. "He's a monster."

Nita shrugged. "Aren't we all?"

"Not like that. Not like him."

It was a fair point, and Nita didn't have a counter to it. Finally, after a moment, Nita whispered softly, "He was on my side. He was the only one on my side. The only one I could trust in an ocean of lies and betrayal. INHUP, Fabricio, my family. Everyone was lying to me. Except Kovit." She raised her eyes to Quispe. "I think you underestimate the power of trust."

Quispe's jaw tightened, and her voice was full of hurt as she whispered, "I was on your side. You could have trusted me."

Nita looked down. "I did. But I didn't trust INHUP, and I didn't trust that you were as wary of them as I was." *And I didn't think you'd be on my side if you knew the truth about who I was and what I'd done.*

They were silent a time, watching Kovit's chest rise and fall before Quispe finally said, "If he survives and the DUL doesn't go back up, I'll testify against him at his trial. I'm not letting him get away with murdering that agent."

Nita nodded. "I'd expect nothing less. May justice prevail."

Quispe's mouth curved in a warped smile that said she

knew exactly how different their ideas of justice were. "I hope it does."

Quispe didn't say anything else, just sat for a few minutes with Nita as they watched a monster sleep, the beep of the heart monitor counting his victims and the hiss of the respirators chronicling their screams.

FORTY-TWO

KOVIT WOKE THE NEXT DAY.

Nita was dozing beside his bed. She wasn't sure how long he'd been awake, only that at some point, she glanced at him and saw he was watching her with those dark, long-lashed eyes she was so familiar with.

He tried to say something, but he still had a tube down his throat, so all that came out was a choking noise. Trembling, Nita reached over, touched his hair softly, reverently, as though she couldn't quite believe it, and called for a doctor.

Kovit was surrounded in a flurry of activity as the medical staff swarmed him. Machines were unhooked. Different machines were hooked. The tube was taken out of his throat, which sounded like a very painful process if Kovit's yelps and groans were anything to go by.

The doctor spoke to him in stilted English, and Kovit responded blearily. He asked for water, and they gave it to him. After a few minutes, the hubbub died down, and Nita returned to her seat next to him.

"Hey," he croaked.

"Hey." Her chest was so tight she barely got the word out.

He gave her a cracked smile. "You look terrible."

She laughed hoarsely. "You should see yourself."

"Who, me?" He attempted a charming smile. "I'm sure I'm the most handsome patient in the hospital."

She laughed a little. "Sure, you'll win the hospital beauty pageant crown."

He took another sip of water, and his smile fell, his expression turning pensive. His eyes strayed to the policeman at the door and then back to Nita. "I get the feeling I missed a lot."

She spent the next hour updating him, careful of what she said in case the policeman was listening. She managed to unobtrusively tell him the story she'd given the police about how they'd met and his relationship in INHUP, worried that the police would come any minute to take his statement and he'd accidentally contradict Nita and put them both in a bad situation.

Kovit listened as she explained, his eyes hooded, and she couldn't tell what he thought of their cover story. Once she was finished, he was silent for a long time before he asked softly, "My sister?"

"Gone. I don't know where."

He nodded slowly, eyes sad, and didn't say anything more about it.

The police arrived shortly after, and Nita was asked to leave the room while they took Kovit's statement. Most of the officers shifted uncomfortably and avoided eye contact with Kovit, and Nita found it a marvel. Kovit was bedridden, near death, and these armed adult men were still terrified of him.

She waited for the police to be done in the small room down the hall. It had a row of black chairs and a small end table, but there were no magazines here to view. Just an old TV that didn't seem to work anymore.

Nita closed her eyes and leaned back against the wall as she slid into a seat, just breathing, letting relief swamp her. Kovit was alive. It wasn't going to be easy, and his recovery would take time, but he was alive. And as long as he was alive, she could fix things. As long as he was alive, her mother hadn't won.

Something sharp and jagged and terrible that had been clinging like a poison leech to the inside of her chest the past few days finally released, and her shoulders slumped, all the tension suddenly going out of them. She let out a heavy breath, tension whispering out of her body and bone-deep exhaustion taking its place. She'd been powering through the last few days on caffeine and desperation, and now that he'd woken, she just wanted to curl up beside him and sleep for the next year.

Not that she could. There was still a lot to do, even more now. Plans to weave, people to bribe, decisions to make. Agent Quispe was going to make life difficult.

"I heard Kovit woke up."

Nita opened her eyes at the sound of the familiar voice, stunned to find Fabricio standing in front of her. He looked different, more mature now, in a button-up white shirt and slacks. His sleeves were rolled to his elbows, and his hair had been combed and parted on the side. It floofed a little, but it no longer had that I-was-just-kidnapped-and-tortured mussed look, which was more what she was used to.

"Fabricio." Wariness crept into her voice. "Why are you here?"

He sat down beside her, a slight smile on his face, and folded his bandaged hand in his lap. "I'm here to make you an offer."

Her eyes narrowed. "What kind of offer?"

Fabricio sighed softly. "Look, Nita. I'm tired. I don't want to fight you. And I don't want to be looking over my shoulder for the rest of my life, wondering if you're hunting me down and trying to kill me." He gave her an ironic smile. "I think you know what that's like."

She nodded slowly.

"We've done a lot of damage to each other. We've lied and hurt and destroyed. I don't want to anymore. I want it to end." He met her eyes. "So I'm offering you an olive branch."

"What kind of olive branch?"

"Legal representation for Kovit."

Nita stared. "Pardon?"

Fabricio's gaze was steady. "Tácunan Law's main purpose was to protect monsters from jail. I personally know all the lawyers who practice that kind of law. I've come into a lot of money from my father's offshore accounts now that I'm eighteen. I can hire you the best lawyer in the world for crimes against humanity."

Nita was silent.

Fabricio's eyes flicked nervously, as though worried her silence was a rejection. "You've won the publicity battle against

INHUP, but there's still video evidence of Kovit torturing people online. Yes, he's young in the videos. But it still exists. He's still a zannie who worked for the mafia. I can get you a lawyer that will win any trial Kovit goes to. Hell, I can get someone who can make sure charges never get filed."

Nita bowed her head. Fabricio was right, Kovit did need a lawyer. For the videos, for the DUL, for Mirella if she chose to press charges. For the charges Agent Quispe had threatened her with.

"And what? I'm just supposed to forgive you?" she asked, voice tight.

"No. I don't particularly care if you forgive me." He smiled slightly. "You don't have to like me. Just stop trying to kill me."

Nita was silent, thinking of everything that had happened to this point. The different faces of Fabricio she'd seen, all carefully created to get himself what he wanted. "You're a serial liar. How can I trust that you won't come after me?"

"I'm a liar, it's true." Fabricio gave her a bitter smile. "I had to be, to survive. I lied and lied and lied to stay alive. I lied so much that sometimes even I don't know what's true anymore." He closed his eyes for a moment and his smile fell as he confessed, "Sometimes, when I'm alone, I think I could have been a good person. In another life. When I didn't need to fight to survive. But that's just another lie. Because no one knows who they really are until they're tested the way we've been — and you and I, we both chose to survive, no matter what the cost. We gave up being good people to be *living* people."

She stared at him a beat, then snorted. "I don't think I've ever been a very good person."

He laughed softly. "Given your upbringing, that doesn't surprise me."

Nita's face fell at the reminder of her mother. The reminder of what she'd done to her mother.

"Sometimes I wonder," Nita whispered, "if we aren't all destined to become certain types of people, no matter our upbringing. The girl I was trapped in a cage with, Mirella, is an activist now, working against unnatural trafficking. If she hadn't been kidnapped, she wouldn't have that cause. But she always had fire, she was always passionate. So would she have just found another cause?"

Fabricio blinked. "I don't know."

"If I hadn't been kidnapped, I'd still be trapped with my mother. I wouldn't be a killer." Nita met Fabricio's eyes. "But I wonder if it was only a matter of time and opportunity before I rose up against her."

"Perhaps." His voice was soft.

"And I wonder if it's only a matter of time before you betray me again."

He winced. "I lie to survive—there's no survival benefit to keeping up this cycle of vengeance with you." His gaze was steady. "Don't trust me, that's fine. But trust my desire to live. I don't care about you, Nita. I don't care what you do, or if you live or die. I don't want or need vengeance. All I want is to be left alone. And if you agree to do that, you'll never have to see me again."

Nita watched the police file out of Kovit's room and down the hall. They were hunched together in a group, whispering, but they didn't look angry or violent, and there was still a guard posted at Kovit's door, so Nita imagined the meeting couldn't have gone too disastrously.

But that didn't mean it wouldn't in the future.

Nita's eyes went back to Fabricio. For so long, he'd been the focal point of her rage. He'd betrayed her over and over and over. She'd done so much to capture him, to kill him, to get her vengeance. Leaving him alive was like leaving a loose end, one more thing that could come back to haunt her in the future. Letting him go went against everything she was.

But Kovit *needed* what Fabricio was offering. Kovit had so many legal battles to face, so many enemies. The truth was, he wouldn't survive without a lawyer. If Nita truly wanted Kovit to get through this, she had to accept Fabricio's offer.

Could she do that? Put her vengeance aside to save him? Could she betray the past version of herself, the desperate frightened girl in the cage who promised herself she'd destroy the one who put her there, to save the person who meant the most to her present self?

She was shocked to find, when she thought about it, that she could.

It wasn't that she forgave Fabricio — she didn't think she was truly capable of forgiveness. But the rage that had burned so bright and vicious when she'd discovered his betrayal was only a dull flame, a slowly burning anger she suspected would never fully leave, even if Fabricio was dead and buried.

So, no, she couldn't forgive Fabricio. But then again, she didn't need to. She just needed to cooperate with him, to make a deal. Like she'd done with Adair, and like she imagined she'd have to do again in the future. She could be practical.

The Nita who first met Fabricio would have hesitated to hurt him. The Nita who found out he betrayed her would have made him scream until he died. But this Nita, here and now, understood that the world was give and take, that sometimes you had to let things go, not hold on, because justice for your past wasn't as important as safety and security for your present and future.

And though she'd never voice it aloud, she'd come to understand Fabricio. She didn't forgive, but she could understand. And with that understanding came the belief that this deal was probably genuine.

So quietly, and without much fanfare, she let her quest for vengeance slip away, into the dark currents of her memory.

"Yes," Nita said finally, her voice gentler than she expected. "I want the lawyer."

Fabricio smiled slightly and rose. "Then it's a deal?"

Nita nodded. "It's a deal."

FORTY-THREE

FABRICIO INSISTED ON telling Kovit himself, and the two of them returned to Kovit's room together.

As the guard checked Fabricio for weapons at the door, Nita watched him carefully. "Fabricio?"

"Yeah?"

"I always wondered. What kind of unnatural are you?" She raised her eyebrows. "You claimed to be valuable for so long. I'm reasonably sure that was a lie."

"Oh." He flushed a little. The guard gestured that he was free to enter, and Fabricio smiled at him, then turned back to Nita awkwardly. "I'm an aur."

He began to glow, flickering like there was a lightbulb just beneath the surface of his skin. On and off.

Nita stared at him, her mouth open slightly. "That's it? You're an aur?"

Dime-a-dozen aurs were essentially bioluminescent people. Pieces of them did make money on the black market, but no one would ever consider them rare or hard to find. Back in Death Market, one of the dealers had been an aur.

"Yep." He grinned. "The most boring unnatural in existence. I can glow so bright you might decide to put on sunglasses. Witness my superpowers."

Nita snort-laughed as he blinked his light on and off. After all the ugly truths she'd been forced to face this week, this simple, harmless truth made her feel light and a little giddy. Fabricio had bluffed himself into making everyone think he was wildly valuable, when he was one of the most common unnaturals out there.

She just shook her head. "I bet you're great at poker."

"Because of my *glowing* personality?"

She rolled her eyes at the pun, but couldn't keep the slight smile from her face. "Yeah. Sure."

They entered the hospital room together. Kovit was reclining in his bed, arms lying loosely at his side, and staring pensively out the window when they entered. It had started raining, and the drops trickled down the windowpane like tears.

"Hi, Kovit." Fabricio stepped forward.

Kovit turned to face Fabricio, and Nita was shocked to see a slight, genuine smile cross his face. "Fabricio? Why are you here?"

Fabricio gave him a self-deprecating smile. "I'm trying make peace with Nita."

Kovit raised his eyebrows. "And she's interested in making peace?"

"I can be reasoned with." Nita crossed her arms.

"Yes." Fabricio raised an eyebrow. "I just needed the right olive branch."

"Exactly."

Kovit laughed. "You bribed her?"

Nita huffed. Fabricio smiled a little and said, "Your words, not mine."

"All right, then." Kovit grinned. "What's this olive branch?"

Fabricio explained about the lawyer, and then at the end pulled out a business card for the person he was planning to hire and gave one to each of them. Kovit was silent, listening, and his gaze was fixed on that small business card.

Fabricio finished, and Kovit bowed his head.

"Why?" Kovit's voice was steady, but there was something underneath it Nita couldn't quite identify.

Fabricio tilted his head. "Pardon?"

"Why are you doing this?"

He sighed softly. "Because you're the only thing Nita cares about, and I have a vested interest in having her not want to kill me."

"But I hurt you." Kovit seemed to be struggling with the idea that someone could do something good for him when he'd done something so terrible to them.

"Thanks, I remember." Fabricio absently rubbed his bandaged hand.

Kovit met Fabricio's eyes. "Aren't you angry at me? Don't you want justice to be served and all that?"

"Not really." Fabricio gave him a bitter smile. "And awful as this sounds, I've had worse."

Kovit was quiet for a long moment, and then he said softly, "I'm sorry, Fabricio."

Fabricio blinked. "Pardon?"

"I'm sorry I hurt you." Kovit's hands were clenched into

fists on the hospital blanket, but his face was calm and his gaze steady. "I wish I hadn't done it."

Fabricio's eyes were wide, and even Nita's mouth was open a little. Kovit was apologizing to someone he'd hurt. Someone whose identity he'd erased in his mind to hurt them had slowly become a person to him, and eventually he'd felt regret. Nita could barely believe it. She hadn't thought him capable of it. She'd thought it would break all his rules, break him, the way killing Henry had shattered something inside him.

But here he was. Apologizing.

She'd noticed the changes in Kovit since Henry had died, but she'd never thought they would lead him here. She wasn't sure what she thought of it.

This apology was different than Kovit's desperate pleas when he'd spoken to his sister. The tone, the action, everything had changed. Kovit hadn't really regretted hurting that INHUP agent, he'd only regretted his sister found out.

Nita thought he might genuinely feel remorse about Fabricio.

"You don't need to forgive me. That's not why I apologized." Kovit spoke quickly, as though he wanted to get this over with. "I just wanted you to know. I wanted to say it. And, if there's anything I can do to make it up to you, just ask."

Fabricio hesitated, and Nita's eyes turned to him. This was all new territory. She had no idea how Fabricio would react, no idea how his reaction would influence Kovit. What had it taken for Kovit to make that kind of apology? What would it be like for Fabricio, who'd been brutally tortured multiple times in his life, to hear that?

The silence hung for a moment, everyone waiting to see what the others would do. Fabricio's face was a careful mask, but she could see the decisions swirling in his eyes, conflicting emotions and thoughts battling together.

Finally, Fabricio took a step forward and put his hand on Kovit's shoulder. "It's okay, Kovit. I forgive you."

Kovit's eyes went huge. He looked so fragile in his hospital bed, so small and breakable. "Pardon?"

"I forgive you." Fabricio's smile was a little broken. "I know what it's like to live in a cage. I know how things that should never be normal become normal. And even when you're out, you fall back on old habits for comfort, just for the familiarity, even when you shouldn't. You hurt people because that's what you've always done. You lie because you can't remember telling the truth." Fabricio's voice went bitter. "I know that better than anyone." He pointedly didn't look at Nita. "And sometimes, in that first while after you're free, all you can do is make mistakes, do the exact things you were trying to escape from over and over, because you don't know who you are and it scares you."

Kovit hadn't missed how similar Fabricio's musings were to his own, and his voice was soft as he said, simply, "Yes."

Fabricio stepped away. "I forgive you, Kovit." Then he cracked a warped grin. "But don't do it again, okay? I *really* didn't enjoy it."

Kovit laughed, a short, scratchy sound.

Nita suddenly had a terrible, dark thought, as she watched that bond of safety click into place around Fabricio, the same way it had for Nita, for Gold, for Henry, for Patchaya. The mental shift in Kovit's mind that meant he'd never be able to hurt Fabricio again.

She wondered if Fabricio had only said those words to earn Kovit's protection.

Fabricio was smart, and he was good at manipulation. He'd spent enough time with them that he could play Kovit like a finely tuned violin. And he had to know that Kovit wouldn't— *couldn't*—hurt people he cared about. Making a deal with Nita was just that—a deal. A deal could be broken. Nita could decide to betray him at any point.

But Kovit? Kovit would never betray Fabricio now. And he'd never let Nita betray Fabricio either.

Kovit awkwardly readjusted his blankets, trying to hide his emotions, and Fabricio turned to Nita, their eyes meeting for a moment. He gave her a small smile, not a smug smile, but a sad smile, a smile of recognition. He knew what she was thinking, he could see the question in her eyes, the angry demand, *Did you manipulate him just to be safe?*

But in the broken cracks of his expression and the grief in his smile, she realized that Fabricio himself didn't truly know either. He'd lied so often and so long, had spent his whole life manipulating people, that even he didn't know anymore whether he said things because he meant them or because they would benefit him.

In that moment, she pitied him, this sad boy who was so lost in his lies he couldn't see the truth anymore, couldn't understand what his own emotions were, had let them all be replaced by whatever person he needed to be in any given moment to survive.

Nita sighed softly and went to Kovit. She took his hand in hers and looked up at Fabricio. She would never forgive him for selling her on the black market. But she didn't have to forgive him to leave him alone and move on with her life.

"Goodbye, Fabricio," Nita said. "Let's never meet again."

He smiled softly and turned away, walking toward the door. "Goodbye, Nita. Goodbye, Kovit. Good luck."

And then he was gone.

FORTY-FOUR

AFTER FABRICIO LEFT, Nita went to the nurses to get a wheelchair and told their guard they were going to go for a walk in the hospital garden. Nita wanted to talk to Kovit, and she didn't want to risk the guard overhearing. She wasn't even sure their guard spoke English, but that didn't matter. She just operated on the assumption the room was bugged.

Nita helped Kovit into the wheelchair, and the guard followed as they made their way to the elevator and down to the first floor. Kovit was conscious and in control now, so even though the pain flowed into him from all sides, it was only rarely that the shaking ecstasy from other people's agony was too much for him to suppress and he'd give a soft, low moan of pleasure, before they passed away from the patient out of range and he'd settle again.

Behind them, the officer shuddered every time he heard Kovit's voice.

It was still raining outside, but part of the garden was covered. Nita politely asked the guard to give them some privacy, and he agreed, looking askance at Kovit. Nita ignored his looks and wheeled Kovit into the garden. The flowers were in full bloom, massive pink and purple blossoms perching on bushes and small white flowers in trees.

The rain washed a petal off a tree, and it fluttered softly to the ground under Kovit's pensive gaze.

"Penny for your thoughts?" Nita asked, sitting on a bench beside him.

He blinked and looked up at her, eyes soft. "Just thinking."

"About?"

"What'll happen now." He watched the rain fall. "Trials. Publicity. I'm never going to be anonymous again."

"No," Nita admitted. "Probably not."

"And for the next while, the world will be watching. Even though I have Fabricio's lawyer now, I'm going to have to be very careful. I'm going to have to behave like the person I'm pretending to be." He made a disgusted face. "I'm going to have to be good."

Nita burst into laughter at the horrified expression. "You are. No torture, no murder, no threats."

He groaned softly. "Ugh. Really? Nothing?"

"Nope."

"I could hide it."

"There's too many eyes on you. You'd be found out." Nita smiled slightly. "You're going to have to put on your tragic hero face and brood for the next few years."

He sighed heavily. "If I must." He looked up, toward the sky and grudgingly admitted, "Maybe it's not such a bad thing."

Nita tilted her head. "Pardon?"

"I wanted a way off the hamster wheel. I wanted a chance to force myself into a completely different life, just to get out of this toxic cycle. Well, there's nothing more different than having to behave like a good person. None of my old habits are allowed. I'll have to completely reform my image."

She looked at him. "You're not actually seriously thinking of becoming a good person?"

"God, no." He burst into laughter. "Obviously, it won't be real. I'd never actually be good. I *like* hurting people. Far too much to ever stop." He shrugged. "But as long as I behave in a 'moral' way or whatever, no one's ever going to know I don't give a shit, right?"

Nita snorted. "True enough."

"And . . ." He hesitated. "I need to prove something to my sister. To all of them."

"What?"

"That *I'm* in control." His voice was hard. "My sister thought it was lack of control that makes me hurt people. That I succumb to my need for pain in dark ways, like an out-of-control serial killer. But it's nothing so excusable. I genuinely enjoy it. And I'm not going to stop." His gaze was intense. "There's a difference between not having control and hurting people because you can't help it, and hurting people because you just don't care. I don't think my sister quite realizes how . . ." His smile turned bitter. "Well, to use her words, how 'evil' I am."

Nita was quiet for a long time. "So you plan to not hurt anyone for the duration of the trial and public spotlight to prove a point?"

"Exactly." He stretched languidly. "And then, the moment

366

it's safe, I'm going to find someone, and I'm going to make them scream in ways they never even imagined."

He closed his eyes briefly, as though savoring the image, and Nita shuddered softly at the expression on his face, dark and hungry and terrible.

She forced herself to crack a smile. "And here I thought you were on your way to a cheesy movie redemption arc."

He laughed, light and free. "Redemption? Me? Not likely."

She smiled a little at that.

He turned to her and sighed softly. "This break will also give me a chance to update my rules."

Nita's eyebrows rose. "I thought you never changed your rules?"

"I did too," he admitted. "But my rules were made in captivity, with very strict goals. And they haven't been working outside of captivity. Killing Henry nearly broke me. I can't be that fragile. I need to be flexible, not rigid. I need to be able to bend when circumstances change."

"Like with Fabricio?" Nita hedged.

"It was more than that. After the video of"—he took a deep breath, and then, to Nita's shock, said the name he'd avoided for so long—"*Mirella* accusing me came out, I realized that my rules weren't protecting me anymore. They were keeping me blind to threats. I couldn't even remember this girl, and now she's pressing charges against me."

He looked up and met Nita's eyes. "Something has to change. *I* have to change."

Nita was quiet for a moment, before asking, "Is that why you apologized to Fabricio?"

"Yes. It was . . . an experiment. I knew why he did the things he did. I pitied him, even though what he did to you is unforgivable. But when I pitied him, I started to regret worsening his life even more. I felt *bad*. So I apologized." He took a deep breath, then let it out. "I made a mistake. I admitted it. And I didn't break."

Nita nodded slowly, understanding more than he was saying. He'd needed to apologize to Fabricio, to bend a rule, to see if he was truly as fragile as he thought, to take that first step into changing the way he worked. She only wished he'd decided to feel bad about Mirella, an innocent victim and Nita's sometime friend, rather than Fabricio, the liar who betrayed her.

"No, you didn't break." She put her hands on his. "You're stronger than you think, Kovit."

He smiled slightly at that, and the two of them were quiet for a few moments, just watching the rain fall, glittering in the darkness.

"I imagine you're happy about my new situation," he said, looking at her from the corner of his eyes. "Less screaming."

She winced. "Guilty."

He was quiet a moment, and then asked, "Why do you stay when it bothers you so much?"

Nita was silent a long moment before she responded, words coming slowly. "I don't like hearing what you do, but I don't care if you do it. I've never cared that you were evil. I think a part of me even liked it, because I could pretend that you were more evil than I was, and it made me feel superior." She sighed. "But the truth is, I'm just as evil as you, in different ways. It's just taken me a long time to see it and admit it to myself."

She raised her eyes and met his. "I don't care about anyone in the world except those close to me. You could skin the fucking pope alive, and as long as I didn't have to see it, I wouldn't care. Because he means nothing to me, and you mean everything."

His eyes flicked back and forth over her face, and then he reached out and linked his fingers with hers.

"Nita," he breathed softly, "what could I ever have done to deserve someone like you in my life?"

"There's no 'deserving' involved." Nita smiled, sharp and sly. "Sometimes bad things happen to good people." His expression of confusion was adorable. "And sometimes," she continued, cupping his face in her hands, "good things happen to bad people."

He stared at her a moment, then burst into laughter, breaking away from her, his sides shaking as he laughed and winced in pain. When he finally stilled, he lifted his eyes to hers, his gaze soft and dark.

He raised a finger and traced the outline of her cheekbone, and she caught his hand with hers and wove her fingers through his so their palms were pressed flat against each other, linking them. She leaned forward so their foreheads were pressed together, drinking in the warmth of his body against hers.

They might both be terrible, and the world might want them dead, but they had each other. Sometimes, that was all that mattered.

FORTY-FIVE

KOVIT SLEPT QUIETLY, his heart monitor beeping softly. Outside, the moon hung high in the sky, and the faint glow of the streetlights barely penetrated the darkness of the hospital room. The door to the room was open a crack, and Nita stood just outside it, in the hallway, bathed in fluorescent lights.

It was the middle of the night, and though the hallway was lit as bright as daylight, Nita was the only person there. The rest of the ward was fast asleep, and there were only a few nurses in this wing, most of them at the desk down the hall and around the corner, chatting. Nita had checked on them earlier.

She stared down at her phone, second- and third- and fourth-guessing her decision, trying to poke holes in it, questioning whether this was truly her best option. But in the end, however many misgivings she had, she knew this was the right choice.

Pride only got you so far. Nita wasn't going to let hers keep her away from her dreams, or from her survival. She called, lifting the phone to her ear as she waited, tapping one foot against the floor in a small physical sign of her nerves.

Adair picked up on the third ring. "Hello?"

"Hey. It's Nita."

Static on the other end of the line, and then, "I haven't heard from you in a while."

"It's been busy here. I imagine you've heard the news?"

"Hasn't everyone?" A short pause. "How's Kovit?"

"Stable. The doctors think he'll make a full recovery, but it'll take many months. They're amazed he survived."

"How *did* he survive, Nita?"

Nita shrugged, fingers awkwardly skimming the flask of vampire blood at her belt. It had her own blood mixed in there too, for good measure. What Kovit didn't know wouldn't hurt him. And she wasn't sure what had kept him going through the surgery, so better safe than sorry.

"Who knows?" she responded, evading the question. "What matters is that he did."

"I'm glad."

Nita swallowed heavily. "Me too."

Adair let the silence linger a bit too long before he addressed the elephant in the room. "I assume you're calling to give me your answer to my proposal."

She nodded, then remembered he couldn't see her. "Yes."

"And?"

She hesitated. "I want to learn. I want you to teach me about the black market. Who the main players are, where the dangers lie. I want you to train me in the information business."

There was a long silence on the other end of the line. "You want to be my apprentice?"

"Yes." The words caught in her throat. She didn't like the idea of working for Adair. She'd fucked that relationship up before, and she didn't want to put herself in a lower position than him, but she sucked in her pride because she knew it was the right decision. "I have the information. We have similar goals. But I can't just trust you to do what's in my best interests forever. I need to learn these things myself, I need to build my own foundation of knowledge to stand on. I'm tired of being ignorant. Knowledge is power, but it's useless if you don't know what to do with it. So I want to know. I'll give you access to all the information I gathered, and in exchange, you teach me about the market. The players, the history, the deals. Everything."

He was silent a long time. "That's something that would be hard to do long distance."

"I know." Nita bit her lip. "The University of Toronto has an excellent undergraduate program in unnatural biology, and their admission acceptance times run much later than American universities. If I get my act together, I could apply next week for September start."

Adair's voice was careful, but not dismissive. "It'll be hard, being a full-time student and full-time information broker apprentice."

"I can manage." Nita was firm. "I'm not giving up on my dream. If I'm not doing this so I can live the life I want, why the hell am I doing it?"

He laughed softly, and she could imagine those swampy

eyes calculating even as he laughed, examining her proposal from every angle.

"All right," he said finally. "We'll try it."

"You agree?" Nita hesitated. "We have a deal?"

"We have a deal." His voice was soft. "I'll see you and Kovit in Toronto soon, then."

Nita clicked off the phone and stared down at it, thinking of the future ahead. She would have her degree in unnatural sciences. She would get a chance to do her research. She would have everything she ever wanted by day.

And by night, she'd study just as hard and learn a different set of skills. She'd work until she knew everything about everyone on the black market, until she could pull their strings and play them like puppets, tearing her enemies down one by one until they were nothing but dust and Nita was the only black market power left alive.

The world would always have a black market. Nita accepted this. And if there would always be a black market, she'd always have enemies. Unless she ruled it.

She smiled and opened the door to Kovit's room. Whistling softly, she stepped into the pitch-blackness and quietly closed the door behind her, cutting off all the light.

The future looked bright.

ACKNOWLEDGMENTS

Here it is, the end of the trilogy. It's been an amazing ride, and I can't believe it's over already. Thank you to everyone who's stuck with me for all these books. I appreciate each and every one of you.

First, thanks to my agent, Suzie Townsend, for all her hard work, as well as her assistant, Dani Segelbaum. And to everyone else at New Leaf Literary who's championed these books and worked with me.

I'm grateful to my editor, Nicole Sclama, for all her work on this series, and all her love for these dark little characters. And to HMH, for picking up my strange little series and putting it out into the world. Thanks to everyone on the team—you're all amazing!

My early readers for book three, I love you all so much, and I couldn't have done this without your brilliant feedback. Special thanks to Stacey Trombley, Erin Luken, Xiran Jay, Yamile Méndez, and Rosiee Thor.

Thanks also to all the staff at WEBTOON, who adapted *Not Even Bones* over the last year into an *amazing* comic and brought more wonderful readers to my books, and who have worked so hard to maintain the soul of the story in a different medium. Special thanks to Stephen Lamm, who's gone the extra mile adapting and remaining faithful to the story, and to Alai Cinereo, whose phenomenal artwork captured the characters and atmosphere so perfectly.

Thank you to all the people who supported me through the good and the bad as I was writing this book, Julia Ember, Meng Tian, Xiran Jay, Erin Luken, among many, many others.

To my family, who have always supported this crazy dream of mine. You're the best.

And to my wonderful readers — thank you for sticking with me so long, and loving my characters so much. I hope you'll follow me along on my next adventure.

ESCAPE TO ANOTHER WORLD WITH THESE

FANTASIES

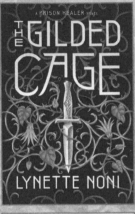

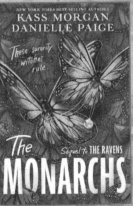

MUST-READ SCI-FI AND FANTASY BOOKS

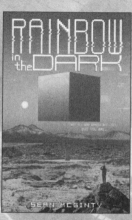

BOOKS FEATURING
LGBTQIA+ VOICES

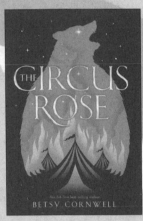